THE WOUND CLOSEST TO THE SUN
NOVEL

THE WOUND CLOSEST TO THE SUN

NOVEL

KARL BERGER

MILL CITY PRESS

Mill City Press, Inc.
2301 Lucien Way #415
Maitland, FL 32751
407.339.4217
www.millcitypress.net

Paperback ISBN-13: 978-1-6628-1190-6

Ebook ISBN-13: 978-1-6628-1191-3

This novel is dedicated to my best friend Maynard Witherell
who died Jan 11, 2021 in a bicycle accident.

Thanks go out to Elayne Masters who guided me in the early
stages and to Kayla Schwerer and her husband Eric. Their help
was on a much deeper level than common editing.

Table of Contents

First Part

Second Part

Third Part

First Part

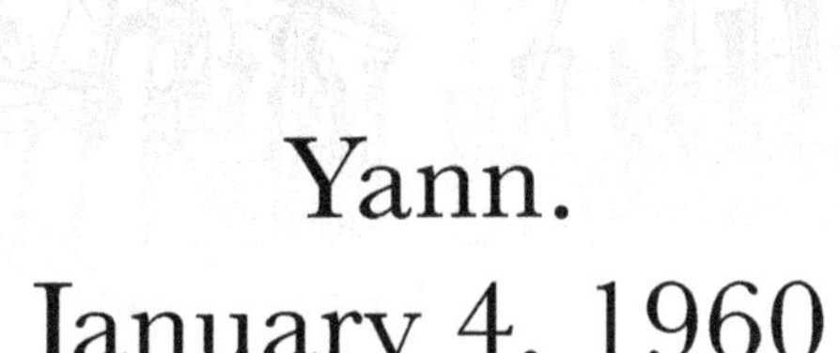

Yann.
January 4, 1960

Monday after the New Year is the least popular of days, but my students at the University of Montpellier have some catching up to do. Before winter break, I challenged them to compose a two-page essay regarding Albert Camus's famous novel *The Stranger.* These theses were to coincide with my upcoming lecture about Camus and existentialism.

That morning before class, I had found two dozen envelopes in my inbox at the university and selected a few of these brief essays for presentation during class.

I tell my students, "My selections are not to be viewed as judgements on the quality of your writing, or your opinions expressed. I rather look for fresh views."

I begin to quote aloud from a student's paper.

"A middle-aged man, working as a clerk in some harbor office in Algiers, receives a telegram that his mother has died in a home for the elderly some distance inland. He acts dazed. 'Maman died today. Or yesterday maybe.' He travels by bus to the funeral, where he reluctantly holds this vigil, his mind very much occupied by minor things, a fly bothering him, doubts about permission to smoke, the heat. Essentials are left out. Where is the father? Are there relatives? Does the author even know? The novel gives no answer."

I stop reading for a moment and look up at my students, back from vacation and looking a little tired.

"Great summary so far, right?" I ask.

A few students nod their heads.

I continue to read. "Just two days after the funeral he watches a comedy movie with his girlfriend; they make love; she asks him if he loves her and he says, 'What difference does it make.' He spends his days in a haze of indifference. Then one day, he kills an Arab on the beach, almost by accident. The judge condemns him to death because of his indifference—" That's quite concise Jacques! Now shall we see what else you have to say about *The Stranger*."

Jacques, a red-headed fellow in a tweed jacket, slowly rises from his chair. "Meursault does deserve his sentence because of his indifference."

"Not because of his deed, the killing on the beach?" I question. " He deserves it because of lack of feeling, lack of faith—is that what you are saying?"

Another student lifts his hand. "Camus inserts the incidence at the beach only as a pretext to have Meursault face a judge—because he needs a judge for the second part of the novel in which he argues against Christian faith and morality."

"I hear some criticism. Alright! Who agrees with Jacques?" I call out. I count a few arms in the air.

After Jacques sits down, I continue. "You booth have a point. In prewar Algeria a white Frenchman would never have been sentenced to death for a killing that was not intentional."

I take a small step. "How many of you are in the German class? 'Der Vorhang zu und all Fragen offen.' Anybody care to translate?"

Jacques stands up again and gives it a try.

"The curtain closed and all the questions open?" he says.

"Yes," I say. "Very good. So, let's imagine that this novel is like theater. You read the last sentence, the curtain falls, and questions remain. *The Stranger* is no different. When the curtain falls, when Meursault walks to his death, you might wonder if we asked the right questions."

Irene, one of my most pleasant students, raises her hand. "Maybe the judge in Camus's novel is a stand-in for God?"

"Interesting!" I say.

There is a hard knock on the classroom door.

The warden bursts in. "Camus has died! It's all over the radio."

The message punches my breath away. I spend the rest of my afternoon and evening in a haze, drinking too much wine in too many cafés and walking through the narrow alleys of the Old Town.

I met Camus in August of 1939.

I was then writing for a weekly journal in Paris. My editor had sent me to Algiers to interview and write about a burgeoning group of young writers led by a certain Albert Camus. Through a series of lucky coincidences, I gained Camus's confidence, and so it had been during a hot, steamy night in Algiers that I skimmed the poorly typed chapters of what was to be published years later as *The Stranger*.

It had been the wrong season to visit Algeria. The ceiling fan churned the stale air, slowly gyrating the paper-strip flytrap whose yellow tape was blackened with dead flies. The heat gummed my shirt to my skin, and even after propping myself up in my hotel bed and pulling the lamp closer I still had trouble reading the faint letters of the manuscript Camus had handed me earlier that day.

I jotted down notes about the interview with Albert Camus and my impressions during the few days I stayed in Algiers. The war had broken out and though the main actions were in Poland, which Germany had invaded in September 1,1939, it was difficult to purchase tickets anywhere in Europe. On my slow way back through Spain and France, I spent a few restless nights in crowded trains that halted on dark planes, their lights switched off because of air raid alarms. I was weary and exhausted. Many of my notes were either lost or stolen and what I eventually left in some drawer in my office in Paris was incomplete. The war was on, and my editor was no longer interested in some unknown group of writers in Algiers. Soon after that, the German tanks rolled in and I fled Paris.

Years later when I had resettled and joined the faculty of the University of Montpellier—at a time when Camus was still living and already famous—I tried again to write my essay, but was unable to publish it. I could have blamed my colleagues' professional jealousy or the limited space in the university presses, but the major problem was that my notes were brief and incomplete. My claim that I had read a raw draft of *The Stranger* as early as August 1939 was met with disbelief.

However, my hopes were rekindled when a few days after Camus's death, I received a call from a publisher friend in Paris.

"Hi Yann! I am George Paran. Remember me? I am the guy who got you the press job for the army newspaper in 1939."

"Oh. Yes. I remember you."

"You see! You still have some friends in Paris! Listen, I found some of your notes from Algiers in a stuck drawer. Are you still a professor in Montpellier?"

"Long time. Still the same job."

"Last time we talked, you were into Camus and existentialism."

"That's me."

"Well, your old notes might still be helpful to you. What do you think?"

"Sure," I said. "Would you send them to me?"

"Married yet?"

"Didn't find the right one."

"Running out of time, old friend...Anyway! It seems that everybody is looking for fresh material about Camus now. Raw lines from a bygone area, you know."

I was hoping that the publishing houses would search out people like me—people who had met Camus face-to-face. The chance to write a new essay using my old notes would present me with an opportunity to increase my academic status. Regardless, and whether my colleagues would believe it or not, I had been the first to lay eyes on the first draft of *The Stranger*.

Klaus.
January 4, 1960

It is Monday when the tickets are half-price and a small group of students crowds into the lobby of the Munich Public Theater. They are rubbing their arms, still chilled by the wintry draft that blows in whenever more fellow patrons enter through the glass doors. Klaus, a German literature student in his twenties, shuffles into the theater wearing a brown coat and a wool cap with earflaps. The young woman handing out programs signals him to take off his cap with a quick sneer. Klaus mumbles an apology, lowers his head, and then nearly stumbles into his seat to see Camus's adaptation of Dostoevsky's *The Possessed.*

A near-empty stage: Two actors lit darkly. One is a bishop wearing a blood-red cloak.

Tihon, the bishop:	*The complete atheist is more respectable than the man who is indifferent. He is on the last rung preceding perfect faith.*
Stavrogin:	*I know it. Do you remember the passage from the apocalypse about the lukewarm?*
Tihon:	*Yes. "I know thy works, that thou art either cold or hot: I would thou wert cold or hot. So then because*

> *thou art lukewarm, and neither cold nor hot, I will spew thee out of my mouth."*

The scene strikes Klaus to the core: *Neither cold nor hot. I will spew thee out of my mouth*. Those powerful words!

After leaving the tramway at Waldfriedhof, Klaus buys a bottle of wine at the Pfälzer Weinstube that he empties on his walk home. It numbs his mind.

Later, when he cannot fall asleep, Klaus listens to the screeching of the last electric tram as it turns its final loop at the Waldfriedhof. For a moment, he sees its grid of window lights racing across the dark street. When he hears the one-hour stroke from St. Canisius, he pulls the small transistor radio from the floor and, sliding his fingers along the wires, finds his headphones and fits them over his ears. The announcer is in the middle of a brief summary of the day's news, and Klaus has tuned in just in time to hear about the tragedy:

> *This afternoon, the writer Albert Camus was killed in a car accident when his car swerved out of control on a road in France. Camus is the author of several novels and plays. In 1957, he received the Nobel Prize for Literature for his novel* The Plague. *We wish you a good rest and, as usual, we will be with you in the morning. This is Radio Bavaria broadcasting live from Munich. Goodnight.*

Klaus's sadness is sharp and poignant. He pulls the headphones off his ears and flings them onto the duvet. He listens to the headphones reverberate with the National Anthem before he fingers the off switch. He lies still, doesn't move lest he tilt the balance of everything in him which is true and actual. The news of Camus's death fills him with a sorrow that hangs over his life like a sour fog.

Meeting Camus 1

Camus was known to be cagey and reluctant to talk about private matters. The very fact that he had trusted me with his manuscript for that one night seemed impossible and made me, at least to some degree, understand my colleagues' disbelief. But it was through a chain of similarities in Camus's life and mine that I could foster a bond. Like everything else in Algiers, our getting to know each other started in a café.

Earlier that day I had landed by seaplane on a new flight route connecting Marseille and Algiers. After introducing myself as Yann Cedak, and, having told him that I was working for *Le Pavé de Paris* and also did freelance work, Camus and I walked up Rue Michelet whose shadowed side was crowded with pedestrians. The massive sandstone buildings had cloth awnings drawn down over narrow balconies, injecting a jolt of red, green, or blue.

Camus and I had been walking for several minutes in the shadow of the buildings. Men with round straw hats and suits filed through the crowds. A few workers were already returning from their shifts at the harbor, many of them wearing knickerbockers and loosely fitted jackets. This was the French part of town, no doubt, and only a few Arabs were in the crowd; most of them wore taqiyahs, square caps made of cotton, and had ropes knotted around the waists of their thobes. As we walked, a passing electric car sprung its pole off the overhead power line. The tramcar came to a halt, and the conductor, in his clean, white uniform, stepped out of the cabin and walked to the rear to pull down the electric pole and nudge it back. A little crowd had gathered and started taunting the conductor, who was struggling with the pole.

"Turtle express," they yelled, and soon some urchins appeared from seemingly nowhere and scampered around the tramcar, spitting and yelling. Somebody threw a soccer ball into the street and a wild rally erupted around the halted tram. Cars started to hoot and a donkey pulling a cart threw itself into a frenzy. When the tramcar finally jolted forward, it drove off with screeches and the loud curses of its conductor.

Camus spread his arms as if calming the Sea of Galilee. An impish look oozed onto his face. He had enjoyed the ruckus, yelling taunts into the crowd while gesticulating as if cheering on his favorite team.

The feeder alley led uphill between houses built of sandstone, but now with fewer stories, not as towering. The windows were less recessed, the balconies even narrower, and beside the entrances I spotted hardscrabble hooded men and beggars. Camus waved them off with a jerk of his wrist. He started coughing and a few times had to stop to catch his breath.

Soon we stepped out onto one of those places in Algiers where the houses were set back to make space for traffic and cafés with thin iron chairs under dark awnings. That day, however, it was too hot to sit outside. Camus opened the door to a room filled with dozens of small tables covered with red and white-checkered cloths. Two wide-bladed fans were blowing air. A waiter walked over from the bar and put two glasses and a carafe with water onto our table, as well as a porcelain bowl with couscous and clumps of sticky rice adorned with small shreds of chicken and fish.

"Where is the rest of the bunch today?" the waiter asked.

"They are piled into Charlot's Bookstore," Camus replied.

"There's barely space for two people and a sardine there." The waiter lifted his chin and then added, "You literati are not frequenting the Facultés, are you?"

"That place. Quel horreur!" Camus opened his mouth in mock terror. "Never! You better believe that when it comes to visitors from Paris, I know where to dine."

The waiter leaned toward me. "We serve only the finest here."

"At least there's not much talk of war here," I said "Not like in Paris where everybody talks of war."

"Maybe not openly," Camus said, "but every week the censors block more from my newspaper."

"This war won't happen, gentlemen," the waiter said, and then he walked off with our order.

"How do you read the signs?" I asked Camus.

"We didn't go to war for the Czechs. Why would we go to war for Danzig or a couple of square miles?"

Camus reached for his glass of water.

For my part, I drank several glasses of water until I felt less parched. The waiter arrived with a big tray of fried smelts and a dish of flatbreads reddened with spices. He then exchanged the empty carafe for a new one and set it beside a large bottle of Cinzano.

"Their beer tastes stale here," Camus said. "I don't dare tell you what they call it."

We occupied ourselves chewing the fried fish.

"Wash it down with the Cinzano!" Camus advised.

He kept staring out the windows as if contemplating that he could get more from life than sitting down with some journalist from Paris who hadn't anything better to do than liven up a pedestrian journal with news from Africa. A young woman passed by our table and greeted Camus. They exchanged a few sentences in an absent-minded fashion.

"She designs the clothes for the theater, but that's on hold now," Camus said after she walked away.

On hold—so, too, it seemed, was our informal talk.

Camus placed another order; this time, flat cakes dipped in honey. Though he seemed disinterested, he showed no intention of leaving and walking to Charlot's Bookstore. He remained, it seemed to me, in some state of muted retreat. Maybe this lingering was in his character (like all the Southerners and Arabs).Or had satiation with food and drink cocooned him? How could I draw him out? They had taught me ways to do it, back in Paris.

But the light here was hard and relentless, indifferent. And what a contrast it was to the mellow touch of the light weakening on the paneled wall behind the ebony-colored piano in my parents' house in Saint-Brieuc. I remember sitting beneath the piano staring at my mother's feet pushing the pedals, this gigantic vibrating dark dome above me, and as I watched the last rays lit up curls of dancing dust.

The waiter returned and served us coffee in small porcelain demitasses. He poured a bitter, dark brew into the cups from a small-mouthed tin can with a long handle.

"Jean Grenier was my high school teacher," Camus said. "He sent me a letter saying you two were just one grade apart at the high school in Saint-Brieuc. I guess this is how your assignment came about?"

Camus sat back in his chair and, for a moment, seemed unhinged by my silence. But then his eyes narrowed and he leaned forward. His hands slid down his thighs toward his knees, where they came to rest, far apart, palms pointing toward each other—a gesture half praying, half reconciliation, but not without boldness and a preparation for bluntness.

"You worked at *La Pavé de Paris*," Camus said. "The censors are worse here than in Paris. They have made it impossible to publish anything but bland dribble in our newspapers. The spirit of revolt and solidarity has died or gone underground. The left is crumbling. The lights on the stage are out. Many nights we are gathering at Charlot's. We talk and drink coffee or cheap wine and then we go home."

"I read your essay and then the *Nuptials*. Neither are political," I said. "Rather contemplative and lyrical, if you ask me."

I took out my stenography pad and cocked my Conklin Nozac pencil, so thin that it resembled a black stinger. I realized immediately that I had made a mistake.

"Ah! Monsieur journalist. The interview begins now!" Camus said as he lifted his eyebrows in an expression of scorn.

"I apologize ...I should have asked you," I said.

Camus's irritation seemed allayed, although his voice remained hesitant.

"In these essays, I tried to sketch a certain sensibility using words that merely touch the boundaries of what we feel. They hint at something beyond but are rooted in the mundane and the real."

"Lucidity, indifference ...the true signs of beauty or despair," I said.

Camus nodded his head. "Sure, I wrote that. You can ask how something can be a true sign of beauty and, at the same time, despair. Use your Cartesian knife and you will never get to the bottom of it. And at the bottom will always be death."

Just two days before, reading through Camus's work, I had underlined a sentence from his essay *Winds of Djemila*. I now quoted it at the table: "'I feel certain that the true, the only progress of civilization, lies in creating conscious death.' What do you mean by that, Camus?"

"Our poverty of ideas about death, of course."

"Christianity emptied the whole field."

"Not quite! Look at the Buddhists! I think there is much to be learned from *The Tibetan Book of the Dead.*"

"Do you plan to travel to the far east?"

"Actually, I have been preparing to travel to Greece, and I have been looking forward to my time on the ship. The wind, the salt spray, and the books I'll bring along ...the rumble of the engines always quiets my mind. It's like a return to the womb. Jonas the whale, but this time benign—you know—in the belly of the ship."

"When are you leaving?"

"The trip has been put on hold." Camus fixed his eyes on me. "The ship brokers are behaving as if war is imminent."

He lowered his gaze and watched me jerking my pencil across the page.

"What else do you want to know?" he asked.

"Just talk!"

"Well, for some time, I did some reporting on court cases, where things are rather dry and factual, and I learned that the system is slanted against anybody with colored skin," he said.

Camus leaned back and moved his hands toward his neck, his thoughts swerving to somewhere.

I took a sip from the dark brew and waited.

Klaus.
Funeral of Mother.
Feb, 1960

Cradled by the car's soft suspension, Klaus slips deeper into his seat. The lights of oncoming cars slide across the windshield and fall off to the side. It's still early, and he's having trouble remembering the name of the small village where the home for senior citizens is located. Petersdorf maybe ...somewhere north of Augsburg ...north of the Alps on a gravel plane spread by glaciers thousands of years ago.

Klaus likes the language of distance.

His mother passed away days ago from a pulmonary embolism. The phone call had come Thursday. His uncle, who lives not far from the home where his mother had been living during her final weeks, apparently had volunteered to make phone calls and work out the arrangements for his sister's burial.

There are ice-related problems across the country. Ice dams have formed on some rivers, and some trains have to be rerouted. Klaus has taken the night train which stops at 4 a.m. in Augsburg where his uncle will pick him up by car.

Klaus prefers the dark for his arrival, anyway—a darkness that is like a cloak he can use to cover his face, his unshaved beard, his red-rimmed eyes, his numbness. The arrival of her only son in the middle of night: dejection and humbleness and unmeasured sadness. Fact is, he cannot remember much of her, cannot feel, and cannot conjure up enough of her life to chafe his soul.

On the night train to Augsburg he is a hollow young man sitting in a badly lit wagon compartment as the train keeps slicing through the cold night. This is the time to smoke, he thinks—to let the din of the wheels drown his senses—but he has never acquired the taste for smoking; no cigarette will ever dangle from his lips the way cigarettes dangled from Camus's in those pictures that have been circulating over the media in the weeks since his death. Klaus stares out the window, watching the lights climb snow banks, flow across sheets of snow, and whip darkly against flowing rivers. Eventually, the train steams into the station, ice splintering off the wagon couplings.

Uncle Otto is waiting for him inside the dim hall of the Augsburg Hauptbahnhof, and he's smoking. When they meet, Otto puts his hand on Klaus's shoulder and offers his condolences. They leave through the main entrance where the Opel, its engine running, curls flags of exhaust out of its pipe. It has been ten years since Klaus last sat in a passenger seat beside his uncle. Klaus leans back, trying to visualize a far memory of swimming in the river Würm. Klaus was raised among old men and women, and Otto was the only one among his relatives young enough to teach him to swim;

"All the informed I have duly noted here," Otto says as he places a steno pad onto Klaus's lap.

Dozens of names are written in Otto's cursive, mixed with gothic runes bleeding at angles thickened with ink. Klaus last saw this handwriting in the letter Otto had written to his mother on the occasion of Klaus's uncle Ludwig's funeral.

Those cold words: *Our worlds are split, our ways separate. Regret of not attending*. There had been so much strife in this family.

"Your mother didn't attend church for years, I reckon," Otto says.

"No."

"A short prayer, maybe."

Klaus and Otto drive through the suburbs of Augsburg, which are filled with industrial wasteland and housing projects. They pass the house where Uncle Ludwig had lived, its triangular sunroom on the second floor jetting out above the railroad divide like the figurehead of a ship. Klaus falls asleep for a while, his head leaning against the passenger side window until coldness on his temple wakes him up. A bloom of window ice is lit by streetlights. A few snow crystals tumble inside the car and land on his eyebrows.

Klaus observes Otto's face, bent over the steering wheel.

"I forgot to bring coffee," Otto says.

"How much longer?"

"On these icy roads? About two more hours."

Klaus conjures a sunrise above the frozen snowfields of Bavaria—some simulacra of depth, hope, and deeper connection appropriate for the occasion—but it's no use. He never felt a genuine affection for his mother. It had been a relation stifled in stiffness, weakened by unease and only relieved by their mutual acceptance of estrangement.

A brochure describes his mother's senior living home as "nestled into a wooded moraine," but there are no moraines this far north. Klaus knows that the building is a former SS compound, some forgotten bastion of the Nazi's breeding efforts. And Klaus knows that Otto had been a member of the SS troops, although nobody ever talks about it.

When they arrive at the home, a narrow, three-story brick building, the rising sun is veiled behind a frozen carpet of clouds. Klaus tries to feel some of its warmth, weak as it might be.

The administrator of the home leads them into his office and sets out cups of coffee. His pants display wrinkles galore; he wears a mismatched pair of socks.

"Long drive from Munich," the administrator says.

"We drove in from Augsburg," Otto says.

"I could never afford the rents in Munich," the administrator says as he turns some pages.

Klaus feels sorry for this man and he doesn't want to bother him more than necessary. But his sadness for the loss of his mother seems no stronger than this man's gloom. There seems to be no difference. Both feelings seem to have blown in from some cold corner of the universe, where neither meaning nor hope reside.

"I need some identification," the administrator says.

Klaus hands him his driver's license.

"Can I see my mother now?"

"Please understand that the embolism has bloated her."

Klaus waits in silence, watching the man's tongue rub his lips, and he wonders for a brief moment how this man would kiss a girl on a freezing night. He disposes of the image in his mind before shame and confusion sets in.

"Your mother wasn't able to make friends during her short stay," the administrator says as he looks at Otto and taps the desk with his fingers to the beat of a hidden timepiece.

"When she fell out of bed, she couldn't reach the alarm button. We found her within an hour or so. An orderly heard her whimpering through the door and we rushed her to the hospital, but the pulmonary ...I mean, it was too much for her. Everything was too much for her. She never had embraced life!"

The administrator stands up and leads Klaus and Otto to the door.

"Please, go ahead. You are permitted to spend time with her now."

His mother's face looks strangely lifted in her casket. That bulbous nose is there; so often Klaus had thought of it as a cauliflower in the making. Klaus notices that Otto's and his mother's lips are much the same: fleshy tubes, oddly hostile. The undertaker has closed her eyes. Klaus remembers their color as that of boiled egg white. He feels like falling, tumbling into a barren place.

How do you act when you judge your life as empty as your mother's? The administrator stands with his back to the door, waiting.

"It is custom here to have a brief prayer at the interments," he says. "But your mother did not make any provisions for religious service and she did not attend our Sunday services."

"Let us leave the son alone," Otto says to the administrator as they both leave the room.

Klaus and his mother are alone now. A thin light crawls down the walls. He walks closer to her body, places his fingers between hers, then slides them across the back of her hand. Is one to touch the dead? Klaus wonders if it is expected, such that the absence of touch may reveal a cold soul? There are stories of Sicilian funerals wherein the son or the daughter throw themselves onto the body and cover it with kisses. Am I being judged for my coldness by God or am I judging myself? Klaus thinks. Aren't tender feelings supposed to come forward during these last moments, some distillation of love and appreciation? Only during episodes of childhood illness, when fever churned him and strangely buoyed his senses, could he render himself porous to the love his mother could give. Lying in bed, his legs uncovered, his mother would wrap his feet in towels she had moistened in the sink. Drawing out the fever, she called it. But beyond these scraps of memories, he cannot conjure the feel of her embrace or the heft of her hand. Her life seemed to have drifted through him like sand through a sieve, leaving barely a memory.

Klaus remains in the room and watches the light on the whitewashed walls. He watches intently as a fly buzzes around his mother's corpse. His head begins to feel heavy as caffeine seeps into his skull. Klaus no longer wants to be alone with himself and the ruinous emptiness in his soul.

Only a few mourners will attend his mother's funeral. Klaus's father died barely a year ago, as did his mother's younger brother, who had thrown himself from the window of the Policlinic in Munich. The administrator returns with Otto and introduces Klaus to an old lady named Beth. "During the short time your mother was with us, Beth talked with her often," he explains.

Klaus tries to fix Beth with his gaze, perhaps in the hope she might finish whatever the administrator intended to express. But Beth just sits there and begins to whimper, flapping her hands in her lap while fingering a rosary, knotting the beads between her fingers, blowing her lips in prayer.

"They were friends in dire times," the administrator says, softly sliding his well-chosen words. "She must have had many friends in Augsburg."

"I couldn't take care of her," Klaus says.

"We understand."

The gloom in the administrator's voice begins to irritate Klaus. But it is not just his voice. From the moment Klaus arrived at this home, a scene from Camus's novel *The Stranger* had clung to his mind: Meursault's mother's burial. It is Klaus's awareness of Meursault's vigil over his dead mother in Algeria as Camus described it in *The Stranger*, a night of flies and numbness, that makes him quickly excuse himself from the room.

Klaus greets the few relatives who have gathered around a table with coffee and other refreshments. Besides relatives, two old ladies living on the same floor have showed up to confirm that their neighboring occupant has actually died, that the lady in her grey socks sitting at the corner table toward the kitchen exit is now gone.

Klaus bends down to speak to Beth who is still holding the rosary.

"You were a good friend?"

"So much for nothing," she mumbles. She looks ghostly with her mouth open and eyes closed.

"We'll all go this way," he says.

"All she wanted to do was run across dewy meadows again. One more time! One more time in the morning fog."

Beth starts sobbing. She remains in the chair, head slumped toward her chest.

Klaus listens to the creaking noises in the walls. The stillness feels as if it's closing in on him, a stillness as undoing as death. Then he hears scraping sounds as the coffin is shoved onto a line of metal rollers and placed into a hearse.

It is a short walk to the cemetery. A black Mercedes leads the way. Beth sits slouched over on the passenger side. The priest has already driven his car to the site, and now he's waiting with the engine running. The burial workers try to thaw the site with torches, but to no avail. They decide instead to use a mechanical shovel, leaving reptilian tracks around the hole where his mother will soon be lowered.

The priest speaks a few words.

"Although I did not know Amalia personally, her friends tell me that she had walked in the valley of grace," he says. "She liked the mountains and Edelweiss flowers and those sacred minutes of Alpen-glow when only the highest of mountaintops are lit. Hers was a simple life, and God will give life to the meek who will inherit the earth. Such said the Lord. We shall now return Amalia to this earth, the earth to which we all shall someday return."

With these words, four helpers in black coats who seem to have appeared from nowhere lower the coffin, but it does not disappear into the ground; its top appears to hover above the surface. On this freezing winter day, it turns out that Klaus's mother is not quite received back into the earth.

Klaus experiences a sudden angst, the realization that everything is strange and stands apart darkly. This instills in him a strange thrill, a frisson, a feeling that is oddly arousing—as if their very existence can deny the meaningless of this world and thus lower the ordinary woes of existence. And maybe that is the way: Nihilism as exaltation, the ultimate sin. This dull grind of despair Klaus is experiencing leads to a yearning for more despair, the strange state of the mind that the scribes described as the despair of not being enough in despair. Hell might look like that: no fires, but an emptiness eternally yearning for more emptiness.

The priest spoke a few words about his mother's life and her love of early morning walks across dew-softened meadows. He spoke with softness, and Klaus has now the urge to shake his hand and sit with him on some wooden table. He pictures eating Weisswursts with him, lifting his eyes beyond fork and knife and asking questions about the nature of God's wrath and condemnation. Klaus wants to break down the wall that separates him from the God of those years when he was filled with religious passion.

The priest, however, strides to his car and drives off. His car disappears behind a low rise, white exhaust flagging the horizon for a while.

"You mentioned my mother's years at the Kneipp Sanatorium to the priest?" Klaus says to Otto.

"She was happy then," Otto says.

"The morning dew meadow walks she loved so much!"

Otto nods. "I saw the priest take a few swigs from his 'flat friend,'" Otto says. "Did you?"

"Flat friend?"

"You know. One of those hip-hugging schnapps bottles."

As tipsy as the priest might have been, he was really the only one who tried to sketch out his mother's dreams. It stings Klaus how far apart he had been from his mother, how he had never been able to get a sense of her way of life.

For a moment, the relatives gather in a circle. Klaus is tempted to cry out: "Hold it. Stay as you are! Don't move. Don't move. Be awake! Be awake! Bare your feet like Jesus did! Walk out into the wet meadows, the crystalline white of the dew as far as you can see, and walk in that field of unending grace!" He feels the urge to tell them to hold hands, but the occasion flicks off, and life whittles back to what it was before, a circle frayed.

They all drift toward their cars and drive off to the inn, where Otto has reserved a long oak table for brunch. Amalia's friends and family lift their Weisswursts from a large terrine filled with boiling water, and they slather them with grainy mustard. They drink Weizenbier and barely talk. None of the gaiety that sometimes takes over at funeral meals comes up. It is as if Klaus's mother's life was meant to be forgotten and discarded from memory as quickly as possible—as quickly as the memories of this frozen week that everybody here in this Bavarian plane has suffered through. The sky has clouded over, and the temperature is rising, and the long-anticipated thaw is ready to begin.

After the meal and a few plain words of goodbye, the mourners' hands meet briefly. As everybody departs, Klaus imagines a bird's-eye view of the small village: cars speeding away, white plumes of exhaust curling across the frozen fields. He senses that all those gathered here today are fleeing away from God, away from their emptiness, from death. He knows that he won't meet these people again. And inside himself he finds nothing but a dull coldness.

Meeting Camus 2

A small crowd of mostly men wearing baggy long pants and silky shirts shuffled into the café. A few women in simple wrap-around clothes with sash belts also surrounded us. The kitchen door kicked open, releasing a smell of sweat, coffee, and badly washed floors. Amid the constant clank of plates, a waiter edged his way around two little boys on the floor who were playing with wooden bobbins through which they had twisted rubber bands, securing them on either side with sticks. Unleashed against each other, the contraptions rolled toward a confrontation like tanks in wars. The boys' father, who wore odd-looking knickerbockers with a bib that reached up between his suspenders, swooped the urchins off the floor and commanded them to sit.

Camus was back with a question.

"What would it be not to intensify your life but rather flatten it and drift into some state of indifference?"

"I figure you know the answer," I said. "Grenier in *Les Iles* hinted at it. He linked the shift of tides, incessantly denuding the earth and blunting all reference, to a peculiar delight and a feeling of nothingness that led to indifference."

Camus leaned back. "But what would it lead to?"

"Possibly a stoic attitude like the Greeks."

"Not quite! The stoics showed a serene outside, a fire contained in a shell. But I am asking a different question: What if a man does not find emotion in himself? Or if he forgoes emotions and chooses not even to kindle the weakest of flames? And what if he has no guilt?"

"I wouldn't value that man highly."

"Exactly! You might even kill him." Camus scowled "In a novel, of course –but wouldn't that man be truer to himself and more lucid than most?"

"Still, why the idea of killing?" I asked Camus.

"Think of all the demands of religion, the tender closeness to God, the warmth in your heart, the fire of belief! What a guilt then if you do not experience them! What then if you live in the knowledge that God condemns your indifference. There is a God for those stricken by sorrow, for those in love, and for those who beg for forgiveness, but there is no God for the indifferent."

"Will you write of this man?"

He nodded.

"Nihilism is a sense of happiness," I said.

"You like to quote Nietzsche! Don't you?"

Again, his pert smile. As if to establish some distance, he turned and called the waiter. "Some fruits, please."

"You write that the sun heals?"

"No. I do not say that." Camus curled his lower lip and almost closed his eyes, his eyebrows pencil-thin. "The African light springs at you, accosts you, hurts you. Think of the sun's reflections on a knife's blade—how it stabs your eyes and dazes your mind."

The waiter returned to our table and set down fruits in a glass bowl, plus a plate heaped with peppermint powder with which to rub our gums. I looked outside where an achromic light burned into the street filled with the agitated traffic of horse carriages, tramways, and tooting Renaults. This Mediterranean light neither sculpted the objects of this world nor bound them; it seemed to be all places at the same time.

"I'm expecting somebody to meet me here, but this person seems to be late," Camus said. "I suppose this will give us a chance to get better acquainted."

"Sure. So, your father died in the Great War?" I asked.

"Yes. I never knew him."

Camus lifted his chin, as if to relieve a choking grief. "My mother still keeps in her drawer a few shell fragments sent to her from a hospital in Saint-Brieuc where he died."

Stillness had crept in. I didn't know how to continue.

"Have you ever seen a rosary made from shell fragments?" Camus asked.

I shook my head.

"The nuns in that hospital sent one to my mother," he said. "War and its blessings, prayer and death."

"My father died in Saint-Brieuc, too. He was of slight build and the Army made him go up in an observation kite. He was shot down right at the beginning of the war."

The ensuing silence afflicted me. I reached into my pocket and took out a small photo with serrated margins and handed it to Camus. "That face on the third-floor marked with a dot is my father's."

Camus sat still, studying the print. "There is a similar photo of my father and I seem to recognize the drab façade of that building...I believe our fathers were in the same hospital!" Camus had an incredulous expression on his face.

The clatter in the dining hall sounded glassy and eerie, as if carrying the sound of distance. "When did your father die?" he asked after a long silence

"October 11, 1914."

One date, and the weary load of history was suddenly upon the two of us.

"Our fathers died on the same day," Camus said. He sighed, leaned back, and ran his fingers through his hair. Then he poured the rest of our Cinzano.

"The light in Africa is unbearable. It is absurd, and its absurdity deprives man of history, burns his core and leaves but the ghost of a shell."

"What do you mean when you say 'absurd'?" I asked.

"Absurdity is that our fathers died on the same day and in the same hospital, that they died in a war for nothing. Absurdity is that God left and death stayed."

I felt the Cinzano. I, too, had emptied my glass and sensed a lightness in my body. I said something about the loss of meaning and that at times all philosophy felt like empty baggage.

"The word 'meaning' always triggers cascades of philosophical dance steps," Camus said. "Lack of meaning is the way we are in this world, the way we live. My response is lucidity and truth."

A middle-aged man wearing a brown business suit, a white shirt, and black cravat approached our table and stood facing Camus. He was sweaty and poorly shaved, the loose skin beneath his chin scuffed raw between stubbles of hair.

"Messieurs," he said, "may I disturb?"

"My lawyer," Camus said. "Please excuse us for a minute, Yann."

Camus and the man walked to an unoccupied corner table, where the lawyer opened his attaché case and spread some documents across the table. They talked agitatedly. The waiter now was moseying up to me. He refilled our water carafe and asked if he should bring another bottle of Cinzano. I declined.

"Came from the mainland today, didn't you?" the waiter asked when he returned to our table with the bill.

I nodded absentmindedly.

"On one of the new silver birds? Well, Monsieur Camus must be famous now that a journalist flies in from the mainland to talk with him."

"Just a small Paris paper," I said.

"Our mayor dislikes his socialist tendencies. Camus might even have been a Communist party member, or so the rumor goes."

"That is up to him," I said. "As far as I'm concerned, your couscous is quite good."

Camus valued privacy. Boundaries had to be respected. It was on that very evening that he handed me his manuscript.

Klaus's Return from Funeral to Munich

Otto had offered to drive Klaus to the train station to catch a train back to Munich. Now, sitting in the damp compartment by himself, Klaus watches the whitened landscape roll by. At the margin of the window, ice crystals have frozen into colorless flower patterns. He keeps staring, thinking about nothing. Between pain and indifference, he has chosen indifference.

Just as he arrives at the main train station, Klaus realizes that he has misplaced the key to his apartment. A Mr. Salomon, who acts as the custodian for the apartment complex, has spare keys, but Mr. Salomon does not answer his phone. It is odd, but Klaus suddenly desires to spend one night in a hotel among people he does not know and does not care about. He wants to stay in a place between his mother's grave and his spare apartment. Maybe doing this will help numb him.

It is just days before Mardi Gras, and Klaus now finds himself in a hotel watching some brainless sing-along special in color. They call it Schunkeln: strangers lined up and locking elbows, swaying sideways to the sound of some Schmaltz music. Germans—the inventors of the wave—all waves, really, carrying their numbed emotions to a pitch.

The next day, a Sunday, Mr. Salomon hands Klaus the spare keys to Klaus's two-room apartment, which is nearly empty apart from a few boxes and two wooden crates. There is a cot with several blankets, a floor lamp, a chair, several large trunks. On the balcony several bottles of beer lean against the wall.

As he settles back into his surroundings, Klaus finds a letter on his floor. He opens it.

We want to express our sympathy for the death of your mother, it reads. It is signed by Mrs. Schnitzel, the neighbor lady, and Mr. Salomon.

Klaus steps out onto the narrow balcony and watches the traffic below. A dry, warm wind, locally called the Föhn, has started blowing across the Alps from Italy and with it record-high temperatures. Klaus knows stories about birds being swept across the Alps. He knows of people—or so his mother had once told him—who smell the scents of the Mediterranean for the first time and are suddenly driven into rueful evaluations of their lives, causing them to commit suicide by jumping from the infamous railroad bridge at Grosshesselohe. When the Föhn blows in from the Alps, people unexpectedly leave their spouses, court hearings turn chaotic, the death rate at hospitals soars. And there is the Föhn's other effect, equally strong, which makes people irritable and lethargic, as if lead has been poured into their joints. All throughout his childhood, Klaus looked forward to the times the Föhn would unleash its winds. It brought an edginess to life, a feeling of impending decisions, of suspense, of clarity and danger.

Klaus turns his face toward the wind, sits down on a pillow, and leans against the wall. He drinks beer and waits for the velvet curtain of inebriation. The swish of the Föhn is steady, strangely demanding, unsettling his mind. He looks down to the terminal trolley station. To see the lights inside the waiting tram always carries with it a strange comfort. It is waiting to go somewhere, he tells himself, and he wonders what it might feel like to be thrown into the rush of aerial forces, to lose himself, uproot his life, and burn the chaff inside his soul.

This evening, Klaus wraps a blanket around himself and sits on the balcony for a long time, just listening, watching the light filter away. The last tram screeches around the loop, and he sees windows light up and being opened. It is getting so warm that people step out onto balconies. For a moment, Klaus wants to rattle the balcony's railing in front of him and yell: "Blow us away! We all want to be blown away!" But he doesn't. Rust has eaten into the iron gridwork of the balcony—it would not be safe, after all—and soon the few restless people on nearby balconies step inside again. One by one the lights go out. The moldy scent of melting snow wafts high in the air.

Klaus walks back inside the almost-empty room and lies down on the mattress, still listening to the wind. He imagines southern bodies of water where this wind was born, imagines himself immersed in a fragrant warm sea he has never seen. His mother's life had been bland. He had always wondered about her resistance to art, to embellishment, to exaggeration of any kind. Her favorite colors were muted sepias and the demure hues of her husband's old-fashioned black and white photographs with their serrated edges. And nothing had ever burned through her skin. Everything had been seething inside her.

The next morning, while leaving his apartment, the wind sucks Klaus right out onto the pedestrian walkway and makes him struggle to negotiate a straight line between the piles of snow. Today is Rose Monday—the day before Mardi Gras—and it's considered a half-holiday, with many offices closing this afternoon to allow their employees to don masks and hats and gather on Neuhauserstrasse in the center of Munich, where they will get drunk and walk in circles to raise mayhem. And the forecast predicts record temperatures.

Klaus steps into the downstairs bakery on the ground floor of the apartment building. A motley crew is crowding in front of vitrine displays of cream puffs, nut horns, and small breads of all varieties. Everything is damp, the windows are fogged, and the tile floor is puddled with a brownish melt of snow carried in on shoes.

He squeezes into a space at one of the round counters and begins to drink his cup of coffee.

"Your poor mother," the man beside him says.

It's Mr. Salomon. His teeth look like a heap of scrap lumber. "Worst time of the year for this to happen—except Christmas."

"She was old," Klaus says.

"For some reason, I still picture her young."

Klaus glances at his cup of coffee and his crumbling Danish. Human relationships are snares. All these expectations of feelings and showing emotion!

"I know it's not going to really set in until later," Mr. Salomon says.

"I knew she would die. In many ways, she had already given up."

"I understand."

He doesn't understand. All Mr. Salomon is doing right now is stirring up the turmoil and the void—always the void—of recent months.

Klaus stays in the coffee shop long after Mr. Salomon leaves. He has no intention of running into him again, but when he steps outside he almost runs him over. Here Mr. Salomon is, struggling with his little mutt. The schnauzer—perhaps held inside the apartment for too long—puts all his energy into one giant leap and lands on a snow pile where he starts digging up his canine colleagues' recently thawed-out excrements, thus releasing a long-suppressed world of scents and odors.

"He's killing me," Mr. Salomon yells.

Klaus tries to avoid them, but the snow piles have narrowed the passage in front of the coffee shop so much that the pedestrians, hurrying to reach the tram, some carrying bags of food from the nearby store, have tangled up into a perfect traffic jam. Klaus would like to bypass this scene, but instead he steps up to the snow pile and tries to restrain the mutt, who snaps at him with gusto.

"Thank you kindly," Mr. Salomon says. "I want him dead. Can you believe he doesn't even want to sleep beside me?"

Mr. Salomon jerks the dog's leash. "Did you know that your mother always had this idea of leaving early on winter mornings and walking across a meadow in her bare feet? The grating of the ice crystals on her feet would be a kind of healing, she always said. I can't imagine, but something must have been in it for her. I don't think she was happy."

Klaus stares at Mr. Salomon before parting ways then walks toward his apartment.

When he steps out onto his narrow balcony, where the snow is now steaming off, he sets down a canvas chair, glances into the gleaming sun, leans back, and rests his feet on the railing. A small group of schoolchildren are walking over to the bus stop. Some disappear behind the snow piles, snowballs start flying, backpacks are used as shields, and wool caps soar in the air, complementing the laughter and screams. And then it all stops. The blue bus's pneumatic doors fold outward and the snow-dotted jackets disappear inside.

A clown appears down at the platform, and he's busy pulling a balloon against the stiff wind that whips the balloon into a twirling dance. An old lady in a grey coat walks along the flower shop's row of glass windows, stabbing the ground in front of her with her umbrella as she goes. Klaus cherishes the fruity flavor in there, the compelling scents of chocolate and lavender, and likes to loiter beside its door. Inside is a paradise of slanted displays of candied fruits among tropic plants. He can still remember his mother shying away from the store. It was too elegant and too expensive. She called it a store "for the fine people of Munich."

Klaus begins to feel hungry, so he finds two Danish pastries and a bottle of old-fashioned Waldmeister lemonade inside the fridge. He sits down on the living room floor and eats the Danish off the wax paper. When he drinks the green lemonade, it reminds him of childhood. He returns to the balcony. A scatter of children, led by their parents, leave the Roxy after a matinee movie. He remembers the Roxy as a livelier place when he was younger. The matinees at the Roxy were cheap American flicks, in which the FBI were always after some Chinese bad guys. The theater would fill with dozens of children, all revved up and yelling and throwing food and jumping off their seats. More than once, the bald-headed owner had to step in front of the screen and threaten to empty the theater.

Nowadays, life has fizzled out. There are hardly any people in the neighborhood. Klaus feels a sense of relief in this emptiness, and a vague awareness of his apathy filters into his mind. He thinks of Meursault, the protagonist of *The Stranger*, who looked down onto the street in Algiers as life too was passing him by.

Eventually, Klaus dozes off, and when he awakes, he lets the cold crawl in below his blankets. There are more people on the street now, their shadows long and slanted in the sinking sunlight. The clown has pulled off his bulb nose. The world is passing by almost soundlessly—a film of plaintive sequences of no bearing.

When the streetlights come on, Klaus folds his blanket and goes back inside his apartment. Suddenly he feels the need to see himself in a mirror—an odd and unexpected urge. He searches for a mirror in his shaving kit, but the metal rim has cracked and the shattered glass splinters away his image.

For a while, Klaus stands in the center of the half-empty apartment as if in frozen torpor, balancing the void against his mind's ruminations. He picks up a sparse bundle of mail. Tucked among the envelopes is another hand-scribbled note from Mr. Salomon, relaying the message that an acquaintance named Rosie had called while Klaus was away for his mother's funeral. She left her telephone number.

Rosie had been one of Klaus's friends, a group of beer-drinking poker players who would bike out to the lakes on summer weekends. But nothing passionate had ever developed between Klaus and Rosie, and thinking of her now gives him the painful twinge of missed opportunities.

Nevertheless, Klaus walks toward the hallway phone and dials Rosie's number. A voice he does not recognize answers, and he asks the lady to please relate the message that he is available the rest of the evening. Indeed, it would be awkward to meet Rosie again. The call has surprised him, and Klaus is not certain he wants to see her again. He will have to listen to stories of love affairs and parties and bus trips to the Mediterranean and ...truth is, Rosie had dropped him because of his bland character—for being repressed and clumsy.

"There's only one thing worse than a bad kisser," she had told him once. "One that doesn't try!"

Maybe it is better to avoid any contact.

Around eight o'clock, the hallway telephone rings. As per customary procedure, Mr. Salomon picks up the phone and then knocks on Klaus's door. Rosie is on the line, he says.

Rosie tells Klaus that she is in Freising, just north of Munich, at a friend's house. She's free the next day, which happens to be Mardi Gras. She proposes to meet Klaus at the heated swimming pool near the power station in Freimann.

"At 10, right when it opens," she says. "We'll talk then, okay? They have a swim-in coffee bar. And you'll get in for free if you wear a costume."

"What are you going to wear?" Klaus asks.

"Is a bikini a costume?"

Back in the apartment a rumbling noise comes up from the Waldfriedhof, a cascade of honking and then the murmur of distant traffic. Smells released by the warmth leach from the carpet, the walls, and the wood paneling. The night is like a mirror, reflecting on Klaus in a thousand ways, and in no ways.

The *Wine Stube*, located at the Waldfriedhof tram station, is teeming with people who clink their wine glasses and carouse under a sheet of wafting cigarette smoke as sleepy dogs under long wooden tables keep blinking their eyes. Klaus walks to the tin-covered bar for a take-out of sauerkraut and Thuringia sausage, plus a bottle of Gewürztraminer. A sweaty, hurried waitress shoves a Styrofoam tray across the beer-puddled surface and stands the bottle onto it.

"Alone today?" she asks.

Klaus hands her twenty Deutschmark.

"Yes. And keep the rest."

He reaches the door right before a group of tipsy men in sheik costumes crowd through. Back at the apartment, he sits on the carpeted floor and eats the sausage from the tray, lifting strands of sauerkraut to his mouth with his fingers. He opens the bottle of wine, steering for a balance of drunkenness, weariness, and indifference. He has laid out a mattress and some blankets on the floor. A softer wind continues to whistle through the open door that leads to the balcony. It is easy enough.

Klaus Meets Rosie at the Swimming Pool

Klaus wades to the coffee bar at the swimming pool just as the espresso machine starts to whistle. He is the first one to use his token to buy coffee.

"If it doesn't taste right, tell us!" the bikini-clad waitress says. She's wearing a baby cap—an adornment that looks like a Mennonite hat—and a bib around her neck that reaches down to her décolleté.

At this hour of the morning, only a few people are in the large pool, but there are sure signs of Mardi Gras: one life guard in a Speedo is trying on a clown costume and one other struggles to adjust his shark mask.

Rosie arrives after a few minutes, walking to the bar in chest-high water. Klaus gives her a hasty kiss on the forehead that feels awkward. A curl of hair has fallen down in front of her face and she tries to shake some order into her curls, which have a tousled look, hinting at mischief. Her eyes still have the deep brown color of chestnut that Klaus so fondly remembers.

"So?" she asks, tilting her head charmingly. If she feels awkward or misplaced, it doesn't show. Klaus appreciates her attention, but recalls how rapidly it waned in the past, and—it is odd—he cannot help but feel that she is pitying him right now.

"It's been years," she says.

Klaus orders a second cup. "Have some coffee."

She takes a sip, smacking the rim of the cup with her lips. "Do they actually chlorinate their brew here?" she asks with a mischievous smile.

Klaus gets ready to order some different drink, but she holds him back. "Just kidding!"

Rosie's lipstick has left red patches on the porcelain cup, and the awareness of it makes Klaus upset in a way he cannot quite describe.

"I have broken up with too many boyfriends," Rosie says. "It just doesn't seem to work out for me."

Before even giving Klaus a chance to respond, she begins talking about other things, like her training as an air traffic controller and how she had to learn English, and how calling for the pilot to "turn to 25" could so easily be misunderstood as, "Turn 225."

"Turn left 30 degrees," Klaus says, fake-talking into a microphone. "'Right?' 'No, left.' 'So, it is left?' 'Yes, that's right.'"

It makes Rosie laugh in a weak way.

"You were never good with confusion," Rosie says.

"What do you mean?"

"I mean that strong feelings often start with a sense of confusion."

Rosie confidently pulls him away from the coffee bar counter to the hot pool to show him her slow backstroke. He watches as her smooth, thin body slices through the water, and, for a moment, it seems as if he's reliving an afternoon with her in the Unger bath: Rosie in her brown bikini, the chlorine biting his nose, the smell of wet grass in the meadows and the far, eerie sounds of children like distant dreams through the trees. Together they spun through the water, folded themselves, then stretched like cats on hot carpets, floated, leaned over, and again and again gave themselves away to the depths.

God! Life can be like that ...one can live like that ...somebody can live like that, Klaus thinks.

They swim to the pool's rim and hook their arms across a concrete lip in the wall—a perfect place to take a break.

"How long can anybody handle that hot water?" Rosie asks.

"I didn't know you could actually feel sweaty inside a pool," Klaus says.

"Well, you can always cool down," she says, pointing to a huge mound of snow at the poolside such that one could toboggan right into the water. They watch a man slide down the glazed chute while his girlfriend gesticulates wildly, yelling, "Freeze your balls. Freeze your balls!"

"Okay," Klaus says, "I'll do it but only if you follow right after me."

"Not in this bikini."

He tries to chuckle then pushes himself over the rim of the pool and walks up the top of the snow mound. From there he takes in the view of the disorganized landscape of urban Munich that's seeping away into rural flats. He looks down at Rosie who waves back then slides down the glistening chute, the ice shaving his buttocks numb in seconds.

It feels good to float in the warm pool again, so he and Rosie float for a few minutes. A clown walks along the rim of the pool, throwing snowballs at the swimmers. They watch as he jams his fists into the wide pockets of his costume's pants and pushes them forward, hinting at a fake erection.

Rosie gently kicks Klaus's leg. "So what's going on with you?"

"Second semester at the university," he says. "I'm studying Romantic literature, some philosophy, and French."

"You should visit me in Nürnberg," she says. "I'll be there for another year. The way things are going, I am free and—hey! We might as well have some fun." She tilts her head and parts her lips, giving herself an impish look. "Today we can take the tram to Marienplatz and roll with the crazy crowd on the Neuhauserstrasse," she adds.

A curl of hair has corkscrewed onto her forehead, partially covering an eyelid. She remains still and closes her eyes. Klaus flicks the curl off her forehead, but she doesn't say a word. Settling her body deeper into the water, she stretches and allows herself to float to the surface, legs paddling gently.

"You've got yourself a nice tan," Klaus says.

"Malta."

"Don't they swim naked there?"

"I wore at least something," she says, chuckling. "Remember your mother making a face when I tied down the sides of my bikini bottom?"

"Well, even showing a belly button was a sin to her."

"So how is your mother doing?"

"Well ...I mean ...it's bad news. She died."

"Oh, Klaus. I'm so sorry ...I wouldn't have mentioned ...I didn't know. What did she die from?"

"A stroke of some kind. Pulmonary embolism."

"When did it happen?"

"Just a few days ago."

Rosie shakes her head. "Hard to believe."

"After my father died I had to place her in a home."

"My mother talked to her just months ago when your mother still lived at the house."

Klaus slides lower into the water, suddenly feeling the need to be alone. His face is now barely above water. He wants to sink like a stone, escape the burden of her silence. He glances at Rosie who stares into the water, biting her lips.

"Well, when my mother called that time, your mother didn't mention anything about moving."

It's obvious to Klaus that Rosie is trying to say something—anything—to break what suddenly separates them.

Klaus turns on his back and pushes off the concrete wall. With a few backstrokes, he reaches the center of the pool. He closes his eyes and looks into the sun. He needs to have the whole sky in his face.

A vision slashes his heart—he has come to the pool's depth so he can be safe and numb because there is not one single deep thing inside him. He is shallow, and all is lost.

Rosie has not followed him, so Klaus swims back to the wall. To his surprise, Rosie is nowhere in sight. After a minute, he sees her return through the glass door of the main building. She casually walks back to the pool, clutching a towel in front of her stomach. She bends over the rim.

"Hey, Klaus. Sorry about that. I had to make a phone call to my cousin. I suddenly remembered that she said something about hosting a party tonight. Kind of ...family stuff."

"What about Fasching in downtown Munich?"

"I'm sorry, but I forgot about my cousin's party. I have to go."

Klaus takes the tram home. The sense of defeat and failure gnaws at his soul. Clowns, sheiks in caftans, witches in black, and a tin man enter the tram. Klaus has never felt so out of place, so out of touch.

When he arrives at his apartment, its sparseness provides an odd sense of relief. He sits on the balcony, thumbing through some old journals and drinking beer. He contemplates lying down, but then decides against it. As the sun sets low and the afternoon air begins to chill, he steps back into his apartment just as I knock on the door.

Reading the *Stranger* in Algiers

Maman died yesterday. Or yesterday maybe, I don't know. I got a telegram from the home. "Mother deceased. Funeral tomorrow. Faithfully yours." That doesn't mean anything. Maybe it was yesterday.

Camus's manuscript was typed on grey paper roughed with tiny wood splinters. Paper was hard to come by in 1939, and so were the spools of ink tape. Whenever I touched the page, I left a smudge.

Camus had handed me the manuscript after our meeting at the café in Algiers when we had gathered with his writer friends at Charlot's bookstore. It had turned out to be a long evening and now here I was back at my hotel in Algiers, reading and fighting sleep.

In *The Stranger,* a young man named Meursault attends his mother's funeral at Marengo, eighty kilometers inland from Algiers. He is alone. He smokes during the night as he observes the traditional night vigil with an empty heart. Only the priest, Meursault, and one old man follow the casket. Meursault has only faint memories of his mother.

Meursault returns to Algiers to continue a hollow life.

I knew I was going to bed and sleep for twelve hours.

The day after the funeral, Meursault runs into an acquaintance named Marie Cordona. They go swimming, and Marie keeps talking about a funny movie with the actor Fernandel. She inquiries about Meursault's black tie.

> *She wanted to know how long ago my mother died, so I said, "Yesterday." She gave a little start but didn't say anything. I felt like telling her it wasn't my fault. By that evening Marie had forgotten all about it. The movie was funny in parts, but otherwise it was just too stupid. She had her legs pressed against mine. I was fondling her breasts. Toward the end of the show I gave her a kiss but not a good one. She came to my place.*

That evening, when Camus had given me those loose pages of his first draft of the novel, he said: "A novel without a father." It was an odd remark, but since we had found out that our fathers died on the same day, there had been an urgency to Camus's voice that conveyed to me some sense of insistence. Or maybe he just figured that I had connections to publishing houses in Paris. I didn't know.

I sat upright in my hotel bed, a wet towel wrapped around my head against the thick heat, trying to avoid the drift of tiredness. I could not decide if I wanted to take a nap and then wake in the middle of night and continue. Luckily, the stack of papers was thin and when I noticed my progress I continued.

Several pages later in the manuscript, I read:

> *Maria asked me if I wanted to marry her. I said it didn't make any difference to me and that we could if she wanted to. Then she wanted to know if I loved her. I answered the same way I had the last time, that it didn't mean anything but that I probably didn't love her. "So why marry me then?" she said. I explained to her that it didn't really matter and that if she wanted to, we could marry.*

It was unreal, lying in bed reading a novel of indifference while hysterical fears of war were whipping across Europe. I was reading a novel in which the protagonist, Meursault, sits on a balcony observing the mundane events on the street—a man dragging his dog; tramways; kids leaving the cinema. The day drifts into night and nothing happens. And then Meursault gets acquainted—and drunk—with a neighbor, Raymond. After Raymond beats up a prostitute, Meursault writes a letter to exonerate him from the pending charges.

I tried my best to please Raymond because I didn't have any reason not to please him.

Maria and Meursault hang out with Raymond and his scumbag friends in a cottage overlooking the water.

I must have fallen asleep. Noises downstairs woke me. I pulled out my pocket watch: April, 1939. The time was 3 a.m.

I shuffled down the hallway, thinking about Meursault, and puzzling out the one thought that would best sum up what I had read thus far: no doubt, Meursault was a man committed to truth and mediocrity!

I kept hearing the sharp voice of some radio announcer and people talking. It was hot in Algiers at the end of August. Life retreated into the early mornings and late nights, and the hotel's breakfast room on the first floor must have opened early. I dressed and walked down. Several men gathered around a radio, hunched over, their heads leaning toward the radio's cloth-covered loudspeaker. One of the men turned his head and waved at me. I nodded and served myself some coffee.

"This is the first time Radio Algiers is broadcasting all night," one of the men explained. "Listen!"

What I heard was the speech Hitler had given on January 30. The calm voice of the translator was almost inaudible over Hitler's shouting. *Should the international financial Jewry achieve to push the world into a new war then the result will not be the world domination by Bolshevism, but the total annihilation of the Jewish race.*

After the speech, a commentator remarked that no world leader had ever used the word "annihilation". And after he stated that the dangers were real and the call upon the nation was urgent, he announced that a partial mobilization of Navy, Air Force, and Army had been decreed.

Everybody was talking at the same time.

"Why are these idiots just now transmitting the actual voice of Hitler?"

"Didn't you see the newsreels in the cinema?"

"They just want you to enlist!"

I did not want to join the caffeinated discussion, which seemed to me a chaotic stirring of hornets. As I left the breakfast room and walked up the flight of stairs, the hoarse sound of Hitler's voice crept after me. And in my mind I could still hear the roar of the masses shouting, Heil, Heil, Heil.

The pitch of rapture! False prophets.

That night, I wrote in my notebook:

This is the reign of epiphany and terror and fear. Make us feel exalted, the masses will cry; they will cry now and they will cry in the future; they will cry in so many ways, but it will be this one cry—always. Blood and fire will reign and blanket the earth. Can a man true to himself in a radical way, indifferent and free, carry the seed for a new world?

I resumed reading *The Stranger* at the page on which Camus describes the beach scene. An Arab who knows Raymond's abused girlfriend stabs Raymond. Everybody returns to the beach house feeling on edge. Later that afternoon, Meursault takes a walk on the beach by himself. He takes a revolver with him, just for safety. There is a chance meeting with the Arab who is still lingering about. The Arab draws a knife. The description of Meursault killing the Arab is peculiar because Meursault, so it seems, does not appear to be an active participant.

> *The light shot off the steel ...the sweat in my eyebrows dripped over my eyelids ...All I could see were the cymbals*

> *of sunlight crashing on my forehead and, indistinctly, the dazzling spear flying up from the knife in front of me. The scorching blade slashed at my eyelashes and stabbed at my stinging eyes. That's when everything began to reel. The sea carried up a thick, fiery breath. It seemed to me as if the sky split open from one end to the other to rain down fire. My whole being tensed and I squeezed my hand around the revolver. The trigger gave; I felt the smooth underside of the butt, and there, in that noise, sharp and deafening at the same time, is where it all started.*

Meursault is kept in jail. His visit to a movie just one day after returning from his mother's funeral is heavily counted against him. He has not kept decorum. One does not do such a thing! Nobody stands up to defend him.

Meursault is sentenced to death. A priest tries to bring him back into the fold of faith, but Meursault, having been silent about metaphysical issues, snaps and starts shouting at the priest.

> *Nothing, nothing mattered, and I knew why. So did he. Throughout the whole absurd life I'd lived, a dark wind had been rising toward me from somewhere deep in my future, across years that were still to come, and as it passed, the wind leveled whatever was offered to me at the time, in years no more real than the ones I was living. What did other people's death or a mother's love matter to me; what did his God or the lives people choose or the fate they think they elect matter to me when we're all elected by the same fate...*

After the rage, Meursault falls asleep in his cell and wakes "with the stars in his face" and the sounds of the countryside drifting in.

> *For the first time in a long time I thought about Maman ...So close to death, Maman must have felt free then and ready*

> *to live it all again. Nobody, nobody had the right to cry over her. And I felt ready to live it all again too. As if that blind rage had washed me clean, rid me of hope; for the first time, in that night alive with signs and stars, I opened myself to the gentle indifference of the world.*

The world was indifferent—that was Camus's truth. No God, no eternal life, no hope or flight into epiphany. And I felt that this last page would not be the end, but rather the beginning. Yesterday Maman died—so it begins. I opened myself to the gentle indifference of the world—so it ends, and in between lay everything.

Coming from the breakfast room, I could still hear a repeat broadcast of Adolf Hitler, his words threatening to drown Camus's "indifference of the world" in a flood of hate.

Post-War *Trip to Munich*

My colleagues at the university have often questioned my claim to fame as one of the first to ever have read Camus's novel. (It is my only claim besides having met Hitler in 1919, but that is another story.) As I stand across my chairman's desk, the bright Montpellier winter sun in my eyes, he tilts his head and stubs his cigar into his ashtray. He wriggles his lips as if some invisible blob needs to be swallowed.

"There are questions, you understand," he says. "Your colleagues have trouble believing that you could have read *The Stranger* in anything like a finished form as early as 1939.

"Yet we know that Camus burnt a number of documents in October of 1939," I counter.

"Tell me again when you visited Algiers?"

"August 1939."

"Still?"

"On May 1, 1940, in a hotel room in Paris, Camus wrote in his diary: *The Stranger* has been finished. Why in the world is it so difficult to accept that I read a rather finished version in September of 1939?"

The chairman looks down; he seems uneasy now.

I can't stop now. "After all, Camus mentions the *Stranger* as early as August 1937 in his diary, and I visited him two years later."

He offers a polite pause. "Well, there's another matter we need to discuss. The University of Munich requests your curriculum vitae. They want you to be one of their guest speakers. But before we get into that, I'm wondering if your malaria has been cured?"

He turns the sheet of paper around for me to read.

"Yann, you state here that after 1946, when you were sent to Mayotte by the Diocese to teach the Catholic minority, you had chronic malaria."

"Everybody at Mayotte had malaria. That island is badly infested."

The chairman nods absentmindedly.

"You didn't see me then, six years ago," I continue. "When I returned from Mayotte, I was skinny like a rod."

"That was my predecessor. I came here in 1955."

"My point is, I have no residual disease."

"The prior chairman got you on the staff based on a recommendation from the diocese? Is that true?"

I have always had the impression that my chairman judges me too old and not enough published for my present position. He rarely misses a chance to hint that I was put on the staff by his predecessor because of politics, the influence of the Catholic church, the financial contributions ...as such, I know exactly where he is going with this.

"I lived on Dzaoudzi right when they built the runway," I say. "I still speak the native language, Shimaore. Actually, I translated one of Camus's theater pieces into Shimaore and staged it at the high school in Mamoudzou."

The chairman looks down and taps his fingers on the desk. It seems to me that he has already shot his arrow.

"Anyway," he says, "congratulations ...things happen when a great one dies ...and with this invitation by the University of Munich, things seem to be getting interesting for you."

"To be a guest speaker in Munich is a great opportunity to shed new light on Camus's work."

A few days earlier, the package from Paris with the lost notes from my interview with Camus had arrived. But the skimpy file fell short of what I remembered, and there were only a few notes about Camus's manuscript.

I had mentioned to the chairman that I expected to recover material from my long-lost interview notes from 1939 and that I hoped these notes would help me flesh out a planned essay about my visit with Camus in 1939 Algiers. But now, with all that falling short, I was relieved he does not mention the interview notes.

But here is what I can say about my notes: the smell is still there, as is the primitive typeset from a typewriter, with the letter "e" nearly worn flat, the rough paper with half the trees still visible.

At the end of February, I travel by train to Munich. Memories rise like the raw smell of water as one nears the coast.

This marks the third time I have visited this city. I first came here in 1919 as a young journalist, seeking action photographs of the civil war that had erupted in Bavaria. I visited a second time during the Nazi reign in 1938 while researching Eugen Gottlob Winkler's suicide.

I feel a lost yearning, so I decide I will search out Karl, a German whom I first met in 1919 at the Bavarian Freikorps, and then again in 1940 when Karl was commissioned by the German occupying forces to build a cathedral overlooking the Mediterranean.

As the train reaches the gentle slope where the tracks funnel down into the main station, I recognize the bridges spanning the tracks and even remember names like Donnersbergerbrücke. My eyes keep panning the walls for the pits and scrapes left by the gunfire that erupted here in 1919. In 1938 I had recognized them—long before the bombing of Munich during World War II. And now, just as then, they are a reminder of events that played out at the Munich main train station in May of 1919.

It was late April of 1919 when I was trudging about the railroad yards west of Munich, where the Freikorps had been preparing their main advance into the center of the city. These units were recruited from all walks of life: young men looking again for the excitement and camaraderie of war; farmers unable to return to stalls emptied of horses and cows, their fields fallen fallow; men looking for a daily ration of bread and some Deutschmark. Mostly, they were reactionaries—right-wing and hateful of anybody leaning toward communism or socialism. At that time, Munich had been occupied for a few months by a thrown-together Communist group with great aspirations and barely a hint of any expertise in governing. Money was printed without hesitation and beer was flowing freely. Garbage was not picked up but the radio station played patriotic marches and proclaimed "World Revolution" while committees lingered for days in cafés, lobbing about lofty ideas. Just a few months prior, they had given the Freikorps a bitter military defeat, forcing them to retreat, regroup, and bring in reinforcements from Prussia. Now the Freikorps had returned, advancing along the railroad tracks west of Munich.

Beyond the embankments where the men assembled, a wide band of allotment gardens separated the railroad from multi-story barracks. These swaths of land were subdivided into tiny parcels of small beds of peas, beans, potatoes, and spindly fruit trees. They barely allowed space for a wooden shed and a few vegetables. Wooden planks rotted beneath drooping beanstalks and muddied potato leaves. Fences leaned away from the wind.

The soldiers started fires to boil water. Some of them sat in the open cargo doors of the railroad cars, airing their sleep-blankets, feet dangling down the sides. A low smoke drifted north toward the barracks, where a few windows were hung with white bedspreads to signal neutrality.

Karl Herrmann was just a face in the crowd that lingered along the railroad embankments. He was very young, with a milky face and pointy nose. Karl kept stamping his combat boots into the water-saturated ground between crags of snow.

"Shit everywhere!" he kept yelling.

Among the mostly tall soldiers my small stature must have drawn Karl's attention.

"Too young to fight, or what?" somebody remarked after I had introduced myself as member of the French Press Corps. I could even hear some hoarse laughter within the ranks.

I told them I was there to report back to the Paris newspapers.

"You speak decent German," a non-commissioned officer said, and after some more conversation, he told me to join Karl Herrmann's detachment. The NCO, Robert Schulig, displayed stitched red piping on his grey field jacket. Uniforms were important.

"So, what distinguishes the French from the Germans?" a bystander asked me. He had a challenging, fierce look in his eyes.

"Maybe we're all the same deep down!"

"Bullshit. You French even shit different. Your shit doesn't even have color. It is white, and ours is brown." He didn't fail to look about with a stupid smile to gather in a few laughs from all the other bystanders.

Amid that awkward exchange, Karl took me aside. "Don't listen to that idiot. At Christmas in 1914, my unit was lined up on the eastern side of a canal in Belgium. My commander had the idea to plant a white flag on a small float. 'Let it drift down the water!' he ordered us. Not long after that, the French on the western side did the same. Next thing we know, somebody throws a couple of hand grenades into the water, and all the fish appear belly-up. We put our hands in the water and just scooped them up. Needless to say, the French on the other side did the same. We all had fresh fish that night."

He paused before adding: "Was the wrong war? Maybe. But I'd rather fight those Communists that occupy Munich."

"I was too young to get drafted," I explained.

"Was your father drafted?"

"He was killed right at the start of the war. He went up in an observation kite and was shot down."

"Sorry," Karl said, and after an awkward pause, "I heard about those kites."

Karl turned out to be a talker. He told me later that the armistice in November of 1918 caught the still-intact German Army by surprise and even more so the storm or shock troops, an elite cadre with a high ratio of officers who had been sequestered from regular troops and trained to rapidly advance through the shell-holed no-mans-land, relying only on pistols, sub-machine guns, and hand grenades. During the spring offensive of 1918, they had almost broken through. No enemy soldier had yet touched German soil, Karl pointed out. But now the Communists undermined German fortitude and resistance. The ships of the fleet had not lifted anchor when ordered. The ammunition factory workers had lain down their tools. The workers in the factories, poisoned by ideas of the rule of the proletariat, had stabbed the Army in the back.

And I learned more: discharged soldiers, at home with their wives, woke up every morning to read of new demands by the victors. Hundreds of airships were to be built and given away, making for a miserly future Army without artillery or tanks. And then there were those many soldiers billeted at their barracks, idling away, waiting. Karl could not understand how they could face such humiliation, living on gruel soup and a meager ration of bread, every day taking the abuses of the soldiers' councils, those stinking red agitprop cells that took over many barracks and intended to paralyze Germany. Hell! Germany would reorganize. Order had to be reestablished and values reasserted. Victory had not yet been ripped out of German hands!

Karl was twenty-two years old—just two years older than I was—and had fought the war from its beginning, as he was to explain to me over the next several hours. Verdun, Somme, Ypres—these were names with meaning to him. He had witnessed reality. He had seen death! Werner stumbling back into a ravine, holding his guts as they spilled out. Reinhold foaming from the mouth, gargling his own bloody spit. Fritz's lung pulsing pink and grey through his burst ribs. As Karl described these horrors, I had an inkling that he was claiming a secret privilege, that all this experience was in some ways a blessing by fire.

"You are born in war and war only," Karl recalled his lieutenant telling them before they climbed out of the trenches at Amiens.

Birth through war! It even was in the Bible: *I have not come to bring peace but war.* And for a thousand years, they will say that they have seen these men fight as the law ordered them to do.

A runner pushed his motorbike across the ballast. "Orders for this day." The two NCOs and about two dozen soldiers and fighters—some of them wearing alpine knickerbockers—gathered around the runner.

"Any beer?" someone asked.

"You bring any beer?" Another voice.

They each took turns repeating the question until they all broke into a fit of laughter. The runner waited in silence and then read the order: the attack toward the center of Munich was better.

In the afternoon, the soldiers lit a fire and brewed the Columbian coffee I had donated, which was quite a change from their usual chicory brew.

"The French may have white shit, but they sure do make great coffee!" an older private blurted out. He had the clipped Prussian dialect, a nasal type of sing-song Karl could not stand.

"You have to turn a Prussian upside-down to find the opening he talks through," Karl whispered into my ear.

An older private standing beside Karl pointed at me.

"What's he doing here?" the private asked.

"He's a French journalist," Karl explained.

"Does he like boys like you?"

"Fuck off!" Karl yelled. He jumped up and drove his face right in front of the private's. "Fuck off!"

Karl was one to be reckoned with.

Over the next few hours, Karl and I sat in the opening of a railroad wagon, and together we watched the fires burn down and fall into embers that were to be stirred again, relit, and banked into flames.

Karl kept telling me about his dreams, how he imagined himself marching shoulder-to-shoulder with his comrades through the arc of victory in the Ludwigstrasse. He had the distant Feldherrnhalle in his eyes already, the two Bavarian lions glistening in the golden sun. What a glory this would be! Streets lined with young women waving flowers, their hands forming a fluttering banner beneath the linden and poplars of Schwabing; women dressed in white like nurses, their uniforms wrapped tightly around their bodies, their breasts heaving in pride.

Karl also talked about his mother, how he remembered standing in the tall, narrow doorway, marking her breaths as she barely stirred beneath the covers. Karl was the oldest of his siblings. He had two younger brothers and the baby, Fritz, was born just a week before his mother bled out and sepsis set in. When the shivers and the convulsions finally abated, she had exhausted herself. Karl said his mother died on March 3, 1907.

He then changed the subject: the rain-soaked craters of Flanders and how soldiers, certain of death, drew the covers over their bodies with a motion of total abandon and despair. For a moment the rain would make their bodies glisten before they sunk into the soaked mud and their faces dipped into the brown brine and muddy waters slushed into their gaping mouths.

Robert Schulig, the NCO who had left in the afternoon, returned in the early evening on a motorbike. "We are not sure who is in those barracks north of here," he said. "The white drapes might be just hung to fool us. The barracks are probably occupied by the 2nd Demobilization Company, which, so they tell me, is now run by a soldier's council under Johann Blüml." Then he pointed to Karl and Sergeant Guenther Puch, who was sitting on an overturned garden bench, smoking. Taking his hands off his breeches. "All right. You both can come. We are going to reconnoiter."

He recruited a few more soldiers, and everybody checked their rifles. After we crossed a line of allotment gardens and a street littered with garbage, we reached the gate to the barracks, where some civilian faces popped up behind a pile of overturned furniture.

"We need to speak to Johann Blüml. I am NCO Schulig, Freikorps Von Epp. 3rd Detachment."

"You can talk to the second-in-command, Adolf Hitler."

"What about Blüml?"

"Sick today."

The man cranked the handle on a phone and spoke into the receiver.

"Straight up one flight of stairs," he said after hanging up the phone.

Schulig nodded and we walked up and entered a room with rows of benches, a teacher's desk, and a lectern in the front. The smell of dust shoved into our nostrils.

"Stay right at the door!" somebody yelled.

"Hitler, I presume!" Schulig said, as he stopped and calmly set his hands onto the top of a bench. He stated unit, rank, and purpose. Hitler, brandishing two rifles, frantically paced between the desk and the lectern. I spotted two soldiers crouched down in the front row, the butts of their rifles set on top of the desk. One of them yelled at the frantic Hitler, "Calm down! Comrade!"

"We shall not have anything to do with your outfit," Hitler growled.

"This is not what we have come for," Schulig said. "We want to make sure that everybody in the barracks remains neutral."

"Why would anybody participate in that Jewish revolt? Communists all!" one of our group shouted.

"Everybody calms down." Schulig spoke with a calm but firm voice. "All we need is reassurance."

Hitler shook his head. I noticed dark patches of sweat puddled underneath his armpits. And what I was to remember most about Hitler—after Schulig issued his demand that all the barracks' south-facing windows be closed—was this agitated jumping jack behind the lectern, his sweaty face, his nutcracker mouth moving up and down and never to the side, mechanical and without any expression but that of fear.

Crossing back over the railroad tracks, the soldiers kept joking. And later that evening, around the campfire, Sergeant Guenther Puch had the incident worked into a nutcracker parody of sorts, which he called "The Hitler Romp." It involved jumping on a garden bench with a rifle butt squeezed underneath each armpit, waggle-wiggling into a limber dance, and moving his chin up and down without making a sound.

"That Hitler was addressed as 'comrade' by one of the soldiers?" I mentioned to Schulig.

"You're right," he said. "I missed that slip of the tongue. We better keep an eye on them and show them some artillery."

Soon thereafter, advancing very slowly so as not to break the timbered railroad crossing, a Platformwagen crawled across the tracks. The silhouette of its self-propelled gun stood out against the smear of a last light in the west.

"That should convince them," Schulig said.

In April of 1919, the snow lay limpid and flat in dirty sheets between the railroad tracks, but now, at the end of February 1960, the tracks are lined by huge snow piles soiled by bulldozers leaving ruts which remind me of giant teeth marks. A recent warm wind has been melting the snow piles, smoothing the crags and hollowing their bases, making them sink and tilt.

After arriving in Munich on the night train from Paris, I enjoy some coffee and Brötchen in a café on the second floor of the train station. From here, I can see into the metal gridwork above the wide waiting hall. In 1919, I had spent a night above those girders; now I want to search for the hidden spiral staircase Karl had shown me, and the narrow metal platform we tried to rest on before the attack.

The waiting hall has been rebuilt, but I can still make out the patches where rusty stains have merely been painted over. The scars of history do not leave that gently, nor do its dreams.

On this first day of May, 1919, as we hunkered down among those rafters, Karl was filled with dreams. Dreams and words. He told me that in September of 1914 he had stood on the floor of that very hall—vendors and soldiers crowding around him—and kept looking up to the skylights lit by the sun. His was a young heart filled with yearning for a noble, adventurous future for one nation united, strong in its industrial might, reborn by the vigor of its soul. He told me of the emotions that throbbed through this hall, throngs of soldiers mulling about, waves of sounds here and there cresting in soldiers intonating the Te Deum: *Grosser Gott wir loben Dich.* He mentioned the flowers handed out by young women in long silk dresses, the piles of knapsacks laid on the floor, soldiers sitting on them, smoking, smiling into the late sun of summer. In one corner of the hall, a juggler had laid out a carpet and was smoothly keeping three bowling pins in the air, one with the colors of Germany the other two with the colors of England and France. Soon enough, cheering soldiers had surrounded him. The fourth one: the Ruskis! And then he launched that one. He was juggling in the air all the enemies of the Reich until, one by one, he dropped each of them until only Germany's pin remained. Cheers ensued. Even the sight of stacked rifles did not distract Karl from the playful mood in the hall, or at least not until the nervous whistle of the train engines called the soldiers.

But that evening of May 1, 1919, the mood was less patriotic. Karl's preparations would take place early in the morning and we needed sleep. So we ignored the activities still roiling beneath us and rolled out our blankets on the wide metal sheet bolted between the rafters.

I hoped to take some front-line pictures of flamethrower action in the morning and rechecked my Leica camera, which I had carefully wrapped into a separate blanket. I had been lucky to purchase one of the first models that used Kino film.

Hans, the second man of the flamethrower unit, had already drifted off into sleep; Karl, too, was drowsy, but when he spotted my bottle of cognac sticking out of my bag, its wraparound label showing the Gare de Austerlitz in Paris, he asked, "Do you know the Austerlitz railroad station in Paris?" When I nodded, he said, "It is more beautiful than this hall. I have seen pictures of the trestle on which the subway enters the station on a separate level after having crossed the Seine River. What is hidden is suddenly revealed, and the demonic is lifted into the age of steel."

Karl sat up and continued talking.

"Ours is the first generation that has found art and purpose in lifting the deep, the heavy, the dark—iron, ore, steel—into the lightness of a future age. Steel bands connecting continents ...flags of steam rising into the sun from iron horses ...just look at the Budapest train station! Ten Romanesque steel arches hold up a glass triangle that towers above all. The old, the tried and sacred, and the new are now joined in spirit."

And then he talked about the mountain in the Alps he climbed with his friend Hans in 1918. It was during a brief vacation after they had been trained in the use of flame throwers and before their deployment in the final German offensive in 1918. "On that mountain, the Höfatz, we swore to each other's eternal friendship and our devotion to Germany until death."

I liked to hear Karl talk. And on that evening, he couldn't seem to stop.

"That's just it, Yann! Steel symbolizes heft and ponderousness, but it can be lightened with playful ornaments and circles, with arcs and soaring grids and steel-wheel ornaments that drop along elliptic tracks to the base of columns rising from large wheels on top and then recreate themselves in smaller and smaller wheel ornaments toward the base. Think about it ...each part relates to the next in some sacred proportion of which only the saints have knowledge."

Karl sat upright and kept drawing circles in the air with his pointer finger.

"German artists will raise steel into the sky," he said. "I shall be an architect and I shall raise cathedrals of steel."

Eventually, we fell asleep between the riveted trusses. The bottle of cognac was half-empty.

I slept through the squeaks of the winches as the sharpshooters hoisted sandbags and crates with ammunition to the upper level of the main ticket hall, but I quickly awoke when light flashes went off somewhere down the hall. My first thought was that maybe there was another photographer at work igniting magnesium powder. Was it Boquot? Didn't he make enough money selling his bloody pictures to the *Illustrious*? He was the frontline photographer I wanted to surpass. In 1919, that was my goal, and the looming battle at the Munich railway station was to be my big break.

But now it is 1960, and, after all these decades, I barely recognize even the very structure of the railroad ticket hall whose iron roof has been replaced by glass panels. From my small perch on the second floor where I'm enjoying my breakfast, I look down into shafts of light and watch the people of Munich hurrying through cones of brightness to step into dark corridors from which they will again emerge, covered in dust that hovers in the air like smoke. Can one wander through life not recognizing those times in the light of grace? And what time of my life am I to enter now that I have a chance to teach in Munich?

I place a call to the university to inquire if they received the copies of my published articles (few as there are) in a timely matter. Then, I take a taxi to my hotel and have lunch near the Feldherrnhalle. From there, I walk the short distance to the lecture hall. The lecture this afternoon is poorly attended, and the auditorium is too large for the dozen students in it. Most of them are sitting in the rear, leaning against the back wall, waiting for the perfect time to make a quick departure.

I tell the students about the evening I heard Hitler's speech in the Algiers hotel, and how I fought my tiredness to keep reading excerpts from Camus's early manuscript. I try hard, but not even the barbed wire scene on the beach and the outbreak of World War II elicit more than a few lame questions.

"Was Camus passionate?" a student asks.

"He was lucid and passionate at the same time," I answer.

"*The Stranger* is the blandest novel I have ever read," one student says.

And another student: "No emotion."

I object. "You can't call Meursault emotionless in the scene in which he rages against the priest."

None of the students seem convinced, and I suspect that only one or two of them have even glanced at my article. The discussion group dissolves after a mere half hour. I sense the undertow of anticipation of a free-for-all evening in a town that's loosening up after a long winter. *Rosenmontag*, they call it, the day before Fat Tuesday that draws everybody into its drunken revelry.

I am disappointed in the lack of interest and want to banish the whole experience from my mind. But, as I walk out of the lecture hall, I keep thinking about the student sitting in the last row. He had left his winter coat open, and beneath it he wore a gray flannel shirt and a blue tie. He had a lopsided face and two bright eyes. His voice was raspy and low, and though he seemed indifferent, his comment struck me.

"Camus wrote *The Stranger* to unburden his soul from indifference," he said.

And that was all he said. When I looked at him, I was almost certain I had seen myself.

All I want to do now is to sink into fluffy pillows, draw a blanket over my head, and sleep. In the taxi cab on the way back to my hotel, I remember Camus having written in *The Stranger* about a young man in the crowd at Meursault's court hearing. This young man-made Meursault feel as though he was being watched by himself. How often have I discussed that scene in my classes, and how strange that it frightens me now.

Maybe life is a court hearing.

Maybe history is judging my life.

The Search for Klaus

This morning, after having enjoyed a much-needed deep sleep, I take a cab to the Einwohnermeldeamt. The very word is an insult to any language (it would not rhyme with any word; I am sure). Einwohnermeldeamt functions as the citizen registration office. Today, Mardi Gras, it will only be open to customers before noon. The police have already closed the town center to car traffic because, due to the mild weather, large crowds are expected to celebrate in the streets.

The official at the main counter wrinkles his forehead when I show him what scant information I have written down.

"Karl Herrmann. Herrman? Are you sure about the spelling, sir? Born in Munich; Freikorps; served in the Army in France ...architect ...is that all you've got?"

He glances past me, almost as if he is looking for another customer who might give him some excuse to send me off. The waiting room, however, is empty.

"Well! If he didn't move a lot, I might be able to help," he says.

He hands my paper slip to an assistant.

"Come back in an hour," he says. "We have to search our Zettelkasten."

Ah! Here is another German utterance of ultimate destructive power. Make a poem out of that one!

I walk the few blocks to the bookstore near the Marienplatz. On my way, I zig-zag my way between crowds of pedestrians and try to side-step piles of melting snow. One of the café owners sets up chairs on the sidewalk with a grin on his face. I can tell he's enjoying this ultimate defiance of the seasons: spring in February!

Upon entering the bookstore, I feel quite claustrophobic. The bookshelves here are leaning precariously. It would only take a faint vibration to make thousands of pages tumble to the floor. The owners have arranged the shelves peculiarly, such that the upper rows have been stashed with an abundance of books, so that the whole store takes on the appearance of an upside-down birthday cake. This shelving defies physics.

In a way, this bookstore reminds me of Charlot's Bookstore in Algiers. Even after all these years, I can still remember it.

Meeting at Charlot's Bookstore

After I met Camus at the café, and after our interview had been interrupted by his lawyer, Camus seemed distracted and absent. The lawyer had left a folder on the table, which Camus kept fingering nervously. And then he abruptly said, "You might as well come with me to Charlot's Bookstore at the Rue Charras. Our writers' group and some artists meet there today. And if you are interested in Mediterranean art, there is a small exhibition of Bonnard's seascapes on display right now. Charlot's is our hangout most of the time. It's a little bit cramped, I must say, but you will see."

Cramped it was!

Charlot's Bookstore was so narrow a place that if you looked for an author whose name started with the letter "A," you'd have to turn left—a sharp left at that—immediately after entering and then squeeze in behind the entrance door and a rickety bookcase. Then, you'd have to stretch to reach the upper shelf, where you would find the "A" section. And only if you made it to "XYZ" in the rear of the store would you note the staircase leading up to a loggia with two desks and a balustrade from which to look down onto the ground floor.

On that August day of 1939, the air in the loggia was stifling hot. The evening had brought no relief, even after Charlot's wife opened the back door to stir up some ventilation. The door opened onto a ledge—not really a balcony—that provided us a glimpse of the Mediterranean, which merely appeared as a thin, green flag cut out between roofs. But it was important to see the Mediterranean. However narrow a glimpse, often no more than of a weak reflection, it was this body of water that had given inspiration to the small group of men that were to assemble on the loggia.

After Albert Camus introduced me to his friends, I took a seat on the loggia with a view down to the main floor, a corner where, so I learned, it was Camus's habit to read manuscripts. Charlot's wife was now downstairs greeting friends, René-Jean Clot, the painter and poet, followed by Claude de Freminville, also a poet, and Professor Jacques Heurgon, the Latin teacher of the gymnasium. They were to join Robles, who was already upstairs.

The formal part of the meeting was brief because the galleys for the Thursday paper hadn't yet arrived; thus, the morning edition of *Algiers Republican* was going to be published without any input from the group.

There were some inquiries among Albert Camus's friends regarding the Paris journal I was working for, as well as the newly established airway connection to Marseille. Once they learned that I spoke German fluently and had traveled there frequently, they shared both their opinions and their fears.

"Hitler won't go to war just for Danzig," one of them said.

"How can he even think of it?" another offered. "He knows that the English and the French are negotiating with the Soviet Union."

"Russia will never go with the Germans," the man to my right suggested. "They hate each other."

Almost everybody had an opinion, even Camus who seemed willing to believe that maybe Goering would eventually run Germany and Hitler would devote himself to his art. Was Camus a dreamer? Even Nietzsche would never have bestowed that much redeeming power on art!

"So, tell us what you think of the situation for writers in Germany," Freminville said. He had been quiet up until then, but he stood out from the others, what with his tight lips and his hawked nose, not to mention the intensity of his dark eyes.

"In October of 1938, I tried to interview a young German writer named Eugen Gottlob Winkler, who had some critical things to say about the Nazis' ideology," I said. "For example, he had written a critical essay about Ernst Jünger and the evil of thinking."

"The WWI storm trooper who kept on writing to glorify the slaughter?" Heurgon asked.

I nodded, then told them about the life of Eugen Gottlob Winkler, as well as his suicide.

The heat was rising even from the floor, there was barely any cross ventilation, and the sounds of the street crowd penetrated through the open windows.

"This war would be a true war against fascism," Freminville said.

"War is always a wrong war," Camus retorted. "Why die for Poland or Bohemia? Three million Germans have been stranded in these newly established territories because of the Treaty of Versailles, and Hitler is now raising hell to fold them back into the Reich. Once that is done, he will slow down. Didn't he say that he has no territorial demands after this?"

Camus lifted his arms to stop the discussion, which had become heated and unorganized. He looked at me, and I was more than happy to change the topic.

"Are you are going to travel to Greece next week," I asked Camus.

"Possibly not," he said. "There are problems with the sailing schedule because of this insane fear of war. Everything seems to be on hold."

"We need you here to battle the censors," Robles interjected. "How is the newspaper going, by the way?"

"Those censors and the suppression of the left and on top the shortage of paper! All that makes it very difficult and the advertisement is now almost zero."

"We are frozen out," Freminville added. "What lifts our spirits are summer, beaches, sun, and water."

Camus leaned forward. "The Mediterranean is life that gives. It does not threaten nor challenge as the sea of Brittany does. The Mediterranean is always there, soothing and forgiving. You can stretch out in it and give yourself over to its simple pleasures and feel the caress of water on your skin. You feel immersed."

Suddenly the sea became our topic.

"The sea purifies man," Camus continued. "Men who haven't seen the sea and don't yearn for it are deprived and given to violent excesses. Hitler, as far as I know, did not see the sea in his formative years."

"Eugen Gottlob Winkler wrote of Sicilian's rugged coast and his last lines are devoted to an island in a Bavarian lake," I said. "Ernst Jünger does not write of the sea. The land pinches your mind; the sea opens it wide."

"So does the light," Camus said. "In Austria, I stopped in a village whose people did not see the sun from November to April on account of the massive mountains. Some of the villagers there crossed the river and made actual pilgrimages to the light. Those condemned to darkness kept talking of national pride, the Olympic games in Berlin, and how all Germans and Austrians would, at some time, unite to heal the humiliation of the Versailles Treaty. They kept drinking, and then they fought."

Camus folded his hands. "Men on these Mediterranean shores refuse escape. This country has no message, and we wake every morning to understand this. It is not only the country ...the landscape with its barrenness, aridity, and lack of greenery ...but also the very lack of history. In this land, no great religion has risen. From this land, no religion has derived its strength. Christ could only emerge far to the east in a boiling cauldron of hope for redemption. We know it has not come to pass, but the illusion has been carried on for centuries, and even when it has exhausted itself, too many will still set their hopes onto the wrong messiahs ...Hitler, and maybe even Stalin. A cry for help: we need to believe and we need meaning! But in the depths where the threads of history and the human soul meet, where fate is negotiated, indifference has risen, and it is the new man who will face it, who will look into the void, who will not flinch."

Nobody said a word.

"It all begins with facing the truth," Camus added. "Nothing will ever sprout otherwise. Lucidity is the first step and not some ideology. The other day, I watched the movies and I saw German stormtroopers goosestep in front of the mustached man. I thought of the frozen sea of ice in man's soul that Kafka has written about. That made me shiver."

"We have to set against their ideology an emotion of equal strength." Claude Freminville's curt remark sliced the air. "Lucidity is not the end of all."

"We have disagreed on that topic before," Camus snarled. "I refuse to pretend feelings as this is the stamp of those who are living a lie. And there is a kind of desperate courage in being lucid and refusing to love."

Claude Freminville seemed shaken.

"On this age, everything will turn," Camus continued. "This age asks for a new, lucid indifference. For man, defaced by ideologies, bereft of benign powers, there is no hope now but this indifference."

"I know you like to provoke by words," Freminville said.

"Enough, you hotheads! If you both agree that man is all there is," Robles interrupted.

"Man can live an ordinary life in genuine indifference. He can be indifferent and true to himself. He can give himself over to the sun, waves, and the caress of the water. But death, even an ordinary, unfelt death, sets down the seeds of dissension. The man of the Mediterranean is suspicious of emotions whipped into passions by politics, propaganda, or pseudoscience. And in this very refusal lies value itself. The value of self-identity, lucidity, and truth."

Camus had spoken now extensively and the long silence after these words affirmed to me his high standing among his friends. Out of which well had this young man's authority drawn such strength? Some lyrical essays and a speech given in the house of culture in Algiers several years ago just did not seem to explain it.

It was Freminville who broke the silence. "I do understand that some philosophical traditions reject the notion that life in its fullest is only life at its most intense," he said. "But how else will be able to resist the furies of ideologies?"

Camus bowed his head and rubbed his temples as if in pain. He stood up. "So let us hold on to the epiphanies of being!"

There was this impish smile again.

Outside, on the Rue Charras, the traffic seemed to have calmed down. Trams screeched through the curve where the track turned toward the hills. The din shook the flimsy blackout drapes ordered by the government. These were times of grave portent.

There were female voices downstairs. Everybody craned over the railing and then hurried down after the women. A quick gesture of Camus's hand made me stay.

"The absurdity of our fathers dying the same day in a war that did nothing but tear men apart," he said.

This was what he wanted to say at the end! He stood up and waved down to the lower floor, smiling. He raised his eyebrows in a mocking way, which was at the same time inviting and distance-holding. He walked downstairs and welcomed two young women with no more than a brief nod of his head. He lit one of his Bastos cigarettes, waved up at me, and before I could even descend the stairs, a bunch of young people crowded into the door. With lots of laughter, pushing, and shoving, they burst onto Rue Charras. I followed.

In the Munich bookstore, I search for books about the turbulent years, when most of the brilliant artists and intellectuals left Germany. The years when those who stayed had been silenced and those who left made me think of light leaving a dying star.

After I leave the bookstore, I eat some Weisswurst, see the Glockenspiel, and then walk back to the—what is it called again—Einwohnermeldeamt.

The official, a mousy, thin man with white hair, tells me he has been able to retrieve my requested information.

"Regretfully," he says, "I have to tell you that Karl Herrmann died several months ago. Karl's wife and their son, Klaus, now live in an apartment at the Waldfriedhof in the western part of Munich."

"So Karl's son still lives with his mother?"

"Yes," he says. "At least, this is our most recent information. I can make you a copy of the registration card."

He goes to the back of the room and returns in a few minutes.

"I apologize for the poor quality of the photo reproduction," he says. "Take tramway line 6 to the end."

"Before I go, can you help me with a phone number?" I ask.

"Sorry, but we have no more information to provide you." The man's eyes shift toward the people waiting in line behind me. "Next, please!"

On the photocopy, Klaus Herrmann's face displays a pale smear of grey, and it strikes me that his face bears a resemblance to the student's in the back row at my lecture yesterday afternoon.

Just before noon, I visit the chairman of the Romance Language Department, who is eager to use his French. He wears black corduroy pants, a white shirt, and I suspect he didn't shave this morning in order to give the impression of the permanently torn intellectual. On display on his desk is a carousel of pipes. He apologizes for the poor attendance yesterday afternoon and asks me if I can delay my return to Paris so we can schedule an additional lecture for Thursday. I thank him for the opportunity and agree to stay. Then, I show him the registration card. I ask if he knows of a student at the university who resembles Karl. He gives me a strange look, and then shakes his head.

"Sorry," he says.

The meeting is short and pleasant enough.

From the administrative building, it is a short walk across the English Garden to the Thomas Mann House. This is where, in October of 1938, the life of the writer Eugen Gottlob Winkler had been changed in a fateful way. Maybe he had been the last of the Dandies, a liberal in love with the spirit of the Mediterranean culture—a man who a German critic once called "the Camus Germany never had". Apparently Winkler's fragile mood could neither tolerate nor survive the rising tide of National Socialism. A few years before his suicide in 1938—he had been studying Romance Languages in Tübingen—a nine-year-old girl observed him ripping advertisements from a Nazi billboard. She denounced him. Frightened to his bones, he attempted suicide in his prison cell. Eventually, he was released because of a lack of proof and then he was admitted to a psychiatric hospital. I had a chance to meet him in his Munich apartment at the end of October of 1938 —five years after the Tübingen incident—but his girlfriend showed up and we agreed to talk later. A day later, he went for a nightly stroll and passed the impounded villa of Thomas Mann—Jewish loot, they called it then—where a police gendarme stopped him for identification. Winkler returned home in a state of paranoia and feared being arrested again. That night, he took a lethal overdose of barbiturates. He held a mirror in front of his face to watch his dying breath. The image of death—this seductive, always-present possibility—had been with him all his life.

I cross the English Garden in the gathering dark. Piles of snow, which remind me of miniature Alps, line the slushy walkways. A cross-county skier in a clown outfit passes me. Tomorrow is Ash Wednesday.

The Thomas Mann house is a disappointment. They tore down the original house years ago—this much I knew—but I was hoping that the post-war rebuilding would closely restore the one I remembered. What I now see instead is some bungalow overgrown with weeds. What had been stately is now inferior; what had been teeming with life is now hollow.

I had last walked by the house in October of 1938, just one day after Winkler's suicide. A gendarme was still standing guard then, and the Swastika flag on a tall pole above us snapped tight in the wind.

On the way back to my hotel, I cross the River Isar and a deep state of discouragement comes over me. I stop and lean over the railing and stare down into the swirling waters. They had warned me that the Föhn—this rare stream of warm air flowing in from the South—could bring on a trance, a deceptive lightness and a state of mind that one may experience before the onset of certain seizures. They had warned me that the wind could make one lose track of time.

And maybe it is the Föhn. Too many thoughts have filtered into my brain to allow space for lucidity. What besets me is a feeling that the young man in the back of the lecture hall during my university presentation the day before was indeed Karl's son, Klaus. Maybe he is the reporter described by Camus in *The Stranger*: the man sitting in the courtroom at Meursault's process, the man who was meant to be Camus himself and at the same time his judge. Is it that Camus's Meursault, *The Stranger*, Klaus, and myself have suddenly become entangled in a circle of judgment, guilt, and history?

I sit down in a café. I stare out onto the sidewalk and follow the haste of people in the streets and the whizzing by of bikers and the blue streaks of tramways. Moods, the philosopher Heidegger had called them ...that which is always already present before thinking. You have to yield to their realm.

Yann and Klaus. First Meeting.

After I knock on the door, I am greeted by a young man with an ashen face.

"Hi," I say. "My name is Yann Cedak. I am trying to find the wife of Karl Herrmann."

The young man—yes, it must be Klaus, Karl Herrmann's son—stares at me, and then closes his fists before drawing them toward his chest

"Do we know each other?" he asks.

"I knew your father during the war. At present, I am a professor at the University of Montpellier."

The young man stiffens. "Wait ...you're ...you're that French professor who gave the lecture yesterday, aren't you?"

"I am," I say. "And you are the student who was sitting in the back?"

"Yes."

"I take it you are Karl Herrmann's son."

He nods.

"I'm sorry to hear that he passed away. I wanted to see him again. We were friends during his time in France."

"When he built that church, you mean?"

"Yes!"

Klaus moves slightly to the side before offering me his hand.

"My name is Klaus," he says. "Come in."

There is silence between us after I enter the room. Klaus takes a seat on the windowsill. With an unsure gesture of his right hand, he offers me a seat on a beanbag. He must have just been reclining on it, as I can see the folded contours and the dimpling where his elbows dug into the cheap plastic. I remain standing in the middle of the room, which is barely furnished. There's a spare bookshelf, a table, and some cooking utensils hidden in a corner. A creepy cold claws to the room's walls. I can't help but shiver.

"I don't want to inconvenience you and your mother," I say, breaking the silence.

"My mother? No, she died just days ago."

"How can I possibly express my condolences?"

"I just returned from her funeral."

"What happened to her, if you don't mind me asking?"

"She fell out of bed, broke her hip, and then developed an embolus."

Klaus looks down at the ground. I can hear the screeching sound of a tramway turning into the end loop at Waldfriedhof Platz.

"How did you find my address?" Klaus asks.

"I went to the Einwhohnermeldeamt."

"I am so sorry," I say again. "Was your father in poor health?"

"He was in good shape until they botched up some surgery."

For a few minutes, our talk hacks on: my splintered sentences explain the occasion of my visit, and Klaus explains the appearance of the half-empty, unadorned apartment, with its frayed carpet and the almost-bare walls. A recent death, the temporary inconvenience, the furniture in storage ...I sense the affliction brought on by unfilled spaces, the unrequited life that seems to suffuse them.

More explanations. The landlord is tied up in litigation; everything is temporary. Just weeks ago, Klaus's mother had moved to a home for older people. Then the funeral. He keeps talking about the frozen landscapes, floods, and rivers dammed by ice.

Only a single photo print hangs on the wall. It shows two men —quite different in age—sitting on a grassy mound near the peak of a mountain. The thought accosts me that Klaus sees in me a judge who, at any moment, might reach into his pocket and pull out a legal scroll of accusations, like in the half-dark of some Ingmar Bergman movie. I do not know what makes me think this way: perhaps it is Klaus's strained voice, the tinny sound of vowels pressed through a liquid, and already an undertow of despair.

"Allow me to invite you for a drink in the restaurant across the street," I say. "It looks like a nice place."

"It is a clean, well-lighted place."

"You read Hemingway?"

"Yes, and I am currently studying Romance Languages. Mainly French."

We walk across the terminal tram station to the Weinstube.

"Today is Mardi Gras," the manager tells us. "Surely you will like to have some privacy away from the clowns. I have a small room in the back."

It is over Nürnberg sausages on sauerkraut alongside a carafe of dry white wine that we both begin to open up.

"My father never said much about his time in France or the Second World War," Klaus says. "I know that he initially was a motorcycle runner and then was ordered to build a church on a mountain in the south of France before he was transferred to Leningrad."

"And what happened there?"

"He was wounded in the abdomen and returned to Munich where he served as an air warden. But tell me about the church project. My father always talked of building steel churches. I sensed that he was frustrated building dairies."

"Yes. I believe that. Your father wanted to build a steel church, but the project was all propaganda, a German-French collaboration, Kaiser Karl the Great, and the Holy Roman Empire all rolled into one. They dug holes for the foundation and built part of a campanile, and then the war suffocated everything."

Klaus stabs his fork into the sausage, and his eyes are cast downward. Laughter erupts in the room next door, and the contrast begins to grate on my mood.

Lifting the beaker, I see my fingertips through the glass and wine. The widening prints remind me of spider webs. I hold the glass between Klaus's face and my eyes in order to hide a sudden chill of memory.

November 1942 on the Massif of St. Baume: the stillness of air amidst the blowing like the holding of some invisible breath! My eyes focused on the horizon and a cloud in the east. The fate of Germany and France having then already tilted into the abyss.

Each turn of fate has such disinherited children to whom the past is a burden and the future a bane.

I take a few sips of my wine, setting the glass down slowly, sliding my fingers off in hesitation, abiding time. A sudden rawness surprises me and makes me keep quiet.

"And what about when the war was over?" I finally ask.

"After Leningrad, my father returned home. The bombs fell and we kept losing the roof shingles off the house we lived in. Then the American tanks rolled into Munich, and then it was all about cleaning up."

"Your family seemed to have been spared the worst," I say.

Klaus shifts his weight in his seat. "Many years later, my father died from his stomach wound. Bowel loops got caught up into some adhesions, and the problem was diagnosed far too late."

"I am sure you and your family went through a lot."

"I was just a toddler then. My first memories are in an air raid shelter our neighbor dug underground." Klaus begins to eat. His silence cuts sharply around us.

"Your father dreamt of building churches of steel even when I met him first in Munich in 1919," I say.

"During the Munich Räte Republic, he fought on the side of the Whites, the anti-Communists, but he never said anything about meeting a Frenchman ...you must have been real young then."

"I was just 20 years old." And then I begin to talk about that morning in May of 1919, the morning after I had spent the night with Hans and Karl among the trusses of the main hall in Munich's train station.

"Tell me more," Klaus says as he leans back in his chair and crosses his arms. He is eager to listen.

All night, I had searched for a totally dark spot to load the Kino roll film. I stuck the camera into my knapsack and pulled out the bottom. I had done it several times before, but I kept fumbling before finding the slit to insert the film, and I had difficulties adjusting the tension of the film before closing the back of the camera.

When the morning finally came, soldiers gathered around a primitive field kitchen that distributed a brown-colored fluid infused with coffee beans. Some tired privates cut slabs of bread onto which they spread thin marmalade.

Robert Schulig gave a short review of the situation, running through some geography. The challenge would be the Bahnhof Platz, a wide-open square stretching between the façade of the railroad station and the massive stone building of the main post office.

"Karl and Hans will advance behind a Kampfwagen, flame thrower at the ready, to reach the post office entrance."

"Never aim straight up," Karl instructed Hans. "The kerosene will come down and burn you."

Together Karl and Hans picked up the canister filled with kerosene; they checked the pressure in the nitrogen tank and the cartridge with the igniting magnesium. As they walked through the hall, Karl spearing the lance and Hans slouching behind him carrying the double tanks, Freikorps soldiers assumed their assigned positions.

Hans and Karl cowered down behind the front-line sandbags. A machine gun had begun to hack from somewhere in the post office building. Above them, one of their own MG-08 heavy machine guns began spraying the post office façade with bullets, lifting yellow powder off its sandstone. Groups of soldiers with bags of hand grenades slung over their shoulders were waiting behind the sandbags. Two light machine gun crews flanked the line of soldiers. I crawled in behind Karl and Hans.

Finally, action! "Watch it! There isn't any cover on that damn square," Karl cautioned me as he looked back over his shoulder. "Stay back, Yann!"

"What if they hit my nitrogen tank?" Hans yelled.

"Are you losing your fucking nerves?"

When the Kampfwagen finally rumbled out onto the Bahnhof Platz, they moved out behind it and the machine guns opened fire. At first, I stayed down behind the sandbags, gripping my camera. Karl and Hans had advanced more than halfway across the square when the Kampfwagen opened fire with its large gun. Pieces of stucco broke off the post office building's façade. I took my first photo, stepped over the sandbags, and ran out into the open square to throw myself down behind the concrete slab of a tram platform. Then the Kampfwagen suddenly stopped. Something had hit the turret. Two soldiers opened the rear hatch to crawl out. The machine gun, somewhere up in the post office, sprayed the tramway platform with screeching metal. A soldier beside me was hit and began to cry for his mother. The two soldiers from the armored car fell and lay bleeding.

How stupid I was! I pressed myself into the small groove behind the platform, not daring to lift my head. That damned machine gun!

Karl and Hans had reached the post office and hunkered down inside its recessed entrance.

"Stupid French asshole!" I heard Karl yelling. "Get out of there!"

But there was no way. The screech of bullets hitting the cobblestones came closer and closer.

I glanced up and saw Karl pull Hans out of the entrance. Both were now running back into the wide-open square, pointing the flamethrower up at the machine gun. They had only seconds before the machine gun would swivel about to target them! I pushed my face into the ground and heard the hiss of the flame. Smoke rushed into my eyes and hot specks of soot landed on my skin. When the din let up, I ran back in panic and threw myself behind the sandbags. The roar of the flame stopped, I heard somebody yelling, "Did you get your fucking photo?"

That very afternoon, some soldiers—livid with contempt—informed me that Karl had burnt his face by pointing the flamethrower too high. He didn't even retreat as burning kerosene rained down on him.

"He saved your goddamn French ass," the soldier said. "Arschloch."

That was a curse word not understandable even to me, who spoke German well.

That same afternoon, the order came from the French liaison to report immediately. I was informed that I would have to draw back from reporting on ongoing military actions.

My short career as a front-line war correspondent had ended.

Klaus looks at me as if, for a moment, he's looking at his own father.

"So what did you do after the war?" Klaus asks.

"I worked as a freelance journalist, mostly in Paris," I say. "I wrote some cultural articles, in addition to book and cinema reviews. Stuff like that."

"Where?"

"Spain, Germany, Algeria."

"You said at the lecture that you read an early draft of *The Stranger*."

"Yes, in 1939, three years before the novel was published." I am pleased that Klaus has channeled the conversation toward my minor fame. That I had crossed the threshold into the Sixties not having achieved much of anything —well, that is quite a different story.

To my surprise, Klaus starts to quote the first lines of the *Stranger* in French: "Aujourd'hui maman est morte. Ou peut-être hier. Je ne sais pas."

"J'ai reçu un télégramme de l'asile. Mère décéedée." I follow with the next sentence and Klaus finishes "Enterrement demain. Sentiments distingués. Cela ne veut rien dire. C'était peut-ètre hier."

I sense a hint of pride in his smile.

"Did you meet Camus again?" he asks.

"I met him in Paris in the Fifties for an interview. We had already shaken hands and the secretary was about to close the door when a woman in a fur coat burst into the office, screaming, throwing up her hands, yelling, 'Bastard!', and the whole interview was off."

"Ah! That must have been his first wife, Hié."

"What a guess! You must know a lot about Camus."

"Over the last several weeks, Camus's life is all everybody at the university has been talking about."

"I am surprised that they appreciate him this much in Germany."

"Oh! There are reasons. Camus's writing is short. It's pithy. A bleached prose. It doesn't yield, and it doesn't pull in God, and it basically levels to our condition of Godlessness."

Klaus puts fork and knife aside and then sips some wine. His face lights up as he continues to talk about Camus. "Meursault's honesty, his emptiness without guilt."

I nod in agreement

"But what keeps puzzling me is the end..."

"Yes! That sentence. *For the first time, in that night alive with signs and stars, I opened myself to the gentle indifference of the world.*"

"He should have ended the novel right there instead of adding a sentence about wanting the people to cry out in hate at his execution," Klaus says.

I think about it for a few seconds. "Maybe Camus feared his own indifference. Maybe that is the dark core of his early writing."

I imagined the day Camus's unpublished manuscript crossed the desk of Colonel Ernst Jünger, who I had met in 1940 in Bourges and who later worked as literary censor in Paris. Camus's manuscript probably triggered a comment from Herr Jünger, who might have looked up from his glass of Merlot and, if only for a moment, ignored the fascinating mirroring of American flares during a nightly air raid on the bridges across the River Seine—a highly aesthetic reflection of war inside the walls of the glass. And maybe he left word with some adjutant about the slim manuscript in front of him, saying that this insignificant story just proved that the French would always find minor distractions. Jünger would not have anticipated that the words would rally the French resistance. It was not that *The Stranger* expressed calls to rise —far from it—but that this novel expressed a pure yearning for truth and authentic living, a call for change that challenged you as it nailed you onto the cross of the human condition.

A drunken man in the next room jumps on top of a table, belching out a marching tune before falling into a tangle of arms.

"That was supposed to sound like Hitler's favorite march song," Klaus says.

"Just look at their age."

"No! No! It's not midnight yet."

More shouts. The manager leans over the counter, and a troubled, edgy look fills his face. The din of excited voices settles back.

Maybe it is in this moment with Klaus, that, in some inchoate way, our lives snag on some unfulfilled promise of life. It is the wine too, of course; we are far into the second bottle.

In the few minutes remaining before midnight, I find myself eager to talk about the early Camus, the one who had a brief and disastrous marriage to Simone Hié, a heroin addict, the Camus who fell out with a fellow actor named Yves Bourgeois during a kayak trip with Yves and Simone Hié on the River Inn in Austria. I talk about Camus the communist! Camus the lover! Camus, who argued with Germans in Kufstein! The Camus who called the Tyrolean "stupid" and continued to Prague to fall into deep pain from which he drew the inspiration to write one of his early masterpieces: *Death in the Soul.*

"I've read that story!" Klaus says.

I wear a stunned expression on my face, as the story was just published last year.

"Was there a real-life event that touched off *Death in the Soul*?" Klaus asks.

"Camus did actually make a trip to Prague."

"So, tell me."

I tell him what I know about Camus's kayaking trip on the River Inn: the wind drifting Bourgeois's and Camus's kayaks apart; Camus waiting under a bridge for the delayed arrival of Yves Bourgeois and Camus's wife, Hié; Camus becoming aware of the remoteness of Hié; Camus sensing the closeness of his friend to his wife, the two extracting some fullness from life that was slipping away from him.

"My mother told me that in July of 1936, my parents visited a town on the River Inn," Klaus says. "There was an incident, and they met a French couple."

That night in the Weinstube in Munich I do not foresee the depth of Klaus's interest in Camus's trip, which is so strong that he is to write a brief theater piece about it that same year, and I don't yet understand that Klaus is obsessed with the thought that he is Meursault, that he is *The Stranger,* that he has been living the indifference that pervades the character of Camus's protagonist. One didn't have to kill an Arab on a beach in Algeria to be condemned. When it came to Klaus's life, the court proceedings had already taken place. There are no Gods for the indifferent and no Gods for the numb.

But that night in the Munich Weinstube, the din of the New Year's midnight celebration blots out any further talk. Sheer drunkenness surrounds us. A clown leans in the half-open door. Klaus and I wait until the yelling die down and all sounds become muted.

Mardi Gras has once again aged into Ash Wednesday. An elder couple enters the Weinstube. They walk between the tables of spent drunks, most of them sitting bent over now, their hands clawing the tables' edges for fear of losing balance. The couple offers to place the ashen sign of the cross on our foreheads.

"No thank you," Klaus says. "We are still working on our absolution."

We walk out of the restaurant amidst the burping and wheezing of drunken men and women, their arms slack with resignation, faces sallow and pale with the recognition that no disguise would now suffice. For a second, I want to say, "Come to France, Klaus!" But I don't. A line of drunken revelers pushes me away, separates me long enough to make me lose my courage.

All the taxis are taken tonight, and the last tram is ready to leave. I ask Klaus to contact me tomorrow at my hotel. The tramway, like a perforated reptile with light streaming from its flanks, moves into the turnaround loop. I find a narrow seat that seems to be pasted against the large window. Through the sheen of reflected images, lights moving up and then down, mirror images of overhead wires cutting into view, I see Klaus standing on dark pavement. Is he waving? Suddenly I am glad, almost elated, that I find myself alone in a well-lit place.

The tram rolls through Munich, a refuge for drunken night travelers with pale faces, their arms slunk limpid into cheap plastic overhead slings. I am staring out the window, taking in the strange relief of a world that, for moments, has lightened itself into shadows and lights and wide stretches of nothing and dark patches of urban lawns. Indifference. I recognize it. I let it suffuse me. I welcome it.

It begins to drizzle. I have to walk only a few hundred yards to the hotel. A bicyclist passes by, the dynamo alerting me with a whizzing sound. I wave.

The hotel bar is closed. Blind, unlit glass. Ashtrays spiked with cigarette butts.

I sleep fitfully. There are drunken night stragglers in the hallway.

In the wee hours, someone falls ...the sound's very dullness could have been death.

Second Part

Day After Having Met Klaus

This morning, the hotel's breakfast room is near empty. Confetti is piled beneath the baseboard, and a single snake roll remains draped over the arms of the chandelier. There's a couple sitting near my table, and I barely understand what is being said in their Bavarian dialect, which could only have been invented by somebody who was born with a bell clapper in his mouth. The Föhn wind is still blowing in from the south, shredding clouds into scuds.

My head feels befuddled, and maybe it isn't just the Föhn. I decide to cross back into the English Garden, clear my head, and maybe revisit the Thomas Mann house. This is the morning of embers and sullen faces. Snow is still crusting the paths and lies in flabby patches. I am alone.

On my walk the day before, I hadn't seen the small beer garden tucked into a corner among the bushes, but today—with the snow having melted fast—I recognize a tacky shed with an enormous Wilhelmina helmet (the one with the piercing spike) as a roof, and a few beer kegs serving as tables. A pole with a sign reads "Biergarten" and some bleached notes on the wooden wall still advertise the price of dark and light beer, plus radishes and sausage. There's nobody around!

I spot a telephone booth, which has to be the loneliest booth in the world—no footprints are anywhere to be found—and the door is frosted over with crusted snow piled against it. I pull the door handle and it gives. A black receiver hangs from a box, the stale smell of beer. I feel a strange attraction to call from this pathetic outpost stuck into white vastness and then I realize that I did not inform Klaus that I have now a whole day to spend in Munich. I close the door and place my call.

It takes a while for Mr. Salomon to get Klaus on the phone.

"Did you have a good night's sleep?" Klaus asks.

"Could have been better. They were still drinking in the hotel."

"Everybody has a hangover today."

"Maybe that's why the chairman asked me to repeat my lecture tomorrow, on Thursday ...because of this massive community hangover."

"So, you are free today?"

"Yes."

Klaus says he has some free time, too, and proposes to meet me in a café at the Ludwigstrasse near the university.

This snowed-in telephone booth exerts a strange attraction. I used to aim my Leica and take picture upon picture—changing the angle, lying down in the snow, replacing colors with planes of plain white, movement with stiffness, hints of connection with bare separateness. "You wallow in loneliness," somebody once told me.

I walk back toward my hotel and cross the footbridge across the River Isar, where I stop and look down into the swirling waters. Ice floes break off, jerk away from their mooring, and gyrate away. Suddenly the world stands sharp, and at the same time, it appears like in a dream. The Föhn has indeed made me lose track of time.

I do not revisit the Thomas Mann house. Instead, I return to my hotel, where the bleary-eyed attendant hands me a note stating that the university lecture for Thursday has been cancelled. No explanation, no apology, and no proposed make-up date.

I am furious.

"Do you all do anything but drink beer in this town?"

I don't even wait for the attendant to answer.

I sit down in the hotel lobby, which is empty aside from two orderlies cleaning the rugs with a vacuum, the noise of which sounds like a saw cutting through my skull. When I try to seek refuge in my hotel room, I find that it is being cleaned. I feel like a nuisance, fighting the strong sense that I have been rejected, that I do not belong.

Since the café where I am to meet Klaus is just a few blocks away, I decide to spend my downtime there. When I arrive, I sink down into one of the café's soft leather chairs and order torte and coffee. It's the first time today that I feel like myself, and my mind begins to settle once my anger over the cancellation wears off. My coffee has a hint of a nut taste that I like very much, and the bottom of the torte is soaked in rum—perfect! Across from me, a young couple blows smoke rings toward the sun-flooded window, and I unashamedly watch as they kiss each other with their perfectly rounded lips.

I think back to the night before ...so many things had been left unsaid. And in the doorway of the Weinstube, hadn't I been tempted to invite Klaus to visit France? But then we parted like strangers, me stepping into the tramway and him crossing the street without waving, locking himself back inside those four walls, totally bare were it not for that large print depicting a man sitting on a steep mountain peak.

I barely know Klaus, and yet I can't help but wonder what moods layer Karl's son's mind. How similar are father and son? What moods snag Klaus's thoughts? What keeps this young man awake at night?

Klaus's apartment is bare and impersonal, as if a cold wind blows through it daily. But there is this deeply obvious ardor when he talks about Camus. I wonder if it helps to ease a hidden pain.

I flip open my notebook and jot down some notes:

Two sacred places, two antique ruins, two temples

Camus's Tipasa and Winkler's Segesta

The pull of the South

The ground of being is the sun

Munich dreams to be the South, but for some, Munich will be what Prague was to Camus: a place and time into the death of the soul

Camus wrote about geography as one form of inequality that rarely is considered, about the sun and the ocean as the gift of his youth, about the grace bestowed on him by the sea's horizon when he lifted his face. He wrote that poverty kept him from thinking that all was well in history, and the sun taught him that history was not everything.

As I continue to wait for Klaus to arrive, I recall some words René Char, the French poet and resistance fighter, wrote in *Hypnos:* "Lucidity is the wound closest to the sun."

But it still stings thinking of René Char's response to my inquiry asking for a post-war interview! Two short sentences like stabs into my heart: "We decline. Consideration is given to those who were with us."

The note was signed by his secretary.

Fragments of the past! Fragments of roads not taken!

When Klaus finally enters the café, his resemblance to the Karl I knew in 1919.

Meeting Klaus and Painters. Photos. They Watch Movie.

Klaus carries with him a backpack and a foldable easel, which he leans against the wainscot. He orders some coffee, but then seems to slide into some state of preoccupation as our conversation turns stale.

"Tell me about the photo on the wall in your apartment," I say.

He doesn't respond.

"I assume one of the climbers is your father."

"Yes. He was always in the mountains."

I tell Klaus about Hans and Karl and their climb on the Höfatz in 1918, the way Karl talked about it that night in the Munich train station in 1919.

When I finish the story, Klaus does not say a word.

"All I know is that Hans had been my father's friend. Hans hated Hitler and my father ...well ...he did not."

"History," I say.

"Yes... history."

Klaus begins watching the couple next to us; they are still blowing smoke rings and kissing. I decide to change the subject.

"So what's with the easel?"

"I'm carrying it for somebody I'll be seeing later this afternoon. He is a member of a group of artists who experiment in ice painting."

"Never heard of it."

"Well, there exists a rare technique in watercolor painting. As you paint on paper right at freezing point the water colors crystallize in some spots, in others they thicken, leading to surprising effects."

"Sounds interesting."

"Why don't you join us this afternoon?"

"I might have time. Tell me more about your group of painters."

"The group meets at a small town south of Munich with some importance in the history of painting. Some call it the cradle of abstract painting because Kandinsky and Gabriele Münter and Franz Marc worked there."

"Yes, I heard about Murnau," I said.

"It sits atop a moraine with a wide view of the Alps. They were eager to experiment, and a few of them came up with the idea to paint in freezing temperatures. They would walk outdoors in the dead of winter or early spring, set up their easels, and apply watercolors to their canvases. As the temperature dropped and the hoar frost spread, unique effects began to take hold.

"So now this group is trying to revive this technique?" I ask.

"Yes, not to mention the whole feeling of an era filled with creativity, friendship, writing, and philosophy."

Later, Klaus and I take the train to Murnau.

The ride leads us through Munich's suburbs and into the humped pastures of Southern Bavaria. Then, halfway to Murnau, the tracks run along the Starnbergersee. Klaus has been quiet and sullen, and he's slouching down on the bench. I have to remind myself of the recent passing of his mother. When a lake comes into sight near Tutzing, Klaus's face lights up. He opens the window, leans out, and points at the shore, which pops into sight between the quick sliding by of hills and trees.

"When Munich was bombed during the war, my mother and I were evacuated and stayed for a summer at the water," Klaus says. "It must have been my happiest time."

This is the first time I see Klaus smile.

I nod as questions edge into my mind.

"I noticed that you're carrying a tripod in your bag," I say.

"I intend to take some pictures of the group."

"You have a Leica similar to mine?"

Klaus loosens the string and shows me his Leica 35mm camera, and then he reaches in deeper and pulls out a twin-reflex Rolleicord sheeted in a leather case that looks worn, some stiches visibly fraying.

"This is my father's Rolleicord," he says.

"Quite a collector's piece."

Klaus cradles the bulky camera against his body and turns the knob, which extends and retracts both lenses. Then he shows me how to slide the levers for exposure time and shutter opening.

He snaps out the optic sight on top—it opens beautifully, like some folded origami flower—then hands me the camera.

"You see the exact picture, and it will not go away even as you take the exposure," he says.

I point the camera, and Klaus's face appears in the dark shaft of his father's Rolleicord.

How often Karl must have held this camera! And now it is in my hands!

"Was the Höfatz picture taken with this old Rolleicord?" I ask.

"Maybe. He took many pictures, mostly of landscapes. He told me that often he would wait hours for the sun to shine just the right light and cast the right shadows. And he liked to walk out early into the cold to catch the first rays of sun."

When we arrive in Murnau, Klaus and I walk out onto the crest of the moraine where easels have already been set up by the group of artists that Klaus has been telling me about. The beauty of the sight stuns me. Beneath us, a flat moor stretches toward the Alps. Millions of years ago, an ancient sea lapped at these mountains which now stand scissor-cut against a slice of blue-colored sky.

It is late afternoon, and fog drapes itself between the slopes, shredding into tattered flags of grey where wind has begun to blow in through hidden valleys. The temperature drops as the painters brush their colors across the canvasses, working with concentration and haste, laying out one canvas after the other once the desired strokes are achieved. I walk from painter to painter, and none of them pay me any attention. They have all been waiting patiently for this moment, for the liquid paints to gel and freeze into crags and fissures and spread into shallow sheets of miniature floes of iced color.

And then, suddenly, it is dark, and our excursion is over.

Later, using a flashlight, Klaus shows me his small canvas that he started after taking photos of the group. He worked with wide strokes to bring out the hills, rendering them smooth, like the backs of whales lazing at the rim of the lake bed, and then eased his brush into green slopes before rolling them up into knolls and hills. But the ice has destroyed this softest of landscapes. Rills have formed between patches of different colors; from the few patches of red burst spider-like splinters; sheets of ocher covering the flat moor have rammed into each other, driven by the chemical forces of uneven freezing and buckled the smooth surface into islands of contrasting color. In some spots, a shattering has occurred; in others, a flutter of what looks like electric charges has spread across the canvas. A hardening of what was soft and a splintering of what was one. The line of craggy peaks rides above all of it, but the glint of a distant blue south has been lost.

Then Klaus says something that strikes me: "They say that Kafka's first story, *The Judgement*, was written at zero degrees."

The thought comes to me that Klaus has frozen out life for a long time.

It is almost midnight when Klaus and I are crammed into the backseat of a 2CV that one of the painters is driving back to Munich. Klaus has not talked at all during this long ride, and, as far as I can understand, the two young men in the front seats are making Klaus the butt of their jokes.

"Painting with freezing piss will be the next project for Klaus," one says.

"That's all you do with your dick," the other says. "Right?"

I lean forward.

"Don't you kids know that Klaus's mother recently died? Give him a break!"

"Oh! Sorry!"

That's all they say, and that's all they will say for the remainder of our drive.

The underpowered car is painfully slow, so the slightest hill throws the engine into terrible fits of droning. It is well after midnight when we finally arrive in Munich. When Klaus is ready to say goodbye, he appears dejected, and a brief stutter clutters his voice.

"Would you come with me tonight to an art movie theater to watch *the 400 Blows*," he asks.

When I tell him that I'll join him, he smiles.

My original plan following my trip to Munich was to stay over in Paris on my way to Saint-Brieuc, but since today's lecture was rudely cancelled I find myself with extra free time. And something in Klaus's voice is telling me to stay; I have begun to sense that in all his silence, Klaus is thrashing about in despair.

I am glad to finally sit beside a taxi driver; the fan of his diesel Mercedes spreads a comfortable heat, and the occasional crackle of the radio gives me some airy reassurance.

At the hotel, I ask the night clerk to extend my stay. I sleep in late, enjoy some Nürnberger bratwurst, and then spend the rest of the day leafing through pages and pages in the many small bookstores that line Schwabing's thoroughfare. I crisscross the district, drink sweet coffee, walk over to the Hofgarten, and sit on one of the benches where T.S. Eliot must have sat when he wrote the early lines of *The Waste Land*. I sit and recall some of my favorite lines and images: "Little life with dried tubers," and "We stopped in the colonnade and went out in sunlight, into the Hofgarten..."

Now, it is not summer and snow-loaded clouds shear in over the roofs of the city. Erratic snowflakes have begun to drift. The ice is coming back to Munich.

Back at the hotel, the chairman of the French Department at the University of Munich has left me a message, apologizing for the unexpected cancellation. It gives me some consolation, but the feeling that my work is neither regarded as interesting or original does not leave me.

I meet Klaus at the movie theater, which is located in one of the suburbs. He seems genuinely happy to see me.

"I know this is a repeat for you, but I might need you to interpret," he says. "French movies are hellish to understand. I mean, French actors swallow whole sentences!"

"What do you think I suffered through while sitting in the back of that 2CV? No one should have to listen to those morons blabbering in Bavarian!"

I have seen Truffaut's film twice before, but the claustrophobic scenes shot in the darkly lit Paris apartment strike me with a renewed, raw force. Truffaut burrows into the family's shackled daily life with thin shafts of light in somber rooms with a camera that must have been held tight to the body as the cameraman funneled himself through a narrow hallway. There is no breath in those scenes, and definitely no escape. In the dark beside me, Klaus sits with thinned lips, and he's bent forward stiffly. On the night when the thirteen-year-old boy, Antoine, is sent out to buy flour in a grocery store, he gets caught up in a group of older women, whose anxious talk about birth and blood and the insults to their bodies he is forced to overhear. I look at Klaus, who keeps pinching his lips with his fingers.

I am sure he cannot possibly understand the rapid, garbled French, but there it is: the terror of torn flesh, the terror of the flow of sexual liquids!

At the film's conclusion, Antoine walks off the soccer field and starts running, breathless. Viewers see the thinning vegetation, the first bulge of sand dunes, and then the sudden opening into the flat immensity of the ocean at low tide. Antoine is still running; we can still hear his breath; we watch as his feet slice into the water. What will be the end?

A state of scouring agitation overcomes me as I sense that Klaus's world, just like Antoine's, is out of joint. The difference is that Antoine runs. The camera is so close to him that we can hear every breath. And then, only then—in that famous still-frame—does he look back.

After the movie Klaus walks beside me, his limbs oddly restrained as if he is wading through some viscous liquid. He reminds me of a tarred bird lifting its wings in limpid desperation. We stop and stand motionless as the crowd of moviegoers disperses. A sudden fear accosts me, a fear of knowing what is best: Klaus must run!

We remain standing in front of the movie house in unexplained silence. Soon even the usher scurries away. I ask Klaus about the large bag he's carrying.

"Camera equipment," he says.

The night is supposed to bring frost. Klaus says that once traffic stops he intends to take photos of the tramway's overhead electric feeder wires at the Stachus, the main square of Munich. He invites me to join him, and he seems surprised when I express interest.

"It doesn't take much to get me interested in photography," I say.

"Yes. I remember you telling me about your photo work during the Munich communist uprising."

"That work got me into lots of trouble," I say.

I'm relieved that Klaus doesn't pine for more information.

He and I take the tramway to the main train station, where we drink coffee in the only restaurant still open at this hour.

I point to the ceiling of the ticket hall.

"When I met your father in 1919, there were trusses wide enough to stretch out upon in order to get some rest," I say, "and that's exactly where he told me the story of him and Hans climbing the Höfatz."

"You mentioned it before," he says. "Did my dad ever talk to you about that copper mine in Sweden?"

"When your father was working on that cathedral, the one he never finished, he talked to me about that mine."

"He often mentioned the copper mine," Klaus says. "And often he put it together with a universe that is mechanical, raw and meaningless. He would then spread his arms wide, as if conducting some cosmic symphony and cite Nietzsche's philosophy, how only an esthetic life—only art —could give meaning."

I have never forgotten the passion with which Karl talked about his visit to the Swedish copper mine. The mine, long inactive and declared a historic site, was known for the intricate network of wooden rods designed to transfer power to the ropes that pulled the lorries. This long line of rods started at a large water wheel, crawled up a hill, and allowed for each crudely hewn beam to ram into the one ahead. Jerking motions, cruel shoves. And then there were relay stations that transferred the energy at right angles—intricate masterpieces of 19th century engineering—sending ramming forces across hills and into valleys, and then onto ratcheting wheels.

"This engineering masterpiece made your father think of a caterpillar helplessly wired into a torture rack, its flesh pierced by hooks and wires. It gave him the creeps, he told me."

Karl heard the water first; it rushed down wooden channels. This was still a natural sound, and so was the squeak of the huge waterwheel as it lumbered into rotation. But then the screech of wood against wood, beams grating and moving, stretching their connecting strips of leather on a rack of torture! Leather strips, which were frayed from abuse, held together the joints of the beams. As the gigantic water wheel began to turn, its axle wobbling in its groove, its knobby wedges pushed on a log, which then shoved away the next log and then the next log. The noise evoked a relentless brutality, the thump of wood on wood, the aching pain of stretched material, sinews and straps of leather and coils of metal yielding to repeat tasks for the rest of eternity.

"Like Sisyphus pushing the boulder up the hill for eternity," Klaus says.

I nod. "Your father told me that he walked up the hill and had a vision of the relentless advance of a soulless age, and that this was the act of final sedition, blasphemy of the holy, the soiling of the Lord. That is how he expressed it. And only in the grip of total terror and total disgust could man resist and save himself. Only from such feeling could come the revolution. Only from this could come the poetry of deliverance."

Klaus looks at me, as if he knows that I have something more to say.

"And this was your father's hope, that Hitler would deliver the poetry of deliverance."

The train platforms are now empty; an orderly in uniform shuffles about, spearing up garbage with an oversized stick. She's also chasing a few insomniac pigeons that keep circling behind her, their heads bobbing incessantly.

Klaus, livened by his multiple cups of coffee, has been listening attentively. Now, he stands up, stretches, and looks at the oversize clock hanging above the ticket hall.

"It is still too early to step out into the square and set up the camera," he says. "The last tram does not move out before 1:30."

"I see that they kept the old clock face with a few bullet holes."

Klaus sits down again.

"My father had a pessimistic, rather dark vein."

"But an artistic vein, too."

"He was a photographer, for sure."

"Didn't he make also some jewelry and encase flowers—Edelweiss I think—in amber?" I ask. "And if I'm remembering correctly, he once showed me a tiny dog figure carved from amber."

"Well, my father was in the Baltic sometime after the 1918 armistice. It must have been in summertime, because he told me about throwing nets into the East Sea to pull out nuggets of amber.

When Hans and my father were still friends, they heated amber in some oil bath and let the liquid amber flow around the flower heads. Too bad that I don't have any of his amber Edelweiss jewelry! All I have is the amber dog you're talking about. It had a special meaning to him, I guess."

His voice trails off.

It is now time to leave and take pictures. We walk the short distance to the Stachus, cross the tramway tracks, set up the tripod, and screw the wire release into the camera. At this hour, only an occasional car comes by, its headlights throwing glares into the black-iced street and reflecting into the wires that hang like frozen spiderwebs above us.

Klaus places his Rolleicord on a tripod, swivels it, and points it upward. He works with concentration. He moves his lips as he counts the seconds—and at times minutes—of exposures. Every so often, he repositions the camera between the tracks. and I take my coat off and shield Klaus's camera from straying lights.

"You're going to catch a cold," Klaus says.

"It's worth the risk," I say.

Above us, the wires glisten. Thin strings of ice spin away toward some free horizon until the cleats of cross-wires, dark blobs of metal, thick and sinister, bend them back into the iron web. I visualize this web suddenly crashing down ...all these wires and cleats and harnesses and weights that obscure a sky withheld. Ice shattering into thousands of shards.

Klaus talks about his fascination with overhead electric wires. As a child, on his ride home from school, he would wait for the old-fashioned tramways that were still put into service during peak hours. He would stand on the open rear platform and stare at the wheel high up at the top of the tramway's feeder pole. He describes how the wheel on top of the pole ran smoothly, but then how it shook and shivered and was flung around corners. On occasion, a trance would seize him as he watched the wheel's dizzying trajectories across a disorienting web of intersecting lines before it would stop and finally rest limply below the cold, black wire.

Not until the rumbling of the city begins, like the slow waking of a beast, do I wave down a taxi. Klaus and I scoot into the back seat, and he drags his camera bag with him. The taxi driver says he will drop me off first, and then Klaus.

When we reach my hotel and I open the car door, Klaus reaches over and places something into my palm.

"I exposed four rolls of film," he says, "and this one is yours. We'll see what comes of it."

I thank him, close the door, and wave goodbye from the sidewalk.

I watch as the rear lights of the taxi smear into the distance. Then I close my hand firmly around the roll of film and, for a moment, I feel its roundness like a promise.

I think of Camus's words: "What a misfortune is the man without a city."

Klaus has a city, but his city is dark, its sky black. And I cannot get the picture of Antoine out of my mind, the boy in *The 400 Blows*, running toward the water's edge, looking back a last time

When will I will see Klaus again? In such a short time, this young man and I have established a friendship almost akin to the one I had with his father.

I hope we'll be in touch before long.

But for now I will sleep in and take the noon train to Paris. I too have a town to visit.

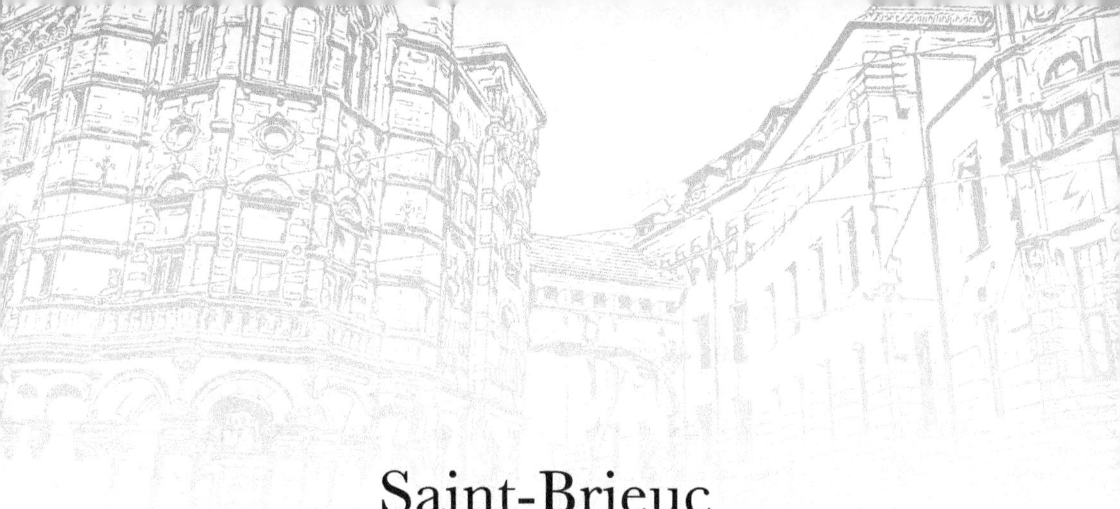

Saint-Brieuc

After I arrive in Paris and stay overnight there, I travel on from the Gare de L'Est to Saint-Brieuc.

Saint-Brieuc: the city on the Atlantic coast where I was born.

On my way, I find an unoccupied compartment where I settle down, gaze out the window, and sleep. My old childhood friend is expecting me over the weekend, but the Munich visit has afflicted me with an unease that keeps edging into my thoughts. It is as if the Munich spring—so unusual in mid-February—has thawed frozen wounds burrowed deep in my soul. The shapeless suffering of Klaus; washes of paint splintering into sheeted ice; his odd interest in tram wires; disinterested Munich students; cancelled lectures—all that melts into a vexing mood. And my past lectures on Camus and *The Stranger* seem beside the point, but what point I cannot say. Camus's death has left too many questions unanswered. It strikes me that *The Stranger's* protagonist, Meursault, was shown as a man without guilt and that Camus's last novel *The Fall*, written decades later, showed a man who laid bare every fold of his soul to guilt. It is as if the sun in Camus's early work has blotted out evil and the tragic undercurrent of life. In *The Fall* man is fallen, guilty of sin, and there is no sun. Maybe that was the reason Camus set *The Fall* in rain-drenched Amsterdam.

It is late afternoon when I arrive in Saint-Brieuc. When Aergard hugs me at the train station, I tear up and, for a moment, bury my face into his Shetland sweater. Observant as he is, he turns and walks to his car. We don't talk for a while.

"Are you still flying full-time?" I ask.

"I run the base operation at the new airport." When Aergard says 'new,' he means after 1939.

Later we are talking of the years before World War One, the *real* old times—the day the Channel winds were so strong a tail dragger lifted off at twenty-five miles per hour and drifted backwards across the airfield, or the day a white-clad flyer took the silk blouse from an admiring lady to mend a torn wing canvas.

Aergard's wife is busy playing bridge, so he suggests that we visit some of our old haunts. He is driving me in his bright-yellow car, with an inscription that reads "Robillard Driving School" on its front doors. Together we travel through the coast village of Cesson, and then down to the Baie de Saint-Brieuc. We take off our shoes and walk a few yards onto the wide mudflat at a spot named Grèves de Langueux. I have not felt mud between my toes in a long time. It creates a pleasant itch that lifts into my spine, but the itch disappears the moment the mud spreads above my toes and becomes exposed to the air. Aergard and I walk silently inside this grey dome of water and sandflats and haze where no colors endure, save faint yellows and pinks run in by a bated sun.

And it all comes back: Cesson Aerodrome, Aviation Day, October of 1910.

This was where I met Aergard for the first time. We both were in our early teens. Both of us had managed to walk close to Busson's monoplane, which was being readied for take-off from the mudflats of Cesson Aerodrome (at high tide, the Aerodrome would be closed). Its wings appeared like extra-wide paddles above a fuselage that seemed glued together from toothpicks and stuck onto some pathetic pinwheels. Our mothers were chatting with

"Grand Busson," the airman extraordinaire who was soon to hold the speed record for a one-passenger flight with a Mr. Alexandre Borie on board, who my father, being so small and lightweight, had unsuccessfully tried to replace. I don't remember where my father was—holding a grudge that day, possibly staying away—but I do remember my mother, Gertrude, standing near the rear aileron in a white crinoline skirt, her blond hair bunched up beneath a black satin hat. The people in Saint-Brieuc always wondered why a shy schoolteacher had befriended a tall, blue-eyed German-Danish woman with the unpronounceable name of Gertrude, and why he would think it funny to roll the "r" whenever he pronounced her name. So, "Gertrrrude" was always making "*rrroast*" or "*rrrolling*" the dough, or "*rrresting.*" The French were accustomed to trilling their "r's" from the back of their palate, while the Germans vibrated their tongues against the upper teeth and, more often than not, ejected a good load of spit.

Gertrude had come through town with a theater group that performed Celtic dances and after the performance she had shown my father how to do the dance. As the cynics in town would later put it: my mother could have easily lifted my father up—his barely five-foot frame against her six foot three torso—but holding him against her bosom likely would have stifled the poor man!

When they got married, some money came in from the well-to-do Danish-German grandparents, and it was enough to purchase a home in Cesson, where I was to spend my childhood. Soren Kierkegaard's to-be-betrothed lover, Regine Olsen, was a distant relative of my mother's, and she was quite knowledgeable in all matters relating to the Danish philosopher whose somber portrait hung in our living room with its dark wainscoting and the even darker piano.

My father was of shy, timid character and not given to soaring ideas—except when it came to be flying. Around 1909, an Englishman named Samuel F Cody came to Saint-Brieuc to demonstrate his seaplane, as well as to convince onlookers about its future uses as a passenger plane. Out of all the onlookers, he chose my father for the demonstration flight. They swooped out over the channel into the perfect blue sky, and when they returned, my father was in a state of bliss.

But more than airplanes, Cody was passionate about his military kite system that he intended to sell to the French Army. He had already constructed a box kite that could carry a man up to a height of two thousand and six hundred feet. When the wind was right, he demonstrated it to great acclaim at a few county fairs.

One day, my father received a note that Cody was planning to show his kite system to military officers near Saint-Brieuc and wanted my father to ascend in the basket. So, one morning, he and I biked on heath-lined roads overlooking the Channel to the field where the horses had pulled the winches and the wooden box containing the kite and now stood scratching the soil, their nares steaming. The crew of twelve young recruits pulled the kite out of its box. They uncoiled the ropes, then secured the basket and the pulleys to manipulate the small wings at the side of the kite.

After several minutes, the small group of officers arrived by staff car, their faces blushed from the champagne breakfast the town had so generously provided. My father climbed into the basket, waving. When the rope was released, the basket slithered across the sand, lifting clouds of dust, and then it jerked up into the air as the kite caught the breeze from the Channel. Several times, my father disappeared into the clouds, but he kept up a steady stream of written notes that he placed into a letterbox then ran down the winch line. "Schooner entering le Val André" and "Two Renaults approaching Erguy." No matter how made up they were, these were messages that might apply to military reconnaissance, and all of us onlookers were thrilled by the box kite's success.

On our bike ride home, my father kept whistling, and he even rode along with his hands off the handlebars. In Saint-Brieuc, we enjoyed a juicy steak, and he went so far as to permit me a taste of the local brew.

"Nothing comes even close to flying," my father said, reveling about the feathery clouds that had surrounded him, the sudden vistas, the hue of pink the early sun had poured into the cloud tops.

My father had found his bliss.

On some Sunday mornings, my parents took me to the beach at low tide. They clamped a triangular-shaped cloth to poles, and I helped them spread a wide blanket on the ground where we would place bread and sausage, cheese and cucumbers. The three of us sat down and glimpsed a pale sun behind the smear of fog. At low tide, the sea bottom lay denuded for miles. That was when my father told me the story of the earthquake in Lisbon. When people noticed that the sea had receded, they walked onto the beach aghast at this wonder of nature. That's when a huge tsunami engulfed them all.

"Don't frighten the little one," my mother chided him.

"I am not afraid," I said. But my answer was not truthful.

"Remember, Yann, that even on regular days, the tide rushes back faster than the hoofs of a horse," he said.

Sometimes I would walk away from my parents and venture out onto the wide, soft flat. I loved squishing mud between my toes and that peculiar, tingling feeling that resulted. When I ran, I watched with fascination as my toes sunk into the mud, leaving rimmed puddles behind me. Then I turned around and tried to make out the tower, the landmark that would tell me where to head back, the gap of eastern horizon where the bay curved into the land.

One morning I walked so far that I could no longer see any of the boats that lay sidewise on the flats. A bank of dense fog had slid between the French coast and England, and I found myself suspended in total disarray without any direction to choose from. I was alone and totally free. I had the sense that the foundation of my existence had been lost, that the sea and the horizon and the land and the sand and the sky had left me anchorless and with nothing to hold onto. I probed my feelings amidst this forlornness, letting in a sadness similar to hearing about a parent's untimely death. Then the water came gurgling in from all sides. When I would manage to reach higher ground, I would sink moments later into ankle-deep water. I felt as though I was running in circles, unable to find direction in the rising water that seemed to surround me from all sides. The thought clutched my heart that I had no choice but to wait for the big wave that was to come and show me the flow. That would be my chance to run for my life.

When I heard a voice eerily deflected by the fog, I squinted and saw a figure waving a black coat. It was my father. He called my name over and over, and that's when I knew I was safe.

In the years to come, I made a habit of walking into the fog and the ocean's wide-open spaces. My intention was to raise my soul against this sense of danger and of being lost. My intention was to search for this shiver of being alive.

Our lives in the small town were orderly—bourgeois—and my father in his yellow cravat and pale teacher overcoat had, by and large, won the respect of his colleagues. His success had even ignited some envy. My mother's German ancestry was overlooked, and she regularly offered dancing lessons. But then came the war. German language lessons in the gymnasium were immediately suspended. My father volunteered for the Air Corps and was assigned to the Kite Corps, which was ordered to reconnoiter the positions of the Huns northeast of Paris. The city was in chaos, and my father had to commandeer a taxi to drive him to the assigned position. The two poilus squeezing in beside him in the back seat of the taxi did not believe his story, and even suspected him of being a German spy. The photo he carried with him, which depicted the kite, the horses, and the French officers, was what convinced them that he was on the French side.

There had been a steady drizzle for several days. The unit was mired in the mud and unable to deploy the kite, but soon after my father reached the unit the weather softened; there was a hazy sunshine and the kite could be released several times with a sandbag placed inside the basket. When word came that the Germans had dug several machine gun emplacements, the kite was loosened first thing the next morning. My father was sent up into the sky with a supply of maps on which he was to indicate the emplacements with a red marker. The wind was strong, and he ascended to more than a thousand feet in just a few minutes. He sent his first marked map down with a scribbled note that read, "The wind is in my ears, the sun is in my face, and God is with my country." It was to be his last message.

Bullets shattered the cross ties, causing my father's kite to lose altitude and tumble to the ground. My father was thrown out of the basket. He landed in a ditch with both legs shattered and his pelvis broken. He was transferred to Saint-Brieuc, where hospital workers encased his lower body in a heavy cast. Days later, he died.

After Aergard and I have walked back from the flats to the higher banks, and after traipsing about for our shoes, we visit a pub facing the quay. Its façade is built of irregular cemented sandstones framed by red bricks, providing a vivid contrast to the white louvers. From each side, a tall building pinches the narrow front of the bar, but the bar's interior, its heavy oak tables and stately chairs, give the impression of a regal place. The ceiling is hung with fairies, Korrigans, Lutins—called "little things"—imps with no redeeming qualities, pranksters one might call them, a literal zoo of winged virgins, lute-playing fairies and gnomes with umbrellas and sickle shoes.

We order buckwheat pancakes folded over fillings of ham and eggs, plus two bottles of Cider Fernier. Aergard looks up at the ceiling and points to one of the fairies, "one of the Lutins known to push bikers off their bikes ...but, he bends toward me, his rugged, wind-ravaged face now right in front of mine, "she is also known to protect unwary travelers from their friends' wives."

"Is your Urraca still as tough and unforgiving a wife?"

"I'd say you are kind of courageous to show up...Be it as it may, our friendship calls for a bottle of Pommeau," Aergard is grinning.

I have lost contact with Aergard for years, but as the Pommeau Schnapps and fresh galettes filled with fruits and jam keep coming, we loosen up.

"I have to wonder why your freelancing opportunity in Paris never took off," he says. "And I still keep thinking about the girlfriends you brought in from there. I had a tough time teaching each of them how to fly."

"Thanks for pointing that out." I am trying to ease the sting with a hoarse chuckle. "You might wonder, of course, why I never found a partner."

Aergard scratches his nose. "You haven't found a partner because no woman wants to marry a man who always comes up short." A mischievous grin crosses Aergard's face. This is how I remember him!

"Are you out to wrack my self-confidence?"

"More than that! I'm out to defrock you, deflate you, shake you up. And you better thank me for that because I'm just trying to harden you for the lioness."

He makes the word "lioness" sound like a suppressed roar, gutting it with low vowels. "So, in all seriousness, why did things never work out with Ingrid ...or was it Sigrid?... and all those other ladies you dated?"

"Well, I never caught on, or they didn't," I say "Or maybe it was that another freelancing gig distracted me, or I lived with an acquaintance from one mansard roof to the other and I couldn't decide. I didn't feel deep enough, wasn't sure enough, except that I knew I had to chase news again and again. It's a shame. Other journalists usually beat me to it, and even when I tried to dive into the literary scene in *La Rotonde*, Hemingway had just left. He wasn't in *Les Deux Maggots* either, and when I tried to camp out at *la Closerie des Lilac*, Hemingway either had a cold or was drunk."

"You made that all up!"

"I wish."

"But in 1936, you did change your life. You joined the Spanish Republican Air Force."

"I was looking for the real," I say. "I had hoped I would find it in the skies over Spain. Death is real. It is the ultimate real. Maybe that was it."

I lift my eyes up to the zoo of grinning fairies that appear to stare right back at me, their black eyes and gnarled fingernails seemingly mocking me.

"It was you who lit the fire in me," I say.

"At least the passion for flying. You were a Republican, after all."

"Yes. I was, and I was young."

"And so was I, and so was Urraca."

"Oh, yes ...the lioness!"

We have reached the time of the night when chairs get flipped onto tables, waitresses move like restless shadows, and the staff lets the cat out to join you so you touch her fur and dream of falling asleep, which you should have done hours ago.

The owner who knows Aergard from old times calls a taxi to shuttle us two drunks downtown in the wee hours of the morning.

We crawl into our beds as clandestinely as possible—I am billeted in the upstairs guest room—and we both sleep in late.

When I come downstairs the next morning, Aergard is making coffee.

"Where is Urraca?"

"Teaching."

"Engineering?"

"Actually, she has now a job teaching Spanish and math. And did you know she has a geology degree, too?"

It has begun to snow into the windless morning, and together we watch fat snowflakes tumble outside the window. We have entered that lucid interval where fairies leave, dreams fade, and old friendships are nurtured into a new day.

After breakfast, we take a bus back to the beach road near the pub we visited the night before so that Aergard can locate his car.

"It's low tide and I'd prefer to walk out into the flats alone," I say.

Aergard just stands there in the mist, his wet face making it look as if he has been crying. Breton winters could do that.

"The Celtic disease," he said.

"For some it's the desert, and for some it's the tide flats."

"I hope you don't stay forty days."

"How about picking me up in two hours?"

He nods. "I'll tell them to prepare a bouillabaisse at the pub."

After Aergard has left, I take my shoes off, set them down beside a streetlight, and step onto the mudflats. The sand riffles in skeins, and in other spots it is lifted into shallow mounds that give the impression that whales are lolling beneath. The water is silently channeling toward the sea. I walk as straight as I can, but all the landmarks are slowly disappearing in the white mist. Snowing on the sea. I have never seen snowflakes tumbling that close to water. Ice to water; water to ice. I feel lost.

Decades ago, and close to the spot where I am wandering, a philosopher walked out into the Baie de Rosaires. He swam to his death to prove that life was not worth living. Camus had known of him, and he knew about the "nothing" that Jean Grenier wrote about: "Every day all things are put in question; every day, nothing exists."

A strange attraction! I keep walking silently into the brume, waiting for indifference to emerge like a secret song. I think of the absence of mourning Camus describes at the funeral of a grandmother, and Meursault's indifference at his own mother's funeral, which was to lead to death on a sun-parched beach. And then I think of Klaus's obsession with indifference, his life drowning in guilt.

Barefoot as I am, my feet numb and cold. I start running, my breath flagging ahead of me. The warmth rises from my toes to my calves and then spreads throughout my lungs, my heart. Exhaustion comes fast as I run through the unwavering mist on shifting sands.

When I return from the beach, Aergard is waiting in the car. Something stops us from talking.

Finally, after glancing at me, Aergard asks, "Wasn't that the spot where Jules Lequier gave himself up to senseless death?"

"Yes! I thought about him out there on the flats."

"Our Celtic disease."

"A vast desert of sand, scoured by the sea and bereft of sun."

"Lequier could have written that," Aergard comments.

"Maybe he did."

The innkeeper welcomes us warmly in his "pub in the mist." The Bouillabaisse arrives in a large terrine, the varied fish cooked to perfection such that the meat flakes off the bones. We drink a tart white wine and cognac.

"While you were at the beach, I was thinking about that chief engineer of the cathedral project. Wasn't her name Madeleine?" Aergard is pursing his lips to sip the juice out from the half shells. "You fell in love with her, didn't you?"

I am taken aback, and Aergard must have noticed my vexation.

"I mean, you did say as much in a letter you sent me just before the war ended."

"Madeleine had already died. But at the time I sent the letter I only knew she was missing."

"Urraca told me that the Germans killed her in an ambush."

My lips suddenly feel parched, and I take a long drink from my glass. "How well did Urraca know Madeleine?"

"Urraca is cagey about it—like about most of her past. All I know is that during the Spanish Civil War Madeleine helped Urraca smuggle weapons across the Pyrenees to support the Republican forces. I do not know how close they stayed after the Spanish Civil War, but I suspect that Madeleine helped some Jews flee across the Spanish-French border once France was occupied by the Germans."

"You didn't live with her then?"

"No. It wasn't always easy between us. With Urraca and me ...well, the Spanish Civil War tossed us into each other like two billiard balls. We kind of liked it that way, but when the war's fervor gave out, Urraca kept her passion for socialism, but I lived in embers."

The innkeeper returns to our table with a bottle of Remy Martin, which he sets down along with three glasses.

"Old Cru," he says. "For a special occasion."

We swivel the golden liquid into slow gyration, sniff the escaping aroma, sip with closed eyes.

"I do not wish to intrude but do let me say that Yann's father is still much talked about in the community," the waiter says. "Those were heady days when men went to the skies in gallantry."

I tell him I appreciate his kind words, which is true. What is also true: I can't stop thinking about Madeleine.

Aergard and I talk some more; it is mid-afternoon when we leave.

At his home, Aergard leads me to the guest room, and I must have fallen asleep because when I come downstairs to the living room, I smell spices. It is dark outside, and Aergard is nowhere to be found.

A wooden stand with memorabilia under glass faces the bay window. Inside are photos of Joris Ivens and Ludwig Renn. Also encased are several infantry medals and the wing medal issued to fighter pilots of the Republican Air Force together with dozens of photos of planes, including the crashed Potez 540 bomber, which led André Malraux to write his novel *L'espoir*. And then there is that sepia-toned photo of Urraca with Ernest Hemingway, not to mention a copy of *A Farewell to Arms*, laid open, displaying Hemingway's signature and dedication: "To a French woman fighting for freedom! Her spirit gives me hope for the future."

On a side table lies an opened copy of my French translation of Friedrich Dürrenmatt's novella *Die Panne.* I recently translated the novella from German to French and had mentioned it in my last letter to Aergard. It was that very letter that led to my invitation to visit during my travels. It gratifies me that Aergard has gone to the trouble to find a published copy.

In the novella, a businessman named Trap is driving through a Swiss village when his car breaks down. He chances upon a group of retired judges—odd local people, at that—who have been making it their hobby to offer a guest to stay for a free night at their bed & breakfast with the condition that they could scrutinize the guest's life story as if it were a trial. Trap agrees to participate. He has nothing to fear, he states. But during hours of alcohol-fueled revelations, the group finds cause for a verdict of murder. Trap has, in their opinion, caused his employer's heart attack. After the verdict, Trap is led up to his guestroom where he sleeps off his liquored befuddlement. The following day, he drives away in his newly repaired car and brushes away the events.

I take the copy of the book into the kitchen where Urraca is spreading the contents of a bag containing garlic, onions, and parsley onto the kitchen counter. She points her elbows toward me and says hello.

"Wet hands," she says. "Excuse me."

She returns to the kitchen with another large paper bag, closing the door with her angled elbow. I haven't seen Urraca in a long time, but she seems unchanged: tall and thin with a pale, worn face that somehow has resisted age. Her dark eyes remind me of the coals that children place into snowmen's faces.

As she heats a huge pan, I watch her dousing mussels with white wine.

"What do you think?" I ask.

"Of what?"

"The Dürrenmatt novella?"

"It's fine."

"Did you know that Dürrenmatt had first written a different ending?"

She shakes her head.

"In the alternate ending, Trap commits suicide. But Dürrenmatt reconsidered, and he wrote a resolution short of suicide."

She stares at me with a fiery look.

"Indifference and detachment wins," she says. "Of course."

Just then, Aergard comes through the door sputtering excuses: some business at the airport has kept him away, administrative duties, paperwork.

"Did Urraca leave you unharmed?" he asks.

I am preparing to respond with a joke, when Aergard continues, "Urraca whips up a royal mussel stew. Let us men withdraw to the couch and leave the kitchen to her." There is a sharpness in his voice.

"You just sit there," she calls. "Gazpacho will be served soon." Her words come out of her mouth like small daggers.

Urraca is a woman of unbent mind. That is how I have always perceived her. In the Thirties, she studied engineering in Montpellier. Beginning in 1936, during the Spanish Civil War, which pitted Royalist forces against the left-oriented Republican forces, she assisted the ground crews of the Spanish Republican Air Corps. There, she fell in love with Aergard, who had arrived from France to fly Tupolev SB bombers for the Republicans.

Aergard returned to France just before the fall of Madrid to the Royalists. Urraca, however, stayed, devoted to fight to the end. Riven by guilt and in love, Aergard returned to Madrid and saved her from certain execution.

After the war, Aergard founded a flying school at the local airport in Saint-Brieuc. When I visited Aergard in late 1944—western France was liberated by then—Urraca had joined an armed incursion of Republican fighters into Franco's Spain with the aim of changing Spain into a Communist Republic. The incursion was unsuccessful, but her passion for a Republican Spain never weakened.

We sit down to eat our Gazpacho soup. Our talk is hesitant, words limping, long pauses. I keep looking down at my bowl and, through the thinning layer of the stew of vegetables, I see emerging the outline of an airplane painted into the bottom glaze.

"Interesting!" I comment.

"Eat your soup and you shall know," Urraca says.

What emerges is a picture of a Potez 540 bomber, a slow and lumpish concoction of mostly wood that was sold to the Republican Air Force in some numbers by the French government. They had been outdated, outgunned, and could be outmaneuvered even in the early Thirties. At the time of the Spanish Civil War, the German Messerschmitt and the Italian Fiats swiped them off the skies over Spain.

"I remember that you flew in one," Urraca says.

"I hoped to pilot them but wound up in the little bathtub built into the belly of the plane to man a machine gun to ward off the German Messerschmitt. I was the smallest of the crew and the only one who fit in that little bay."

"Not only the Potez, even the Tupolev was crammed," Aergard comments.

He puts his spoon aside, sets his elbows on the table, and circles the air with his fingers as if to reel in memories.

Urraca lifts a large terrine with mussels onto the table, places small plates with spices and leek in front of us and invites us to fork out the orange-colored meat from the black mussels, mixing it with leek and sponging off the broth with chunks of bread.

It would have been a friendly dinner, sharing food and conversation, reaching out for the plenty and sipping white wine, but Urraca intended otherwise.

"You fought for the Spanish Republic and against fascism. So, I don't understand why you worked for the Vichy government a few years later."

Aergard slides back in his chair, takes a deep breath, drops his head. "Not that old record again," he says with a strained voice.

"It's all right. She wants to know." I turn toward Urraca, "I read Andre Gide's pamphlet, *Retour de L'USSR,* just after it was published in 1936. That changed my opinion."

"That was the opinion of one man—and a pederast, at that."

"And a Nobel Prize winner," Aergard says.

Urraca looks at him with an angry expression.

"Don't forget that Gide witnessed hunger and suppression of ordinary people under the whip of a murderous regime while the Paris intellectuals discussed dialectic materialism on the Left Bank," I say before dropping my dainty fork onto my plate with a clang.

"But why join the Vichy pigs?" she asks.

"I really didn't see it coming, Urraca. How could have I predicted the murders and the transportations to the concentration camps and Drancy—all of that?"

"You worked for the diocese and you knew it all and you read the encyclicals. Hell! They knew."

"I did help the Resistance, Urraca. You know that well."

"And when the Germans turned rabid, your resistance—or whatever you want to call it—turned indifferent, lukewarm, and coward. When the Allies finally liberated us, you sat at a desk while my friend and your lover lay in a shallow grave—and France with it!"

My throat is parched dry. I cannot utter a single word. Urraca has sunk the blade of history into me.

"As they say of some. Not even the love of a woman can make them a man." Urraca's voice is loud and hoarse.

"Fuck!" Aergard yells. "Enough!"

"Find the ending to your Trap story!" Urraca bolts out of her chair and leaves the room.

"Nobody has the right to insult my guest," Aergard says. "Not even my wife."

He walks into the living room, where he keeps circling the table, fists balled and arms bent like a pugilist. I cannot move; it is as if I am being held to the chair by strong waves of irate feelings.

"You don't go anywhere tonight," Aergard finally says.

He has guessed my thoughts.

Once Aergard and I settle on the couch, he pours us calvados.

"I don't know what to say, but I want to apologize for her behavior."

"She went to Spain because her eyes could see no other way," I say.

"Her eyes still can't."

Our conversation ends there. History is suddenly like a dark cloud boding a riven friendship. And that is just it! I cannot talk it out. I cannot overcome the feeling that Aergard knows, that he holds back, and that today's fury is nothing but the beginning of a spiral of contempt.

Walking on the mudflats had been balm; the mist closed me in, relieved me of time's burden, and settled me on plain ground. There was the absence of a judging sky, the shelter of fog, and the sand at my feet. In those moments, only hours ago, I was at peace.

"Tomorrow I shall fly you to Bourges," Aergard says. "The forecast is calling for sunny skies and, besides, I need some fresh air."

The next morning, Urraca stays in her bedroom as I pack my bags and leave the house with Aergard.

I tell Aergard that I need to return to Montpellier to prepare some papers on Albert Camus. It is an outright lie. Fact is, I have quite a few more days to myself. Munich has been a disappointment, and Urraca's outburst did me in. It is time to leave. Once again, I feel as though I don't belong.

"My wife is still bitter that I followed you when you quit the Republican Air Force and returned to France." He speaks as he is readying the plane.

"But you rescued her just months later."

"For Urraca it was and always will be honor over life!"

There is still fog and Aergard files an instrument fly plan.

Soon the plane pierces the bank of fog, thick and dense at first, then lighter. Shredded clouds swipe across the plane's windshield and then we burst into unwavering blue.

I think of Camus's return from Prague in his short story *Death of the Soul*. First he sees grey skies over the spires of Prague, and then, finally, after a long train ride, he sees the light and has the whole sky in his face.

As sunlight pours into the cabin, Aergard and I look at each other and smile.

After we land in Bourges, Aergard stays in his pilot seat. We shake hands and call out goodbye over the engine's noise. I crawl out onto the wing, stumble away from the plane, and wave as he taxies off.

Within minutes, Aergard is back in the sky.

I take a taxi to the train station and check into a hotel nearby. I have time to kill. I crawl into bed and stare at the ceiling, noticing all the spider cracks that have been poorly plastered over. I imagine all the sleepless eyes that ever have gazed up toward that ceiling, yearning for a lost fullness of life.

It always happens like this: I cannot empty myself for sleep and I barely hold on to a pale replica of real life. I cannot empty myself of history and, if I could, what would I be? I am the rubbings of past hurts and failures.

After Germany invaded France in 1940, it established an administration for the southern third of France which it then declared as an unoccupied zone.

I was in my late thirties. Many fled Paris when the Germans came close, and the tattered remnants of the former French government had fled to Bordeaux. Among the turmoil and confusion, I participated in the formulations of proposals and speeches and, finally, in the wording of the armistice. There was a hopeful shape to this hesitant cooperation, a wish cast out like an anchor into the future: a united Europe under the umbrella of a powerful Germany, with French art and lifestyle easing the sternness of Teutonic temerity.

I was captivated by the sense that Germany was young and France brittle, that Germany was exuberant and France stale, and I was hopeful that hate would not uncoil and peace would prevail. Now I see that former self through the blurred glass of recollection. At this remove, his thoughts appear incredulous and naïve, and yet I can explain him better than my present self. But I cannot empty myself of him and, for sleep, I need to empty myself of him.

He was I and I was he.

After my visit to Aergard and Urraca I knew I was to reside as much in the past as in the present. Past and present were inseparable now.

Yann and Jünger

In June of 1940, after the German Army had surrounded all major Allied forces near Dunkirk, they poured into the south of France. There was no resistance to speak of, and the German advance was only limited by the speed of their half-tracks. Nobody imagined how fast they were progressing into the South.

As I left Bordeaux, I drove my car against the stream of refugees fleeing south. My skin felt glued to my crumpled suit, and I hadn't slept for days. There were signs of confusion and hesitation among the refugees. Then, on June 26, 1940, the wireless broadcasted the news of the armistice with the Germans.

Four days after the announcement, the refugee's haste had ebbed; carts were ditched on the sides of the roads, and tattered canvases were strung from trees to shelter people from the heat.

There was hope that Pétain, the French General from World War I, would be able to keep the Germans out of the south of France and establish order. There was hope for an honorable peace.

Many refugees just stood around talking to find information. Others walked away from the dusty road across fields to beg for food.

I saw the first German helmets when I stopped in Bourges, hundreds of miles south of Paris. Two German privates spotted the gasoline cans stored inside my car.

"Raus!" they yelled.

I tried to argue, tried to use my German as well as I could, but I couldn't do anything but stand beside the car as the soldiers removed the cans.

An officer stepped in.

"Stop!" he shouted. "Leave them!"

His voice was as firm as the man was tall. He had chiseled cheekbones crammed in beneath steady blue eyes that were rimmed by sickle shadows.

He watched me with those cold eyes and waited for my reaction.

I explained that I had been recently hired to work for the exile government—now led by Pétain—as a speechwriter and press contact.

"You, sir. Where did you learn German?"

I told him that I had studied German literature.

"And your name?"

"Yann Cedak."

The officer introduced himself as Hauptmann Ernst Jünger. I immediately recognized the name. He was a well-known German writer and highly decorated World War I officer. I felt quite star-struck.

"I just read your novel, *On Marble Cliffs*," I said.

The officer's level lips, not easily bent in any direction, widened.

"I published *On Marble Cliffs* just months ago," he said, sounding surprised.

Then, he called an adjutant.

"Monsieur Yann Cedak can take his car into the courtyard," he said. "Someone get him a room, and tell him how to contact me tomorrow."

The next morning, I met Hauptmann Jünger at his office at the end of a narrow alley that opened into a wide courtyard. Cars with mattresses tied onto their roofs blocked the entrance.

A few young women were carrying water from the courtyard's fountain where a group of German soldiers had taken off their shirts and were taunting the women with whatever French they could muster. Other soldiers stood atop the hood of a Kübelwagen, holding bottles of champagne with outstretched arms. And then there was the constant yelling of kids running between cars, chasing cats or sitting inside the carts, kicking their feet out between the spars while chomping strawberries.

Ernst Jünger and I sat down in a corner where beams were laid across stacked coffins, creating a makeshift table. There was plenty of food: dark bread (from German supplies), boiled eggs, ham and cheese.

"You mentioned writing for Pétain," Jünger said. "That sentence in Pétain's speech, the one about 'the soil itself is your fatherland' ...if I'm remembering it correctly ...who wrote that?"

"Well, I did have a hand in it!"

Later, Hauptmann Jünger took me to the library. It was empty, aside from an elderly librarian who kept staring across her reading glasses into the stale air.

"Tell me where you come from," he said. "In French. This is my lesson."

I told him my background, even managing to add that I had once met Adolf Hitler. I, however, left out the parts about the hysterical rifle jostling, armpit sweat, and Hitler's hammering voice, not to mention the disgusted reactions of Hitler's comrades. I felt it best to keep those details to myself.

Hauptmann Jünger stood up and pushed his hand into the small of his back.

"Forty kilometers marching every day!"

He waved me toward the window, and together we looked down to the welter of cars and carts, kids, and shouting soldiers. Everyone was jostling into each other, squeezing through the alley. And everyone was driven by fate, history, and fear.

"Hitler, for sure, could agitate a beer hall full of drunken Bavarians," he said.

I wasn't sure how to respond, so I just nodded.

For a moment, Jünger rocked on his boots and wrinkled his lips.

"I prefer the firm discipline and regularity of the military life ...its outer sparseness, its inner devotion," he said. "This is also what has attracted me to the Catholic life. I'd prefer an enlightened military regime like the Prussian to democracy, which always bends to the will of the crowd."

He asked me where the Pétain government was located.

"In transit right now, heading for Vichy, as far as I know," I said.

We also talked about the Freikorps. I told him how Karl had saved my life, plus the long talks I had with Karl and Karl's dreams of building cathedrals.

"Here we are in a library, and we haven't looked at one single book," he said.

I pulled Rimbaud's *The Drunken Ship* off the nearest shelf, and we discussed it briefly. But what grabbed Jünger's full attention was an 1898 edition of Joris-Karl Huysmans's *The Cathedral*, in which the author describes the esthetic pleasures the art of Chartres confers to a passionate Catholic.

I had never read the book.

Hauptmann Jünger was obviously fascinated by it.

"I like Huysmans," he said. "I yearn for a world in which beauty is lifted to heights not reached in modern times. Cathedrals are fired with beauty."

"My German friend, Karl, dreamt about building a steel cathedral."

"That is interesting," he said. "In 1875, Gustave Eiffel had actually designed a steel cathedral in Manila, Philippines, using eight shipments of French prefabricated steel. The frames were filled in with sand, gravel, and cement, and the cathedral was built in one year. Record time. And that was not the end of it: Eiffel also built a steel cathedral in Chile that was partially assembled in Paris and then shipped to the Pacific coast town of Arica."

"They built one recently on French soil," he added. "It was in Crusnes, near the German border. I visited in 1939, just before the war. I must say it impressed me as rather boxy, but inside the church you could feel the clinking hum as if the steel itself was breathing."

Jünger took out a leather notebook and pressed me for more details about Karl. He jotted down some notes, and then suggested that a new steel cathedral—maybe somewhere in the South of France—could stand as a great symbol for the future European order. "I'll talk with Alpert about it."

That was the first time I had heard of Alpert, who was to serve as German envoy to the French government.

There was a dark passion in Jünger's discourse. The corners of his mouth quivered almost imperceptibly. I observed him as he guided a cigarette to his mouth, his elbows angled out, his fingers sliding upon an invisible plane.

"Germany can lead a new Europe," he said.

I felt a deep power radiating from this celebrated German officer.

I yielded.

I would leave for Vichy the following day.

Yann Drives to Pic

In my bed in the hotel room, I kept staring at the cracked ceiling in search of elusive sleep. I turned and turned, and with each turn came Urraca's piercing words: 'You were sitting at a desk while Madeleine lay in a burning grave.' Those words—the truth in them—knifed into my heart. Finally, in the wee hours of the morning, I saw that my whole existence hung on these years I knew and loved Madeleine.

I had not driven up to the Massif de St. Baume since the end of World War II. I had avoided it, had tried to efface it from my memory for almost twenty years, but in Bourges, my recollections flooded in raw. Just months after I had met Ernst Jünger in Bourges in 1940, my job as a journalist employed by the Vichy regime had brought me up this mountain, where a few storage sheds had already been built and the foundations of a cathedral traced out. Madeleine was the engineer supervising the project. The Germans, drunken with the glory of easy victories, were funding the project as a prime example of the architecture of their master race.

For thousands of years, men have gathered on high plateaus, mesas, tepuis, and buttes to offer sacrifices to the gods, to pray, to sing, to dance. And for thousands of years, men have built fortresses on top of plateaus with names like Massada, Geshen, Aradi, and Kachaghakaberd. In their dreams, God told them to build tall monuments that reach like fists into the emptiness of an unanswering sky.

The Massif de St. Baume rises twenty miles northeast of Marseille. On my way back to Montpellier, a visit there would be merely a small detour, and so I took an early train to Lyon, spent the night, and rented a Renault the next day.

It was already late morning when I reached Plan-d'Aups-Sainte-Baume. I stopped at a small café for a plate de jour and a glass of white wine. There was nobody else in the restaurant, and the owner joined me for a drink. He was an older man with a big build and an eagerness to talk.

"I hope your car has decent tires," he said. "I bet there's still snow up there, and you really have to watch the hairpin curve near the Monument of the Lost Travelers."

"I'll make it. Not the first time up there for me."

"So, what's up there that interests you anyway?" he asked.

"Memories."

"Ruins, I bet."

"During the occupation, the Nazis wanted to build a church up there."

"That's what I heard. Were you involved?"

"I was as a journalist."

"For the Vichy regime?"

"Yes. A bunch of liars and buffoons."

"And what are you doing now?"

"I teach journalism and European philosophy at the University of Montpellier."

"My daughter studied geology there. But what she is really passionate about is taking photographs."

"Photography is an interest of mine as well," I said. "I couldn't help noticing that big camera bag in the corner."

"That's hers. Hey, keep me company for some calvados, if you'd like."

I pointed at the wall behind the man, where a framed painting showed a delicate white flower with five white leaves surrounding a yellow kernel.

"I recognize that flower," I said. "Its name is Sabline de Provence."

"My daughter painted that picture. She's always in these mountains, walking the rock falls, looking for caves."

"I once knew somebody like her."

"An old love?"

"Yes. She also enjoyed exploring the Massif."

"Another reason to have some calvados on the house! It refreshes memories."

Just then, a woman in her twenties entered the restaurant. She was carrying a brand-new Polaroid camera that was about the size of a small rabbit cage.

"Hi, Lucienne," the man said. "Say hello to mister..."

"Yann Cedak."

The woman greeted me with indifference but then grew interested when I told her about my interest in photography and my plan to take some photos of the Massif.

"I want to assemble an album full of black and white photographs of the Massif," she said.

"Well, today's not exactly the perfect day for picture-taking," I said.

"But that's when you take pictures that stand out! I am interested in the off-season, the snow up there ...and the fog ...the very bareness of it all."

I had started the day sullen, but the complimentary calvados or Lucienne's enthusiasm for art lifted my mood. I found Lucienne's presence refreshing. In her thick parka, blue jeans, and baseball cap—through the back of which flooded a small cascade of red hair—she looked young and adventurous.

I carried my photo equipment from the car and she looked over my Leica and its exchangeable lenses.

"Dad! Can I please join Mr. Cedak for his trip up there? It's a perfect day for what I want to do, and I think he could show me a thing or two."

Her father had his doubts; there was the problem with the snow, the cold, the early darkness. And then there was me: still a stranger to both. I assured her father that I would have her back in a few hours. Lucienne's enthusiasm—she was already fully dressed and waiting—plus whatever gut feelings he had about me, allowed him to eventually agree.

But then, just before Lucienne and I headed for the door, he briefly grabbed my arm. I turned toward him and saw a determination leavened by sadness in his face.

"What is it?" I asked.

"We are of the same generation. We should talk."

I stared at him, not knowing what to say.

"You see I was a sailor on one of the torpedo boats that made it out of Toulon Harbor."

"I was on the mountain when the sailors blew up their ships," I said.

"Yes, Dad," Lucienne interrupted. "Yes, Dad. Later!"

"Just don't return too late," he called after us as Lucienne and I were leaving through the door.

"His mind is still too much with the war," Lucienne remarked as I started the car. I liked Lucienne's father, but his last words had made me afraid. As if he was judging me, as if he knew something about me, and the dull grey of his eyes, this regard so full of heft, had stripped me of all comfort.

It began to snow as Lucienne and I traveled up the road. We continued through stands of beech, scrub oaks, and yews. After the hairpin curve, we headed toward the east where the road is precipitously carved into the north-facing cliffs. Soon, we reached the plateau, where it once again turns toward the west.

At the crest, snowflakes skittered between small boulders before the wind tossed them up and drove them off in wavering sheets. The sea lay in the distance in deranged grey, barely visible between the tattered clouds. Lucienne was thrilled to be at the crest. This was exactly the landscape mood she had been looking for. She left the car and took an exposure with the Polaroid. Back in the car, she pulled the exposed film from the camera, set it between two metal plates, and asked me to hold it for one minute under my armpit.

"The best way to keep it at the right temperature," she explained.

Satisfied with the trial exposure, she stepped outside again and set her Leica on a tripod. I watched as she lined it up with the narrow crest of the Massif. Even on the trial exposure, I could make out dense curls of wind-driven snow rolling over the crest.

"Why do you bother with those trial shots?" I asked.

"I loaded a black and white film into the Leica, a new type of film that can show the most minor variations of grey. And don't ask about the costs! I have to be sure I don't waste the roll."

"But we aren't even at the ruins yet," I reminded her.

The ruins of the church were located at the far western outreach, where the Massif fell off into a cliff a thousand feet tall. When we arrived, the sun was obscured by grey yellow fog, which reminded me of an egg yolk thrown into a pile of ashes. I looked down the cliff in the direction of Marseille as Lucienne climbed on the boulders to set up more shots. I thought of midnight laughter in well-lit places and the clinking of wine glasses, and I tried to evoke the sounds of tugboats, the chafing of wooden keels on quays, the clucking of waves splashing about between the moored boats in the old harbor.

It was October of 1940 when I first stood on this cliff. I still remember how I turned away from the wind and saw Madeleine for the first time. She was dressed in one of those jump suits; in 1940, they called them "siren suits" because Churchill wore them during German air raids on London. The suits, made from crude cotton, had a zipper in front. Madeleine wore a real ugly one: the legs of her garment were oddly short, revealing ankle socks and clogs padded with cork. Her hair was bundled toward the nape of her neck and held in place with a turban. She had a soft smile that tugged at her taut, drawn cheeks. Her lips were full and delicately curved just far enough apart to make a man think of kissing.

To my surprise and delight she approached me.

"I am Madeleine Cardini," she said. "And you are Mr. Yann Cedak from the press corps, I presume?"

"That's right. I'm the one commissioned to write about this cathedral project," I said.

"You see a cathedral here?"

"I suppose I'll have to make one up."

Madeleine showed me the foundations of the vestry and tower; only the sleeping quarters, a large kitchen, and the administrative building were standing at that time. She told me that in the woods to the north, the Vichy government led by Pétain—which would never amount to more than a puppet regime installed by Germany—was building camps to fabricate industrial charcoal, and many of those workers would be happy to lend a hand.

"So you have two industries: charcoal making and cathedral building?" I asked.

"We also have ice factories. During winter, we freeze water in huge basins at the base of the mountain and store the ice in caves. In the summer, it will be transported to Marseille. The fisheries buy every single bar of ice we make."

Madeleine pointed to a diesel engine that pumped in water from the ice cave.

"Fuel is scarce," she said, "and we shut off the generator at ten."

We passed a row of well-stocked cupboards full of large hams, wheels of Swiss cheese, and barrels of wine.

Madeleine must have seen the look on my face.

"Believe it or not, we like you guys from the press," she said, smiling. "Sometimes, we even serve you dinner."

The sleeping area in the next building had dozens of bunk beds with lavatories at the end of the hallways. A few men clustered in a corner had their ears pressed close to a large, fabric-covered loudspeaker.

"My God! How often do we have to listen to Pétain's speeches?" Madeleine asked.

Somehow, I missed the irony and blurted out that I had some part in writing them. Madeleine turned her face away from me and shrugged her shoulders. A sudden silence cut in.

"What is your training?" I asked, hoping to quickly change the subject.

"Engineering and geology."

"You stand out, I must say."

Madeleine then led me to the engineers' drawing rooms above the living quarters.

"Yann, I'd like to introduce you to our architects: Jean Jacques from Paris, Karl Herrman from Germany. Federico, from Italy, is presently outside admiring the sunset from the cliff."

Ice crystals scraped my face, and I buried my cold hands into my pockets and leaned into the wind. Down in Marseille the masts of fishing boats surely had to be tilting wildly now, whipping through the harbor air like hundreds of disjointed pointers. Once I turned away, the wind was at my back and it nearly blew me into an unhinged door that flapped in the gusts. The door hung onto the remnants of a wall, which, for the most part, had crumbled into a pile of bricks.

I returned to the car. I had left the motor running, so the heat comforted me. Lucienne came back with another trial exposure and seemed quite excited about its potentials.

"I need your armpit again," she said, chuckling.

Lucienne leaned back and pulled the Rolleicord from her bag. She handed me the boxy camera, its two lenses stacked on top of each other. This one had the manual knob, but I did not notice the engraved letters *DRP*, which stood for Deutsches Reichspatent.

"Almost looks like a war model," I said.

"You are right," she said. "It is a newer version Rolleicord, but their appearance has hardly changed."

On the day Madeleine introduced me to the architects, it was a Rolleicord camera that caught my eye. It was set on a table, and behind it stood Karl.

I recognized him by the burn on one side of his forehead—a patch of glazed skin pulled taut into a rim of tissue that was folded like the peel of ripe prunes. His nose had widened, so it seemed, or was it just that his cheeks had filled in and softened the harsh features of a peaked Freikorps fighter?

"Karl! Is that you? München Hauptbahnhof, I am Yann!"

Karl's expression was full of disbelief.

"What are you doing here?" he asked.

"I'm working for the Vichy Press. And you?"

"Colonel Jünger has ordered me to build a cathedral."

I now made the connection between Colonel Ernst Jünger's leather book and our chance meeting in Bourges just weeks prior, during which I had mentioned Karl's passion and interest in building churches made of steel.

"Wait ...you two know each other?" Madeleine asked.

"Karl and I met in 1919 in Munich..."

Just then, Federico, the Italian architect, came into the room.

"Federico! The brain behind the campanile project," Karl quipped.

"Which you just love to sabotage!" Federico replied.

Madeleine flashed a fierce glance at both of them. "Cut it out, guys!"

Later, when I sat with Madeleine at supper, she told me about unresolved arguments between Karl, who wanted to build a steel cathedral— a construction regarded as unique in Europe— and the Italian architect, who insisted on building a marble campanile, a glazing white tower reaching out over the sea.

A kitchen orderly served us bread and cheese, plus warmed up chicken slices, which I washed down with water and wine.

"So, what happened in Munich?" Madeleine asked.

I told her about Karl's fearless use of his flamethrower, which saved me from getting killed in front of the train station.

"He aimed the flamethrower straight up, kept torching the machine gun, and didn't stop even as flaming kerosene poured onto his face," I said.

She lowered her head.

"So, that's where he got the burn..."

After a long pause she asked, "What happened to you after that?"

"Well, I was demoted and prohibited from taking any more war-related photographs. I moved to Paris to write freelance essays, mostly about culture, German literature, and movies. And two years ago, I volunteered for the Republican Air Force to help fight the German Messerschmitts in the Spanish skies."

"You're a pilot?"

"I used to think so."

"Why do you say that?"

"All they did was stuff me into the rear gun turret of a Russian bomber which, at best, was nothing but scrap metal."

"I know all about that. The Russians and their outdated bombers were no match for the Germans and Italians. That Franco would win in the end was obvious. It was a wonder the International Brigades held out until 1939 in the first place." Madeleine's voice had taken on a grating pitch, but then she stopped abruptly, sat back, and sipped some wine. "Tell me more about Karl Herrman."

"Honestly, I have not seen Karl since 1919."

"You said he saved your life."

"He certainly did."

"I'm surprised you didn't keep in touch with him."

Lucienne stepped out of the car and into the cold again, setting up her tripod and her Rolleicord to photograph the landscape smeared into a grey-white wash. I watched her through the windshield. The snow came in so thick that I had to use the wipers.

Eventually, I left the car—no sense playing the old man—and walked over to the dilapidated administrative building. Neither history nor weather had been kind to it. The roof had tilted in, and gypsum had powdered the floor along the walls. A few tables and chairs remained, and the stairs to the drawing room where I had been reunited with Karl still seemed somewhat intact.

I looked around downstairs. The wind had blown filigree lines of powdered snow through crevices in the walls and patterned the floor like Naztec desert lines. I heard wind roar through the upstairs. There might be loose panels, caved-in ceilings, and blown out floor boards, I thought. It could be dangerous up there. I just stopped and stood there, taking a few minutes to take it all in, taken aback by the realization that I was close to the spot where Madeleine and I had enjoyed dinner together.

When Karl had joined me and Madeleine at our table, and as the conversation went on, I quickly learned that I had to choose my words carefully. When I complained that I could not visit my birthplace in Saint-Brieuc because it was in the restricted coastal zone of the English Channel, Karl snapped, "You're lucky the whole damn country isn't occupied."

Madeleine was quite accomplished in soothing rhetoric, although it took me some time to recognize that.

"You see, Yann," she said, "Germany plays it safe when they close off a belt along the Atlantic Coast." Then she turned to Karl.

"Although, with the way the war is going, they shouldn't be worried about the English at all."

Later that evening, Madeleine went outside to find a better spot for the car. That's when she spoke more candidly.

"I'm lucky that I live where the Germans don't step with their black boots. I'm glad they've kept their troops in the north and left the administration in the south of France to the Vichy government."

"I still think the Vichy government under General Pétain might carve out some independence," I said.

"We have to wait and see about that. One thing is for sure: I am glad my family stayed in my hometown in Corsica."

"I saw a Cursinu dog outside," I said. "Is he yours?"

"I brought him over from Corsica just before the debacle." Madeleine's eyes suddenly narrowed, her voice low and hoarse.

"The Italians have occupied our land," she said. "They marched from the harbors with opera music blaring from their overblown marching bands. They are destined to destroy our culture. One letter from my cousins managed to come through. They write that they can no longer corral their sheep in the mountains and lead them down to the coastal plane in the winter. This year they will be hiding in the stazzus—those primitive stone bergeries—hoping to keep warm by burning asphodel stalks and stuffing sacks with asphodel leaves to make mattresses."

"The Italians are worse than the Germans," I said. "At least the German soldiers are straightforward, klutzy in all but warfare. They're a somber bunch, and predictably boring."

"And not that visible here in the south, thank God."

"And Karl?" I asked.

Madeleine shrugged her shoulders. Her mind had to have been reeling, what with having to deal with the defeat of the French Army, and now a France subdued and humiliated. It was no great comfort that the Vichy government openly collaborated and licked the conquerors' boots.

"Even then, leaving for Corsica was on her mind. She had what Albert Camus liked to call 'the Mediterranean mind.'"

What came to my mind that evening—and what I shared with Madeleine—was Camus's story of those ancient Greek soldiers who returned from ventures in Asia to their home countries, starved and thirsty, cast into despair by so many failures. How they climbed a mountain, and at the top admired the sea, and how they began to dance, thus forgetting about their weariness and frustrations.

"I can't imagine those clunky Germans dancing on mountains," Madeleine said.

As we walked back to the mess hall, the setting sun slipped below a bank of clouds and sprayed Madeleine's eyes with gold.

It was in that moment, I believed, that we had begun to understand each other.

"Yann says I look as bad as Churchill in my siren suit," Madeleine jokingly said to Karl, who, back in the hall, gave her a big smile.

In 1919, Karl couldn't have produced a smile like that; he was much too skinny, intense, and scared. But now, in 1940, he looked confident. He kept hooking his thumbs into his suspenders, and I noticed a bulge around his waist. Middle age had caught up to him! It crossed my mind that he might have eaten his way across the vineyards near Lyon, the Bourgogne. I pictured him stopping his motorcycle and gumming up the pole in the center of the market square, holding some clipboard and announcing the proclamation of collaboration.

When Madeleine left to talk to some workers, Karl cast aside his stop-and-go French for the time being and we began to inquire about each other's lives.

"Married?" I asked.

"Yes. My wife and I live in Munich. She is pregnant."

"At the train station in Munich you told me you dreamt of building a church."

"I'm surprised you remember that!"

Now I had mentioned the Munich Hauptbahnhof! What was I to say? Should I thank him for saving my life? Skip the subject entirely? My heart began to race. Karl, however, didn't even notice. He was too distracted by Madeleine, who was looking at us from across the mess hall.

"Man, if I just could peel her right out of that siren suit..." he said.

I could not hear Lucienne's steps through the roar of wind-blown snow. When she came suddenly into view, her face appeared animated, almost radiating, in the wash of light.

I must have looked at her in a startled way.

"Ruins attract me," she said. "It's as if they are a way of placating history. Distilling beauty out of what kills us, you know?"

I couldn't grasp what she wanted to express, and she didn't seem to expect a response. She grew even more enthusiastic when she saw the stairs.

"What a picture of the opening into the sky!" she said.

She stood at the base of the stairs, and then walked up a few steps, carefully testing each one as she went. When she felt comfortable enough, she spread open her tripod and tried several camera positions to capture the sulfa-yellow sunlight smearing through fast-paced clouds. I was watching an artist at work.

I could still picture Madeleine walking down these stairs wearing a stunning checkered dress, its middle hour-glassed by a wide belt. I could still picture the way she angled her elbows as she reached into the pockets; those dimples that opened in her cheeks like nascent rosebuds; the box hat that was pinned to her abundant hair.

The occasion had been a formal presentation by the architects on a sunny morning in October of 1940. It was an important meeting. The kitchen workers brought out sweets and, this time, real coffee, not the usual chicory wash.

Federico, the Italian, went on and on. This tall, black-haired Italian kept supporting every sentence he uttered with a cascade of writhing movements, ascending and brilliantly culminating in a swerve of his head. All I could understand was that he insisted on building a campanile first. His argument was that visitors, especially influential ones from Vichy, Berlin, or Rome, would be impressed. He also proposed installing bells at three different heights and installing them sooner than later so that visitors would be greeted by the ringing of the bells.

Karl's speech, on the other hand, was rather dour; he detailed supplies and wind factors and freeze-thaw cycles. But when he revealed a large blueprint of his vision of a steel cathedral, his voice became full of unbridled excitement. I had expected a gothic-style structure, which, from its base to its very peak, would strive toward the sky, toward God. Karl's blueprint, however, showed a jumble of cubistic blocks at the cathedral's base. At first glance, they appeared unordered, and then, at half-height, there was this horizontal interruption that gave way to a needle-like tower. But the needle almost appeared to be an afterthought. In Karl's church, the drive to heights did not instill itself from the base; rather, it was grafted onto a base that had lost its purpose.

I could not shake the impression that I had seen this church somewhere. Maybe a photograph? Maybe a painting?

The French architect a mousy manikin wearing high-waist baggy trousers and an oversized jacket, looked as if he had just stepped out of some jazz club in Paris. He spoke in favor of short-term results, although he conjured up the proud history of French cathedrals such as Sens, Poitiers Amiens, and Beauvais.

I suspected even then that I was witnessing the creation of a three-humped camel, a failure in the making. But the Vichy government—those puppet masters of Nazi Germany—expected news of progress, cooperation, and collaboration. I saw an opening for my services and I needed to make myself indispensable because

I had learned that Emmanuel Berle, my mentor at *le Pavé de Paris*, had retired. My old job in German-occupied Paris was gone.

The enthusiasm of the workers that day was catching. Madeleine, sweetheart that she was, had even ordered extra food and wine. I was asked to stand up and was greeted again with "Maréchal, Nous Voilà": the national anthem of the French Vichy regime.

"Down with perfidy Albion!" some of the workers cried out in unison. "The Mediterranean belongs to France, Italy, and Germany!"

Madeleine's generosity and the outpouring of support kicked Karl into a good mood. He drank too much and vexed Madeleine with some remarks and she scowled at him.

Lucienne, having climbed the stairs part way, was now determined to climb up to the very top and take more photos. Her enthusiasm drew me in. But when she started to hurry up the stairs again, I held her back.

"Wait! I am the scout," I said. "First let me go to the car to get my camera, and then let me check to see if it's safe all the way. Stay right here."

When I returned, I carefully went up to the top. The wood had splintered, and the nails were rusted and protruding, but it seemed safe enough.

"Has the scout cleared the stairs?" Lucienne called from below.

"All clear!" I said.

She and I walked into the former drawing room. The wind blew through large openings and knifed into me. Lucienne began kneeling on the floor, scouting out picture angles. The hesitant light drifting through the broken wall, the pattern of blown-in snow, and the fallen-in roof would be great vistas.

There were some shattered drawing tables piled along one wall, their wooden legs splintered, their surfaces cracked. A few curled blueprint papers had been wind-driven into the corners and I knelt and unfurled one of them. It almost cracked apart in the cold, but despite having been drawn twenty years ago, it hardly had faded. I could still see the blue lines of the design. I took a picture of the print with the fallen roof in the background. Then I took more, and soon I found myself stirred by artistic urges that I had not felt in a long time.

When Lucienne walked over to me, she said, "That composition looks interesting."

"Design and decay," I said. "Idea and demise. What happens to man's dreams. That's what this photo may be about. If it comes out all right, that is ...now, why don't you take a shot?"

Lucienne was hesitant, and even mentioned artistic rights to originality, but after more friendly prodding, she caved in and began taking some of her own exposures.

"This was fun," I said, "but I give up visiting the bell tower. I am freezing."

Lucienne, having underestimated the freezing wind as well, nodded her head in agreement. With stiff hands, we gathered our equipment and went back to the car.

Lucienne looked out the car window.

"You know, I think it is still standing because it is so stumpy," she said.

"When they started the project in 1940, the tower was supposed to be the immediate showpiece. But even at that, they never raised it to more than a third of its planned height. They installed the bells on the lowest level right away, as if they knew it would never amount to any height ...would never rise."

For a while, we sat in the car to warm up.

"You must know this mountaintop very well," she said.

"With interruptions, I was up here every week from 1940 to 1944," I said. "For some time, I even lived in that dilapidated building."

"You were reporting on the progress of the project?"

"The building site never really took off because the war ground everything to a halt, but I became pretty inventive in putting together fake presentations. They called me *Graf Potemkin*."

"Ah! That's the Russian count who lined up wooden facades of whole villages to fool the eyes of the Czar of Russia as he traveled by in his train."

"You got it!"

The unease that Lucienne father's words had sunk into me had not dissipated. I asked her what happened to her father after he escaped Toulon. She briefly explained that he was first stationed in Algiers, then reassigned to torpedo boat units operating from Corse and that during the last weeks of occupation had joined the Marquis. "But he thinks too much about it," she said, and as if not to go too deeply into the past, she unpacked a few Polaroids cartridges and kept busy repacking her camera equipment.

"I can't imagine that it's warm up here even in summertime," she finally said, waving her hands in front of the heater vents.

But it certainly was warm during those autumn days in 1940. Near the same spot where Lucienne and I were now warming up in the car, Madeleine had showed me a magnificent creation (or so she called it) that had been driven up to the Massif de St. Baume for use in a propaganda movie to be titled *Glory of Vichy*.

The car, a Peugeot 402 Gazogene, was pitch-black with wheel wells sculpted like Greek helmets. It ran on gasoline in its glory days, but Madeleine told me that it had recently been converted to burn wood gases. Even the stacked boilers on the back and the car's wide roof box, which looked like an ugly calcium hump on a mollusk, could not detract from its underlying beauty and grace. It was easy to imagine how, after the war, this car would shed its burden and, like a snake shedding its skin, be reborn as the elegant Parisian sculpture it once had been.

Madeleine was leaning on the swooping incline of the fender, having set one foot against the door hinges. She wore a tight black top and a long crinoline skirt with a flowery pattern. Overshadowing it all was a hat, its top dramatically folded. In the slant of light, Madeleine's high cheekbones seemed to lift her eyes and widen her lips into a slightly amused smile. She held a cigarette in her left hand. That was just it: here was this beautiful woman, engineer, administrator, country girl in a crinoline skirt with a cigarette in her hand. She was perfect, right down to her slim legs and her pumps with pyramid-shaped heels. I was taken. I must have exposed a whole roll of film that day.

Madeleine walked to the back of the car and explained the Imbert burner, how the wood was burned almost without air, then underwent combustion and reduction, creating gases for the intake manifold of the carburetor.

A woman in an elegant dress explaining the fine points of chemistry; my majors in philosophy and journalism hadn't prepared me for that!

Karl had now joined us.

"*Glory of Vichy* will show all over France...and I will be the star," Madeleine quipped. When she sat down on the backseat, flanked by me and Karl, I could feel the spot where our hips connected, and I felt an unsure buzz in my groin.

"Can't say that the movie industry is a field that lies fallow, can you Yann?" she asked.

In the summer of 1940, Pétain had broadcasted those very words: "A field that turns fallow is a part of France that dies." I had penned much of his speech and made no secret of it. Now her irony stung me, but I stayed quiet. My knowledge of Kierkegaard and Heidegger—not to mention my grasp of German, Spanish, Italian, and English—all that philosophical heft suddenly seemed to be nothing but baggage.

In the fall of 1940, the war had slowed down. Germany occupied Norway, the air war over Britain lost intensity, and a cross-channel invasion was delayed. The friendship pact between Japan, Italy, and Germany had been signed in September, and diplomatic efforts between Romania, Bulgaria, and Hungary stabilized the eastern countries. Hitler, for once, seemed to have called back his panzers.

Looking back now, I remember the fall of 1940 as pleasant enough. But then, on October 28, 1940, Italy invaded Greece from its bases in Albania. Albania, then occupied by Italy, was located just across the Adriatic Sea from Italy, and Mussolini decided to march his divisions across the mountains southward into Greece. And now everybody sensed that the lull in the fighting that could have led to negotiations had officially been ruptured. And in our small world on top of St. Baume, the relative peace and calm was to break when the bishop of Marseille, Monsignor Delay, invited Madeleine, Karl, and myself into a meeting in Cassis, a small beach town to the east, to discuss further details about the cathedral on top of the Pic de Bertagne. I had no deciding voice in the discussion, but Madeleine had insisted to have somebody from the Vichy press at the meeting. We four had a dinner of stewed rabbit and roasted eel. Karl kept staring at the small den of eels inside the round pie with a terrified expression. This was not exactly sauerkraut and liverwurst, and Karl had his problems.

It got worse.

"Forgive the Italians," the bishop said, his expression hovering somewhere between a smile and a frown. "The shining city on the hill! Maybe it should start with a tower."

"Karl and the Italian architect haven't yet worked out their disagreement," Madeleine said.

"I am aware of that, but, for now, let the tower be built and the nave may follow."

The bishop spoke softly, but his message came through loud and clear. "Cassis was founded on rocks in just the way Christ's church was founded on the rock of St. Paul," he continued. "We are more modest, of course, but our quarries supplied the base for the Statue of Liberty—just one more reason the Italians wouldn't mind our quarries being shut down to give their Carrera Marble the competitive edge! And may I suggest that our German architect may include in his progress reports the importance, quality, and beauty of the local limestone."

Karl acted as if, at any moment, the eels might come back to life and invade his food pipe in ever-increasing spirals of choking.

The bishop quickly changed the topic. He looked at me. "Madeleine mentioned that you wrote parts of Pétain's speeches?"

"In part," I said. "Only in part."

"Pétain told us to go back to the earth for the soil does not lie, to revere the land, to draw from ancient wisdoms, and yield to the chills that only a child's devotion to God can give."

"You are so right, Monsignor," Madeleine said.

"The bickering and posturing of the Third Republic is past, and now that its brittle empire has fallen, the Germans have given us an opportunity to refresh in our hearts what is viable, living, and founded on the words of God."

"France is being reborn in a new way," Madeleine said.

"We all yearn for epiphanies," Monsignor Delay said, his voice low and distinct.

"And what if a whole nation has an epiphany?" Karl snapped.

"Epiphany belongs to the inner life," Monsignor Delay said.

Karl slid his elbows back onto the wide arms of the chair. "To attain fullness, man has to recover and relive history. We Germans believe a nation has to be embraced, lived, and our lives sacrificed to it."

"Personified in one man?"

"Heil Hitler!" Karl said.

Madeleine stiffened as Karl leaned forward.

"May I quote a verse from Rilke? 'For beauty is just the beginning of terror / We can barely endure it / And are awed / When it declines to destroy us.'"

"We all pray for peace," the bishop said. "I am sorry to cut this short, but I must leave. Tomorrow, Jules Saliège, the bishop from Toulouse, will be gracious enough to stop at this small outpost on his way to Rome. If you desire to have a nightcap and a walk around the harbor on an unseasonably warm night like this, I recommend a glass of Pernod at Chez Gilbert. Now, please be careful on the road back up to your quarters. Goodbye for now."

The sudden gusts and swirls of snow took away the view through our car window. Driving alongside the mountain's spine, I kept looking for the single tree that stands near the sharp bend where the road curves back into the northern flank of the Massif down to the villages. The flurries were nearly blotting out all landmarks.

"Tell me more about Madeleine!" Lucienne said.

"She was an engineer, a hydrologist, and an expert spelunker."

"I, too, am a spelunker," Lucienne said. "Caves do not frighten me."

"I've been told that every year, a few people die in the caves."

"I've heard stories about people disappearing after entering the lesser-known caves and then, decades later, surfacing in some other country, their names and appearances totally changed."

"They cheated history and I envy them," I said.

Lucienne turned her head and looked at me in a curious way; it was if she was startled.

"Why do you say that?"

"I've often thought about wiping history away and redoing everything. I guess age has made me think that way."

"It isn't age," she said. "I must admit that I've pondered the idea of disappearing to Corsica."

"That's where you're from?"

She nodded her head, but then, as if to discourage me from asking any further questions, she pointed out the window where the landmark tree at the bend—a fir standing all alone—had finally appeared. The flurries had stopped and rays of sunshine now grazed the mountaintop.

I stopped the car and asked Lucienne to set up her remote trigger to take a Polaroid picture of us standing next to the tree. When the print slid out, its surface first appeared milk-colored, but within minutes the image sharpened, stretching into each corner. Before I knew it, I saw the tree and me and Lucienne—the two of us smiling, surrounded by rocks and scraggy vegetation.

"Don't touch it," she said.

It had taken just minutes for the present to appear on the surface of some piece of plastic, a chemical figment so fragile it could not even resist the pressure of a thumb. The past, however, was indelible. And for some the past is more real than the present.

It was in the fall of 1940 that Karl and a small group of German soldiers nailed wooden signs on that very tree, pointing out directions and mileage.

Berlin–800 miles
London–1500 miles
Moscow–4500 miles

The soldiers then stood there, their arms raised in the air. They drank beer and sang "Tomorrow the World."

The next day, the signs were found shattered on the ground; a German helmet had been nailed to the tree.

Hate was already simmering.

The events were still seared into my mind even after I had been away from the cathedral project for several months.

The Vichy government had sent me to report on the invasion of Greece from Italian bases in Albania. It was winter, and the offensive turned into an embarrassing rout for the Italian army. There was no good news to report—fascist Italy was losing the war. After a few months I was recalled back to St. Baume.

Right after my return, Karl announced that he had been deployed to a different theater of war. During those last days he showed me his artwork. He had acquired ground amber from the Baltic, a powdery substance which was easily melted and made to flow around flowers and other small objects. He had encased an Edelweiss flower so artfully one could trace fine hair stretching from the felt-like leaves into the amber, which glowed like liquid gold when held up to the sun.

Madeleine had been learning the technique from him during my absence, and when she showed me her Sabline de Provence flower in amber, I could see the pride and pleasure in her face. Even after Karl's departure she would continue to encase flowers in amber until she ran out of the powder Karl had given to her. I, too, received a gift; Karl left me several rolls of difficult-to-obtain Agfa color film.

But these gifts did not make up for Karl's arrogance and anger during his last days with us.

It was an unfortunate coincidence that Karl's beloved Zündapp motorbike was delivered to the mountaintop right before he had to leave. Karl started the bike, mounted it, and then spun the rear wheel so violently that the front of the bike lifted off the ground and sent him dashing off. He didn't get too far, as the back tire spun out in a sandpit. But somehow Karl managed to force the bike into gyrations, such that the scene turned into some circus performance that was dangerous, crude, and clumsy. Eventually, Karl slid off the bike and stepped away, laughing.

"Now, allow me to present something more artsy," he said to Madeleine, who had joined the small group of onlookers. Karl used his feet to snap out the two footsteps that extended to both sides of the front wheel hub. Then he asked Madeleine to stand on them, facing him. "Hold on to the handlebars!"

Madeleine's face cringed with hesitation when Karl yelled, "That's an order!"

When Madeleine stepped on, Karl pulled onto the flat and straight part of the road —very carefully at first—but then returned and veered off onto the roughs. Madeleine now was jerked up and down, and it was obvious that she was barely able to hold on. At one point, she began crying out for him to stop. Karl refused; instead, he yelled, "Heil Hitler!" After the bike came to a stop, Madeleine hurriedly slid off the footsteps and limped back to the office without even looking up.

The onlookers began to silently disperse, their faces drawn in fury and disgust.

The next day, as Karl was preparing to leave the Massif de St. Baume, I watched as Madeleine pushed Karl aside when he tried to say goodbye. It was as if they both knew they could never live together, could never make things work. This scene remained in my memory like ink in a deep well.

After Lucienne had taken the picture of us standing at the tree which marked where the road left the crest, bent sharply, and lead down into the valley, she wanted to know what its importance for me was. She must have observed that I looked at the tree quite intently—not knowing that I was looking for the nail marks the German direction signs had left—but I did not want to evoke those memories and so I pretended to suddenly remember something about filmmaking during the Vichy regime and spun out a story in which Karl played a quite unintended comic role.

"You'll absolutely have to hear this. It's hilarious," I said, raising my voice to muster as much enthusiasm as I could. "You, Lucienne, who is interested in all things photo and film! Telling the story to

Lucienne, I left out the parts that did not fit. Because even during these rather easy-going weeks I had noticed a kind of mindfulness in Madeleine's eyes when she and I would walk to the cliff to look out over the Mediterranean. Was it already the anticipation of the collapse of goodwill, a vision of suffering and sadness, a moment in which some essence had been preserved before history would rupture all seams?

"A thousand-foot drop," Madeleine had said, pointing down to the corner of the ice reservoir that had been cut near the base of the cliff.

"Do you know what Kafka wrote about ice?" I asked.

She shook her head.

"Literature is what loosens the floes of ice in your soul. And now Germany has driven an icy pick into the heart of Europe."

Camus had written that truth would arrive with the softness of the feet of pigeons. Karl's truth came on iron heels.

So, I kept the story light hearted and I told Lucienne that, truly, our spirits were lifted when the long-awaited Paris film crew finally arrived and set up their cameras in the Cantanque de'Vau, a narrow fjord at the Mediterranean coast.

Karl and Madeleine and I had been one of the first on the beach. Madeleine and Karl climbed a steep path that led to an outcrop of rocks overlooking the Cantanque de'Vau, which was already lit by the full sun when the narrow beach still lay in shadows. When they rounded the outcrop and disappeared from view, I sat down on the beach, looked down at my knees, feeling old now among this revelry of young people beginning to arrive in trucks and small buses. But I felt restless, couldn't get my mind off Madeleine and Karl hiding up there. A state of vexation had begun to simmer in me.

Several minutes later, I walked up a short path on the opposite side of the fjord. From there, I could see Karl and Madeleine beyond the bend. They were both sitting, and Madeleine had slouched her back against Karl's chest. I watched as Karl lit her cigarette and reached his arms in front of her before resting his face on her left shoulder. They seemed to be one body, and they did not move until the camera crew finished setting up their cameras and silver-coated umbrellas.

The cameraman corralled the actors and ordered them to set up chairs and tables and plenty of food. Then he instructed them to gather and sing "Nous voilà Maréchal" around a campfire. He also instructed them to lift girls above their heads in joyful play, and briefly after, to solemnly pray while holding hands. That was followed by pulling a boat onto the beach. It went on and on like this.

When the cameraman needed Madeleine for a brief appearance in the water, Karl somehow managed to wade in beside her.

"You! Yes! You! Out of the water!" the cameraman yelled at Karl. "We're rolling!"

Karl turned around, put his hands on his hips, and yelled back, "So what?"

What the cameraman said next was far beyond Karl's French comprehension and even more effective because he managed to stretch his wide lips around each and every curse. Karl was suddenly the center of attention. Everybody was looking at him, and, finally, he grunted, threw up his arms, and walked out of the scene. For a while, he just sat on the shoreline, water leaking from his swimming trunks, digging his toes into the sand.

I walked over and sat down beside him.

"This guy is just full of it," Karl said, "and where the fuck does he get that food from?"

Karl remained sullen even after the film crew started repacking their equipment, sat there even as the chantiers recruited from the north and the girls from Cassis kept diving into the bay, splashing about and turning like eels, making the walls of the fjord reflect back their yodeling and yelling as their bodies slapped the water.

I ended the story right then and did not tell Lucienne that Karl, Madeleine, and I spent the night after the filmmaking at a youth hostel together with the crew. That there was food and wine, and the party turned into a drunken revelry. That in the middle of the night, traipsing about looking for a bathroom, I passed Madeleine's room and heard Karl's muted laughter. That Karl had saved my life, but now, years later, he was occupying my country and trying to charm my love interest!

The film crew would end their work just as the colder season set in. Shortly after I was sent to Albania and Greece to cover the disastrous Italian offensive. Other events were to take over my life.

Lucienne and I had driven about half-way down into the valley when we reached a sharp curve where the rocks close to the road ended and a wide view opened. It was the site where the Massif ended in a precipice.

Lucienne asked me to slow down the car. "What are these impressions in the grass right there at the base of the rock wall?" she asked, pointing at two round recesses in the ground. "It looks like there's some old wood lying around."

I stopped the car. "These are remnants of ice-making equipment we used during the war."

"I want to see that?" She picked up her camera, opened the car door and walked into the shallow impressions.

I left behind her and pointed out the circle of disturbed ground still visible where decades ago an ice basin had been located. "The most efficient one, the one that still had ice in September, had actually been inside a cave," I explained.

"You made ice," she said in some disbelief. "I have to come up here when there is more light but you have to tell me what this is all about."

Which I did when we were back in the car and continued down into the valley.

As the summer of 1941 scorched the coastal plain, the fishermen in Marseille needed ice to preserve their catch, and so the business of transporting ice bars to Marseille harbor picked up. Madeleine managed to obtain an exemption of the curfew, and the truck loaded with ice bars rattled down to the Marseille harbor on most weeknights. On some occasions, Madeleine would ask me to help.

To this day, I still can hear Madeleine's voice: "Thanks for helping, Yann! The bars of clear ice go to the bottom. They are for the German Kommandatur! The remaining bars are for the fishermen."

We spent entire afternoons cutting into the ice that was left in a trough dug beneath a rocky overhang at the base of the Massif de St. Baume. A segmented tile roof pivoted on a central pole that covered the round basin; this was a set-up that Madeleine called the "ice carousel." We had a routine: pry the precut ice bars loose, grab them with iron thongs, and slide them onto the back of the truck. There was often only one other helper.

One evening, when the truck's flat was covered with two layers of clear ice bars, Madeleine took me aside and pointed to a white, coffin-sized box in the corner.

"A colonel pilot of the Royal Air Force has been shot down by the Germans," she said. "He parachuted out and then was hidden by the Resistance. Tonight, we shall fit him into this box, hide him amidst the ice bars, and get him loaded onto a fishing boat."

"What?"

"Yann, I really need your help!"

"You didn't tell me! Why me?"

"Besides you, there is only other person I can trust." She looked toward the helper.

"How dare you involve me in this!" I hissed

"I depend on you. I need your help."

I was aghast. I stood paralyzed by fear and shock when the pilot limped out of the darkness like a ghost and Madeleine helped him to settle into the box.

We worked with the light of two acetylene lamps for another hour before the rear of the truck had been stacked with ice bars, the box with the pilot hidden in their midst. Madeleine kept looking at her pocket watch.

When the truck bumped down the unpaved access road—with Madeleine at the wheel—her face looked worn and worried, her lips drawn and strung tense. I sat beside her in silence. The man who helped us had left. Shortly before we reached the paved road, Madeleine stopped the truck, walked toward the back, and shouted, "Watch out! In a minute, we'll be on the main road to Marseille."

The first sign of a checkpoint arrived when we saw the black glaze of militia helmets.

"Those helmets look like shoe-shined chamber pots," Madeleine whispered.

"Ah! Madame, driving herself tonight," the guard said as he checked the official curfew papers with a small flashlight. An assistant walked to the back of the car and pulled up the flap.

"Cold in there," he said. "Allez-y! They want their beer cold, cold, cold at the Kommandatur."

After they granted us permission to carry on, we drove into Marseille, reached the Rue Breteuil, and then turned left on Quay de Maréchal Pétain into the old harbor. A grinning guard waved us through. Madeleine parked the truck close to the hull of a fishing boat and a primitive gangway was heaved across the side. With the crew's help, we pushed the ice bars down, eventually sneaking the airman in between the ice bars and sliding him down to the deck. The box landed with a dull clunk.

Only when the fishing trawler had lifted its anchor and we could hear the *tuck-tuck* of the diesel engine as the boat went out for an early catch did my heartbeat finally slow down. We supplied more ice to two other moored boats, plus the last few ice bars to the Kommandatur. On our way back, Madeleine was relaxed enough to make jokes. "At a meeting, Hitler slams his fist on the table and yells: Enough of the Nazi jokes; they make me *fuehrerious*." But my lips remained tight, my mouth dry, my fear unabated.

Shortly after the rescue mission, Madeleine arranged a meeting between me and the bishop of the Marseille diocese who remembered me from the prior meeting with Karl and Madeleine. The bishop made his office schedule two follow-up interviews. To my surprise, I was offered a job as a photographer for *Catholic Weekly* and as a teacher (I crammed the Bible in fourteen days, drinking all the supply of real coffee there was to be found). The position would allow me to use the press pass issued to me by the Vichy government, plus a wood-gas fueled Citroen that I could use to drive up to the project site where I continued to meet with Madeleine and compose more reports which made the cathedral appear to grow.

On a sunny weekend, I even recruited a few young workers from the wood camps to erect a fake wall that stood just long enough for me to take pictures before it tumbled in the breeze.

It was evident that Madeleine was active in the French Resistance. Soon after these events I was contacted by another member of the Resistance when Pére Marie-Benoît called me to the Capuchin's headquarters at 51 Rue de la Croix de Régnier in Marseille. He was a Franciscan of huge stature, with dark, sunken eyes and a nose that jetted out above his waterfall of a beard. He trod heavy, his cloak billowing as we descended into the basement of the massive brick building.

"You can help us," Pére said. He pulled up a floorboard and retrieved a box. "These are passports of Jewish French citizens. We must help them escape. On some documents, we just need to change their nationality, and for others, we need modified photographs. Some even need the federal stamp that we cannot procure."

"Where are they all going?" I asked.

"Switzerland and Spain. At least for now. "

"And what about bishop Jean Delay?"

"I hear he is quite open, but I don't know where he really stands. We have to keep things secret from the bishop so that in case of trouble he can maintain that he never knew what was going on."

Father Benoît continued, "The situation in Marseille is unpredictable and corrupted, Yann. Everybody is trying to get a permit to leave German-controlled territory. And with your expertise in photography, you can help!" Father Benoît then pointed to a room hidden behind a coal bin. "There's water, heat, and electricity. Just be aware of the coal dust! And look on the bright side. We won't have Vichy officials sneaking around—they don't want to get dirty—and being Capuchins we have some protection."

Father Benoît must have noted my surprise. "If you have any doubt, Madeleine has vouched for you."

"How do people find you?" I asked after a long pause.

"Word is spreading. We have been serving meals almost every day, and then joining hands in reciting the Lord's Prayer. Among those who seek bread and sustenance are those who seek freedom and those who fear for their lives."

"Jews."

"Not a word against them in the Lord's Prayer or in the Holy Bible," Pére Benoît said. "I ask you to think about my request for help, to pray, and then to make your decision to walk with the Lord."

I know now that Pére Benoît would have given me a blessing and a worn smile even if I had refused, but I said yes as he traced the sign of the cross on my forehead and then sent me on my way.

"Such is the power of those who believe in what lies beyond the reach of those chained to this world," he said, and then he sent me on my way.

Soon I began working with a small group of forgers, falsifying exit visas and baptismal certificates. Initially we could not effectively forge the federal stamps, and thus replaced them with similar-looking mail stamps. At the border of Spain or Switzerland, the refugees were to show their documents and explain that there was a shortage of paper ...regular stamps had to be used temporarily. Incredibly, their chutzpah worked for a while, although permission to cross the border always depended on the daily whims of the border officials. (It was at that time that Walter Benjamin, a German journalist and philosopher, was sent back by Spanish border guards and committed suicide.)

In May of 1941, a Belgian Jew, a coworker of mine, managed to develop superb color copies of the federal stamps using Karl's Agfa rolls. One day, however, he disappeared, leaving me with quite a few color prints of the federal stamps. The colors were good—deceptively good—but the paper on which the stamps were printed was far too thick to be pasted beneath the photographs in our falsified Vichy transit documents. The copy stuck out just enough that, with the swipe of a finger, a border guard could detect the edge and reject the document.

Soon after, Madeleine handed me a silver gadget as she and I stood near the cliff, looking toward Marseille.

"Yann, this is a microtome," she said. "It's designed to make incredibly thin slivers of medical tissue. Why don't you try to embed the prints of the stamps in wax, and then slice the paper thin?"

I could see in her eyes the line traced by the distant sea's horizon. She turned slightly, snapped a twig off a dwarf pine, folded her hands around it, rubbed her hands against each other, and then placed her hands on my face. I closed my eyes.

"You can open your eyes now, Yann.

Her face was near mine, and she was smiling. I felt a sharp sting of passion, of desire.

"We are now fighting for the same cause," she said.

"That last day, when Karl humiliated you in front of everyone, I thought that it would mean a kind of beginning for us," I said before I pulled her close and kissed her.

Madeleine pushed me away and her body grew stiff. My heart ached. A cold phlegm worked its way into my throat.

"I didn't..." I stammered.

She stepped back. I felt this awful fear in the pit of my stomach as I watched her walk away.

"Come back," I said, not sure if I had yelled or if my voice had even reached her.

I didn't see Madeleine much over the next few days. We met only briefly at lunch, but she sat away from me, and we exchanged only a few furtive glances.

Then, from mid-summer of 1941 on, Madeleine was absent. Vichy officials had sent orders to keep progress at the cathedral to a minimum. Our main workforce was now to concentrate on producing wood chips and fuel for the coming winter.

Things were changing for me, too. I had been preparing for my position as a teacher in the diocese and had already visited some outlying parishes when I was called to the bishop's office.

"There will be change in your position, Yann," he said. "But it will be temporary, I am sure."

I was to take a position in Stalag XII-D in Trier, a town at the French-German border where French prisoners of war had established a university inside the camp. The Vichy government judged me to be good match: teaching German, writing reviews for the International Red Cross, and even sharing some German philosophy with the French prisoners of war.

The bishop ignored my hesitations and barely looked at me. On my way out, despite my consternation, I asked him about Madeleine. He shrugged his shoulders. "You know it is war and nobody knows a thing," he said. "We shall have your transfer papers tomorrow."

In the letters that I sent from Trier to the diocese I often inquired about the cathedral project and about Madeleine. I received word that eventually I was to return to Marseille. But not a single word about Madeleine.

While in Trier, I gave a few lectures about German philosophy, taught language and journalism, and, on Christmas Day, helped stage a theater piece about the birth of Jesus Christ. A young philosopher named Sartre had penned the piece the winter before.

In this heartland on the border between Germany and France, the war seemed far away. German troops had not achieved to occupy Moscow, and the Russian front had been frozen into the tundra. But surely, come spring, the Germans were to unleash their tanks and Stukas to finish off the Russian Army. And spring would again send out the French prisoners into the fields to help German farmers plow the land and plant their crops. The winter semester that crowded us all into the compound was to eventually come to an end.

In the spring of 1942, I boarded a train to Paris, and then the express to Marseille, where I moved into my small office at the Saint-Victor Diocese.

At my first opportunity, I drove up to the cathedral site where Madeleine greeted me with a firm handshake. I stared at her.

"Surprised?" she asked.

"Very much so," I said. "Did you hear that I was teaching POWs in Germany?" She nodded, and a weary smile crossed her face.

"What about you? How did you get through fall and winter?" I asked.

She told me that the Vichy administration sent trucks up to the building site every two weeks to supply food, fuel and the paychecks for the few permanent employees.

"Where did you live?" I asked.

"I managed," she said.

"But tell me!"

"Sometimes it is better not to know too much."

And that was it. No further explanation. Madeleine was a mystery.

Parish work kept me in Marseille, but on the few occasions when I found time to drive to the building site I always felt a wonderful sense of relief when Madeleine greeted me warmly. It was obvious that she was feeling cheerful. Work on the cathedral had begun again. The wall of the campanile was being built, and the foundations of the nave were to be poured as soon as the weather improved.

On one visit I asked her to join me for dinner and she accepted. I had managed to buy real coffee and salami smuggled in by Italian masons on the black market. We sat down in a small private area. Olives, black bread and wine, thereof was plenty. Madeleine wrapped slices of salami around feta cheese and kept joking that her recipe would survive the war.

But then she spoke seriously. "It is in the woods that you can hear songs and poetry. Resistance is hope and tomorrow we will have visions in the passage of poems and the light of lucidity, the wound closest to the sun. Yann, believe me, there comes a clarity of the mind when life is scaled to the essential, when the eternal is laid bare."

"I think I do some good here in the service of the church," I said.

"Still the hesitant one.." She sat back in her chair and took a long sip of wine. "So, how do you keep your fires burning?"

There again appeared that impish smile—the one that narrowed her eyes, and carved little dimples into her cheeks. "Enough wood chips in your car cylinder for the way back to Marseille?"

"I'll make do."

We walked out to the car. She gave me a kiss on the cheek and I could feel her warm breath.

"You have to think about these things," she said.

After this dinner Madeleine and I resumed our little excursions to "Stonehenge"—that is what we named the circle of boulders—where we shared cigarettes in the lee of the wind. One time, when our faces came close, she pushed me away and said, "There will be a time."

The gentle push of her hands felt like an invocation of good things to come.

One evening, Madeleine and I walked out to our Stonehenge. We watched as swallows dove above the cliffs.

"Join the armed Resistance fighters," she said. "The Maquis would love to have you. Disappear from Delay's staff—or don't. There are ways. What's holding you back, Yann?"

Her words came like a rupture, and I was short of an answer.

"I ...I ...I can still be helpful in the diocese," I said.

She took my hands in hers.

"Don't you see? We must face it. We have to accept that armed resistance is inevitable."

Interrogations

When I had finished my story about the ice making we were near the village. Lucienne told me that she was going to buy some bread in the local bakery, but that later she wanted to hear more war stories from me. "My father does not talk a lot about the war," she explained then suddenly asked, "But what about your old lover?"

I stiffened in my seat, cleared my throat.

"You were talking to my father about her when I came in."

"Will we arrive at the bakery soon," I was trying to change the subject.

Lucienne persisted. "Wasn't it unusual for a woman to lead a team of architects and draftsmen and workers?"

"Men were in the war or working for the war industry."

"What happened to her?"

"She joined the Maquis ...those who wore arms and rose against the Germans. In 1943, she was killed by the Germans."

"Oh no! What happened?"

"An attack on some convoy. That's all I know...there was fighting going on all over the mountain range."

"And what happened to you?"

"I helped Madeleine, but I never was in the thick of it. My job was with the diocese, teaching children the Bible, and teaching religion in school."

Never in the thick of it. Those words suddenly stuck. And I thought of Klaus, how he quoted the words of the angel of Laodicea in Revelations, the same words Camus used in *The Possessed*: "Because you are neither hot nor cold, I am to spit you out of my mouth."

"I'm really sorry," Lucienne said. "I didn't mean to upset you. I asked too much."

I wanted to say, "Asked too much? You interrogated me!"

But I didn't.

She didn't know any better.

In 1942, nobody had any illusions about what interrogation meant when members of the French paramilitary groups knocked on your door and wanted to have a "friendly chat" to find out what was going on in the neighborhood. Sometimes these brought a bottle of wine or some ham or eggs—that was a good outcome, but most often they arrived at the door with only a cold stare. Fear was spreading across the land.

Still, there could have been a good ending to it all, or so it looked in those balmy days of 1942. Russia could be conquered by the Germans, and in the new European order there could be a place for France as the natural arbiter between Germany and Great Britain. People believed it.

October of 1942 was mellow, a month of last fruits and of distant smells and tastes. Up on the mountain, the dwarf mountain pines filled the hills, and even the winds could not diffuse their heavy sweetness.

One of the canteen workers introduced us to her toddler, a little curly haired girl who giggled in delight when she smelled the resin pearling out from broken twigs.

One morning, I tied together a kite from packing paper and cheap strings, and I hung it with a long tail of knotted-together cloth strips. My father, quite a master of box-kite construction, had won a few of the local competitions in Saint-Brieuc, where crowds assembled on the beaches and marveled at the hundreds of kites fluttering on thin lines hung out over the ocean. My father had taught me the art of tying together the strips of wood and balancing the triangle of strings in order to locate the exact spot upon which to fix the kite to the line.

The steady updraft lifted my kite quite effortlessly, and it hung steady in the currents. The girl squealed as the kite hovered and waved in the air. Occasionally, however, she lost interest and busied herself by collecting wooden sticks that she used to craft a bed for her one-eyed puppet.

"Dog bit it," the girl said when I inquired about the absent eye.

She held the maimed puppet firmly to her chest.

We didn't see the small all-terrain vehicle until it had almost rounded the storage barn. A tall man in a dark brown trench coat stepped out. He had a dark bristle of hair, thin lips, and the high cheekbones recognizable amongst Slavs.

"Milice, Marseille detachment," he said. "Papers!"

The little girl started crying and ran toward her mother, who lifted her up and into her arms.

I handed the man my ID papers. Madeleine did the same.

"I see," he said. "Employed by the Diocese of Marseille. What are you doing here?"

This idiot had no clue.

"We plan to winterize the building," I said. "It's a joint German-French project. We're preparing for inspection in the coming week."

"That's it?" The Milice official turned his head and looked around with an incredulous expression on his face.

"We are building a cathedral in the spirit of French-German cooperation," Madeleine said. "This project is being overseen by the Vichy Cultural Affairs Department."

The little girl kept burying her face into her mother's chest. Meanwhile, the man in the trench coat coughed and straightened his back.

"That kite could carry a message to the Maquis," he said. "You must understand. Take it down. Seen any Jews here?"

"This is a barren mountaintop," Madeleine said.

"You find that Dreck hiding everywhere."

A man waiting back in the vehicle flicked his cigarette stump into the Krummholz and laughed. The man in the dark trench coat laughed, too, and then he pulled out a knife and cut the kite string. The kite flew off and away.

"We leave it at that," he said.

After the Milice men left, Madeleine called them "dirty ravens" and "worse than the Germans." She repeatedly shouted such insults as the little girl continued to wail.

Rumor had it that the Germans had rounded up thousands of Jews in Paris, corralled them into a velodrome, and locked them into cattle wagons with destinations unknown.

And still, I kept dreaming of a future, a post-war life, with Madeleine by my side.

The bakery finally appeared out of the fog which had enveloped the valley.

"Won't you come in?" Lucienne asked.

"I prefer to wait in the car."

"Maybe that's better. Otherwise, you might buy some of his excellent bread and ruin your appetite. I bet that my father has prepared his favorite rabbit stew in buttermilk for you."

She left the car before I could answer. A sudden angst welled up in me like choking fumes. I didn't want to talk to her father.

Back in the car, having returned from bakery with two baguettes under her arm, Lucienne told me that her father had married a Corse woman, her mother, who died of tuberculosis shortly after the war. And as she was telling me all this I searched for some way to extricate myself from something I was flinching from.

"I am so sorry," I finally said, "but I must get going. I must make some headway to Lyon where I rented the car."

"He's going to be disappointed, I am sure."

"I really have to get going when we get back."

"I think I'm beginning to understand you," Lucienne said after a long pause. "This mountain was difficult for you. There are places where my father won't go, and I don't know why, and I'll probably never know why. I think I kind of pushed myself into a trip that you needed to take alone."

"Believe me," I said, "I enjoyed this little outing with you. You're a good person and a good photographer."

What I said was true, but the passage of time has ways of wearing down the soul and cutting a man off from his fellow travelers.

When I stepped out of the car back at her father's small restaurant, I said goodbye to Lucienne's father and offered him myriad apologies. Before I left, I handed Lucienne two of my exposed film rolls to develop in her optic lab. She seemed grateful.

Then I was on my way back to Lyon.

Night had fallen. I stared into the light cones that the headlights drilled into the fog. I knew I was fleeing, fleeing from the memory of that fateful day. It was the day I couldn't pass thru the eye of the needle.

November 27, 1942, a warm wind was blowing in from the east, and the flowers down on the coast were blooming. Madeleine and I were sitting behind a rock that oversaw the western slopes of St. Baume, taking in the honey-sweet smells of resin and fruity air wafting up the slopes. I pulled out my watch: it was 7:02 a.m.

Suddenly, we heard a sound that made us turn our heads toward the east. It started as a deep rumble, but then we heard distant popping noises.

"Toulon?" I asked.

"I don't know," Madeleine said.

"Explosions..."

"No! Except..."

"Oh, my God! They are blowing up the fleet in Toulon!"

The swell of distant rumblings, which seemed to emanate from the earth's very core, continued for a few more minutes. I felt a ratcheting unease. In front of the cathedral-in-progress, groups of workers had gathered, some still chewing pieces of dry bread.

"Toulon," somebody said. "That's where the French fleet is moored."

And another: "But the Germans agreed to leave the ships untouched as long as they stayed neutral in the harbor."

"The Germans broke all the agreements by occupying the free zone, and what's preventing them from going any further?" Madeleine asked, her voice trembling.

A billow of smoke had risen to the east, and it rose beyond the hills of Toulon before thinning into a grey scarf laid across the horizon.

Madeleine put her hands on my shoulders and looked deep into my eyes.

"Join the Maquis," she said. "Yann, please. Quit your job! You have no children. You have no wife. Please. You have nothing to lose."

"What can I possibly offer them?"

"Don't be silly, Yann. You speak fluent German."

"So what?'

"You can eavesdrop on their conversations."

"But I am old."

"A daredevil like you? Dodging bullets in Munich?"

"You know as well as I do that that was a long time ago."

"Take up the gun!"

"I'm sorry, Madeleine. I just don't know if I can."

I began to step backward—fleeing, really. I knew I was compromising myself for a regime I detested; I knew I had thoroughly scraped my soul for every imaginable excuse from acting, from being courageous, from putting my life on the line for justice and for freedom.

Madeleine lowered her head.

"What do you know?" she asked before turning and walking away.

Days later, we learned that French sailors had managed to explode all major warships before they could be taken over by German forces. It took several weeks to learn more: the cruiser *Strasbourg* ignited its fuel stores first. Minutes later, the cruiser *Colbert* exploded, and then the *Algérie* erupted in flames. *Algérie* would burn for twenty days, the *Marseillaise* for seven, and the cruiser *Duplex* for ten. Rumors were spreading that the Russians had encircled Germany's 6th Army in Stalingrad and had closed their pincer grip at Katach, which was located to the west, behind German lines. Names of Russian villages lit up with the glimmer of hope; the Russians were back at the Don River.

History came rushing in with the news of far-away places in the Russian steppe. There had been no acts of effective resistance in Marseille, but when I returned, my papers were checked three times by German detachments. Soon the city was to boil over with anti-German sentiments. A laborer named Tavernier had been shot by the Germans when he did not stop when called upon to "halt." Turned out, he was deaf. The news spread across town like a wildfire.

On December 2, 1942, bombs exploded at the Hotel Astoria and the Hotel Rome. Nobody was hurt, but the Germans demanded hostages. The demand was refused by the police commissioner. On December 16, the harbor was closed to all French fishing vessels. New identification papers were required for all dockworkers. Curfews followed, only to be lifted for a day or two and then promptly reinstated.

On January 3 and 4, 1943, assaults at the hotel Splendide and a nightclub frequented by Germans led to another round of curfews and demands for hostages. Again, the police commissioner refused, but this time he was forced to comply on account of an order from the German Kommandatur at Rue de Paradise.

The diffidence I had shown toward Madeleine dimmed my life; sounds thinned with tinny hollowness; the world seemed daubed in sour colors. And my position at the diocese seemed threatened by forces even I could not fathom.

Nobody knew exactly what Madeleine was doing. Rumor persisted that she used a motorcycle. I saw her less and less. Early in 1943, I received word from Bishop Jean Delay's office: any activity that might provide pretext for a search of buildings at the bishopric had to be stopped immediately. It was around that time when German-French police razed the Old Marseille Harbor during a major police action that was led by Himmler. And Himmler, leader of the German Special Forces, made sure it was conducted with utmost cruelty. It put an end to all clandestine activity.

Temporarily, at least.

In February of 1943, Madeleine wrote me a letter from Montpellier, stating that even after a temporary extension, the fishing area in Marseille was confined to such a narrow zone that rescue and smuggle operations had to be suspended. Not that she couched the message in those words; she used the word "money" in the letter as often as she could. Any German Gestapo eye—monocle or not—would glance over it and think, *Those French! Nothing but money they can think of!*

Madeleine also wrote that her Cursinu dog was homesick. Of course, it too was code, and I suspected that she was planning to get involved in operations in Corsica.

The good news was that the trains between Marseille and Nice were full of Jews fleeing the German occupation toward the areas that had been newly assigned to the Italians. When the Germans occupied most of France, they carved out an additional region to be occupied by the Italians. It was no more than a sliver of land—a token gesture toward the Italians, no more— but it helped Jews reach areas where their prosecution was less rabid.

Rolf Mühler, at his headquarters at 425 Rue Paradis, was so busy cleaning up the Old Harbor that thorough checks on identity papers in trains did not begin until April of 1943. Word of mouth was that the regional prefect of Nice was viciously anti-Jewish, but the Italians refused to cooperate with him. There was now—so it seemed—a safe haven because Pére Benoît had negotiated an understanding of restraint toward the Jews with the Italian Commissioner of Jewish Affairs.

I was quite puzzled about the entire cathedral project. I knew it was at a near standstill, but there were still work crews regularly coming up from the valley. They had to be supervised; papers had to be filled; paychecks had to be signed. Once a week, Bishop Jean Delay sent an employee with administrative experience to the site to do paperwork, and I was sent up, too, but there was no word about Madeleine's whereabouts. I even wondered if there was somebody in the Vichy government secretly working for the Resistance, some unnamed official bent over a dusty typewriter cranking out letters and money-drawing documents that could be cashed.

Visits by some obscure commission were announced, and then canceled.

In the summer of 1943, the Germans were on the run. The German counteroffensive at Kursk on the Eastern Front had failed. The Germans had thrown everything at it: hundreds of tanks, elite troops, and thousands of planes. But after the largest tank battle in history, German forces were exhausted, and the Russians kept coming. German and Axis forces were attacked from all sides. General Patton was to take Sicily, and everybody knew that Sardinia and Corsica were next. After the defection of the Italians to the Allied Camp, those islands were guarded by the remains of the once-powerful Africa Corps, now shrunk to a few battalions, licking their wounds, and soon to be shipped back to Italy.

Still, Marseille seethed with frustration and hate. The old harbor had been destroyed and thousands of people caught in the Nazi dragnet had been shipped to the north. Life was from day to day now. But I knew that in the hills, people with vision and determination had gathered, that *Lysander* planes from England landed on secret airstrips when the moon was full and dropped weapons, ammunition, and radio transmitters. And on dark nights PT boats from Corsica beached supplies in rubber rafts. I could have joined the Maquisards and gained Madeleine's respect. I thought about it often, but I just kept writing vacuous letters to the flock, helping with sermons, and approving official pronouncements that afforded the Catholic Church some sanctuary.

Communications were very difficult, and most packages arrived ripped after they had been filched for contraband. An old friend in Paris must have remembered my stay in Algiers in 1939 because he had successfully managed to send me a copy of *The Stranger*.

I opened the book immediately. The note enclosed inside read, "Is this what you've been writing about?"

I read in one session what I had glimpsed in Algiers back in 1939.

It would take a few more years, the liberation of France, the dominance of Camus and Sartre in post-war intellectual life before I learned that *The Stranger* had strengthened the moral of the Resistance. But how could it have? A call to action it was not! Rather, it was the tale of a bureaucrat named Meursault—a bureaucrat not unlike I had been in wartime Marseille—who heeded no sentiment and no emotion, to whom love was fleeting, who decided he would join no religion and no cause. But Meursault was a man who would not lie. And I had not lied when I told Madeleine that *I didn't know if I had the courage to join*.

In 1943, the Vichy administration sent an order to shelve the cathedral project. All personnel were to report to the administration, and all materials were to be repositioned. The bells in the partially finished tower were to be removed as soon as possible. A short line of motorized equipment made its way into the valley one day, and all that was left was the wind.

With the cathedral project shelved my duties were to change too. I was still employed by the Marseille diocese, but was soon transferred to Cassis, a small fishing port which was located at the coast about 20 miles east of Marseille. I still had my limousine with the all so important Vichy license plate, and my duties—penning press releases, teaching in the schools and doing clerical duties—had not changed. But the tides of war had changed, and at the end of 1943 there were almost weekly PT boat runs from Corsica—now occupied by the Allies. Commandos beached their rubber dinghies in the narrow fjords between Marseille and Cassis and unloaded radios, machine guns, rifles, incendiaries and dynamite for the Resistance. However, transporting those supplies from the beachheads to the mountainous interior of the region where the resistance was strong was dangerous.

When the cathedral project had ended I expected a secure desk job in Marseille. I could wait out the war, I thought.

It was not to be.

On that day I spent with Lucienne on the mountain taking photographs and after I had left, I stopped and ate in a small restaurant. It was a well-lighted place full of plastic tables and chairs and a friendly enough waiter who seemed exhausted.

I found a cheap, suitable inn along the highway. One small room stuck in between all the others, and the incessant noise of cars rushing by. I needed that noise. I needed numbness

Drive Back to Montpellier

After Lucienne and I had spent most of the afternoon on top of the Massif, I returned to Lyon and spent a night in a faceless motel. I rose early, returned the rental car, and took the morning train back to Montpellier.

The chairman of the philosophy department had left a note at my university office, requesting that I give a short presentation during the inter-study's lunch group meeting the following afternoon.

We met inside the cafeteria near the esplanade in a back room, which was separate from the spacious student lunch hall. It turned out to be a disjointed meeting. The chairman left the room to stop a bread fight among some students, who kept ripping pieces off their baguettes and throwing them across rows of tables. When he finally stepped on top of a table to make himself heard, a pandemonium of catcalls followed.

"We should stop serving wine at lunch," he said. "And bread, too."

I reported to the chairman the disappointing lack of student interest at the University of Munich. When I mentioned the Föhn and the unusual winter thaw in Bavaria, a discussion about sirocco, prevailing winds, and the new sailing classes near Maguelone ensued. But then he wanted to know more about my stay, and I told him about Karl and my meeting his son, Klaus.

"I wonder how that post-war generation copes with their fathers' crimes?" he asked.

I was relieved when he didn't wait for an answer, and he continued almost absentmindedly, "So, what's the name of that German writer you've been researching?"

"Eugen Gottlob Winkler."

"That's right. And didn't you tell me he was 'the Camus that Germany never had'?"

"I believe so, but I couldn't find out a lot during my stay in Munich."

"I know the feeling."

Later that evening, I met a colleague at a pizzeria in the main square. Gastyb and I took a seat outside beneath a cluster of heaters hung from the canvas roof. Gastyb was of slight build, with a spare face and a marine haircut; he squinted whenever he talked, and always acted as if he was giving in to some pressure. He could sit in one of the leather chairs in our faculty room, smoke a pipe, and fit in just fine.

"Louis Malle plans to make a movie based on a novel by Drieu La Rochelle titled *The Fire Within*, and they asked me to review some philosophy parts in the script," he said. "I thought of Camus, and then I thought of you."

I sipped my Sangria and gave no response.

"So, did you know Drieu?" he asked.

"I know of him," I said. "Who wouldn't? I lived in Paris in the 30s, and Drieu was the director of *La Nouvelle Revue Française*."

"Was he the one who got executed in 1945 because he was a Nazi collaborator?"

"No, that was Brasillach. Drieu committed suicide."

I watched a crowd of students pass by on the sidewalk. I fought a pinch of irritation about Gastyb bringing up the topic of Nazi collaboration. He would not let me forget that in times past I had crafted speeches for Marshall Petain.

Our waiter placed a bowl of shrimp-topped couscous on the table and dropped more ice cubes into our pitcher of sangria.

"You have to eat with your fingers, Yann," Gastyb said, his wide lips lighting up his face.

As we spooned the couscous into our mouths, Gastyb continued to attempt to make friendly conversation. I, however, was feeling rather annoyed. Maybe it was because he kept chipmunking his food, filling his cheeks and muffling his words, barely looking at me, and all the while working his hands into the air as if to distract me from the real message, which clearly was that he wanted me to do some work for him.

"So," he said, "Louis Malle's movie is about some burnt-out drug addict who visits his friends with the hope they will talk him out of blowing out his brain."

I thought of Camus's *Myth of Sisyphus* and those first lines that Camus wrote: *the only real question is why we do not commit suicide.*

"I just can't wait for the scene when they roll the rock up the mountain," I said.

I was surprised when Gastyb picked up the thread of my thoughts.

"You told me about that philosopher mentioned in *Myth of Sisyphus* ...the one who denies that life has any meaning and swims out into the bay at Saint-Brieuc to a point of no return. Saint-Brieuc. That's where you were born, right?"

"Broken heart, unrequited love, a sure dose of depression, and then a poem published by a relative that makes everything look, well, philosophical," I said, straightening out in my seat and vainly hoping that this conversation would not last any longer.

Gastyb then flashed me a letter from Louis Malle before stuffing it into my jacket pocket.

"I knew you would do it," he said, patting me on the back.

He lifted his glass. I ignored the gesture and continued chewing the couscous while Gastyb sashayed over to lighter topics, what with his real concern out of the way now.

"When can we really swim again at Montpellier Beach?" he asked.

"Are you referring to the department outing?"

"Outing. Sure. If you want to call it that. And as we are on the topic do you have your little talk ready?"

I shrugged my shoulders.

"I remember windsurfing at the end of March," he said.

"That's great."

I finished my couscous and said I needed to get home. I didn't think I could handle another minute of Gastyb's company.

Gastyb insisted that I walk with him to the bus station. He stepped into the rear bay of the waiting bus, turned for a moment, and called back: "Let's wait for the secretaries to lie out in their bikinis!"

"There goes the philosophy department," I yelled as the door closed.

As I was waiting for the bus to Celleneuve, a pack of students came trouping by. Among them was Albert, one of my most motivated and intelligent students. To my delight, he had just begun a study of the German Freikorps after WWI. I did not spot him right away because he was surrounded by a trove of giggling girls.

Albert walked up to me and intended, it seemed, to politely introduce me to the three girls who were now lined up beside him. One of the girls, visibly drunk, elbowed her way in front of Albert, pouted her lips, and said, "Honey! You're going to tell your professor that the Germans are afraid of sex, aren't you?"

Even in the dark I could see Albert blushing. He threw his head back and ran his hand through his hair.

"I apologize, Professor Cedak," Albert said. "Please take no offense. I handed a first draft to my chairman just days ago."

I barely understood his last remark, for he was being tugged away by the girls.

Meeting at Place Bresson

I could not blame the young woman for blurting out the same sentiment that I had expressed in Camus's company years ago. It struck me how this topic of Germans fearing sex, love, and softness surfaced now in almost the same way it did back in August of 1939 at the café at Place Bresson in Algiers.

That evening, after I had met Camus and his friends in Charlot's Bookstore, we all walked toward the harbor, passing groups of young Arabs loitering in the haze of cigarette smoke and jestingly shoving each other into the rush of pedestrians.

Some of the men wore djellabas, others long trousers and white cotton shirts, while a few women in burkas slunk by close to the buildings, kids in tow. The smell of fried fish and cheap smoke was in the street. Whiffs of air blew up from the harbor, carrying a smell of tar and kelp.

We took a shortcut, leaving the Rue Charras and entering a maze of alleys. We were surrounded by tall houses with cobbled facades where garments of all colors and sizes were draped along the balcony railings. Arab women crouched on doorsteps with their burkas drawn across their faces and ankles, making them appear boulder-like—lifeless but creepily secretive and vaguely lethal. The men huddled in dark corners, their lit pipes and cigarettes etching glowing circles. They turned quiet, and their voices hushed the moment we passed. We, the French; the Europeans; we, the occupiers.

We walked into Square Bresson, which was dominated by three massive buildings: the bar Tantonville, the Café des Facultés, and adjacent to the latter, the theatre, with its open terraced square used only for the occasional self-congratulatory parade of the French ruling class. Nobody was walking across its barren sandstone steps that were lit by bright lanterns. People seemed to prefer the half-lit corners. The building facades looked dour, grim, and senescent. Down on the square only a round, fenced-in palm garden broke the monotony. In front of the stately facades, horse-drawn carriages were lined up against the harbor wall from which a narrow road led down to the boats. I recognized the buildings as part of the celebrated harbor frontage, which so impressed visitors entering the harbor. These facades resembled a fortress' bulwark, and though adorned with fake stucco and windows and filigree balconies overseeing the harbor, they were set precariously against the cliffs that threatened to push them back into the water. Europe had a foothold here—but no more—and the French who settled here clung to the sea.

We stepped onto the terrace in front of the Café des Facultés, where potted plants and small islands of grass loosened the harshness of the stones. Camus pointed out that René Jean Clot, a painter and good friend, had reserved two tables here simply by spreading his paintings across. Camus and I walked up to René, a stout fellow with a red beard and dark, buried eyes.

"Can't sell them, but I do excel in using them to my advantage," he said.

One of the paintings that was lying face-up did impress me. It was a watercolor featuring the bend of the harbor of Algiers as viewed from the hills. Some mist infiltrated the landscape, like a whiff of unintended wistfulness. It was stunning.

A waiter soon arrived with dishes of olives, feta cheese, fried calamari, sardines, a basket of baguettes, and bottles of Algerian wine and anisette.

"Wonder of wonders! The world comes to an end. Jean Clot must have sold one of his paintings," Camus said.

Amidst all the cackling, everybody at the table reached for the morsels and clinked their glasses in revelry.

"Don't forget that soon we'll have a blackout," the waiter cautioned.

"Everybody show your candles!" Robles shouted.

"Robles is our philosopher on call," Camus whispered into my ear, and then his voice rose in volume. "That ridiculous blackout against German U boats doesn't bother me, but with all that war hysteria, the officials keep censoring our newspaper!"

Right then, the lights went out. Somebody struck a match, and we all lit our candles.

We stood up and gaped across the low hedge onto the Square Bresson, which now appeared sunken and forlorn. The lanterns in front of the theatre were out, and so were the ones where the horses were tied. The lights that cascaded down to the harbor and the lantern in the central palm garden were all extinguished. We sat back down and moved the chairs closer, huddling against the darkness.

"Our eyes will adapt shortly," Camus said.

"To this darkness—maybe," Fréminville said, "but never to the German darkness to come."

"My twin—the pessimist," Camus joked. Then he turned to me. "Fréminville and I founded a small publishing company, and he keeps my optimism in limits."

I didn't have a chance to respond; the topic quickly changed to National Socialism and the Freikorps.

Camus stood up. "Yann Cedak, our guest here today, is the one who knows most about what goes on in the German mind."

The darkness—not to mention the multiple glasses of wine—began to loosen my tongue. "The Freikorps were the well from which National Socialism rose. They denied defeat and instilled in everybody a sense of siege and betrayal. And they had a sickly attraction to blood, death, and honor. Germans look upon themselves as the victims of a fate beyond them—a fate to which they yield as long as deep devotion to the character of their nation prevails."

Someone responded: "And we have no conviction to match their conviction."

Another voice emerged from the darkness: "That's T.S. Elliot!"

I had to admit, they were a well-informed literacy bunch.

During my time with the Freikorps, I began to understand that history is driven by man's yearning for meaning and ecstasy. For years, these men in the Freikorps had experienced the thrills and adrenaline rushes of battle. Though they suffered episodes of dread, boredom, and mulling doubts, they believed in the final victory. But that victory never came. In store for them instead was surrender, and they didn't even know it as they slept in their trenches with their guns at their sides. They marched across the bridges of the River Rhine in ordered columns, drums thumping and trumpets soaring. Waiting for them back at the barracks were weekly rations, daily soups, and gristle from a large kettle in a barren courtyard. Their hearts yearned for the thrill—any thrill—and so they always found a way back to war.

And I continued to talk about my experience advancing with the Freikorps along the Munich railroad. I told them that I sensed that those soldiers needed death and mayhem to feel the rush and the quickening of their pulses. They could not stop fighting. They cherished the edge; they cherished steely weapons and unyielding rock. To slide into bed with a woman and caress her softness—that was what they feared most. In a sense, it was as if the fighting and the company of men relieved them of giving in to the softness of the world. If only they would have surrendered to the void, surrendered to the lack of meaning—only then could they have sensed the very tenderness of the world.

"The tender indifference of the world," Camus added, turning his head toward me. "I think that Yann has it right," he added. "For a long time, war has represented meaning for Germany, and the tenderness of women a threat. But they kept insisting on ways of being invigorated, of being drawn into some form of epiphany."

Everybody at the table was quiet.

Camus continued. "The negotiations of tenderness demand the ebb and flow of feelings, which might, at any time, be negated, counteracted, or dimmed by guilt and fear of indifference. And it is this fear of indifference that drives our yearning for epiphanies and thrills, and shivers of the mind."

When the lights came on again, everybody applauded. Somebody even jumped on a table and started yodeling, making fun of the Germans. Fréminville walked over to me and whispered into my ear.

"What I fear, Yann, is that the Germans will light the century on fire, torch civilization, and smother all hope."

Party on Beach Day after Meeting Gastyb

That night, after having met Gastyb at the restaurant in Montpellier, I took the bus to Celleneuve, the suburb where I live. I stared out the window as the silhouettes of stately patrician homes receded, and I watched as fields opened, dark and stippled with lights from distant gypsy wagons. I didn't want to yield to jealousy, but I couldn't stop thinking about the young women who clung to Albert. And I kept imagining Gastyb at home with his young new wife, a freckled Norwegian, her handing him one last glass of champagne before pulling him down and drawing him into her softness, making him forget about everything.

The next morning, an envelope arrived in the mail. Klaus had sent me a theater script that he wrote based on Camus's short story *Death in the Soul.*

When Klaus and I met in Munich, I had mentioned that I treasured *Death in the Soul* because it draws inspiration from Camus's life and provides insight into his first marriage to Simone Hié, a glamorous morphine addict. The story was written after a 1936 kayak trip Camus took on the Austrian river Inn with Hié and a friend named Ives Bourgeois.

Klaus attached a note to the script: "You made me wonder about details Camus did not flesh out in his story. Camus visited

Kufstein—this is known—but he might have spent time at a small river town called Rattenberg. This is a town—one of only a few in the world! —that no ray of sun touches all winter.'

Rattenberg surely would have intrigued Camus, who had been living in the light of coastal planes. And here was an Austrian town that, because of surrounding mountains, would not be touched by a single ray of sunlight from November through April. All winter long, its residents suffered from darkness.

I knew *Death in the Soul* quite well and had taught it many times. Maybe it was my upbringing in the gloom of Brittany that made me sensitive to a language—so rare in Camus—that evoked the northern latitudes, the lack of sun: *Coppery light from the grey sky; birds passing in the thick, misty morning; roads bordered with sour plum trees.* And those prophetic words: *the music of the world finds its way more easily into a heart grown insecure*—and the image of the man next door who died alone in his hotel room. *He was dead. I knew it was not suicide.*

I opened the envelope just before I had to leave for the department's "Death of a Beach" meeting. In a hurry, I skipped to the end of the script, where I found a few stage directions:

Everybody in the Stube sits or stands frozen. A deep silence hushes over the stage and the audience hears nothing. The people separate into two groups and then face each other. The lights dim.

The River Inn ran through Camus's story, drifting him toward his stay in Prague, his darkest hours, where he spent his time alone in a hotel room or aimlessly walking narrow paths.

Suddenly, I had a sense of foreboding that Klaus, too, had entered a state of despair.

On the drive to the beach east of Montpellier, I regretted not having taken the time to read through Klaus's entire script. I should have thought to bring it with me, but back in my apartment it remained: the envelope ripped open like an accusation of sorts, unashamedly displaying my indifference and my reluctance to face my worries about Klaus. Signs had been appearing. Had I not seen them, or had I been ignoring them? Klaus had outright told me he thought he was The Stranger ...the ice painting ...his forlorn walk beneath Munich's electric tram wires in the darkest part of night ...and now, now this fascination with Camus's most private and desperate short story!

I spent the rest of my drive trying to convince myself that my worries about Klaus were just part of a hangover from last night's meeting with Gastyb. Besides, it didn't help that Gastyb wanted me to be the Camus-inspired expert on suicide.

But maybe Gastyb had a point. Camus did start *Myth of Sisyphus* with that precise question: Was life worth living? And hadn't Camus based his essay on the strange death of the philosopher Jules Lequier who, on February 11, 1862, walked to a beach not far from where I was born, shed his clothes, threw water on his chest, and jumped into the bay to swim beyond the limits of his strength until he was visible only as a dot among the waves?

This year, the journalism and philosophy departments had united to stage a beach rally against "betonization." For years, a powerful lobby of real estate developers had issued proposal after proposal in hopes of building beachside hotels and luxury homes. The blueprints depicted a string of concrete stretching miles to the east of Montpellier. Vauban, the famous French fortress designer, could not have dreamt of a more impressive line of fortifications. This year, the department had properly notified the press of the rally, and so the members arrived with reporters and microphones in tow.

By the time I arrived, the chairman of the philosophy department was already giving his first interview. He was a wiry man in his fifties with a thick tuft of hair rimming his otherwise bare scalp. They called him "Porcupine" because his straight hair burst out from his scalp as if it was driven by some hilarious magnetic force. The comparison of the chain of beach hotels with Vauban's fortresses had been his idea, and as I stood by and listened to what he had to say, it was clear he was in his element.

The Germans pitted our coast with their concrete bunkers, behemoths that never can be removed, shaming the natural

> *beauties of our beaches for a thousand years! ...and now we, the French people, we who love our country, we who cherish our huddled medieval villages, we who tune our ears to the song of millions of beach grasses swaying in the gentle winds that cross our estuaries—we—yes, we the proud French—now bend down to the vile and greedy machinations of a short-sighted coterie of interests that will degrade what is sacred and defile what is whole a thousand times more efficiently than the Germans could ever have.*

"How melodramatic," Gastyb whispered into my ear as he joined me to listen to Porcupine speak into the reporter's microphone.

"As far as I know, they have tried to stop the project in the courts, in public hearings, and with impact studies, but the developers bribed the hell out of everybody," I said.

"Mind me saying that I thought for a moment you could have written Porcupine's little speech."

Gastyb was doing his squeeze–eyes, let-loose-of-your mouth corners, I-didn't-really-mean-what-I-just-said performance. He would never let me forget my part in setting up Pétain's speeches that put the sheen of false poetry on the shameful collaboration. Twenty years later and the curtain of forgetting had yet to fall! I had quickly learned that in parts of this world, wars are fought over insults that happened a thousand years ago.

My colleagues and I had gathered around the shack on the beach, which happened to be the only structure for miles. Nobody knew how the ramshackle hut had been placed there, nor when or by whom. It seemed that some Russian emigrant was the only human ever present. Everybody knew his ruddy face: a molded bag of potatoes, stuck with two cauliflower ears, his lips as rough as the skin of lizards. His French rattled with consonants, a song withheld. On sunny warm days, Rasputin—or so they called him—would bridge some cinder blocks with wooden boards, drape the boards with a white tablecloth, and serve everybody drinks. And on windy, cold days, one could find shelter inside his hut at a few tables and a primitive bar. He would always talk to you, spread out the most recent picture postcards he had acquired, and then ask you to tack them onto the wooden beams and the walls. Over the years, he had received so many postcards from all over the world that they had wallpapered the entire place.

"Send me a postcard from where you live" was his usual way of saying goodbye to all visitors.

The hut itself consisted of two parts that seemed to be in eternal conflict with each other. The "bidonville" part was made of corrugated sheet metal flaked with orange paint and loosely bolted into wooden boards. The "ski hut" looked more promising, but upon closer inspection, one could see that the walls thinned into mere clapboards, with tilted windows and doors.

Over the years, the hut took on symbolic meaning: the annual blessing of the ocean was usually performed there, and preservationists referred to it as an example of individuality and originality that would be sniffed out by soulless concrete.

The weather during the meeting was sunny without much wind. The ocean waves lapped softly, carrying faint lines of foam up the gentle slope. Near the escarpment where tables had been placed, blue smoke curled off the row of fish baking over heaped charcoal. Bottles of white wine were aplenty, and so were Greek cheeses, tomatoes, cucumbers, and broiled chicken. I began to believe that everybody was having a good time.

After the meal, members of the faculty gave a presentation in which they quoted favorite excerpts with the theme of beach and sea. I had selected the swim of Rieux and Tarrou, characters in Camus's novel *The Plague.* These were quotes I held dear, and the quotes I shared with everyone in attendance:

"Do you know?" Tarrou said, "what we now should do for friendship's sake?"

"Anything you like, Tarrou."

"Go for a swim. It's one of those harmless pleasures that even a saint-to-be can indulge in, don't you agree?"

...Once they were on the pier they saw the sea spread out before them, a gently heaving expanse of deep-piled velvet, supple and sleek like a creature of the wild ...

At the end of my recitation, I received some applause.

"Yes! Monsieur Camus!" somebody cheered. I suddenly felt proud and content.

For a while, I sat down in the dunes. The wind had blown out shallow dips no larger than a body. I glanced into the sun with half-open eyes and let the shadow of swaying grasses dance across my lids.

As I sat there all alone, I couldn't help but recall the day on the beach near Algiers in 1939. Sun and gentle, lapping waves ...it was the last day of peace.

Meeting Camus's Friends After Manuscript Reading

The morning after reading Camus's draft of *The Stranger,* I was eager to join him at the bus terminal, where two cobble-stoned ramps widened into a level place. One ramp led up to the main harbor boulevard, and the other down to warehouses at the waterfront. I bought pita breads and bottles of water and stored them in a sack. The bus we were to take to Tipasa was one of the older Renault models with exaggerated wingtip fenders. Its square back reached out far beyond the rear wheels and the roof was used for storage. The conductor was busy heaving duffel bags, packages, and even a small cage with a chicken in it on to the roof.

Camus came hurrying up the ramp mere seconds before the bus was scheduled to depart.

"Louis Benistine and Blanche Balain will join us later," he said, sounding quite out of breath. "How was your night?"

"Rather short, considering I spent it reading your manuscript and listening to the reactions of a group of businessmen huddling around the wireless." Then I added that I had left the manuscript with the owner of the hotel whom Camus knew well.

"The Soviet Union has betrayed us," Camus said. "I am disheartened. If we would have considered the legitimate German grievances and not have punished them with the Versailles Treaty, this German-Soviet relationship would never have come to fruition. As you can see, the international brotherhood of man has evaporated into the politics of power and opportunity. One more reason to walk on the beach at Tipasa and see the ruins of man's follies."

The bus conductor waved at us, and we hurried to seat ourselves in one of the back rows.

"What do your friends think?" I asked as the bus rattled up the cobblestone road to join the coastal highway.

"I for one urge restraint and peace. But just listen to Fréminville and his praise of socialism and it's obvious that he doesn't understand that Communism and National Socialism are at their core religions."

Fumes belching from its exhaust, the bus wheezed and rattled toward the heights of west Algiers.

"This is precisely what I fight against," Camus added. "These ideologies that are nothing but schemes to fill man with some vague notion of filling the void with throbbing emotions."

When the bus stopped at the university, Blanche Balain jumped aboard and joined us, just as Camus had promised. Blanche wore a long, white dress that was bunched up over her tightly belted waist. She held a basket in her left hand, and I watched as she gave the conductor her ticket, waved, and then sat down behind Camus.

"Blanche, this is Mr. Yann Cedak from Paris," Camus said.

She reached her arm forward above the back of the seat and I shook her hand. It all made me feel awkward.

"Camus told me about you," she said. "Fascinating that you came with the seaplane from Marseille. I never was in one ...so, what's the name of the journal you write for?"

"Le Pavé de Paris."

"You heard the bad news about the censors going out of control," Camus interjected, nodding toward Blanche. She rumpled her nose and began talking to Camus, lifting her chin above the top of the seat's back, which looked uncomfortable to me. I offered to switch seats, and she gladly accepted.

"He didn't sleep much last night," Camus said.

Over the next dozens of miles, I dozed off and on as the coastal road wound into some shallow hills until it reached the coast again at Douadoudo. There was monotony to the clutter of white houses that stood like clumps of chalk against the Mediterranean's blue. Bou Ismail and Bou Harouna passed, and only when the road began to run close to the coast at Ain Tagourait did I wake up. I remained still, clinging to a pleasant dream state in which I lingered in a world with eyes half-closed. Camus and Blanche rumbled on in a Spanish-French dialect they called Cagayous. *Et alores et oilà, faire figo.*

All that numbed me, and smells and sounds melted into a netherworld of delight that was hard to fathom. For a while, I kept squinting at a landscape where small beach coves alternated with hills of sand. I did not want to let go of this dream, but Blanche's hand reached back and knocked me on the head, forcing me out of it in the rudest of ways.

"Oilà," she said. "Tipasa ahead!"

We three debarked the autobus across from the entrance to the Roman ruins. Camus took the basket that Blanche was carrying and announced that this was, for him, a moment of freedom, deliverance, and remembrance.

"I might not return to Tipasa for a while, as my life will shift to Oran," he said.

Blanche gently took the basket back.

"You both go ahead and join Louis," she said.

"His usual spot?" Camus asked.

Blanche nodded.

I followed Camus as we filed our way between knotted trunks of cypress trees until we entered an opening where the light from the opaque sky laid a milk-colored carpet across the floor of a Roman temple. Only the stumps of columns remained: stelae asking for the roof that once sheltered them, asking for colors, the lives and faiths long dead. They lined up twenty in a row, which might have been of interest to archeologists seeking a pattern of reason and clarity now lost. What remained was a carcass of what was once alive. A carcass and a warning, not to mention a sparseness within which lay a resolve of some kind.

I had recalled Camus's lines: *In the spring Tipasa is inhabited by the gods. And the gods speak in the sun and the scent of absinthe leaves, in the silver armor of the sea.*

It was August, so the flowers were desiccated, long shriveled into dried tubers. The wormwood trees and mastic, however, stood so thick that their leaves built a grey wool that fluffed down to the Mediterranean; in spots, the wool reached in between the stumps of columns, only sparing the floor of the temple, its bare slabs of sandstone starving their roots.

Then: *... We stand in the light breeze, with the sun warming one side of our faces, we watch the light coming down from the sky, the smooth sea and the smile of its glittering teeth...*

After exploring the temple, Camus introduced me to Louis Bénisti at a promontory that jetted out into the Mediterranean. Louis was sitting on a narrow, smooth slab, creating a pastel of the ruins as viewed from the outcrop. He lifted his head to acknowledge our presence but continued drawing in silence.

"Calebot," Camus said, a grin widening his face. "*Faire figa. Faire fissa. Vinga taper un bain.* Calebote Bénisti!"

Bénisti smirked, grabbed his sketchbook, and outlined Camus's face with a few pastels: nose a thin line, a struggle of shades around his lips, and the uniformity of his black, dark hair. For his final touch, Benisti imprinted a small cat onto Camus's forehead with a fine pen.

"Give Yann the sketch," Camus said. Then, with a wave of his hand, he added, "This is Yann Cedak, a journalist working for the *Pavé de Paris*."

"Of course," Bénisti said. "Camus told me of your visit. Welcome to my ruins."

A strange opposition in Bénisti's half-finished pastel clamped to his easel struck me: the stumps of the columns and the grounds of the ruins were sketched as wide blocks of static color, well outlined and demarcated, whereas the sea and vegetation seemed fluffy, quivering in muted mist.

"So, what is real?" I asked him.

"I have painted this same scene quite differently before," he said.

Bénisti pulled a finished pastel from a briefcase at his side. He held the painting up with both hands. It depicted the ruins as if reflected in wind-driven water, as if seen through a shaking lens. The temple's floor was warped and shifted such that no mortal would ever dare set foot on it. The sea, however, was drawn in blocks of solid colors, firmly anchored and stable, unchanging.

"You see that in this pastel, I turned upside-down how painters usually make you see land and ocean," Bénisti said.

"It still is not an answer," Camus said. "It still is absurd."

"Answer to what?"

"Man's total and nonnegotiable search for meaning."

"The universe will not yield an answer," Bénisti said. "Only art does."

"Only man," Camus countered.

"Botcha!" Benisti said, his hand swiping the air.

"Calebote!"

They chuckled.

These two must had carried on like this before.

Benisti turned to Camus with a prankish look in his face.

"So, how is that novel of yours coming along?"

"*Monter l'aubergine*," Camus said.

Bénisti turned to me.

"In Cagayous, that means he's putting both fingers in your eyes if you dare talk about it."

I moved my fingers toward my eyes.

Blanche suddenly appeared between the columns, her white skirt driven in between her legs by the sea breeze.

"That rising hot air makes you look like a quavering ghost," Bénisti said once she stepped closer. "Why don't you three go down to one of the rocky points while I finish this painting? But don't open the wine bottles just yet."

Near an outcrop, a group of men in grey suits and straw hats strolled about penciling into their notebooks, and, in a cove, French soldiers skipped flat stones across the water. A few of them were lying in the sun, having removed their uniform jackets.

"I have to say that it doesn't feel like there is a conflict pending," Blanche said.

"There won't be war," Camus said.

The strange force of the place took me in. Men in Northern Europe had built stone monuments ...had built them on plains, on mountaintops, and in dark woods. The grace of sea, of rock, and of sun was never granted to them.

For a time, we looked out onto riffled silver waves and happily listened to the sucking sounds of water sliding under rocky overhangs.

"I read your essay about Tipasa," I said to Camus. "There, you give yourself totally to experience. *This is red, this blue, this is green. This is the sea; these are the mountains, the flowers*."

Camus looked at me with a puzzled expression, which prompted me to tell him that Edmond Charlot had sent my editors in Paris a sample of his essay collection, *Noces*.

"They printed only two hundred and twenty-five copies of *Noces*," Camus said.

"It is one of the reasons I came to Algiers," I said.

Camus bent forward attentively and folded his hands between his knees.

"You could have read further," he said. "*Yet even here, I know that I never will come close enough to the world.*"

"Is this why you love this place?" I asked.

Camus did not answer.

Nobody, in fact, said a word, even after Bénisti joined us and took the inaugural swig from the bottle.

"Silence is my favorite language," Bénisti said.

"I have makoud and zlabia in my basket," Blanche announced.

I opened my backpack, laid out a small blanket, and set down flatbread and bottles of water. The honey-drenched fig cakes melted on our tongues, balancing the harshness of semolina cakes that grated our palates. The bread, too, was welcomed, easing away strong tastes and reopening our taste buds to the sweetness of the wine.

After the meal, we reclined on the sun-warmed rock and closed our eyes. Bénisti sat with his legs dangling over the rock's edge, staring down at the sea, listening to the slurping sounds of the waves breaking. When he turned around and spoke, I sensed hesitation in his voice.

"I overheard Camus talking about 'never coming close enough to the world,'" he said, "but as a painter, I try to do exactly that."

"Paul Klee, the German painter tried to do the same," I said.

"I've heard of him. Bauhaus, wasn't he?"

I shared with him Klee's epitaph: *My limits are not of this world. I reside as much with the dead ones than with the unborn. Somewhat closer to the heart of creation than most, but far from close enough.*

"Closer than most, closer than most," Benisti said.

Then, silence.

I stretched out again, settling my head into a smooth hollow in the rock. A jacket served as a pillow for Camus. Rolled into a bundle, it was even wide enough for Blanche to rest her head beside his.

A life that tastes the warm stone. I could still remember that quote from *Noces*.

I kept reflecting on my task to report back to Paris what this group of French writers in Algiers was all about. And how would I say it? The *taste of warm stones*—I surely would use that, and *the scent of absinth flowers ground between your palms.* That, too.

I glimpsed Blanche's face, her fluted lips, the subtle heaving of her breasts beneath her moiré blouse. *Here I understand what is meant by glory: the right to love without limits.*

My thoughts reeled back to the nightly broadcast on the wireless and Hitler's voice—raspy with hate and emotional drunkenness—as he called for elation and abandonment at any price and promised the enchantment of the world by the sword. And how frangible the writings and paintings of these French expatriates were, how exploratory and hesitant! And Camus's manuscript: a young man living in Algiers, dragging himself through a bureau job, not really loving, not really hating, drifting, detaching even as he pulls the gun's trigger four times. Meursault, a stranger, a victim of the sun's reflections! I remembered the vacuity of the balcony scene in Camus's manuscript: How, after lunch, Meursault was a little bored and wandered around the apartment.

I considered that the Paris establishment might hack Camus's novel to pieces were it ever to be published. Not even the title was finalized; Camus told me he was going back and forth between *The Indifferent* and *The Stranger.*

The draft had some issues that I wanted to discuss with Camus. For one, the protagonist, Meursault, hasn't earned anything and he doesn't shape his life. He is a buoy, incessantly tilted and heaved by random forces. And in the second part—barely even sketched in the draft—there is far too much preaching, and all that struggle against long-exhausted philosophy and religion. A kind of straw man is built up here, I sensed; the priest with his barnacled truths; the judge with the cross!

But there was this lingering sentence near the end of the novel: *I opened myself to the gentle indifference of the world.*

How to wrap one's mind around that line?

Indifference leading to murder at the mercy of the sun's reflections on a knife's blade ...which meant that Camus was trying to mark indifference as the real and deepest scourge of our times...

Or, to the contrary, Camus declaring indifference as the shield against the flood of emotions unleashed by ideologies?

Or was this all an illusion? Maybe the novel did not claim to depict more than some insignificant life in Algiers.

I heard some stirring beside me. Camus was now tickling Blanche's ears with a twig. She shivered slightly, chuckled, and pulled up her legs. When he persisted, she sat up, shook her head, and suggested that we all walk down to the beach.

"You haven't given me the tour of the ruins yet," I said.

Camus, twig still in hand, responded, "Ruins, ruins, and Roman ruins at that! The deeper you dig down between those sun-scalded columns, the more you conceal the message this place whispers: truth lies on the surface. And only the Greeks knew how to celebrate the surface. They were the masters."

"Which means?"

Camus smiled, got up, jiggled his legs, and stretched. Bénisti, meanwhile, gathered his brushes, paints, and the easel.

"I'll visit a friend who lives nearby and see you later," Benisti said.

"Meet us at the creek," Camus said.

Camus, Blanche, and I packed our bags. We passed a rundown restaurant, its wood pitted and splintered by wind and sun, now no more than a timeworn shack barely held up by rickety stilts at the edge of the Roman temple mound. From there, the hill lowered to a wide stretch of sandy beach. Camus left briefly and returned with a paper bag filled with pears. We filed through a last stand of wormwood tress, absinth bushes, and knotty cypress, and, after having changed into our swimsuits, we eventually walked out onto a beach with white-bleached sand.

We spread the towels and set on them what was left of the bread, the bag with the pears, several chunks of hard cheese, four bottles of water, and two more bottles of wine, which Bénisti had added from his bag.

"He never tells me where he buys that cheese," Camus said.

He stepped out of his canvas shoes and waded into the water. I noted how skeletal he appeared, with his jutting ribs and legs sticking out beneath his swimsuit like toothpicks. Camus strode into the water, he didn't run, as if to celebrate every layer of coolness rising. Eventually he did slide into the surface—and for a moment it seemed to me as if the sea had folded open—and he swam off in slow, measured strokes.

Blanche hesitated at the edge of the water, but then raced in, legs angled, splashing white tongues of water left and right. Her body tilted into the sea so powerfully that, like a seesaw's, her legs bounced in the air behind her. With reaching strokes, she was beside Camus in no time. I spotted their heads near where waves rose and curled into white collars of foam.

It reminded me of a scene that I had just read in Camus's manuscript, when Meursault and Maria swim out into the sea: *The water was warm with slow, gently lapping waves. Maria taught me a game.*

When a child at Saint-Brieuc in the Bretagne, I had to walk hundreds of yards into the water to reach a depth that would allow me to swim. But if you lingered at low tide, the returning waters could suck you in, and, paralyzed by clawing wet sands, you could not escape. The sea did not comfort me then, not even on days when the sun seemed to slide a silver drape across the smooth surface, when the seagulls pivoted in the sky for sheer joy, and children splashed in tidal ponds, their far cries mingling with the shrills of seabirds.

I looked around. The beach was near empty; to my far left were two women in burkas wading in ankle-deep water; and to my right, three French soldiers lingered where the hill from the Roman temple eased down into the flat of the beach. Behind me, a few stilted shacks with warped porches stuck into the side of the folded dunes, and a solitary rock stood near the stony bed of what might have been a brook in spring, but now was a dry wadi with a few reeds crumbling in the heat.

At the far end of the beach we finally came to a little spring running down through the sand behind a large rock. There we found our two Arabs.

Could this have been the beach Camus described in his draft? The beach where the murder occurred? Where the sunlight fractured into little pieces on the sand and water? Where Meursault's world shattered?

I bundled my clothes and then placed them on the scorched sand. I walked toward the water, hot grit chafing between my toes, and then, suddenly, I felt the smoothness of a narrow mudflat, a first caress of the sea. I wanted to slide into the water just as Camus did; there was a strange attraction to his ways. Languid waves lapped up on me, spreading a pleasant chill into my groin. The first feel of weightlessness, relief of denseness! Then, having walked further into the sea, I resisted the urge to sink in, to suspend everything. There was still the small fear of immersion, of losing yourself, until you roll onto your back in abandon, certain that the water will lift you, and you drift in the sea, the full sky in your face. I closed my eyes and floated, feeling the heat of the sun on my face and on my knees, and all was suspended; all was immersed. There were no tides here, no sucking currents. Time had vanished.

I stayed in the water for a long time. When I walked back onto the beach, I found Camus and Blanche sunbathing.

"Have some wine!" Camus said.

We passed the bottle around.

"Where is Bénisti?" Blanche asked.

"He's always meeting somebody," Camus said.

Our appetites had returned. Camus cut off pieces of cheese and wrapped them into the remaining flat cakes. For a while, we sat in the shimmering sunlight of the early afternoon. The sea seemed to grow lazier than before, spreading panes of silver beneath the sun, sliding in waves that barely bulged the surface. The sea's skin glistened like oil. We made the wine bottles last a few rounds between the three of us.

Eventually, Camus and Blanche decided to eat the ripe and sweet pears, allowing their juices to drip on their chins, forearms, and hands. They tried to fling the syrupy liquid off, but then, out of sheer pleasure, started slapping each other and swiping the sugary liquid over each other's faces until they finally had to return to the water to wash off the stickiness. I stayed behind, stretching out on the sand, sinking into drowsiness. Off and on, I managed to glance through half-closed eyelids out to the sea, locating their heads that kept bopping up near the white hem of waves.

When I woke, I did not immediately open my eyes. Instead, I listened to the gentle slapping of distant waves.

They did not raise in me the uneasiness of the channel tides I listened to in my childhood, water edging into crevices and secret holes with slurping, threatening sounds. I wiped my forehead to remove the sweat, flopped my arms to the side, and slackened every muscle in my body. I felt the grit of sand on my calves and a pleasant grating into my back. In the depths of my eyes, I imagined the mark of the waves, the horizon a wire between sea and sky. I saw a perfect whiteness.

Suddenly, I heard distant yelling coming in from the sea. It became more insistent, louder. I sat up. Searing light shot off the steel in front of me. The sun was reflected in hundreds of blades. My head was full of noise and vertigo. Dazzling spears of light scorched my eyes. I jumped up and stepped backward to get away from this terror when somebody yelled, "Attention!"

A soldier in battle fatigue stepped into my view.

"We're installing barbed wire," he said. "Orders from Paris."

To my right, I spotted Camus and Blanche gesticulating at a group of soldiers that were rolling a second line of barbed wire parallel to the coastline. There seemed to have been a heated discussion without resolution.

Eventually, Camus and Blanche filed through a gap in the barbed wire-fence and came walking toward me. Camus was visibly irate.

"These idiots want me to believe that German commandos intend to land here," he said. "They might as well fence off the whole Mediterranean."

"I don't understand," Blanche said. "There is no war."

I stood frozen, staring at the soldiers who rolled off barbed wire, lifting thousands of singing blades of steel toward the sun. This was the unfurling of the steel-studded beast separating man from the sea. This was the final hour.

I recalled a line from Camus's manuscript about the *shattered harmony of the day.*

We tried to suppress the moment's terror but could not do more than helplessly watch as the sea was cut off behind thousands of blades of steel. Camus gathered our belongings and put them back into the backpack. He was the first to gain his composure. Blanche and I kept standing there, transfixed by the glinting steel. It was as if the sky had been split open.

We agreed to walk back to the bus station, and though I did not know it, a telegram from Paris was waiting for me at the hotel, instructing me to return to the mainland.

The silvery seaplane I had boarded to Algiers would not return to Marseille. Instead, it had flown off to some unknown destination. The boats serving the Algiers-Marseille line had been ordered to stay in harbor.

The next day, I took a train to Oran and then reached Tangiers. From there, I took a ferry to Gibraltar. I wrote down what I experienced in Algiers. I wrote it down in darkened trains and at night in cheap hotels. Europe was in turmoil. A curtain had fallen.

Klaus's Theater Piece

At the end of the department's "Death of a Beach" meeting, I drove three inebriated secretaries back to their apartments. They insisted on crowding into the backseat, giggling while they made a bottle of Port wine change hands. Then, suddenly, they stopped.

"Hey? Why aren't you married?" one of them asked.

"Well..." I began.

"We never see you anywhere having any sort of fun," another said, interrupting.

"He's professor of philosophy!" said the redhead in the middle, causing all three of the ladies to burst into an annoying fit of laughter.

I wanted nothing more than to kick them out of my car, to tell them to find their own way home. The whole scene reminded me of being in the car with those drunken Bavarians who kept ripping into Klaus for no good reason.

Back at my apartment in Celleneuve, I uncorked a bottle of wine. Gastyb's veiled remark of me having penned Pétain's speech was still irritating me. And those remarks by the secretaries! At least they were drunk. Gastyb wasn't.

I decided to spend the evening reading Klaus's play. A letter tucked inside explained that his parents might have met Camus and his wife sometime in 1936 in an Austrian town named

Rattenberg at the River Inn. I tried to remember what details I had told him in that noisy Weinstube in Munich about Camus's short story *Death in the Soul*. But I could not have mentioned anything about Rattenberg—I mean, I didn't know the town—and now here was this theater script in which Klaus's parents meet a French couple and there is a drunken fight.

Rattenberg

A Play in Three Acts
By Klaus Herrman

Cast of Characters

KURT (later, the father)
KURTS'S WIFE (later, the mother)
KURT'S FRIEND
WAITER
DRUNKEN MAN
IVES BOURGEOIS (Camus's friend)
ALBERT CAMUS
SIMONE HIÉ (Camus's first wife)

Setting

A beer Stube in Austria near the German border (Rattenberg)

Time

July 1936 and 1944

ACT I

(A row of wooden tables, wet and sullied by spilt beer. Dim recessed lights. Drinking songs in the background. A group of rough-looking hikers back from a mountain

tour. Sporadic servings of radish, beer, and sausages. From the stage, a dark tunnel goes into the wall, and a small fence separates the tunnel from the tables.)

KURT

I wonder where that tunnel leads?

KURT'S WIFE

We are sitting right under a castle where the larches are, Kurt. Remember? Or are you already that drunk?

KURT'S FRIEND

Memory distorts.

KURT'S WIFE

Time is like a tunnel. You lose your way. (*points to the tunnel*)

KURT'S FRIEND

Forward ...to 1939!

KURT'S WIFE

Dare further!

KURT'S FRIEND

To 1960!

KURT'S WIFE

Everything that may happen in this tunnel will pull in the future.

(***KURT scoffs)***

KURT'S WIFE

Would you enter the tunnel?

KURT

Nonsense! Kauderwelsh! All I know is that the tunnel will belong to Germany! (***looks about him carefully***) **The future is us, Germany, Hitler!**

KURT'S FRIEND

Want to bet a shilling?

(They both retrieve shillings from their pockets and place them on the table. KURT'S WIFE takes them and puts them into her pocket, and then continues to casually sip her wine.)

KURT

We'll get the Sudetenland and Pommern and Alsace Lorraine. And we shall stand like a solid rock in this muddy swamp of small thinkers. That's what they are: small thinkers!

KURT'S WIFE

Things always get murky with beer.

KURT

But you say the truth only when your tongue is loose.

KURT'S WIFE

Mountains, alpine roses, and Enzian. That is my truth.

KURT'S FRIEND

On the Höfatz, you needed spiked shoes because it always felt like you were sliding backwards. The most beautiful meadow in the world, lush, and believe me, I lay down and it was like this corner of the world was open to everything and all things human.

KURT'S WIFE

At the Kneipp Institute, we burst out from under the cold showers and then toweled each other dry in the morning mist, and in the dewy meadows, we spread our toes as wide as we could in order to slide the moist blades of grass between them. We ran and ran behind the flags of our breaths. And when we reached the height of a hillock, there was a small collection of fir trees, and I remember how the waft of resin came to life in the first light of morning. We rolled about in the soft needles and then reached back through the meadows laughing, gasping, choking in the denseness of life.

KURT

(***taps his fingers on the stein***) **You should have stayed there.** ***(pause)*** **Waiter! Another round!**

(Beer arrives. Noises—and some broken Italian— come from an adjacent, cave-like room.)

KURT

Italians!

KURT'S FRIEND

Hold on to yourself. We aren't in Germany.

KURT

Tomorrow ...(***KURT gives a hint of the German salute***)

KURT'S FRIEND

Stop it!

KURT

Why hold on? Those bird fuckers haven't ever done any good in war.

KURT'S FRIEND

But we have peace now!

KURT

War was pure shit. I didn't have dry feet for months. Trench-foot, we called it. A brown slime building on your toes. They wrinkled like prunes and then came the ulcers, some with rosy rims like baby mice. Yes. The color of baby mice. But we had only rats. Some tried to shoot them, but they were always too fast. Damn, those rats. Somehow, they survived the gas attacks.

KURT'S FRIEND

Can't we just talk about something else?

KURT

At Verdun, I saw soldiers carry their own guts in front of them across that gully. They carried them like a mother carries her baby. Once, I even saw a man trip on his own guts. Have you ever seen that? Could you imagine?

KURT'S FRIEND

I know you went through a lot, Kurt.

KURT

Words, words! (*KURT stabs the air with his hands)* You didn't see that squishy misery in his hands! He gaped at his own guts and wondered what he was seeing. Could it be true? And then he began to convulse, and then came that awful burbling noise. That was the only time I was relieved by the sound of the artilleries. Shells were more human than that! More human than dehumanized humans! That's how it was.

KURT'S WIFE

You shouldn't get this upset, Kurt. C'mon. We had a great day together.

KURT

So what did you do during the war?

KURT'S WIFE

Can we please leave?

KURT'S FRIEND

I think she's right.

KURT

Stay out of it

(Fragments of laughter and talk in the adjacent room get louder.)

KURT

Fuck it! They are coming over to us!

(Loud noises and rowdy sounds. DRUNKEN MAN comes into the room. His pants are gray, the color of carabineer pants.)

ACT II

WAITER

Ladies and gentlemen, we must close the other room. Please know that your section here will remain open until midnight.

(KURT checks his watch and seems satisfied, but only for a moment. Two men, ALBERT CAMUS and IVES BOURGEOIS, enter the room. They sit down at an empty table. DRUNKEN MAN slides into the empty chair at the table and begins talking to IVES BOURGEOIS.

IVES BOURGEOIS

You forget that I am French. Translating from Italian to German gives me such a headache.

(DRUNKEN MAN calls for the waiter, who arrives swiftly.)

DRUNKEN MAN

A round for all the gentlemen ...uh, uh! The lady too! Let's hear it in German!

(SIMONE HIÉ enters. She is striking. She wears a white dress that does not fit in with the atmosphere of this place.)

SIMONE HIÉ

You have a Baston, Albert?

(ALBERT CAMUS lights SIMONE HIÉ a cigarette. She sits down, and they both begin to smoke.)

IVES BOURGEOIS

(***leans over to the DRUNKEN MAN***) **Why do you want me to do this? This is it! You understand? Just the last paragraph of this fucking story!**

(IVES BOURGEOIS studies the last paragraph in a book. He tries to speak in a low voice, in German, but DRUNKEN MAN laughs rowdily whenever he quotes a particularly dirty passage. At times, SIMONE HIÉ joins in the laughter, but her husband, ALBERT CAMUS, remains silent. What the audience hears onstage is the voice of DRUNKEN MAN.)

DRUNKEN MAN

(laughs) **Fucks her through the cheese cloth ...Brhhh! They sawed off the top rungs on the ladder and (*slaps his knees*) the Teutonic asshole knight is prevented from sliding down by his large schmeckel and it goes clickedy-clack, clack click clack all the way down.**

(DRUNKEN MAN reaches between his knees and makes an obscene gesture. There is a ladder nearby and he clumsily tries to demonstrate the scene.)

DRUNKEN MAN

The Germans think only of the coming Olympic Games. That's all they write about in their newspapers. That and occupying Austria.

IVES BOURGEOIS

My friend thinks Hitler will resign and devote himself to his art and Goering will take over power.

DRUNKEN MAN

The clutches of power, once dug into your flesh, will never let you go.

IVES BOURGEOIS

Is it true that in Rattenberg from November to April there will not be a ray of sunshine in town?

DRUNKEN MAN

Yeah. Just that drinking hole! That's all!

IVES BOURGEOIS

We live in Algiers in plain sun every day. You think that the sun changes peoples' souls …I mean, changes cultures and hearts?

DRUNKEN MAN

No idea.

(***Seemingly talking to himself***)

It's true. Ideas grow in sewers. They grow in the dark. Sun incinerates illusions.

ALBERT CAMUS

Et le Nazis?

DRUNKEN MAN

Lack of sunshine. (*laughs*) *Pas de soleil.* (*nods*)

ALBERT CAMUS

Pas joie de vivre.

DRUNKEN MAN

All dark. Götterdämmerung. Wagner.

(He intones the first notes of Wagner's opening theme. ALBERT CAMUS funnels his hands into a megaphone. He appears more lively once he realizes DRUNKEN MAN speaks some French.)

ALBERT CAMUS

Nietzsche. Le mort de Dieu.

DRUNKEN MAN

Ah! The death of God. That's what the Germans can't get over. But the death of God is their invention!

ALBERT CAMUS

Coincé.

DRUNKEN MAN

What?

IVES BOURGOIS

***Verklemmt*. Hung up.**

DRUNKEN MAN

But they get drunk on this ...and they get drunk on their hate of the outsider, hate of anybody ...Jedermann without blue eyes. If they ever get into Austria, they will be the poison in our wells. They will hollow our culture with their wordy tirades, their hysterical outbreaks. And the Olympic Games ...believe me, they're just a delay in Hitler's invasion plans.

IVES BOURGOIS

***(nervously looks around, as the conversation begins to turn too political for his tastes)* Albert dreams of a Mediterranean culture.**

DRUNKEN MAN

Exactly what the Germans lack.

(KURT returns from the restroom with an unsteady gait. His suspenders hang down across his leather pants. He is entirely visible to the audience now.)

DRUNKEN MAN

Too drunk to pull up his suspenders, but yet he wants to occupy Austria!

(KURT walks right in front of DRUNKEN MAN, pulls up his suspenders, and snaps them, catapulting pieces of shit into DRUNKEN MAN'S face.)

DRUNKEN MAN

You bastard!

(DRUNKEN MAN stands and punches KURT in the nose.)

DRUNKEN MAN

Cleaning you up a bit!

(KURT trundles backward briefly, then steadies himself and stands again in front of DRUNKEN MAN'S face.)

KURT

We'll continue this outside. Into the tunnel!

(KURT overturns a glass of beer. Foam pours onto the table. KURT'S WIFE stands up to hold KURT back, but KURT'S FRIEND steps in front of her.)

KURT'S WIFE

He will hurt him!

(Everybody sits or stands, frozen. A deep silence hushes over the stage and the audience hears nothing. The people separate into two groups and face each other. The lights dim.)

The script stopped there. Klaus had scribbled a note at the end, mentioning that he had not yet finished the third act.

Klaus's play was certainly not about Camus. The play was about a tunnel into Klaus's past—a dark tunnel full of pain.

His writing stirred unease in me, and I didn't know how to best respond. I had to give it some time; maybe it was better to wait until Klaus sent me that third and final act.

Freikorps Affair

The faculty's beach party had taken place earlier in the week. A dinner and dance were scheduled for the coming weekend. It was already the season of mellow afternoons. Lawn chairs had been taken outside, and the pizzerias in town had begun to set up their white and red tables in gardens beneath trellis flecked white with blossoms.

One morning, I was called to my chairman's office, and I immediately knew that it had to do with Albert, the student I had met after visiting the pizzeria with Gastyb. I suspected that Albert's first draft of his Freikorps study had rattled some nerves. I had proposed the topic to Albert, and when he had started reading post-WWI novels, I offered him help with some of the difficult and ambiguous texts. These action novels, published in the 20s and 30s, glorified the immediate post-WWI period. Right-wing soldiers wrote them; the writing was anti-Communist and glorified the Freikorps's role in the civil wars that broke out in Germany. The titles reflected the tone: *The Last Rider*; *Gun Above the Town*; *We Bear the Life*; *Up Goes the Flag*. Among these titles was *Battle as Inner Experience*, written by Ernst Jünger, whom I had met briefly in 1940.

I hadn't even taken a seat in his office before the chairman slid a few pages across his desk.

"Look at these quotes! Is your student going bonkers?"

He was not smiling.

With a quick snap of his fingers, he turned the pages.

"Listen to this quote: *Her nakedness assaults him with a sudden glowing shudder, a wind across a placid lake. He says nothing, but with a jolt his breath rushes into his blood, filling it with pearls of pure, quivering bubbles, a gushing froth like a man shot in the lung.*"

"What is this drivel?" the chairman asked, looking up at me.

"Those writers knew nothing but war," I said, irritated.

I knew that his critique was targeting me, the preceptor.

Something was up. The chairman was usually a man of measured words and gestures. He liked to wear sweaters whenever the climate or air conditioning allowed, and I easily could picture him in a leather chair in the backroom of a Scottish golf club reaching for a pipe in a rack leaned against dark wainscoting.

I began reading some circled quotes, but he interrupted me.

"I need to speak to you about this."

"Just let me look at it," I said.

"Eros of warfare," I read. "*His hands tighten around the gun, but he still feels this young woman... Whipped naked buttocks...A club thrust into a hole...Beaten into a bloody mess...Flares sent underneath skirts.*"

"These are just quotes," I said, setting the pages back down on his desk.

"Albert writes that those Freikorps soldiers were afraid of women," he said, eyebrows raised. "Did you know about that? This is a history project, Yann, not some wooly Walter Benjamin sex arcade."

He had to have known that his remark would upset me. Writing about Benjamin's life was one of the ideas I had mentioned to him. I felt heat pushing into my neck and I narrowed my eyes. "Something original from the department—finally," I quipped.

"Look who's talking!"

I turned around and left.

As I made my way down the hallway, I noticed that the chairman of the psychology department had his door open. I knocked.

Bernard liked to cultivate the persona of a liberal progressive: late Thirties, small mustache, always more than a 5-o'clock-shadow, the only one in the department who spoke fluent English, not to mention the most rumored about in terms of love affairs. He had his legs stretched on top of the desk and I was relieved when he waved me in.

"What's up, Yann?"

"My chairman just chewed me over..."

"I know," he said.

He took his legs off the desk, opened a drawer, retrieved some papers, and handed them to me.

"Chairman is ruffled. Huh!" He pouted his lips. "He sent me a copy just yesterday and talked an earful ...that seemed to have calmed him down ...fact is, your student might be up to something."

Bernard stood up and closed the door.

"Albert's take is simply accurate," he said. "Those Freikorps soldiers had no real relationship with women. Softness, no! Skin and touch, no! Being attracted and feeling that sweet helplessness, absolutely no! They would rather have built dams. They dreamt up ideals of white nurses and virgin sisters and acted out their deep fears of communist rifle women, the hussies, and prostitutes whom they turned into bloody mush."

There was no stopping him now. After all, psychology was his specialty.

"Sigmund Freud overlooked the turmoil boiling in all of us before ego rises. Before ego, there is only the All One. In that realm, no world exists yet. No, 'I am here; the world is there'... Think of the terror a baby must go through losing the All-Oneness with the mother, the caretaker, the breast, the touch and warmth of skin—language fails here!"

Bernard slapped his hands on the table and bent over. He was known to easily get lost in esoteric dissertations. His black eyes were looking straight at me.

"These men had a most violent rupture when as an infant the "All One" cleaved into the I and the objective outside world, as it had to do eventually. It must have felt to them like: What's going on? Why is everything impinging on me? Why is everything so unreal? What's that crawling, ever-moving brew and why is everything changing so fast? And why the hell can't we psychologists express it this way? Surely there's always the short version—that they are afraid of women. But we have to explain more here. We have to explain the near-psychotic drift into violence that has remained with mankind for thousands of years."

He looked at his watch.

"My lecture about Michael Balint is coming up," he said. "Balint brings up some of the same questions. Stay tuned!"

As I turned and reached for the doorknob, Bernard called me back.

"There will be future fascists," he said, "and they will have different beliefs. Their faces will be different, but their women will be kept away and veiled. They will rape, they will commit atrocities we can't even imagine. They will claim to spread justice in the world and they will be non-corruptible and—like the Freikorps—deep down they will love death."

When I left, I wasn't even thinking who Balint was—or future fascists, for that matter. I sat down in my office and jarred my memory so as to set free what I remembered about Karl that night in the Munich train station. Karl and his dreams of steel towers and cathedrals ...dreams of the strong, of the rigid, of the hard.

Rattenberg

A postcard from Klaus, which followed closely after the envelope containing his theater script, arrived unexpectedly. It was in a mail jacket labeled "Urgent Delivery," and the front of the postcard pictured Hotel Schloss, located in Rattenberg, Austria. On the back of the postcard, Klaus had composed a brief message to me: "I'm searching out the darkest town south of the Arctic Circle."

I was struck with disbelief that Klaus might really be in Rattenberg. But the proof was in the postcard.

What was his strange attraction? In Rattenberg, the town where the sun would not shine all winter, April was the month the sun would finally climb up over the mountain and break the spell. I imagined Klaus in a gloomy hotel room looking out over the relentless clutter of cobblestones, the last drunken patrons of the bar waddling abandoned streets, the few lights still on like torches on sinking ships. Camus in Prague, close to self-annihilation if he would not have had the littoral light in his soul! Camus later would remember the smell of pickles they sold in the streets. Oh, the bitter taste of loneliness!

I put in a request for a few days off, even though I had recently come back from Munich.

Genève, a young and brilliant assistant, reassured the chairman that she could take over my lectures. And he agreed to our plan—but not without adding with a tinge of acid in his voice that the ladies surely would miss me.

But I knew better. Maybe I was well known as "Professor Camus," but lately I was feeling more like a mousy intellectual moping about in the university halls.

I called the telephone number listed on the back of the post-card and left a brief message for Klaus.

Then I proceeded to select a route to Rattenberg through Northern Italy. Less than an hour later, I got in my car and began my journey.

Some of the alpine passes had just been opened for cars without snow chains; at one point, some officials in green uniforms even checked my tires and noted the summer threads. They cautioned me about proceeding.

I reached Rattenberg late at night. The narrow alleys were barely lit and poorly plowed; worse, the snow piles made it almost impossible for me to turn around whenever I lost my way.

Sometime after midnight, I finally knocked on the side door of the Schloss Hotel.

The owner answered.

"Yes, yes," he mumbled in half-drowned diction when I reminded him of my message.

I walked up the stairs and settled into my room. As I drifted toward sleep I thought I heard a child whimpering, but the drive had made me tired and I quickly fell asleep.

Sometime after I fell asleep, I heard sharp knocks on the door. I opened it with some hesitation.

"Monsieur Yann Cedak?" the gendarme asked.

"Yes, that's me."

"Your papers, please."

"But I just arrived..."

The gendarme merely raised his hand. I opened my bag and handed him my passport.

"We have to ask you some questions downstairs."

As I entered the hallway, I couldn't help but notice the happenings in the room opposite my own. I glimpsed some official-looking man holding a camera. He was dressed in a long black coat, his body foreshortened as he bent over a small corpse. The child might have been three years old, at most. The child's face was covered with blisters, and his lips were parted to reveal ugly brown teeth. When the man pulled back the white linen that they had draped over the child's body, I thought I saw scarred legs cratered with sores. For a second, the child's eyes pierced me with blackness so dense that it forespoke the fall of all reason and hope.

In the downstairs breakfast room, frigid at this time of the morning, and with chairs still set upside-down on the tables, a few guests gathered with bleary eyes. Klaus happened to be sitting across from me, but his face barely gave way to any expression of surprise when he saw me. In fact, he merely nodded. One after the other, we few guests at the Schloss Hotel were questioned by the gendarmes.

"Did you hear any strange noises around midnight or after?" one of them asked me.

I said that I got in late, but I had heard some whimpering.

"Did you hear anyone fall? Anything like that?"

"No."

"Did you meet a child upon your arrival?"

"No."

Could I think of anything suspicious that I heard or saw in the room across from mine?

Again, I answered no.

The body of the small child was carried downstairs on a stretcher and put into a van built of corrugated steel. The vehicle reminded me of pictures I'd seen of those mobile killing units used during WWII, with openings in the roof wherein the Zyklon B gas canisters were dropped.

I looked about in order to gauge the light. There are some birds—or so they say—that can perceive the subtlest shades of grey, but my eyes saw nothing but the undifferentiated color of dingy brine. It was almost noon when I was finally able to sit down with Klaus.

He told me that he had been questioned at the police station separately and that he had been talking to the little boy and his mother the evening before.

"He had a rare disease that made him break out in severe boils at the most minor exposure to light," Klaus said. "So the mother brought him to Rattenberg quite often, and the owner of the hotel knew them well."

"How did he die?"

"They're saying the mother stifled him with a pillow because she couldn't stand his whimpering and crying anymore."

I had seen a woman sitting inside the steel van, but she had been bent over such that I could not see her face. They had carelessly thrown a raincoat over her pajamas.

"I did hear some whimpering during the night," Klaus said. "They were not welcomed. The child was crying throughout much of the day, and people do not want to be reminded of God's indifference."

A silence sunk in between us. I rubbed my cold hands. Klaus rested his forehead in his palms and placed his elbows on the tabletop. He avoided eye contact. "All morning, I lay on my bed thinking of nothing. It's like everything has been sucked empty," he suddenly said. He took a deep breath. "I counted over and over the cracks on the tiled ceiling. I tried to rearrange what I saw and what I experienced into some pattern of reason or meaning."

Klaus's face was drained of color.

"Isn't that what we're all doing?" I asked. "It's what Camus had called 'our unceasing questioning of a universe that remains silent.'"

"Yesterday the owner of the hotel showed me the tunnel in the basement," he said. "There is a fence there now. I could feel the musty cold air leaking in, and it made me shiver. It is not used anymore, he said, but in the 30's, it was a lively establishment."

"And that is where Camus would have met your parents?"

Klaus nodded. "I believe so."

I imagined Camus waiting for his wife, Simone, and his friend, Ives Bourgeois, beneath the arc of the Inn Bridge. It was quite possible that they had spent some time here.

"You know, Camus did not feel well when the trio arrived near Innsbruck," I said. "Days of fighting erratic winds had exhausted him. Ives and Simone had Camus's kayak in tow. Camus might well have traveled by train to Rattenberg to await their arrival. And while waiting all alone at the banks of the River Inn, he entered darkness."

"Where did you read that?"

"A colleague of mine interviewed Ives Bourgeois after the war."

"Do you realize that you could write a biography of Albert Camus?"

"Yes, I do," I said.

Klaus and I started walking down the sloping alleyway toward the bridge across the River Inn, which, on this sunny afternoon, was halfway bathed in light. When we reached the middle of the bridge, we stopped at the spot where light and darkness met and looked up at the sun skimming the top of the ridge.

"*L'envers et l'endroit,*" I said. "*The wrong side and the right side*, as they would translate it."

Klaus understood. He knew Camus's early lyrical works rather well.

We settled in a nearby café, sat in the sunroom facing the river, and drank Glühwein. The mountain, named Rat Mountain, rose across the river. The sinister hump of rock leaned over the small village like an ogre blackened in soot. Silver had been in the earth, they said. Zinc and copper, too. But now there was only darkness.

Klaus looked around in silence and then said, "These are the last days of the dark period, as they call it here. I doubt the guests in this cafe know what happened at the hotel."

The café was crowded with folks who had walked across to the sunny side of the valley. Dogs were sleeping beneath tables, and baby carriages were wedged in between chairs. A giddy mood filled the air.

"A murder like that?" I whispered as I bent over the table.

With a sudden chill, I thought of the last lines of the second act in Klaus's theater piece the premonition of affliction and doom. But I did not want to ask. I leaned back in my chair, unsure of where our conversation would go next.

"My father wasn't a violent man," Klaus suddenly said. "The most daring thing I remember my father doing was sneaking through a fence to check on the progress of a construction site for an old folks' home, the one where he planned to spend the rest of his life. On some Sundays, we would walk over to the former heavy anti-aircraft gun emplacement in a small copse of birches, and he kept talking about things that had happened during the war ...the war, the war, the war ...the dividing line between men and children, between those who understood and those who didn't. He convinced me—without ever saying it—that war was what made a man."

There in the café, Klaus reached into his coat pocket and took out a photo of his late father. It struck me then that during my Munich visit he hadn't shown me any photos of his father aside from the one that he had hanging on the wall—the photo depicting Karl on the Höfatz, his face distant and barely recognizable. Now for the first time since the Forties, did I see Karl's face up-close. The years had furrowed Karl's eyelids, burying his eyes in a riffled sea of flesh. His lips had thinned out; his nose had sharpened; his abdomen had ballooned in size. Karl's body had metamorphosed into a barrel on leggy sticks—a far cry from how I remembered him on his Zündapp motorcycle, his foot tipping the kickstarter.

Klaus continued to speak of his parents. How they quarreled and how his father drank too much beer and slouched to the bedroom in numb glumness, the newspaper still spread on the table, its pages barely turned.

A sense of failure had oozed into his parents' lives.

His mother would not let go of the accusations. If only Karl would have followed her advice and invested in a house, real estate, a *homestead*, as she preferred to call it. Though WWII had come to an end years ago, every afternoon they still broadcast a list of missing soldiers: "Corporal Conrad Meyer, 11th tank grenadier company. Last seen at Rostov on June 3, 1942." On and on it went, for hours.

Klaus's sentences just kept gushing out, and I had to continuously interrupt him so as to keep the timeline straight in my mind. He recalled his mother holding a small painting she purchased from a cripple seated in a small carriage no larger than a Radio Flyer wagon. The man had lost all his limbs and now painted postcard-sized aquarelles with a brush that he held between his teeth.

Klaus said he remembered holding his mother's hand as they watched another amputee sketch the horizon of some steppe landscape in ocher colors. He hastily added some clouds, shuttling the brush across the canvas in order to catch the color before the paint drifted downward. The man used his tongue to curl the brush inside a rectangular cup of green to lay the color base for a low copse of windswept trees. He held the brush in his jaws, dipped it into a can of water, and moved it across the cloth.

This was also the year food became freely available overnight. Klaus's father started to eat too much. When his mother silently served the evening meal, Karl lifted the newspaper just briefly enough to allow his wife to slide the large plate of food in front of him. A cigarette went into his mouth, and with a swift movement of his arms, he held the newspaper overhead and folded it deftly. He stared at the plate piled with sauerkraut, which was topped with two large sausages, the one red and the other a glistening gray. One was called "blood sausage" because it contained the clotted blood of cows mixed with diced potatoes and other ingredients. The other contained pieces of lard, stomach, and brain.

What followed must have had a deep foundation in tradition. One might think of Spanish bullfights and the picadors, who, with an overhead throw, jetted lances into the bull's neck. Granted, Karl's execution of sausages paled in comparison, but there was still to be carnage. The hulls of the sausages ripped open and gave way to an avalanche of red and gray matter pouring over the mountain of sauerkraut. Properly executed, the sausages would empty. Forks came in handy to lift and turn the sauerkraut and thoroughly mix the strands with the released torrent of the sausages' ingredients. Only then would Klaus's mother carry her own food from the kitchen and sit down and eat opposite her husband.

Klaus sensed that his parents forced themselves to be good parents and tried hard to stifle their irritable spirits and bury their frustrations of unfulfilled lives.

Klaus's openness stunned me. I couldn't tell what brought it on; perhaps it was the child's death, or Klaus's visit to the cellar where his parents might very well have met Camus, or the tunnel where something bad was to happen.

"So ...I read the first two acts of your theater script," I said.

Klaus's lips immediately tightened.

"I finished it," he said.

"You did?"

"Here you go," he said, handing me a large manila envelope containing the final act.

I was about to comment on the first two acts when Klaus began talking about his parents again.

"Once, when my mother was drunk, she called my father a murderer. When drunk, my parents usually put me to bed early. I couldn't help but stay awake and listen to them fighting."

Klaus fell silent. His shoulders sagged.

The shadow of the setting sun hadn't reached the café yet. There was still a faint light on the River Inn, but it was as if the shadow had already thrown darkness onto Klaus's face. We had been sitting in the café for a while now. Other visitors had also noticed the mountain's shadow crawling across the bridge, soon to cover the café in darkness. Many were getting up and leaving, beginning their walks across the bridge toward their houses, which lay huddled in darkness below the ruins of the castle. There were lit pylons on the bridge. It looked like the people were crossing a burning bridge.

Klaus and I sat in silence as the darkness crept in.

I knew what I had to do.

"Come to Montpellier," I said.

"I can't," he said.

"Leave Munich!"

I continued to try to convince him. I had three rooms; my apartment was too large anyway; he could look for other accommodations ...but Klaus's face remained frozen and his answer remained the same.

He was listening to voices and fighting battles I was not privy to.

Soon we crossed the bridge and gathered our few belongings. I drove Klaus to the train station because he said he wanted to return to Munich.

In the car, it seemed that he and I were both feeling dispirited, so we barely talked.

To my surprise, before he stepped onto the train, Klaus turned around and hugged me. I sensed that walking together across the bridge into the light had been a new beginning of sorts.

That evening, I drove into the higher altitudes of the Alps and spent the night at a hotel near a lake that lay dark like a fish's eye surrounded by bald peaks. The sun was still touching the tops and through some of the notches in the crests, light fanned across fields of crushed stones. I strolled around the lake and sat down for a leisurely dinner. The owner, who was greeting all of his guests, complemented me on my fluent German and then added, "I saw you walking around the lake. You probably figured the purpose of those cement basins at the northern rim."

I told him that they were used for making ice, which, at higher elevations, would be clear and, thus, of a higher quality.

"May I join you for a moment?" he asked. "You see, we don't make clear ice anymore, but you have me wondering if you were once in the ice-making business?"

I told him that, indeed, for a time I was. But when he pined for more information, I excused myself. I had Klaus's final act to read

ACT III

KURT and KURT'S WIFE are now referred to as MOTHER and FATHER. It is obvious that both have aged since Act I and Act II; KURT, in fact, has turned gray. The furniture strewn throughout the set is reminiscent of the Forties. The time is just before the end of the war (1944).

MOTHER

You know, I would have stuck with you, even in jail.

FATHER

You are so superior. That is really what you want to say.

MOTHER

Not at all.

FATHER

Jail. Jail. Which didn't happen because ...?

MOTHER

I must admit that you frighten me.

FATHER

What?

MOTHER

Stop! You are mad.

FATHER

Not because of you, fair damsel lounging on a sofa, sitting on a white horse.

(MOTHER shakes her head.)

FATHER

"Anschluss" is the word. Political power. Hitler marching into Austria and taking care of it! The judge was a Jew and the man I fought was a Jew, but the judge was gone in no time. I tell you that they would have turned it against me whichever way.

MOTHER

I believe you didn't kill the man.

FATHER

What I did do was ram into him ...I heard his skull crack ...and I think I let go then. All this darkness spilled out of me, the bitter milk of one——and now——another war.

MOTHER

Bitter milk?

FATHER

My mother apparently brushed soot onto her breasts and rubbed salt on her nipples when she wanted to wean me.

MOTHER

That's sad. I'm sorry.

FATHER

No. Don't apologize. It made me strong. That's how my mother told me that I didn't need her, that I could make do without all those old wives' tales.

MOTHER

Aren't you sad about it?

FATHER

No. I am strong.

MOTHER

Yes, you are, but ...don't you care about us?

FATHER

The war is over.

MOTHER

You know I'm not talking about the war.

FATHER

All you want to talk about is that wound that split you when the baby ripped you open!

MOTHER

Everything hurts right down there. Don't you care what will happen to our lives?

FATHER

(*stands up and gets visibly angrier*) Down there! Down there! La! La! La! No! Why would I care?

MOTHER

You really don't care?

FATHER

Have it repaired, leave it alone ...I don't care. Whatever!

MOTHER

We're just married, and you tell me...

FATHER

(*struggles to stick by his words*) I don't care. That's what I said. Have it your way.

MOTHER

But I want you to decide with me.

FATHER

These are hard times.

MOTHER

The operation can be carried out and then everything will be like before ...

FATHER

Well. Big deal.

MOTHER

The war has changed you.

FATHER

What don't you understand, woman?

MOTHER

You seem so distant.

FATHER

But I always take care of you, didn't I?

MOTHER

You are a cold, cold man.

FATHER

Don't you ever forget it. *(walks to the couch and stands with his hands on his hips, calling to mind a military gesture*). I pulled you out of the gutter and now you are the bitch that even the devil cannot ride.

MOTHER

You did kill that man. You are a murderer! A murderer, I say!

(MOTHER closes her eyes and keeps them closed—as the lights dim and a toddler is heard crying in a room nearby.)

-END

Return to Montpellier after Rattenberg

That stay in the icy hotel up in the mountains brought back memories that chafed my being. I slept badly.

My mind raced through dreams that, though barely remembered, left the taste of bitter ashes in my mouth. Rattenberg was like Camus's Prague, the stone city of his despair. Suddenly a detail of his essay *Death in the Soul* struck me: the room where Camus had stayed in Prague was blue, as was the room wherein the child had died in Rattenberg. The town had left an afterimage, as if I had been staring too long at a Bruegel painting furrowed by lines of peasants trudging over frozen ponds.

The third act that Klaus had handed me filled me with vexation and foreboding. I kept trying to tell myself that Klaus was now finally able to express himself, but nothing seemed to lift my spirits. And my life, or so it seemed, was all about erosion, about the small accumulation of forces that ultimately dried the soul and built nothing. And that Nothing had an unlikely quality: heaviness.

As I drove down from the mountains and into the widening valleys, among hills that were to eventually flatten and breathe out into the sun-drenched planes of Italy, I thought about how Camus described his return from the bleak Prague to the Mediterranean *I enter Italy ... the first houses with their scaly tiles, the first vines flat against a wall made blue by Sulphur dressing, the first clothes hung out in the backyard ...the first cypress, the first olive tree, the dusty fig tree.*

The soul exhausts its revolts in the shady piazzas of small Italian towns, Camus wrote, and, as I drove on, windows wide open, my elbow resting on the car door's rim, I marveled at the strange airiness that had entered me. I did not dare change a thing; I barely moved on my seat; I drove on and on in the exaltation of this lightness.

Late evening, I crossed into France and made the small detour into Cassis to pass the night. I strolled in the harbor and, in the shades of evening, walked up Rue Frederic Mistral to St. Michel Church. They had added some administrative buildings and still tended to the lovely garden, which I had so much appreciated during my visits in the 40s. The church had not changed. The square tower still impressed me as not more than a plump reach for the playfulness of Italy's church towers. The church was white, efflorescent even in the late light with the glaze of Cassis' limestone, which had been the economy and pride of Cassis for decades. I opened a small gate and stepped into the courtyard where, in 1943, I had often parked the official limousine of the Marseille bishopric. But then memories from the war years edged in, vaguely threatening first, then more so, unhinging me, and I turned and went down to the harbor and drank wine and tried to lose myself.

After I passed the night in Cassis, I did not drive to Montpellier directly but decided to take a small detour to the beach shack where, just recently, the faculty had gathered for the "Death of a Beach" meeting. A soft wind was blowing in from the sea; I squinted my eyes against the soppy sun behind a rare fog bank. Inside the shack, the Russian was cleaning cognac glasses. I was surprised that he recognized me.

"I listened to your little speech the other day," he said.

"That was just a brief quote."

"Come here!"

He opened a drawer and showed me the back of a postcard that read: *Bin gar keine Russin, stamm' aus Litauen, echt deutsch.*

He translated right away: *I am not really Russian, come from Lithuania, I am truly German.* "T.S. Eliot." I said, "*The Waste Land*, and, by the way, I know German."

"This is the last postcard my daughter sent to me," he said. "I was in Switzerland then. Where her ashes are, we do not know."

He offered me some cognac. We sipped it in silence for a few minutes. "You worked with your camera during the war, I heard."

"Yes," I said. "I forged identity papers."

"My daughter must have thought that the Germans would not deport her if she quoted that German line from *The Waste Land.*

"What a belief in the power of words!"

"How can you believe otherwise if you are a professor of literature?"

"In war-torn Poland?"

He nodded.

"The blood lands."

"They took the very best, didn't they?"

I sunk my eyes into the bulbous cognac glass. I gave it a small shake, watched as the golden liquid coiled into billows that reached for the rim. Then, the swirl calmed.

Some memories, I thought, will never calm; they swirl in unending circles.

A young couple poked their heads through the half-open door.

"Sorry," the Russian said, "we're closed."

"So what's your name?" I asked him as the couple walked away.

"They call me Boris," he said. "But my real name is Saulé, which means 'sun' in Lithuanian."

It suddenly struck me that his daughter would have been of the same generation as Madeleine—a generation diminished by war and murder. My life—Boris's, too—took in the span of the Twentieth Century. We were the survivors and, thus, the guilty ones; it was our responsibility to mend, heal, and understand the motives of a murderous generation whose violation lay like soot on the conscience of their children. Now the children were entering the maze of unexamined despair, of repressed questions, of wondering what would have been their prior incarnations and what would have been their unconscious experiences that gave rise to such evil, and what elations would have driven them away from simple decency, and what were those words that encouraged their fathers to agree to murder and a complicity fanned by the fever of the irrational?

"You don't have a strong accent," I told him.

"In my time, speaking French meant being educated. In 1919, when the Freikorps invaded Latvia, the French sent a small expedition corps and pushed the Freikorps out. I fell in love with a French nurse—she was actually from Corsica—and we lived in Paris for a while, had a daughter, and returned off and on to Riga ...the rest you know: war, fleeing from the Huns, taking up arms. I was lucky to be out of town that day."

Boris sat quietly, biting his lips.

"What about that submarine photo on the wall?" I asked.

"I was in Algiers in November 1942 when *Casiabianca* reached the harbor. The French had blown up their fleet in Toulon, and she was one of the few boats to make it out and reach safe harbor in Africa."

"I know of a submarine that ran supply missions for the Resistance," I said. "Heavy machine guns and all those clunky weapons they could not fly in with Lysanders."

"Yes! That was the *Casiabianca*."

"And those English MAS boats?"

"How did you learn of all that?"

Boris placed his elbows on the wooden table and poured us more cognac.

I remained silent.

"You're going to tell me, aren't you?"

Coastal Road Task

And so I told him about the reconnaissance along the coastal road with Madeleine.

The year was 1943, and Madeleine hoped that the German's increasing brutality had lowered my reluctance to devote myself to the armed Resistance.

"The Germans have lost all their humanity," she told me. "They are rounding up Jews in cattle cars. There is no longer any pretense. They are shipping Jews by the trainload from the Drancy internment camp."

The military situation had also changed. The English already had a base of PT boats in Corsica; the battle for Corsica was over; the Germans had been flushed into the sea by a Moroccan mountain division at Ajaccio.

"But the devil will not leave without a fight, and it won't happen by knocking off a German soldier with one of those laughable Liberator pistols the British keep air-dropping," I said.

She looked me straight in the eyes. "Yann, I have been assigned to reconnaissance the coast line. We anticipate torpedo boat operations from Corsica to supply the Maquisards and ship out fugitives."

She must have seen just enough expression of interest to continue.

"When the Italians left a number of MAS boats in Corsica, the British ripped out the torpedo tubes, lowered the bridge structures, and added inflatable tanks," she said. "These boats usually go out on moonless nights for the trip to France. They switch over to their electric motor miles out, and then launch rubber dinghies. The headlights of cars passing on the coastal road have lit up these dinghies during past reconnaissance missions, so we need detailed information about how to best avoid these areas for landings. This will involve studying the headlights on cars driving up and down the coastal highway."

"But they opened new checkpoints, and the curfew is still on," I said.

I bent forward and took a deep breath. I knew what Madeleine wanted from me, and that sudden insight stuck in my throat like a block of ice that refused to melt.

"It's clear that you need the official limousine of the diocese," I finally said. "And some pretext, of course."

I was stunned by my own words. A felt a shift inside me, and a feverish ball seemed to expand in my chest.

I must have nodded, said yes, or given Madeleine some sign, because she took my hand, clicked her tongue, and smiled. I had never seen her do that before.

A few nights later, Madeleine and I drove the wood-burner Citroen—its official metal plaque displayed on the dashboard—into the hills. The road wound into a few serpentines east of Cassis, then, having reached the barren escarpment above the Mediterranean, straightened and slowly lowered along the coastline. Along these stretches, the road turned near perpendicular to the coast such that a car's headlights would indeed light up a small boat in the distance. Off and on, I steered the car onto the shoulder to shake the charcoal fire alive.

I stopped at the first overlook and Madeleine dutifully noted the reach of the headlights while I walked to the rear of the car and closed the levers for the air intake in order to avoid burning off too much charcoal.

"Now, the kiss," she said, revealing a solid block of lipstick cleverly tucked into a paper canister.

I watched as she ran the lipstick in an oval around her lips.

"Hard to believe that they label this 'non-smear,'" she said. "Of course it is all black market."

I stood between her and the cliff with my mouth agape.

"Now it's your turn," she said. "Kiss me for the sake of the country."

I folded my lips around hers, and, as these matters go, it went a bit further. I pulled her to my chest and squeezed her breasts. She took her time and then gently pushed me away.

Intimacy may start in many ways. If the English writers of the last century are to be believed, lifting a handkerchief from the floor may break the ice. During our past smoking excursions among the rocks, Madeleine would put her head in my lap, and I would listen to the wind, feel rocks pushing in my back.

But this time, the night was on us—a night on a coastal highway patrolled by Milice. This meant danger, and what it also meant was being with her, unconditionally. This time, I wanted to be her equal; I wanted to be as courageous as she was.

We drove on, and at each turn of the coastal road, we memorized the mileage and the angle of the headlights skimming the sea. After a few miles, we encountered a roadblock: several Kübelwagen, notched helmets, and Milice.

"*Vos papiers*," a young soldier demanded.

In the coastal fog, his face appeared to be suspended in milk.

We were ordered to leave the car and spread our hands on its roof. A flashlight was thrust into our faces several times. A few men huddled around the Kübelwagen at the side of the road. Hoarse laughs erupted as a German soldier tried his French. He had trouble understanding my detailed explanation: urgent transfer of wavers and wine and blessed olive oil for extreme unction. Had he noticed the lipstick smears? I couldn't say. He checked our identity papers and the transit permits issued by the diocese of Marseille. He lifted away the backseats, bent away the wooden sheet separating the wood burner, and then crawled under the Citroen.

"Nobody hidden and no contraband," he said, duly reporting back to his fellow Milice men waiting in the shadows at the side of the road. Then he turned to me and ordered us to return to Cassis.

I drove off. For several minutes, Madeleine and I didn't say a word; we just allowed our heartbeats to settle. We drove back through the abandoned streets of Cassis and rang the doorbell at the sacristy, for it was too risky to negotiate the rutted road up to St. Baume in the middle of the night, and, besides, the charcoal had burnt down to its embers.

The caretaker who knew us answered and led us to a room. She did not ask any questions; after all, on occasion, people sought shelter there. The Germans still avoided searching property of the Catholic Church as a gesture of restraint and prudence.

After having listened to my story, Boris asked, "So, what happened to your friend?"

"I lost contact with her," I said, "and late 1943, she died during an ambush of a SS convoy."

"That was your last night with her?"

I nodded.

"I understand," he said, his expression withdrawing into some distant melancholy. And in that moment, in his silence, I sensed the beginning of a friendship.

That last night at Cassis, after Madeleine and I had returned from the coastal road, I walked out to the car to close the louvers on the burner and choke off the oxygen. I couldn't be sure that there was even enough charcoal left in the burner to get us back up the mountain in the morning.

When I came upstairs to the room, Madeleine had made the beds. I lit two candles and put a bottle of white wine on the rickety table.

"That pale-faced German who stopped us on the road didn't even notice the bottle when he searched the car," Madeleine said, smirking.

"Missed the lipstick, too," I said.

I sat down at the side of the bed and stared into the half-shadows.

"I know what you're thinking, Yann, but sometimes you have to choose the gun," she said. "We are not helpless anymore. Every month, we receive Sten submachine guns and pencil detonators, and silencer pistols."

There was a breathing silence between us.

"Take up the gun!" she said.

Then she sat down beside me, took my head into her hands, and gingerly kissed my lips. She slid her hands into my hair and gently drew me onto the bed. Her mouth was soft and inviting. I put my hands under her blouse to feel her nipples, which firmed under my caresses. She let me kiss her skin down into her wetness until she started shivering. And then everything was to change—our breathing, our bodies; all softness was gone; our rhythm had given to hardness.

The two candles started to flicker, and then went out. I kept fumbling for matches to relight them. Madeleine and I sat down at the table and managed to uncork the bottle with a knife. We drank in silence as I held her hand across the tabletop.

What my silence tried to preserve was this all-too-transient lift into a realm where passion and danger merged into a unity beyond which there was no other realm.

Our candles were the only light for miles, and though our light was enough, beyond us there were cries of tortured pain deep in the cellars of Rue Paradis, and somewhere, on a winding road, a German dispatcher on a motorcycle was riding toward his certain death, riding toward that steel wire resistance fighters had strung across the road.

That morning, we woke to gutted candles and a grey light filtering in from an overcast sky.

"You know that I joined the Resistance with my blood and with my soul," Madeleine said.

But I couldn't express more than a lame question in response: "Will I see you?"

"For some time I shall keep my boots up at the cathedral, or whatever you want to call that site. I shall file fake papers and write requisitions and report of phantom planning meetings. And then there will be a time the Germans will pull their tanks with horses, when they will eat their horses, and then they will sink into the morass of history—and I shall not have stood by idle."

She waited in silence for my word, and she was still waiting even after I had returned from stirring the charcoal in the wood burner in preparation for our departure, and she was still waiting when we had arrived at the top of the mountain.

"Join us!" she said.

"I don't know if I can."

The kick of being was not in me.

I had arrived at Boris's shack at noon. Now, it was already late afternoon, and my mind, pierced by memories, staggered in drunkenness. The long ride down from the Alps had worn me, and the content of Klaus's third chapter had deeply afflicted my mood. When Boris offered me to spend the night, I was thankful.

"I don't live here," he explained, "but I often stay overnight myself. The patter of the waves puts me to sleep, and in the morning there's nothing more refreshing than a swim in the sea."

I didn't need the patter of waves or the whistle of the winds in the dunes to drift off. When I woke in the night and listened to the subdued rumble of the waves, it was like stillness.

Next morning, I took a swim and arrived back at the auditorium in Montpellier as the authentically disheveled associate professor of journalism and philosophy. I sat down in the back row, a gesture that—for me, the well-known Camus specialist—I reckoned would be regarded as a sign of sincere humbleness.

Genève was confidently leading a discussion about the late works of Camus. I was taken aback that she so conscientiously had prepared her lecture without my help.

For some reason, I always had shied away from Camus's later works. *The Stranger* had always been my favorite, but, as I sat in that auditorium, I quickly realized how much I had limited myself and how much I had fallen into a rut. Genève was charmingly brilliant, and her Irish accent gave her French a kind of ratcheting ring that everybody loved. She knew how to please.

Genève was relating the theme of Camus's *The Fall* to the story *Traps*, written by the Swiss writer Friedrich Dürrenmatt.

"Class, Professor Yann has just joined us," she announced. "His translation of this story into French was just published."

And so I took it upon myself to explain that it was a story of a successful businessman driving through a small village in Switzerland when his car engine stops. He spends the night at some retired judges' bed & breakfast, where a tight net of interrogation shows him guilty of having caused the death of his superior. Next morning, he drives out of the village and shrugs the experience off as a drunken episode without meaning and consequences.

"Dead end!" a student remarked.

"Quite true!" I said. "Dürrenmatt wrote a version in which the businessman committed suicide."

And that's when Urraca's spiteful words in Saint-Brieuc flooded back to me, unhinging me, stirring in me a tripping unease that did not let up even as Genève continued her thoughtful presentation.

"I sketched out some thoughts about how to compare this brief work with another brief work," Genève said. "Let's now begin our discussion of Camus's novel *The Fall.* I'll summarize it for you. A retired judge sits in a dim restaurant in Antwerp. What he tells the listener during his monologue encompasses his whole life, which has been one of egotism, debauchery, and the easy seduction of women. But the core of his misery is the failure to rescue a woman, who, years ago, he witnessed jumping into the River Seine. He failed to act, and now his life is nothing but living the guilt. No matter what he does, and no matter how easy his life looks from the outside, his soul's writhing around this failure is his existential problem. On a ship-voyage, he spots far on the horizon a black speck, which reminds him of the woman who jumped to her death. There is no escape, and Camus gives no answer."

I began to feel sick. It was a vertigo that made things seem to fall away into some abyss that I could not see. Black specks rotated through my field of vision, and I felt nauseated. Genève quickly summoned a nurse, who led me out of the room, gave me cold drinks, and took my blood pressure. She invited me to rest in the medical office, and I did. It was some time before I was able to stand up and drive home.

When I arrived home, I realized that I did not want to feel better. It was as if I had been presented an opportunity to work it all out by yielding to my senses, suffering, and disassembling this chaotic world of my thoughts.

But work out what? *The Stranger* depicts an act of careless murder on the beach and *The Plague* a physician's resolution to set his whole being against the indifference of God. In *The Fall*, the aging Camus writes about the failures of man, failures that will sink into man's soul a gnawing guilt.

My insights came in wisps of admissions, a slow backward progression into my own past and marches of failure. Urraca's words haunted me over and over again: "You sat at a desk as my friend and your lover lay in a shallow grave—and France with it!"

After my attack of vertigo, and with the help of a sedative, I had a decent night.

At breakfast in the cafeteria the following morning, I set my tray down beside Genève's as if nothing had happened. And she acted the same.

"We had a lively discussion about religion after you left," she said.

"Why does that topic come up so often?" I asked.

But that was the extent of our conversation, as we were interrupted by a few colleagues who had decided to join us. The usual banter took over. Guilt and forgiveness were not on the menu.

I had hoped that my visit to Munich would stir their interest, but that didn't happen. In addition, my off-and-on efforts to pen a paper based on the remnants of my notes from 1939 Algiers lead to nothing publishable. Apart from a long title—*Camus, The Stranger, and The Last Day of Peace*—it was all air.

At the university, I left my door open to encourage students and colleagues to walk in, consult me about their ideas, and soak in my advice.

But nothing of that sort happened that afternoon.

Party at Gastyb's

The next day Gastyb handed out invitations to his olive garden estate near Montpellier, where the most coveted party of the semester was scheduled to take place. This year's invitation was inscribed on thick, felt-like paper, upon which was embedded an olive leaf imprinted with my name. Though Gastyb had frustrated and annoyed me during our most recent outing, I couldn't argue that the man had good taste.

Gastyb's estate was situated on a sloping hill where the Mediterranean plane folded up into the cliffs. His house—and the vineyards and meadows surrounding it—always seemed to be bathed in an azure blue that softened the dark and divined the succulent carpets of lavender that in a few months would spread across the landscape. At night, guests like me could look out over parapets toward the Mediterranean that lay sickle-silver in the moonlight. The scent of earth, flowers, and budding seeds was in the air. Professors of philosophy may get a chance to enjoy such a life if they publish successful books, but, in Gastyb's case, he married a woman who was heir to an estate.

On the day of the party, I arrived at the estate in the early afternoon. Gastyb introduced me to his wife, referring to me as "the colleague who had met Camus in Algiers in 1939, and specializes in his work." He turned to his wife. "You surely have read Camus's novel, *The Stranger.*"

His wife smiled in a worldly way—it was a smile I could appreciate.

"I heard good things about you, Yann," she said. "Nice to meet you."

"Yann is also helping me with Louis Malle's *Feu de Follet* project."

"When is that movie coming out?" she asked. "I want to go see it with you."

"Louis Malle has barely begun the script, Chérie!"

She cocked her head, stretching the white silk of her dress.

Benice, Benice. Allez-y! Allez-y!

We overheard a swell of cheers coming from the main building.

"It's tradition that she starts the swim," Gastyb said.

When Chérie walked away, Gastyb did not follow her. Instead, he took me aside.

"I read your first draft, but I think you should leave the cinematography to Louis. We aren't the ones who decide the details of the scenes."

I had suggested a café scene with the soundtrack switched off, showing people sliding by as if they were moving behind a glass panel, and I felt that this was how the world might appear in the eyes of a man destined for suicide.

"You're better off just limiting yourself to the philosophical content of the script," he continued. "And don't forget that the words should complement the mood of the scene."

I thought about Klaus, the grid of overhead tram wires, frozen water paints.

I shook my head to ward off my irritation and suggested that Gastyb read Malle's instruction about the word "suicide" not being spoken in the movie.

"Well ...I'm not sure I..."

I watched Gastyb stiffen. He scratched his head.

"We have to discuss that some other time," he said, turning and walking toward the farmhouse in silence. I followed several steps behind.

With the pool now open, the party seemed livelier than ever; raucous bursts of laughter kept erupting, and wet pants and shirts were proof of some intense naval battles. Most of the philosophy and journalism professors were either bare-chested drunk or hiding in corners with sullen faces. Some leaned across the back of chairs like limp, over-hydrated sacks. Some awkwardly nibbled on plates of food, and only where the make-believe of intellectual life had to be kept alive—where the next assignment or the next publication in the university's quarterly publication would be decided—did I note hints of competition: tilted heads, fingers pointing, and feet tapping on the floor for that prepared-for moment that might decide an assistant's career.

I was surprised to find Genève all alone in a corner, drying herself off with a thick towel.

"They threw me into the pool," she said, looking up at me like a sad puppy. "Newcomer's luck, I suppose."

I was sure that Genève was up for these sorts of poolside shenanigans. As young and well-built as she was, how could she have minded being thrown into a pool? But now here she was, sitting all by herself as the crowd circling around the pool bawled *Sur le Pont d'Avignon*, and every time they ran out of words—which happened frequently—there was a splash, and some drunken philosophy fellow or some barely-clad secretary went under.

"Yann, if you don't mind, I'd like to ask you about the documents you lost in Spain on your transit to France in 1940," Genève said. "You had your notes from the interview with Camus and all your other material in your luggage, right?"

"Yes, and my luggage was stolen in a seedy hotel near the Madrid-Barcelona rail line."

"Well, did you know that Hemingway's first full manuscript was stolen in almost the exact same way in Spain?"

"I did not know that."

"And it didn't keep him from writing."

As if suddenly becoming aware of the sharp sting that her words had inflicted, she added, "Let me also ask you about Sartre.

Do you think that all that whining about despair and emptiness and authenticity is just a front? That it all comes down to lust, jocular kicks, and whoopees? Sartre admits in an interview that he never experienced anguish or despair—maybe boredom, maybe misery—but never the soul-scarring alienation he expresses in his literary work." She wrung her hands in some fake expression of angst.

"But why would he put on the mask of despair?" I asked.

"To drape himself in that gilded charm that despair and the hunger for seriousness lend to intellectuals at those Left Bank cafés."

"Intellectuals all over Europe flock to him," I said.

"They copy Left Bank all across Europe."

"Actually, I must agree with you. Sartre's life is quite different from his work. I have been told stories, too. His wife, also a philosopher, keeps befriending young women in the university circles, and then she flips them over to her co-conspirator, who promptly beds them. And let it be known that most of them are stressed young women who let themselves be lured by his mumbling philosophy and the advanced placements that even a casual connection to Sartre will give them. Rumor has it he spends his savings renting multiple apartments close-by, all occupied by some nervous and stressed woman he can visit at any time."

"I heard similar talk about Camus," she said. "Which brings up the question—if even Camus..."

"Camus knew real happiness," I interrupted. "The deliverance that the sea and the sun and women's smiles could give. In his work, he expresses a clarity in happiness. Camus invokes light to make us feel his deliverance and bliss after leaving the dark clefts of Prague's streets. There is nothing like it in Sartre's work. Sartre does not show readers the light."

Genève nodded.

"But," I added, "Camus's happiness does not allow for a belief in the God of the sparrows."

Genève and I kept quiet for a while, allowing our thoughts to simmer.

Out of all the drunken guests, there remained only a few still standing and conversing; philosophy had finally settled into its Dionysian blur. The bus soon arrived and whisked everyone back to Montpellier via the coastal road. I stared out the window at the hills of salt, saw water; saw foam stirred up by a rising wind. Genève sat near the back of the bus with a younger colleague. I recognized him from the theater department. When she got off the bus, she didn't wave goodbye to me as I was hoping she would.

"I'm sorry," she said a few days later at lunch, "I was very tired that night."

To my surprise, Genève timidly handed me a small envelope containing two theater tickets.

"Samuel Beckett's play *Waiting for Godot* ...first time in Montpellier!" she said.

I was well aware that tickets for the play were sold out, and I thanked her repeatedly for thinking of me.

"From one tramp to another," she said, smirking as she bit into an apple that may as well have been my heart.

Klaus's Sudden Visit

A few days later, Klaus stood outside my apartment, ringing my doorbell.

"Couldn't find your number," he said as he stood in the cold light of the hallway. He looked rough.

I offered him a glass of Pernod and warmed up some pizza in the oven before we lounged on the beanbags in my living room. Klaus's voice was raw as he told me about his travels from Munich.

"I couldn't sleep on the night train to Paris, and then when I finally arrived, there was a strike and nothing but delays."

I hesitated to ask why he had come to Montpellier. What had made him change his mind?

I folded out a sleeper, encouraged him to take a hot shower, and told him to make himself at home. Then I excused myself from the living room, walked out onto my small balcony that overlooked rows of vines peeling off into the dark hills, and breathed in the aroma of the spring night. I thought of Klaus's balcony in Munich and how I had stood there looking down into craggy piles of snow. For a moment it was as if I had the musty smell of his hallway still in my nostrils, the screech of tramways turning in the Waldfriedhof loop still in my ears.

A few minutes later, when I walked back into the living room, I felt as if my body was the bow of a ship heading into troubled waters.

Klaus was already fast asleep. I sat down and sipped my Pernod. Here was a child whom I wanted to gently cradle and pick up and make coffee for in the morning. His shadow had sunken into my life, forcing me to recall history, not to mention my own fears and guilt.

His father had saved me. Could it be that Klaus wanted me to save him?

The next morning, I called Genève. She happily agreed to take on my role in the morning roundtable, and even offered to teach my two lectures scheduled for that afternoon.

"I have your outlines," she said, "and Fridays are usually light days anyway. You just have to face the damage Monday morning, okay?"

I didn't laugh, didn't thank her, and it didn't occur to me that I hadn't until minutes after I hung up the phone. I considered calling Genève back, telling her that I was sorry for not being in a lighter mood, but I was immediately pulled back into Klaus's world when he awoke and sat down at my kitchen table.

His face appeared slacked and drawn as I poured him some coffee.

"I'm hoping we can go to the beach," Klaus said, reaching for the creamer on the table. "Then we can talk."

"You're lucky I was able to take off today, you know."

As we walked to my car, the sun was steaming off a rare morning fog. I picked up some croissants and coffee on the way to the beach. When we arrived, I spread a blanket within eyesight of Boris's shed. A half-dozen chairs were stacked against the wall of the shed; Boris's opening times were always a guess.

I watched Klaus step into the water. His skin looked as milky as the haze that still draped far out over the water.

"What made you come here so abruptly?" I asked when Klaus returned to our blanket.

"Everything in Munich has been driving me into despair," he said.

"You have lost a father and mother. What you're saying is understandable."

And that was it. Klaus clammed up and looked away. He sat bent over, his forehead supported by his arms, and then he kept slowly grinding his heels into the sand, almost imperceptibly first, then with increasing force. It seemed as though he wanted to bury himself in the ground.

"I just need to listen to the ocean," he said.

I knew that was a lie. We were on a beach facing the open sky, and all Klaus wanted to do was disappear. Even in the fullness of the sky and the sway of waves—he was *The Stranger*.

After Klaus fell asleep, I strolled along the beach and kept an eye out for signs of activity at Boris's shed. Eventually, I watched as Boris set up the tables and chairs and raised the Corse flag, which vexed some visitors—which was exactly what he intended.

At lunch, Boris carried to our table two wooden plates. The first was piled high with dark rye bread and dried mushrooms and the other with slices of veal and deer sausage. He said he wanted to share with us some Corse and Lithuanian food.

"Here's to France," Boris said as he pulled a bottle of Cognac from his satchel. "Yann, this is the bottle we didn't kill last time."

We drank and ate almost without interruption. Boris had a young helper working for him that day and there were few visitors along this remote stretch of beach. Klaus listened intently to Boris's stories about Corse; how the spine of mountains inside this island had preserved an indigenous culture to this day; how invaders came to the coast; how ships brought merchandise and foreign customs and songs in strange languages yet never touched the core of a fiercely tribal society that populated these steep valleys and dizzying heights. I was taken in by Boris's accent and his clacking meter, which laid the stress on the beginning syllables and was so different from the lilting French singsong. Klaus did very well with his French throughout the conversation, and the brief runs of German that Boris came up with made Klaus chortle.

Boris invited Klaus to view a number of maps and photos of Corse that he had collected over the years. Meanwhile, I sat in the background, listening to Boris talk about Corse—about the freedom, the ancient trees, the hunts in the mountains, the families, and the meals one could find there.

"Boris wants to forget the past," Klaus said on the drive back to my apartment.

"What do you mean."

"He yearns to disappear into the ragged interior of Corse," Klaus said. "He wants to extinguish history, he wants to change his name, his character, even his face."

"I have to admit that I hadn't seen that side of Boris until today," I said.

In the evening, Klaus and I attended the performance of *Waiting for Godot.* It had taken a long time for the university to obtain permission to perform this adaptation, at least according to Genève, who had explained over lunch one afternoon that many formal letters were written and phone calls made. *Waiting for Godot*, playing to full houses all over Europe, had finally come to Montpellier.

In the play two tramps—Estragon and Vladimir—meet on some swampy plane dominated by a bare tree with one branch. Why are they there? They are waiting for Godot, who never shows up. The first line of the play reveals the tramps' tragedy: *Nothing can be done*, while the last line tells us why they are still on the stage: *We have to go on.*

Following the performance, a reception was held inside the cafeteria, where a cold buffet had been set up. The actors—still in their costumes—were shaking hands and appeared happy to socialize. Klaus, however, positioned himself far away from all the giddy happenings, and although I introduced him to several colleagues, he appeared disinterested in everyone. It wasn't until Genève came up to me to ask how I liked the performance that Klaus began to lighten up a bit. She was impressed to hear that Klaus had seen *Waiting for Godot* at the Munich Schauspielhaus and that he had also seen the movie *The 400 Blows*.

After the reception, many of us walked into the main square to drink coffee, eat honey cakes, and continue the lively discussions that were started at the reception. The actors and stage hands joined us, the actors' faces still glazed from the ointments they had applied to remove their make-up.

"So what did our German friend think about the play?" the actor who portrayed Estragon asked.

"The lone tree on the stage symbolizes death," Klaus said.

"No," someone at the far end of the table said, "it symbolizes life."

"It remains undecided, like almost everything in that play," Genève said. "Estragon and Vladimir plan to hang themselves on the single branch left on it. Estragon fixes the rope first because he is the lighter one, but if he dies, he can't be sure that Vladimir will go through with it."

"And if Vladimir ties the rope first, the branch might break, eliminating the possibility of committing suicide altogether," said a bald man with glasses, whom I had recognized as an adjunct. "That's why they talk about jumping off the Eiffel Tower."

"Meaning they can't die together," Genève said. "They have to die alone or live alone."

Everybody kept talking now. Klaus was listening intently.

The actor who portrayed Estragon spoke up again. "There is yet another meaning. Vladimir says that hanging will give them an erection, and it is at that moment that I say, 'Let's go ahead!'"

"Dying for an erection?" Klaus asked.

"Klaus, what are you getting yourself into?" I asked with a stern voice. Why was I feeling so irritated?

"Yann!" Genève said, "this play is all about interpretation. Let Klaus talk." Her voice was soft with the lilt of sirens of mythology.

"Couldn't it mean that they would die for the one single moment of feeling that forever remains true and unadulterated and unchanging—the one moment that no God or inner voice could ever trammel upon?" Klaus asked.

"Are you suggesting that suicide is a most authentic decision?" Genève asked.

"Suicide cuts out all the chaff," Klaus said.

Genève's face froze.

"Cuts out life," somebody else said.

The conversation was suddenly back on, with nearly everyone at the table joining in: "Cuts out future erections." "Nothing to be done." "Klaus may have a point."

"Stop it!" I shouted. Klaus's words, spilled in his gravelly voice, frightened me. What young man speaks like this? What pain had led to this? All this yelling as if this were a joke horrified me.

As it turned out, my interruption wasn't well-received. In fact, it caused the gathering to swiftly peter out. Klaus seemed annoyed at me, but I didn't care.

Everyone diffused out into the square, where engines cranked and horns honked. The party was over.

That night, back at my apartment, I complimented Klaus on his progress with the French language. Then I tried talking to him about Boris. But none of my efforts to get Klaus to talk were successful; he remained silent and told me that he wanted to go to bed.

Early the next morning—acting abruptly and without any explanation—Klaus took the first train to Paris. When we parted at the train station, he said, *Der Vorhang zu und alle Fragen offen.*—"The curtain closed and all the questions open."

Ever since I had visited Munich and met Klaus, an unexpected cold wind had blown into my life, and what came with it was a weary sense of unease. Its sidling powers had stiffened into a cage that had begun to close around me.

The self-doubts that I had been feeling of late cut me off from other people, woke me from my sleep and, at times, made me feel like a ghost standing beside myself—a self no more than an empty shell, sick to the stomach and spent.

Days later, a small envelope from Klaus arrived in the mail.

Inside was a note that explained that he had started writing—this time in earnest. Also included was a diary-like confession that caused me tremendous anxiety:

The French name it "merde"—it lacks a punch—the Germans call it "Scheisse"—that's an improvement—and the English have the shortest version—as usual— "shit."

You step out of the tramway and it feels like you slip on blubber, but how you feel you can't say because you feel nothing, having numbed your mind into a whiteout and ground all emotions into silt and muffled all feelings and lied to your mother, telling her that you would again see a French movie, The 400 Blows, in which a boy runs away from home and is put into reform school and in the last scene runs toward the sea as if to drown himself. And visiting a prostitute without being the least in the mood is merely bizarre and lacks all drama, even though you planned it for weeks because nothing spontaneous has happened, or will happen, and this makes everything seem understandable—or so you tell yourself—and why you want to achieve a state of no pain, no feeling, and why you liken this winter day with its fading Munich light to the day in Algiers in the novel The Stranger *in which Meursault walks on the beach in the glint of a cruel sun, and why you need to have this mental deception, this literal vision, is because not much else is real in your life and in some obscure way you sense that you are on your way to killing something inside you because only total despair will save you and you sense that you are Meursault with a history, Meursault after the fall of his God, and quite different from the Meursault of Camus in* The Stranger, *who has no history and hasn't read Kierkegaard's* Sickness Onto Death, *which bit you like a snake as you worked your way through the chapters about despair and all its variations, among which you recognized your version of despair as not being deep enough, of living in this strange desert where you can live only in the full anguish of your thirst, but you have no thirst, and so you keep walking away from the train station, where the late light of the afternoon throws a greenish gloom onto the glass ceiling above the tracks and that's when the prostitute steps into the taxi, her legs angled. And she rocks on her knees and opens her black leather jacket to reveal a red halter and then the whole maneuver just seems to freeze into one gesture of her sitting there in front of you, blocking your advance, blocking your retreat, and you nod, sensing nothing, and you can see in plain sight her thighs flash white as she reaches over and rocks her hand across your crotch to reveal your penis until she gives up and pulls back her hand and stares out the window and it is exactly that curving away of her body that chills you to the bone as your dying father turns his face away from your mother, a gesture that will haunt her for the rest of her short life and this can best be described as a terror you don't know of yet. Somehow, you manage to temper the chill in your heart with a vague hope that biology will take over and some muscled atavistic force will carry you away from this numbness, which still sears in you as the taxi rattles across some cobblestone streets and comes to a halt in front of a dimly lit bar located on the ground floor of a dark brick building. The prostitute knocks on the rear door and reaches around the corner to pull a key from a wooden board and you realize that her eyelids look like a turtle's, leathery and cragged, as she sticks the key into the lock, saying, "Call me Elsie," and as she leans into the door and enters the room and clicks on the center lamp in the ceiling, you now see the wide bed that's flanked by nightstands, and then there's the lamp, with her silky red underwear hung over the lampshade to dry, and you watch as she bends over—you can see the crack of her buttocks as her black skirt slides upward—and switches on the lamp, she tells you to lie down before she turns away from the bed and steps toward a chest of drawers and two chairs and asks you facetiously if you can undress yourself and then steps out of her mini skirt and takes off her jacket and you can see her bra now and now her naked body, which comes too close to you as you kneel awkwardly on the bed. The angling of her belly and that rocking movement she is putting on frightens you. She desperately tries to enliven your flaccid penis, which lies on your belly like a comatose snake, and then she starts asking if you are getting anywhere and that her time is limited and that's when you are finally able to admit to yourself that she is merely going through the motions, and then it will eventually stop. She rolls off the bed, mumbling that she never went through anything like this, and it all proves that your despair is deeper and never lessened by carnal desires, so as you pull your pants off the floor, she stays standing in the corner of the room, where a small window lets in some daylight and makes the room appear sickeningly bare and then she puts on her coat and waits and you know that she's longing for the company of predictable voices downstairs in the bar because she's frightened by you, frightened by what just happened, and how unnatural it was, but even so she must ask you for her pay. In the bar, she flicks a few dollar bills toward the bartender and orders a Bloody Mary, which seems like a soothing enough drink, and all of a sudden she looks up and makes eye contact with you and for a moment you feel convinced that she wants to reach out and hold your hand, to take pity on you, but there's no reason to believe that she would ever do this, considering how badly a lost cause you are, and now you must go, now you must enter the streetcar outside, and when you step in, you are comforted by the thud of the pneumatic door, as if there's a chance that it could bring you some closure.*

When I put the paper down, a thousand thoughts sprinted through my head. I bit my lip. I felt nauseated.

Was this the final thrashing about of a tortured soul?

I quickly retrieved Klaus's theater piece and reread the last word of the last line: "murderer," as well as the final stage direction: "A toddler is heard crying in a room nearby."

I paced my living room, fighting a sense of impending doom until long after midnight.

The next morning at the university, Genève took me aside and asked me if there was anything wrong with me. I looked distracted and aloof, she said, and that's when I told her that Klaus had sent me a disturbing letter.

"I have some questions of my own about this young man," she said. "Klaus's words at the café meeting after the performance were odd. Very odd. In any case are you free to talk this evening? We must meet to sketch out the curriculum."

"Yes. Yes. Sure."

"Yann! You could not possibly have forgotten that we needed to do that!"

"No. Surely not."

Later that evening, Genève came to my apartment to discuss the business of scheduling next semester's coming lectures. She also shared with me an idea that involved locally recreating Charlot's Bookstore the way it had existed in prewar Algiers, and she wanted to give it the original name: *Vraies Richesses*.

"We'd place you right up there on the balcony above the row of books where Camus would sit reviewing manuscripts," she said. "Guru on site!" she exclaimed.

When I didn't respond with even a smile, she asked what was wrong.

I slid down into my seat and reached for a lighter. "I am worried dead about Klaus." I handed Genève Klaus's theater piece and his most recent letter. Then I went out on the balcony and smoked.

I needed that cigarette more than anything.

When I returned to the living room, Genève looked concerned. I told her that I owed my life to Klaus's father, and how Klaus thought he was *The Stranger*. The more I talked, the more I could not stop talking. I told her about Klaus's isolation, about the recent death of his parents, about his total lack of friendships, about his odd obsessions.

She didn't interrupt me; she listened. But when I finished, I didn't feel relieved. Rather, I felt worse, as if I had fallen out of the present moment and into some timeless, empty abyss of dull indecision that allowed me to sink back into indifference.

Genève stood up and hugged me.

"You owe him one," she said. "Off to Munich."

Second Trip to Munich

The next morning, Genève and I stood outside our chairman's door.

"Any word from Klaus?" Genève asked.

"No," I said. "Nothing as of this morning, at least."

"Don't worry. You'll be in Munich before you know it. And if Gaspar gives you any grief about leaving, remember that I have your back."

Genève always seemed to know exactly what to say to me.

When Gaspar finally stepped into view, I experienced a strange sensation as I watched him walk down the hallway; it felt as though there was a clock hanging over my head, its second hand ticking with such brutal force that it made me feel nauseous.

"Genève and Yann," Gaspar said with a sigh. "How can I help you two this morning?"

I told Gaspar that I felt compelled to travel to Munich right away because I was worried about Klaus.

"And you," he said, turning to Genève. "You are ready to cover for Yann?"

"Yes, I can take over all of Yann's lectures. I'm fully prepared."

"Well then," Gaspar said. "Yann, go and take care of what you need to take care of so that you can return to Montpellier and concentrate on your job."

He patted my shoulder as Genève and I turned and left.

"Please keep me updated," Genève said. "But don't worry about your students, okay? They are in good hands with me."

On my drive to Munich, I didn't even make an attempt to phone Klaus. I couldn't tolerate imagining the hallway phone ringing off the hook or listening to Klaus trying to talk me out of this visit.

When I arrived that night at his apartment at the Waldfriedhof, Klaus seemed to be expecting my visit. He opened the door and barely looked at me.

"How did you get time off?" he asked, as if under obligation.

Klaus's eyes were swollen, and it was clear that he hadn't shaved since leaving Montpellier.

"I'm worried about you," I said.

Klaus's apartment was in disarray. Manuscripts were strewn across the floor and the bean chairs dotted with marker streaks. A half-eaten pizza lay on the floor in its pathetic box; the grease had eaten through the cardboard, giving it a glassy sheen. My eyes drifted once more toward the photograph hanging in Klaus's apartment—the one that showed Karl and Klaus sitting on the sharp pinnacle of a grass-covered mountain, Karl's hat casually draped over an ice pick.

"How come you guys used an ice pick?" I asked, pointing to the photo.

"It helped us hold onto that tricky mountain."

"Your father loved the mountains, didn't he?"

"The Höfatz was his Hausberg."

"Who took that photo of you two?"

"Some fellow climbers who were more experienced and better equipped."

"So...did you and your father climb together often?"

"Yes. Father was happiest when he was climbing, and I was happiest when I was climbing with him."

"Do you have any more photos from your adventures?"

Klaus proceeded to retrieve an old photo album from his bedroom.

"Take a look at these," he said.

Klaus turned the album's pages, showing me his collection of black and white photographs. Many were grossly overexposed, and others dark, out of focus, and smudged with fingerprints. But each was special to Klaus because it captured their happiness in the mountains.

Klaus recounted his adventures with his father and, while doing so, became so alive and animated that, at times, I had to interrupt and ask for explanations.

The massif of the Höfatz, he said, was known as the most beautiful in the Allgäu Alps; it resembled the majestic, triangular shape of the Matterhorn. But the Höfatz was also the most dangerous. Its slopes were steep and covered up to the peak with only grass. If you slid backward, nothing would stop your plunge—no Krummholz, no knee-pines, no dense undergrowth of cyclamen that covered other mountains at that altitude.

Klaus pointed to a photo of the Älpelesattel, a deep notch between two mountain peaks.

"When we made it to the halfway point, we incorrectly assumed that the sun had burnt off the dew," he explained. "From there, we reached the craggy spine of the ridge that led to the peak. But we made such slow progress because its upper part was devilishly steep and still considerably wet."

"So what happened?"

"We had to either crawl up the steep grass flank or climb into a dangerous ravine. Besides our ice picks, we had nothing: no pitons, no rope, no crampons."

"Wasn't that too much for you?" I asked. "I would have been intimidated by the mountain at your age."

"Yes, but that was my first big mountain excursion with my father. I felt the danger, but I also remember feeling safe because every time I slid backward, he'd push my feet up."

I pictured Karl protecting his son like he had protected me.

"It was late when we reached the peak," Klaus continued, "My father spread food on a small blanket for us. Dark bread,

Bretzen, radishes, Pressack, liverwurst, Opatzten and chunks of Emmenthaler. He always placed a special emphasis on food, and our food never tasted so good as on that afternoon." Klaus paused.

"But then my father told me we had to spend the night on the mountain because it was too late to descend. I can still remember watching the sun ...it was just above the western reaches of the Alps, then it slid behind a bank of low clouds above silvery Lake Konstanz. We could see the little thumb of the isle of Lindau jetting out from the coastline."

"What did you do about shelter for the night?" I asked.

"There was a primitive shelter a few yards down from the cross."

"A cross?"

"All the major mountain peaks in the Alps are topped with a wooden cross."

"The shelter," Klaus continued, "was nothing more than two wooden coffins bolted together, with a small opening between them and steel cables grounding them on all four sides. We lowered ourselves into the coffins and wrapped ourselves in blankets my father had carried in his backpack. I remember the wind whistling through the steel cables that held the cross. There was an opening between the two coffins, and he handed some schnapps through to me."

"Very nice," I said.

"The next morning, I stayed in the coffin, breathing in the scent of melting sap before crawling out and into the open. My father was up already."

We kept quiet for a while.

"Would you be up to climbing the Höfatz again?" I asked.

He looked at me suspiciously.

"I don't know. Maybe."

That night in Klaus's apartment, I slept fitfully. Drunken revelers kept shouting obscenities in the street and throwing stones at traffic signs; the sharp clinking of metal jarred me out of my drowsy state. Even the distant toll of the church bell—one beat for each quarter hour—tensed me up, as if it signified the beat of a metronome taking the pulse of my life.

When the morning light eventually seeped into the apartment, it cast light upon the dirty socks on the floor, smudged wine glasses, and one of Klaus's dog-eared manuscripts. I fingered for my watch on the floor and listened to Klaus's raspy snore. Then I tip-toed out of the apartment and walked to the coffee shop downstairs. I needed some time to think, not to mention breathe the aromas of coffee and baked goods wafting through the air.

An hour later, I carried two coffees and a few croissants upstairs, so Klaus and I could enjoy breakfast on the balcony.

"What do you remember about the war?" I asked.

"I remember the bunker at the neighbor's house, the musty air, and the uncovered concrete that oozed water," he said. "I remember my father lifting the iron hatch after an air raid and me, just behind him, staring into the red wall that rose on the horizon. Munich burning. From afar. Everything always from afar."

Were these memories of war—remote as they were—uncharted territory that continued vexing him? And, if so, how was he coming to terms with it all? Klaus didn't just consider himself a stranger, but *the Stranger*—the character from Camus's novel. *The Stranger* was distant and indifferent, and he always saw everything from afar. He was a man who might as well have pointed the gun on himself.

I took a deep breath.

"I have to leave soon," Klaus said. "I have some errands to run and I must help somebody with French lessons."

"What about your studies?"

Klaus got up and went inside. I took the tray with the empty cups and followed him.

"Klaus?" I asked.

"I quit," he said.

"You quit school?"

"Weeks ago."

I didn't know what to say.

"Listen," Klaus said, "late this evening, I've been invited to a fencing association's recruitment meeting. I'm allowed to bring a friend. Would you like to join me?"

The fact that he thought of me as a friend gave me a sense of relief. I was starting to see the sprigs of deeper connections.

"Sure," I said. "Let's go this evening."

We took the tram to the town's center, and Klaus seemed genuinely happy during the ride, asking me random questions and pointing out not-to-be-missed sights. It occurred to me that perhaps he was glad to have finally let me in on his pain.

When Klaus excused himself—to help a student prepare for his French exam, he said—I made the decision to visit the recently opened heated swimming pool. It was the talk of the town—the newspaper described it as a tropic lagoon, a perfect way to pass the time.

I spent most of the morning soaking in the heated open-air pool. As the sun strengthened—it was an unseasonably warm spring—I lay on the soft grass, giving myself over to lassitude, my ears to the ground, my mind drifting off to the distant rumbles of the far city and the dreamy cries of children playing. I had lunch at the swim-in bar and hoped that through the somnolence of a languid day I could forge some idea as to how to help Klaus.

Hadn't he given me a hint when he told me about the climbing excursions with his father?

When I left the pool, I took the tram downtown to visit Sport Scheck, the biggest sports outfitter in Munich. I met a seasoned mountaineer who worked there, and he said that he had climbed the Höfatz. He showed me a detailed map, gave me lots of advice, and sold me two pairs of adjustable crampons and two ice picks.

In the evening, I met Klaus for dinner at the Rathaus Weinstube. He didn't tell me much about how he had spent the day, but that was fine. It was my turn to talk.

"I want to climb Höfatz with you," I said.

"Climb the Höfatz?"

"The picture of you and your father and the stories you told me last night really got me interested."

"That climb with my father was dangerous."

"I have a solution."

"What do you mean?"

I showed Klaus the crampons that I had purchased.

"Les cramps," Klaus said, switching his dialect to French.

"You just said "cramps." What you meant to say was *crampons*."

That's when Klaus cackled in a way that I had never heard before, and though it was all trivial—all too trivial and trite—and though we both had shared a bottle of wine and I could write it all off as inebriation, I had a feeling that Klaus might open up and consider making some changes in his life. I hadn't proposed it yet ("Come to France! Come to France!"), but I was beginning to feel hopeful that Klaus would soon be happy to call France home.

The fencing session was to begin just before midnight. To pass the time until then, Klaus and I watched Antonioni's *L'avventurie*, a black and white Italian tear-jerker filled with tragedies, big gestures, and barren landscapes.

A few minutes before midnight, we walked down the stairs to a cellar located beneath a restaurant. Two combatants stood still, facing each other, and the outlines of their shoes were marked with chalk on the wooden floor once their required distance had been measured. The distance was established such that the tips of their swords—held with outstretched arms—could just barely reach their faces. I had witnessed one of these fencing sessions before—it must have been in the Thirties—and remembered that the duelists were to stand still, hold their swords overhead, and then swing them downward toward the opponent's face. The measured distance was so precise that nothing more than a superficial scar across the chin or cheek could possibly result. Repeated flinching or *recul* (they loved to use French words) would lead to some form of disqualification. Klaus and I watched as assistants circled around the two combatants, their movements choreographed by ancient runic rules.

I looked about the room with its low, smoke-stained wooden ceiling. The paneling on the walls was dark and cracked open in spots, revealing bricks underneath. This was no doubt a cheap knight's hall, and it reminded me of *The Song of the Nibelungs.*

Two fellows hammered a copper spigot into a keg of beer and lined up several dozens of glasses along the bar, carefully avoiding any clinking noises so as not to disturb the seamless preparations. Maybe it was the faded smell of spilt beer that had soaked for decades into the paneling and floorboards that suddenly gave me the vertiginous sense that I had seen this all before.

I walked to the back wall, from which a broken tin trough stuck out, its connecting copper tubes strung grey with spider webs. And then the recollection broke over me like a wave: I had been here before! In 1919, to be exact. In this very spot. I had witnessed the blood in the tin troughs and the beer kegs, and I had heard the cries of wounded soldiers piercing the bawling of drunken Freikorps soldiers.

After the battle in front of the Bahnhof Platz in Munich, I had tried to run over to Karl—I understood what he had done for me—but a group of soldiers pushed me away.

"You bastard!" one of them yelled. "Why would Karl save the life of a stupid asshole like you?"

They ripped my camera out of my hands, and one of them struck me with the butt of his gun. Meanwhile, Karl was carried away on a stretcher, and Freikorps soldiers swarmed into the nearby post office like ants. The firing had almost stopped. Flags were being waved out of the windows of the building, and I held my breath when I saw some soldiers dangle a combatant out the window, his upside-down body thrashing as the crowd below chanted, "Let him bounce!"

Groups of soldiers ran toward the Matthäser beer hall, gesticulating wildly as they overtook a group of medics carrying wounded soldiers in bulging canvasses. I followed, only to find an equally chaotic scene. The soldiers had pierced a wooden beer keg, and out flowed its contents. They made a game out of sliding beneath the spout for a drink, their mouths gaping. One drunk in particular filled his glove with the liquid, making as big a scene as possible. One other pulled down his pants and let the beer wash over his ass. Everybody laughed.

When the officers arrived, they tried to elbow their way between the drunkards, yelling, "Don't eat any sausages until the dogs tried them!" The dogs tore into the sausages thrown at them, and when finished, slinked away to lick the floor, sopping off the blood pouring from the soldiers' wounds as the soldiers groaned in pain and called out for their mothers.

As the wounded died, the drunk got drunker. Like bees swarming to their hive, the men clustered around the kegs, filled their steins, and saluted the dying.

I could not find Karl and did not want to draw attention to myself. Instead, I kept to myself in a corner, staying unnoticed until a group of officers burst into the beer hall, shouted commands, and fired shots into the ceiling. An officer spotted me and yelled, "There's some French prick waiting for you at the *Hotel Vier Jahreszeiten*. Get your ass out of here!"

Had I had a tail, like those blood thirsty dogs wandering around the hall, it would have been between my legs that evening.

Klaus must have noticed that I was in a daze. He rested his hand on my shoulder.

"Are you okay?" he asked.

"They brought your father here in 1919," I said. "It was a huge beer hall back then."

"Right here? Are you sure?"

"Yes."

"After he got injured?"

"I'll have to tell you more about that."

Klaus seemed bewildered and was eager to talk, but the German national anthem, "Deutschland Über Alles," began to play, and an orderly hushed us in no uncertain terms.

After the anthem, a parade of participants entered the scene: combatants, adjutants, sub-adjutants, knaves, water boys, swordsmen, tissue holders, and arbiters. The procession made for a sea of tussled swords and wide belly bands and feathered hats and caps adorned with skulls and hands in white gloves. Off to the side, two medics stood at their table with sutures and curved needles in hand.

The two combatants faced each other while being outfitted with protective steel glasses that would serve to shield their noses and eyes. They held their swords overhead, their elbows supported by their respective adjutants. This was a choreographed dance of violence.

During the third round, one of the fencers jerked his face back ever so slightly, indicating cowardice in the face of battle. The move led to long discussions between the arbiters and adjutants. They eventually agreed to resume the duel, but not without giving the combatant in question a stern warning.

The fifth round was by far the most action-packed; one of the combatants suffered a gaping gash in his cheek. The fight was stopped, and the medic called. The stitching of the wound was carried out in silence in the back of the room while the crowd waited for the wounded combatant to re-appear and give the "all clear" signal. When he did, both fencers stepped on top of a table in the middle of the floor, holding their overflowing steins in front of them.

Some elder with a deep voice offered the incantation.

"It is an honor to initiate this drinking competition, for which there will be no winner," he said. "May honor and tradition be upheld, and may Germany live forever! Heil!"

The combatants emptied their steins with long, sustained gulps before triumphantly holding them up in the air. The arbiters inspected the competitors' steins, solemnly declared them empty, and with a rising chorus of hoarse voices, the carousing began.

There were no women here. These men were afraid of real women; they were afraid of insecurity, ambiguity, of questions left dangling ...afraid of what was natural and moist and warm. These men built dams and wrote novels about nurses in white coats who attended to dying soldiers. And they wrote about the mess of Communist women who bled like pigs in the trenches of Riga, and when peace set upon the lands again, these men fled to Munich's dark beer caves to take part in hours of ecstatic inebriation, which in the clear of the coming day would again be set against the stiff and regulated camaraderie, black leather boots, strict rules, chalk lines on the floor, tussled swords, and sacred words and traditions. They were prepared to keep the faith, keep dissolution in check—at least until another cataclysmic war could come and ease the tension.

After the Munich revolution, I had written about the Freikorps. My writings allowed me to better understand how hollow and distant the words of those Freikorps soldiers were, and how pain and disillusion cast a sickening spell over post-war Europe. The war had torn their minds asunder, had filled their hearts and souls with a brew of hate, aggression, and murder. Thus, across those threatening waters, they had built their dams and their symbols: white nurses in their sterile uniforms, and men standing unflinching in the face of death. When inchoate feelings crept up on them, they numbed those feelings through rituals and incantations that reached back a thousand years.

When two orderlies began casting sawdust onto the floor with wide and confident arcs of their hands, it made me think of peasants spreading seeds. A drunken assistant, his feathered hat slit back enough to reveal the scar across his forehead, stepped in front of me and blurted, "En garde!" His scanted smile melted off his face when I responded, "Touché." And that was the end of the festivities. Bleary-eyed young men shuffled up the stairs into the day's soapy first light.

A recruiting assistant cornered Klaus on our way out. "I hope our group convinced you of our values, of how we will raise our fatherland back to its destined glory and power," the man said, reaching out to shake Klaus's hand. "Can I be reassured that I shall hear from you? Our stern and unwavering defense of the values of our fatherland will guide you, especially during this difficult time of loss."

To my disgust, Klaus shook the man's hand.

"I thank you," Klaus said. "You will hear from me, I assure you. Your display of bravery and friendship has greatly impressed me."

The assistant handed Klaus a brochure, and then lumbered up the stairs.

I fought a baffled sense of defeat and couldn't hold my tongue.

"They are all idiots. Nothing but blood and sawdust! Don't you realize that all we witnessed in that musty dungeon was a game of charades?"

"They stand for something," Klaus said. "There is order, and there is chivalry."

When I looked into Klaus's eyes, I saw a sullen face and empty eyes that could not hook into life. I couldn't stand it anymore. I felt irritated, and I started yelling.

"You told me that you are *the stranger.* You told me that you are not home in this world. Life is a festering wound, you said. Reality chafes you. And you never feel what you are yearning to feel. Something needs to change, Klaus. Something needs to change, and fast."

Life wasn't flowing strong in Klaus; he hadn't seen the dance. Something carried me off. There, amidst the poplar trees, standing in the grey of an ordinary morning, my voice continued to rise.

"Those pale-faced kids in that musty cellar don't want to face anything. They convince themselves that being able to unblinkingly stare at a lowering blade gives them knighthood, but all they are doing is denying that they are empty. They spin out bizarre cults and run dark dreams of hate so they can continue to deny, deny, deny. They have no roots in life but only death!"

"*The Stranger* is empty, too," Klaus said.

"Empty, sure, but he recognizes the truth."

"God condemns him. Man despises him."

"No," I said. "He is man who cannot lie, who cannot pretend. He is a man without ideology."

We had come to a stop in front of a café.

"Let's go in and have a seat," I said.

Klaus appeared bled white by some inner turmoil. We sipped our coffees in silence and stared at passersby.

When I felt prepared to say more, I leaned across the table as I cupped my coffee like a sacred potion. I wasn't through just yet.

"Klaus, the German Nation once erupted into feeling—feeling as a value by itself—and they called it the Romantic Age, and it wasn't before long that they sharpened it with their demand for ultimate intensity and purity. They called on the God of Laodicae, sprung from the feverish sayings of zealots. But God was dead, and still there was this fever. So, they created a piper who was to lead them out of the valley of indifference. They revived myths and instilled hate and resentments so that the nation would feel again. Feeling, you know, Erlebnis, excitement, the pulse of the Lord!"

"What are you talking about?" Klaus interrupted, his face appearing redder by the second.

"Listen to me, Klaus. Are you listening to me?" I was almost yelling. "Meursault looks through all of this."

"Meursault is empty. He is the evil. He is what has to be fought against."

"No! No! Camus said that Meursault is the Jesus Christ we need."

Klaus flung his head back and pushed his chair away from the table. A rejection of everything I had said poured into his posture. But ticking in the background of this moment in the café in Munich was a clock I was not privy to—a clock that summoned humiliations, confusions, and painful absences. And so it was that Klaus's incredulity had begun to fizzle.

I took a deep breath.

"A man who stares at his soul and sees a wound, sees emptiness, nothingness ...he is authentic ...he is lucid."

Klaus remained silent.

"The whole history of the world should be rewritten as man fighting the intrusion of emptiness, as man's reaction to the silence of everything around us and to the flight of meaning. Only when you feel bled dry by some cold wind blowing in from some corner of the universe ...only then are you a man, Klaus, and only then are you with the living as well as the dead."

Klaus sank his gaze. I had gone too far.

I paid for our coffees and called a taxi to drive us to Klaus's apartment. We both slumped into the backseat; Klaus fell asleep within minutes. The long night—and our tense conversations—had finally taken their toll.

When I awoke the next morning, I found Klaus standing in the middle of the living room in his hiking boots with the crampons clamped on.

"A climb on the Höfatz might not be such a bad idea." A restrained smile crossed his face as he walked toward me, for the moment forgetting that the spikes were leaving a trail of clefts in the floor.

"Damn!" He set boots and clamps aside and assessed the damage, shaking his head in disbelief.

"How could I have been so stupid? My landlord is surely going to notice."

"Don't worry. Maybe we can fix it later," I said.

And hopefully, I thought, you won't be living in this apartment too much longer anyway.

Klaus pointed to the large photograph on the wall that showed him and his father on the Höfatz.

"You know, when my father was photographed, he made a point to only show the side of his face that had not been burned. That scar was just too prominent. But in this picture, he didn't seem to mind. You can see his scar clearly."

"It's a picture of truth," I said.

Klaus nodded.

"My father climbed the Höfatz often, and he thought it was one of the best ways to spend time with his friends," he said. "But the man my father considered his closest friend—the friend who used to climb mountains with him—eventually stopped talking to him."

"The friend in the photo you showed me in the album?"

Klaus nodded.

"Why?"

"Apparently, they had a falling out over Hitler's politics."

"I see. Well, if you are taken in by that beer-fueled dueling we witnessed last night, you and I might have a falling out, too."

"They're trying pretty hard to recruit me."

"I know."

As we prepared our hiking gear Klaus tossed a bottle of schnapps into his bag.

"Not many people I know could sleep soundly in a coffin without a little schnapps," he explained.

I laughed, and our moods lightened in unison.

Höfatz

Following the advice I received from the mountaineer at Sport Scheck, Klaus and I took a taxi to Obersdorf and made our way to a primitive chalet near the base of the Höfatz.

The company picked us up at the train station with a Puch Geländewagen and drove us to the Alpine dairy, whose owners had a few primitive beds available for overnight guests. That evening, both the young and the elder Alpine herdsmen drove up and sat down with us. They said they were preparing the hut for the flock of sheep's summer grazing.

"What do you think about us taking on the Höfatz?" Klaus asked one of the elder herdsmen.

"I think it's a bit early in the season to go up there," he said. "I hope you two know what you are doing."

"Look," I said, pointing at my hiking boots. "We've got crampons and everything."

"Good," he said. "I see you've also got your ice picks. It's good to be prepared."

"We're even prepared to seek shelter in the coffins up there," Klaus said.

"How do you know about the coffins?"

"I've climbed the Höfatz before," Klaus said.

"Must have been a few years ago then."

"It was. How did you know?"

"The coffins started to deteriorate years ago, and they haven't been in use since."

The man instructed his son to retrieve some beer from the ice cellar.

"I reckon you're ready to tell me some of your stories," the man said, extending his hand. "By the way, my name is Alex Sebald and this is my son, Reinhold."

In addition to sharing their beer, the herdsmen offered us a large plate of cheese and meats. We tucked in late that evening, but not before Alex and Reinhold bid us farewell and good luck.

Our hike commenced the next morning, and our first rest stop took place on the Älpelesattel. There, we ate some of the Landjäger with rough pieces of dark bread, and we each took a swig of cherry schnapps.

"So far so good," Klaus said.

When we reached the steep part of the mountain, we took another break and attached the crampons to our boots. Klaus and I walked around for a few minutes to get used to the feeling. This was the steep and technical part of our climb, and we were making good time. And what a relief it was to find that the grass was dry enough to give us a good hold.

On our way up the steep, grassy slope, I spotted a few Edelweiss flowers sticking out from rocky crags. That flower reminded me of Karl. It was the flower he had artfully encased in amber and given to Madeleine as gift.

Klaus and I took our time; the slope was nearly thirty degrees, and it stressed our calf muscles.

We reached the peak shortly after noon. I looked around for the two coffins that Klaus spoke of and was disappointed to find that what the herdsmen had said was true: they had been rotting. It was nonetheless interesting to see their deeply rilled wooden sides slicing a rectangle outline into this rare, level spot. I thought about how, for years, mountaineers sat and rested on these wooden sides. Though the coffins were now filling with rocks and soil, I marveled at the idea they might still give shelter to an unfortunate climber forced to stay the night.

When we sat down, Klaus pointed out to me all the surrounding peaks, including Hammerspitze, Nebelhorn, and Grosser Daumen.

"That name ...Hammerspitze ...it sounds quite aggressive, doesn't it?" I asked. "And it translates to hammer and pickaxe, right?"

"Yes, it does," Klaus said. "That's how the Germans make their philosophy: with a hammer and a pickaxe."

An oblique smile hung on Klaus's face for a while.

We sat down with our backs pressed against the cross, which was secured with a set of new-looking tie-downs. Our meal consisted of ham, sardines, dark bread, radishes, and cheese, which we washed down with water and a measure of cherry schnapps.

"Yann look at this," Klaus said.

He pulled a print from his pocket; it was the photo of him and his father on the mountain. Klaus canvassed the panorama surrounding us, pivoting as he held the photo print firmly in front of his eyes.

"Right over there!" he pointed. "That's where my father and I sat for our photo. Can we take a picture of us both sitting right there? What do you say?"

I had with me my Leica and an extra-slow delay trigger for the wire release.

We placed the camera between some small rocks, triggered the release, and then crawled along a narrow ridge to a nearby mound. I returned and took several exposures, just to be sure we'd get the shot.

That Klaus had insisted on taking a picture of us where he had sat years ago with his father made me feel lighthearted and grateful.

We remained the only ones on the peak that afternoon. And though the herdsman had told us that the coffins were "out of use," we lay down dozing inside their shallow rims where we were cradled away from the wind.

When we woke up, Klaus made a grand gesture of taking off his hat, looking inside it, and then twirling it in an odd way before placing it back on his head.

"Reminds you of anybody?" he asked.

"Vladimir?"

"As in Vladimir in *Waiting for Godot*?"

"Yes."

"Great," he said. "Here are your lines."

He handed me a few pieces of paper that were bound together.

"What?"

"I present to you my version of *Waiting for Godot*. You are playing Estragon today, so please take off your shoes."

Klaus looked determined, and as absurd as this situation was, I felt obligated to play along.

"We have to go on," I improvised. "We are grounded here as we stand."

"Grounded in coffins."

"In death, the oldest wound."

I bent down as if to take off my shoes. "A wound. Let's step out of the coffins!"

"I can't," he said.

As singing sound was coming off the cross's metal tie-downs.

"Was it the one on the right who got lifted to Heaven to see Jesus that very day?" Klaus asked.

"So says Luke, but none of the others mention the episode."

"It is the episode where Jesus promises eternal peace and eternal life."

"Jesus promises deliverance on the same day," I said.

"Deliverance from what?"

"Hell!"

"You should say death!"

"But he says hell."

"Who says hell?"

"Luke!"

"That's enough," I said, surprised by how quickly we had invented our own version of Beckett's play without having read from the script.

"Not bad!. Now take a look at the title!"

And there it was, in Klaus's unmistakable handwriting: *Enough of Godot.*

"The first line's for you, Estragon!" he said.

I looked at the script and hesitantly began to read Estragon's lines.

E: Like the scene in Waiting for Godot.

V: Too much for one tree!

E: We need a cross.

V: Which consists of two trees.

E: Up here on the mountain peak?

V: Crosses are everywhere.

E: Right. Just like silence, boredom, and having too much void between feelings.

V: Or no feeling or—or emptiness.

E: Emptiness is the ground of Being.

V: Oh! How original, Estragon!

I paused for a moment because the thought came to me that Being might just be grounded in the bottom of a coffin.

"Continue!" Klaus said.

E: So we think there is nothing and then they prove that even empty space has something in it ...some weird quantum fluctuation ...and that the whole universe or the conglomerate of what we can imagine or see or dream of is never nothing—and why should it be?—the beginning of the universe is from nothing but not really, as there is no nothing—have I said that?—and so it is on us from the beginning of time to never think of nothing.

V: Which we do right now.

E: Don't the wise men keep thinking, Why there is something rather than nothing?

V: Which of course is something.

E: Something filling the void between the times when they do not ask this question.

V: Have you studied philosophy, Estragon?

E: Something filling the void between feeling nothing.

V: Didn't you just say that?

E: With all the privileges bestowed on me by my education ...so I did!

V: But how can you fill the void between feeling nothing?

E: Feeling nothing can be changed to something.

V: And that would be?

E: Putting yourself in despair about feeling nothing.

V: Something tells me that would be something.

E:But there's a problem.

V: I see it. I see it. Give me time to think, Estragon! ...Because that despair might just not be enough of something.

E: But nothing again!

V: So you would have to replace it with something again which would be...

E: Despair about feeling nothing.

V:You are a great interpreter of the Copenhagen school of philosophy.

E:Despair eating despair eating despair...

V:Which would lead to...

E: Finish it all.

V:Or step out of the coffin and leave the stage. These were the last lines Klaus quoted—the last lines of the script.

We silently stepped out of the coffins, gathered the manuscripts, and put them back into the backpack.

"You wrote that piece just days ago?" I asked.

"Yes."

"At the end Vladimir leaves the coffin, doesn't he?" I looked at him. "Will you leave and come with me?"

"I will come to France with you."

"Come closer to the sun," I said.

Klaus nodded, and then turned and walked toward the cross. He sat down at its base. The wind whistled as it blew across the steel ties holding the cross in place. I picked up some stones and rolled them around inside my palm, listening to the clicking sounds as they collided.

Third Part

Munich to Saint Zacharie

Late afternoon I leave the Auto Route north of Avignon and take the road toward L'Isle-sur-la-Sorgue. We are not taking the direct route to Montpellier, but rather a detour to Lourmarin and L'Isle-sur-la-Sorgue, which is where Camus spent many weeks near the end of his life.

The mountains are distant here; the flat country is criss-crossed by irrigation canals and stern lines of poplars that fragment the plain.

Klaus folds and refolds the Michelin map. He seems restless. Only days ago, we stood on a mountain in the Alps. Since then, Klaus has changed his life with a resolve and speed that astonishes me. Storing the few pieces of furniture, signing papers, gathering his application documents all that took just days. When he stepped into my car back in Munich, he hollered, "Let's go! Let's get to the coast!" He was finally reaching out to soothe his soul.

Père Benoît has contacted me through university channels—the message reached me in Munich—and proposed to meet in Cassis. I have not seen him in years and gladly said yes. Our meeting, however, will not take place for days, providing time to visit the countryside Camus loved so much ...the countryside where Camus found peace, where he met his friends.

I tell Klaus that the poet René Char, a very close friend of Camus's and a well-known Resistance fighter, lived in these villages, writing poetry while he was on the run from the German Special Services. Char was a magician of insecurity, I tell him, holding out against the weight of history.

"Magician of insecurity," Klaus repeats. This description strikes him, and he churns over the meaning as he sits stiffly in his seat beside me. We drive deeper into the wide valley. As we progress, the mountains that rim the horizon seem to recede as if to offer a kind of respite. I do not know why I think this way. Anticipation of the sea, maybe.

"I'd love to pull that off," he says.

"Pull off what?"

"Live and conquer anxiety through poetry."

"Poetry is magic," I say. "But life is more. Camus admired René Char's closeness to real combat, the nights in the mountains evading Special Services units, lighting gasoline-soaked sand to guide the Lysander planes down into the valley."

"Poetry of combat," Klaus says. He speaks in short phrases now, which is new. In Munich, he talked effusively, spilling words and thoughts in tangles, but now he lets the meaning set in before he ratchets to the next word. I am reminded of Karl talking about the copper mine in Sweden, where he became frightened by the rack of mechanical reality.

We stop in L'Isle-sur-la-Sorgue at a restaurant with a terrace reaching out over a small channel of water. A waterwheel's wooden paddles slap the water, discharging the flow in streaks of foam. The sun is cresting distant rims, and the chatter of voices eases the tiredness of a long drive into a dreamy cadence. I don't want to leave, even as the sun slips away and the wet smell of grasses bordering the water drifts up in cool pockets of air. I let Klaus do the ordering; he enjoys his considerable fluency in French and smiles. I feel at ease, but later, when we reach our bed and breakfast at the Route D'Aups, I sense that Klaus is restless. He acts as if he wants to say things that only now are edging into his mind.

"Tell me more about that cathedral my father tried to build," he says.

"There are only some walls and a half-built tower standing," I reply, and continue to describe the mountain crest and its very barrenness. "Not much left there."

The next morning after breakfast, I phone Genève for really no reason. She tells me that I might enjoy some additional time away from campus. Sometimes I can't help but wonder if she thinks it best that I keep my distance, that my presence at the University is no longer essential, that I am to become a relic.

"Take it slow," she says.

Before I hang up the phone, I begin to realize why I called her; I desperately wanted to hear that I am needed, that the courses without Professor Yann are just not the same.

It didn't happen.

I decide to book a room for another night. Klaus and I use the morning hours to visit Le Rebanqué, an old stone barn in the hills above Lagnes where Camus spent many of his summers before moving to Lourmarin. Lavender is grown here. It climbs the gentle hills, its scent mingling with the perfume of orange blossoms. As we drive the road to Apt, the fields of lavender snake up the hills in blue streaks, bursting millions of spikes and blossoms. Soon I find Palerme, the house Camus had rented for a few summers. Workers are busy restoring façade and foundation; just a few months after Camus's death, a minor industry is being built around his name. And somewhere in these hills, in front of some stone house, Camus shook the hand of a most trusted friend, Henri Mathieu, on that fateful third day of January.

Klaus and I walk narrow paths lined by oak trees and apple orchards before we break out into the open lavender fields. We enjoy a spare lunch on the roadside. I watch the sky, a deep blue—*lapis lazuli*—the most appreciated and expensive color in the palettes of medieval painters.

I can see more signs of lightening in Klaus's face, his lips less tense, his cheeks drawn higher, his eyes wider. A kind of ascension has taken place.

"I never imagined this to be his landscape," Klaus says.

"Camus found a connection with Algeria in this mountain-rimmed plain the locals call sweet and tough, a land that never is somber or dark."

"I can imagine how he felt about Prague and how sadness tore his heart."

I thought of the darkness in Rattenberg, and that morning when the police stood by heavy oak tables asking questions. I thought of the cloth barely having been drawn across the body of the child the mother has stifled in despair. And I thought of the rain-splattered facades in Munich, the frozen snow piles on the sidewalks. What is a man who lives with sea and full sky in his face, and what is a man in cities where skyscrapers pencil shadows? I remember 1939, when Camus led me up to the small balcony atop Charlot's bookstore and pointed to the small sliver of sea in the distance. Later, he wrote that the sea taught him that suffering was not all to life.

I do not want to leave this checkered, fragrant plain.

After we walk the river that encircles the center of town, giving it the name "The Venice of the Luberon," Klaus and I return to our restaurant in L'Isle-sur-la-Sorgue. Klaus buys a notebook in the restaurant's gift shoppe. I gift him my favorite pen from Faber Castell.

"My contribution," I say.

Klaus starts writing at our table overlooking the river.

"I'll show you the first page," he says.

I begin to read: "I feel like Camus on his train ride from Prague to Venice. Waiting for the cries of the gulls, the first olives trees, the first flat vines against the walls, dusty fig trees. (I must reread! I must memorize these pages!)"

I hand the notebook back to Klaus and tell him that I like what he wrote.

We hear the hoarse cry of seagulls that evening. "They come with the fish trucks," the waiter tells us.

During our drive the next morning, I lose my way near Bonnieux and turn west by accident. But Klaus and I make the most of it by eating a second breakfast at a corner café that seems to face every direction at the same time. Klaus pulls out his notebook again, but this time doesn't invite me to read his freshly scribbled words. The sun slants in pleasantly.

When I negotiate the first tight curves climbing into the mountains, with the Renault leaning wildly, Klaus starts yodeling in high-pitched guttural sounds that I have only before heard on recordings. He does not get it right. It seems displaced and touches me in a strange way.

As we enter Lourmarin, we park the car outside the center and right away walk the *La Grande rue de L'eglise* to see the house Camus bought in 1958 with the money he received from winning the Nobel Prize. We stand in front of the narrow façade, hemmed in by the adjacent houses with barely a space between. Klaus inquires if one even can walk between the walls. The street is narrow, and every building is a fortress. The windows of Camus's house are slits with faded green shutters. The house doesn't stand out.

"How could he choose this cramped site?" Klaus asks.

"Wait until you see the other side when we visit the castle."

The view from the castle proves that Camus must've chosen the site for the garden, which gently slopes down into a plain. From there, he had a beautiful panoramic view. He essentially had both worlds: the village of man and the wide-open sky and view of the mountains.

I ask him to guess what Camus's house had been originally used for and, of course, he doesn't guess that it was a silk farm. Klaus, however, doesn't even seem to be interested in the details. It seems he'd rather just breathe the air and enjoy the sights.

We venture on to a restaurant called Ollier. This is where Camus liked to drink his favorite cocktails. Klaus is quiet, but his eyes take in every frame. Often, he seems to retreat into some sullenness. Except that it isn't; it is more like the hem of unhappiness giving way; and that's when he writes in his notebook.

As we leave Lourmarin, Klaus points out a blue line he has drawn on the Michelin map that—to my surprise—connects the most winding roads across the most rugged mountain ranges to our destination: Plan-D'Aups-Sainte-Baume.

Initially, Klaus had wanted to reach the coast as quickly as possible; that was before he changed his mind. Now it is me who insists on the direct valley route through Aix-En- Provence. However, accidents and stretches of road work slow us down, and Klaus keeps making snorting noises and shaking his head.

I open the sunroof, and Klaus eventually falls asleep despite the stop-and-go traffic. When he wakes up, he reaches for his copy of *The Stranger*.

"Yann, do you remember what you told me in Munich?"

"We were both drunk."

"You said every sentence in *The Stranger* has meaning." Klaus opens his copy of *the Stranger,* which he has highlighted in places.

"Where I grew up in Saint-Brieuc, we had friends who made a habit out of opening the Bible at random, selecting a sentence or two, and then spinning the words into some interpretation that would guide their lives that day or week or month."

"My father used Marcel Proust's works to find some deep connection to 'the all'" I continue. "That's what he called it, at least. He and the others believed that every word contained a universe of meaning."

Klaus has been riffling through the pages of *The Stranger.* "I found the quote," he exclaims. "It didn't mean anything. Besides, you always feel a little bit guilty."

"That's one of the few places Camus uses the word 'guilty. Meursault says these words after his girlfriend, Maria, learns that his mother died just days before," I explain. "And remember how they keep laughing through a Fernandel movie? There are some passages where Meursault hints at emotion, but here I would say he is just shrugging his emotions off as inconvenient and wearisome and inauthentic. I think he's trying to say that they are common and not genuine to the individual."

"Meursault is authentic when he has no emotion," Klaus says.

"Right."

"Camus never was this way."

"Because Camus was afraid of that."

"Of being the 'Stranger'?"

I lift my right hand off the steering wheel to hold him off. "There is a passage where Camus writes in the nuptials: 'Yet even here I know that I shall never come close enough to the world.' And in another passage he writes: 'To balance an inborn tendency to indifference, I was thrown between misery and the sea.'"

"The sun," Klaus corrects me.

I startle. I am losing my edge. Now I can't stop thinking about Genève, how lively and competently she has taken over some of my lectures.

Klaus looks down on the book on his lap. "How could this book, published in 1942, grow into a bible for the resistance? "he asks. "After all, it describes profound indifference, and it doesn't rise above it."

Klaus's question is valid. I've always been puzzled by how *The Stranger* could incite motivation to resist the Nazis. I do not remember talking of *The Stranger* to Madeleine in any detail, but maybe I did. What I do know is that I did not follow the call when I read the book in 1943.

I choke and clear my throat. I need to answer him, say something.

"Morvan Lebesque is a writer who recently gave a talk at the University," I say. "He is from Breton, and he's currently working on a biography of Camus. He and I have talked about this effect of *The Stranger.* Morvan believes that the book, in showing the life of a coward, ignites in the reader the will to resist ...except, of course, that Meursault was no coward. What you think? I must admit that it remains unclear to me."

"The very notion of cowardice is based on the command 'you should,'" Klaus says. "And nothing of that is in the first part of *The Stranger*. Death at the beach changes that. In my opinion, the novel has two parts."

Klaus is right on, I think.

We are finally passing by the site of the accident that has had held us up. Three overturned cars, an oil slick on the road. The ambulance—a boxy Renault—reminds me of the coroner's van I saw in Rattenberg.

A gendarme speaks to us through the open window and warns of more delays ahead. Something dark settles and corners me. I change my mind and decide to head toward the roads that Klaus has outlined on the map. I turn around at the first occasion, take a shortcut, and drive into the mountains.

Soon we're weaving up mountains and descending into plains, taking on range after range, slowly getting closer to the Sea.

Saint-Zacharie to Cassis

We make it to Saint-Zacharie that evening and find a suitable bed and breakfast. From this town, we must cross just one more range to reach Plan-d'Aups-Sainte Baume.

Klaus loves maps, loves to trace the roads, anticipate hills and curves and valleys, but when I spread the Michelin map and trace the windy road across the mountains from Saint-Zacharie to Plan-d'Aups-Sainte Baume, he barely pays attention. He has a stomach ache, he says.

Klaus informs me that he does not want to have dinner this evening; he'd rather go upstairs and lie down. He says he feels nauseated and keeps pushing his fist into his stomach.

At dinner in the dining room, I am almost alone; only two older couples are present. After my meal, I stop to check on Klaus and find him in a deep sleep. When I return to the terrace, I notice I am all alone now. The owner brings cheese to my outdoor table and invites me for an drink. It is a warm evening. We sit down on the porch, where he serves fried caramels and Pernod. He is in his fifties—a stout figure indeed. His skin runs in folds below his eyes; his cheeks are chafed and rubbed raw by the wind and sun. Life has worn him out, but his eyes flicker with a sudden energy. I can imagine him in a field of wheat, throwing out his scythe.

"I overheard you talking about Camus earlier," he says. "Everybody here is shocked about his death. And you might know that he spent the best time of his later life right here in our mountains."

"My friend and I both love Camus," I say.

"I noticed your friend's accent."

"Yes. He's German and will study in Montpellier."

"Just a bit more than a two-hour drive."

"We plan to make a stop in Cassis." I lift my glass. "To Camus."

"His last months were spent in the company of René Char, so let's also lift a glass for Camus's friend—the war hero, the poet, the lover."

"I suspect Camus envied him for his courageous fight with the Resistance? Being in the thick of it."

"René was fighting the Germans in this area, but even he could not prevent the boches from killing civilians."

He sweeps his hand in the air, as if to trace the mountain-rimmed plane. In the last slant of the sun, the water in the irrigation canals shines a silvery-white.

"The SS stood them up against the slope of the canal, shot them, and let their bloated bodies drift through town."

"You had to witness that?"

He nods, and then puts his hands onto the railing, as if our conversation has physically weakened him.

"I worked for the Marseille diocese during that time," I say.

"Yes! 'That time!' This is the dread underneath everything, the black seed, the words that gnaw at our age."

"I helped with the smuggling, too," I say. "I falsified transit papers and passports."

"I heard that this was very effective."

"It was. Until the Germans caught on."

"How did you do it?"

"A group of Jewish artists worked with me in secret."

"What happened to them?"

"Most escaped over the French-Spanish border."

"And then?"

"The Germans got rabid. Armed resistance was necessary."

His large body turns towards me; his face comes out of the shadows.

"The biggest action near here was when they blew up the Lysander," he says.

"That was the type of plane that flew in most of the allied supplies..."

"And the Germans could never get their hands on one until end of 1943, when one crashed not far from here. The next days, the SS was swarming all over the place. It was as ugly a plane as you could think of, but there must have been something about it that it could fly so well under their radar. I think it was built of wood."

"You may be right," I say.

"Just three men fit into the Lysander. You could get it down on half a soccer field."

"I've been told that."

"It took the Boches some time to disconnect the wings. They brought in two half-tracks and one of those eight-wheelers. The Resistance fighters knew they had to ambush the convoy before it could reach the main highways in the Rhone Valley. I worked as a lookout then, and had to stay on a mountaintop for two miserable, cold nights. The Germans secured the whole area, but any delay would work for the Resistance because, so they told us, the British had beached a supply of heavy machine guns on the coast. With all the German armor gathered in the small area, the Resistance fighters needed the heavy machine guns. But they never came."

Something dry heaves into my throat. I suddenly cannot look into the man's eyes.

The Germans surrounded the plane with heavy armor and the fighters had no artillery. The Resistance fighters thought of blocking the road with a flock of sheep, but the shepherds didn't want to have anything to do with it. Herd sheep across the road to block a SS convoy? We all will wind up dead in a ditch, the shepherds told them. So they had to herd the sheep themselves and had to face heavily armed Germans ...and let me tell you, these Germans were rabid."

"You stayed on the mountain?" I ask.

"That was my order."

"Nobody survived?"

"Nobody."

I listen to the rustling sound of the small creek that passes by the porch. I yearn for calm and peace.

The owner takes a long drink from his Pernod, breathing audibly.

"It's difficult to talk about," he says.

"And difficult to hear."

"Did you know that they received help from railroad workers who had joined the Resistance? At a railroad crossing, there was a water station where they could position a steam engine without causing suspicion. They would pack the engine with sandbags and ram the blocked convoy."

He continued with a raspy voice.

"It was a beautiful morning, with dew on the flowers in the fields. When the leading halftrack crossed the railroad, the sheep panicked and slid sidewise down the roadside, and the soldiers on the halftracks started firing into the flock. The resistance fighters advanced the steam engine into the crossing. They opened fire. Then the Germans opened up. Steam exploding. The canvas covering the plane flew off in tattered shreds. Somebody threw incendiaries. The side of the mountain erupted in dust. Bleeding sheep lay spread on the road, mouths gaping, bleating with pain, their legs shot off. They say that a woman fighter had been hiding among the sheep and held on to their hides, and that the sheep dragged her back into the hills." He holds his breath and bites his lips. "But nobody knows for certain."

A sudden vertigo throws me back into my chair.

"Are you okay?"

"Yeah."

"Are you sure? You look quite pale ...can I get you a glass of water?"

I wave him off.

"A woman?"

"Yes, a woman."

"What was her name?"

"Her code name was Fox. That's all I know. Why do you ask?"

A sudden recognition. I can't breathe.

"Are you all right?" he asks again.

I nod.

"After the war, I spotted a woman walking through the hills, sometimes carrying a little girl on her back. This always perplexed me. She never talked to anybody, but I sense she was on a mission to find the Fox."

I slump over and set my elbows onto my knees. I can't talk; all life has spun out of me. I find some excuse to go to bed and bid the owner farewell. Back in my room, I keep staring at the ceiling with dry eyes.

I toss and turn long into the night, try to slide into some sleep, but his story haunts me.

Klaus does not wake up when I put on my shoes and leave our room. I pray that with each step I can ease the guilt that reaches inside me with an icy fist. I start walking along the irrigation canal toward the mountains. I walk, not paying attention, tottering as if to give drowning death a chance. I could drown like those women and children who, decades ago, tumbled into the water that runs below. I keep stumbling over bunches of grass, and I find myself running across the dry land and then standing still and listening to dogs barking. I cannot lose myself under this sky, which will forever speak of my failure to bring in the heavy machine guns, without which the courageous fighters had no chance to penetrate the German armor. I think of Madeleine, of the moments we had together gazing out over the Mediterranean and waiting for silver to spread across the water. As I look around, the moonlit bands of irrigation canals seem like metal bands cutting the landscape, and I sense nothing—nothing but an empty hum. I want to feel Madeleine's hand on my shoulder again, her cheeks on mine. I want to hear Madeleine's chortle as we kissed and her cursinu dog came sliding in between us, wagging his tail.

I sit on top of one of the levies and rub my palms across my eyes.

When I return to the bed and breakfast, Klaus is still sleeping soundly. The morning hours do eventually bring me a short rest.

At breakfast, I ask the innkeeper if we can stay another night.

"Yes," he says, "and if it is of any interest to you, I marked the site we talked about yesterday. It is almost on your way to Cassis. You could easily drive there today."

He opens a regional Michelin map and marks the site in red. The color of blood.

"I better stay here," I say.

"I'll take care of your young friend," the innkeeper offers. "If anything would happen to him, I know the local doctor well. The doc and I have a deal, you see: life-long medical treatment for my family, and life-long free wine for his crew. He got the better deal so far.

"Think of it. You, too, look kind of peaky," he continues. "If you want to sit down at the brook, that might help. Are you sure you are not coming down with the same bug?"

At the innkeeper's suggestion, I walk down the meadow to the brook and find a hammock. The gentle rustling of the brook lulls me to sleep. I wake on and off, with memories of Madeleine pushing into my mind. And I feel guilty that such memories do not destroy me, feel guilty that indifference and numbness take hold of me so easily.

It is afternoon when the owner serves me and Klaus a concoction he has named "Lazarus": scrambled eggs with morita chipotles, and tomato juice with vodka on ice.

"You both will rise," he jokes, and indeed, his secret concoction does the job.

Klaus now declares himself cured and ready to join me on the road, and I decide to leave that afternoon. When we reach hands through the car window to say good-bye, the innkeeper says, "We can all learn from these hills."

I put my hands on the steering wheel.

"Our friend in Cassis is waiting," I say.

He nods and says, "A friend from difficult times, I presume."

The judging slant in his eyes seems to frame all my life.

I'm aware that Father Benoît has arranged a room for us at the church for the night. It is afternoon, too late to visit the Pic de Saint Baume before arriving in Cassis. Still, I have the urge to watch the sun set in golden armor, just as I used to do with Madeleine when we stood at the western precipice dreaming of peace and love. But Klaus and I are now too far to the east, and we would have to descend the treacherous road from the Pic at night.

Klaus keeps tapping the dashboard.

"I cannot wait until I see the first sliver of the sea!"

He looks at me. His face shows excitement, and the tension of great things to come.

"Will it be silver; will it be blue?" he asks.

He almost sings the question, which surprises me because, apart from yodeling on top of the mountain, I have never heard him sing.

"Will it show between olive trees or flip into view between two houses alongside the road winding down into the plain? Or will I first smell it?"

He asks me to leave the sunroof open.

Why remind him that he swam in the Mediterranean when he visited Boris in his hut at the beach? I know that his mood was dark then, shuttling from obsession to obsession, and this time I sense that he will not arrive as a stranger. And the sea cannot appear too early.

When I detour from the direct highway to Cassis, Klaus starts frowning.

"Let's get to Cassis. I want to swim today! Today!"

"There is a scenic country road I want to take first."

"A slow road, I bet."

Klaus grunts and sinks back into his seat.

I still feel some vertigo and rather would stay on the straight and level road that leads down to Cassis, but my mind is in turmoil and I will have to visit the red road, the road the innkeeper has marked on the Michelin map, the road that will lead by the mountaintop he had been looking out from in 1943, the road where Madeleine must have died.

I keep thinking about the woman and child the innkeeper had mentioned.

Klaus acts peevish.

"You tell me when we are finally getting closer to the sea, okay?" he asks.

I just nod my head. I am in no mood to talk. Klaus will visit the sea, will find reprieve and experience the softening of things.

The road winds up into mountains and then descends into a narrow valley. Where the valley widens, the road crosses an abandoned railroad right of way. The road is pleasantly bent across a brook. A historic marker near the parking lot points out a bulging stove pipe-like structure that is now crusted with rust. The railroad tracks have been removed and the right of way padded with limestone to create a biking trail.

I stop, beg Klaus to get out of the car, and together we sit down on a bench. I bring out the coffee the innkeeper gave us for the road.

What remains here is the open meadow and the brushwork from where the sheep poured onto the road. I imagine a locomotive approaching from our left, steaming toward the crossing, the few Marquis crouching inside the cabin, guns ready. I imagine how the German soldiers rapidly turned suspicious, the first flare of gun fire, their heavy guns ripping open the side of the cabin, steam flaring out of the tank and blotting everything out in billowing clouds and the turrets all trained at the engine, which screeched to a halt. Maybe it happened this way, and maybe Madeleine had even anticipated it and had run out from between the brushwork on the hill. Maybe she ran along among the sheep pouring across the road, animals frightened by the whistle of the steam, panicking, as German guns trained the fire into the exploding engine. Madeleine, half-hidden, perhaps opened fire toward the airplane from her spot among the sheep. Only seconds would pass before the German halftracks turned their turrets and their bullets poured into the herd of sheep.

Sheep torn into burst flesh, tumbling over, their convulsing legs jerking into the sky; sheep still running, not yet feeling the lead in their entrails; some scramming back across the road and throwing themselves up the escarpment into the hills to safety between the boulders and in the ravine from whence they had come.

"Are you feeling okay?" Klaus asks. "I can drive, if you want."

"I'm fine."

"You keep staring about. Is there anything here?"

"Believe me. I am fine."

I get up.

"From here it will be just minutes to Cassis."

Klaus gives me a questioning look.

The drum of memory in my mind does not leave me, but now the road needs all my attention, serpentines and sharp curves and rock walls jetting out close. Klaus has moved forward in his seat and has his hands on the dashboard. Attentive. On the lookout. After a sharp curve, the view opens and Klaus jumps off his seat and throws both his arms over the rim of the sunroof, shouting: "The sea! The sea! That's it!"

We had talked in Munich about who would first spot the ocean, and even considered some reward for the winner. Minutes ago, I spotted the first sliver of ocean, but I had kept quiet. My thoughts have been back in the mountains where Madeleine died, and the sea now looks insignificant and stale, its waters pale.

"Let's drive to the beach first. Please!" Klaus pleads.

We pass by the church and park at the Esplanade. The sun has already set behind the outcrops of rock in the west and the lights in the restaurants are on. The cooling air brings out the smells of kelp and bait. Nobody is on the beach except two boys wading in the water. The lifeguard is walking away slowly after having locked the equipment shed. All this: a calm scene of things shutting down.

Klaus dashes toward the waves, tosses away his shirt and pants, and then dives in. He buoys, flings his arms, and repeats the whole sequence in a wild manner. I sit on the sand and try to go with the feeling this young man displays—the enthusiasm, the relief, the clarity. But there is a weight on me that will not release.

Later, when we arrive at the church, Klaus's wet hair still dripping water on the ground, I learn that Father Benoît is unable to see us. The priest who hands us Father Benoît's note is in his twenties, a young clean fellow who speaks clipped French and has a habit of drumming his fingers.

Father Benoît's note reads: "Dear Yann: The sickness of a dear friend has called me away this evening. I hope that you and Karl's son have arrived safely. I shall see you tomorrow at the church."

The young priest leaves most of the talking to his secretary. I cannot imagine engaging with this priest, discussing the times German Kübelwagen rolled down the very street where the church now stands. And when I mention the war times, he cuts me off.

"Algeria is our problem now," he says.

From the moment I drove into the churchyard I have been feeling weary. I ask him to secure us lodging at a nearby motel, but he insists that he lead us down a hallway to our guest room.

"Père Benoît would be disappointed, to say the least, if you were to decline this room," he says. "There is a bottle of Cassis Bagnol Rose on the table. Feel free to dine down at the harbor. Please, make yourselves comfortable."

I have trouble orienting myself. Even decades ago, the outline of the church premises was confusing to me. The architect who had taken on the challenge must have believed in stacking blocks in unending varieties on top of each other, beside each other, across and askew from each other. I look out a small window and reacquaint myself with the street outside—that surely cannot have changed—and with the window almost at street level (the parish is on a hill), I guess that the room Klaus and I are sharing has been built above what was formerly the underground garage. The room's walls are bare, although where the walls meet the ceiling hangs a crucifix: Jesus's body slack and bent, his head flopped downward, his arms spread wide and half-loosened from the nails. He is no God; he is flesh. His crown is tilted.

Klaus stares at me and it vexes me. I felt afflicted by his silence during our drive, and now I'm feeling afflicted by these narrow hallways and the bare walls and the crucifix. Klaus remarks that he has seen a Jesus like this one. It is located in a Bavarian cloister where visitors enter a long, narrow room whose ceiling lowers progressively until visitors must crawl in beneath a huge cross with Jesus's limp body nailed to the ceiling beams.

At the harbor restaurant, the local band plays so loudly that I am relieved of making conversation.

Lying in bed that evening, a feeling of dread enters me yet again. Klaus has fallen asleep. I cannot coax myself into sleep, so I stay awake after having emptied the Cassis Rose Father Benoît had left for us.

In the middle of night, I step out into the hallway and search for access to the garage

Delivering the Machine Guns
Cassis. Late 1943.

I roll the two heavy machine guns out of their oiled paper wrapping. A young priest named August helps me. He has a burst of red hair and a brimming smile, which he can make tumble off his lips to such effect that its appearance makes me laugh, changing the world for a better for this fleeting moment. August is an enthusiastic, ardent Catholic, who, over the past few days, has been assigned to accompany me. He wears the blessed wafers, the flesh of Jesus Christ, in a silvery box hung from his neck.

I do not know through what chain of command in the Resistance he has been sent to me, but what I do know is this: we take to each other as soon as he shows me a smuggled poem by René Char that the writer has penned in hiding. One of the lines in the poem reads: "We are torn between burning knowledge and the despair of having known. The thorn will not relinquish in fire and we will not relinquish our hope."

Sparing no time, August and I work together to hide the machine guns, which have been expertly disassembled, between the large wood burner and the frame of the car. We cannot stack in more than a hundred rounds of armor-piercing ordinance, or else the tires will appear flat—a sign that patrols look for and will make them search even a car with all the insignias and official papers from the diocese of Marseille.

I know of developments in the Luberon, of intensifying actions against German Special Services that increasingly use lightly armed halftracks to back up their sweeps. They roll into the village at dawn and place their halftracks at the square. From there, they spread out into small groups, tearing into houses, leading away young men and lining them up while their collaborators wait in the halftracks, identifying Resistance fighters. Then the shooting begins, along with the hanging, the victims' feet just dangling above the ground so that they are able to tiptoe away from their stifled deaths until their feet give out, must give out, and they helplessly string themselves into the tightening noose.

The Resistance currently has no weapons to penetrate the armed personal carriers; they cannot risk a fight and must wait until The SS leaves town amidst the smoke of set fires.

Through channels in Marseille, Madeleine has sent an urgent note requesting help to transport heavy machine guns to a site further north.

"We need help fast," she writes. "We gather around fires in the mountains; we have songs and we have poetry; we dance and we make love."

Two days before August and I plan to carry out the transport, he disappears. A Milice official soon stops by and inquiries about him. One of the aides assigned to me in the Cassis church takes me aside and whispers, "Be suspicious! They give you the impression of not knowing about his whereabouts, at the same time he is already cracking under torture."

The Milice has a request. "The German Kommandatur demands your presence at a bell dedication," he says, with a fierce determination in his voice. "In the spirit of cooperation, a church community in a nearby village donated their church bell to the war effort. No bells will ring until final victory!" A grin draws into his cheeks. "Now, you come with me!"

When his — arrives at the village square—a group of German soldiers has already lifted the bell onto a flatbed truck. The bell is partially draped in black cloth, and a swastika is painted on it.

A German sergeant approaches me. His left arm has been amputated; the stump hangs loosely in its dirty sleeve.

"Isn't it your job to do the public relations? If we can ever find you doing your job!"

There's spittle in his mouth. I can tell he's drunk.

"Just stand there and sprinkle your holy water. We have our own photographer and I insist that goddamn picture of you be published in your gazetteer! And with a hearty good smile on your face! Verstanden?"

I glance into the sun, hoping that nobody in the future perusing this picture—after these ogres have been defeated, that is—will recognize me smiling at this one-armed fiend.

Soon the flatbed truck bumps off across the cobblestones, the covering cloth billowing in the wind, and the sergeant's empty sleeve dangling out the car's window.

"Keep to your teaching job!" the Milice says as we part. "Spiritual needs of the believers and nothing else!"

On the ride back to Cassis in the Kübelwagen, I fake a migraine, and even manage to make myself throw up to avoid the Milice's incessant questions about August's whereabouts.

I try to get to sleep early; the drop-off point is hours to the north, making for a long drive in the morning. I lie down on a cot in the basement in front of cabinets stocked with hymnals and Bibles. There is a musty smell —the sour trail of days permeated with guilt and oppression. Red cloths —thread-markers for verses —hang loose from the sides of bibles like strings of blood. The night filters in through the mire. Darkness is everywhere, like gossamer that fills me with dread and fear. Distant sounds come through the walls and wake me: halftracks on the coastal road with their metal tracks shrilly scraping the road and shots ringing out near the harbor. I also hear shouts: "Achtung. Halt!" I keep tossing my head, and then lie still, listening to the pounding of my heart pouring fear into my body. My eyes feel like two bruises in my head. A leaden wire has strung itself into my throat. I do not dare to close my eyes; it feels as if, at any time, the walls could close in on me. So I get up and walk into the garage.

With my finger on the light switch, thoughts roll about in my mind—thoughts about my future, the war, France, destiny, Resistance fighters situated somewhere in a valley or on a mountain. And somewhere in the dark Madeleine readying her gun.

When my finger pulls the switch, I stand in the pitiless light of defeat. I gather some tools and crawl beneath the car's chassis. I loosen the bottom shields and slide out the machine gun barrels. I disconnect the wood burner and remove the cartridge belts, the magazines, and the tripod. The guns I store beneath a clutter of garbage in the root cellar.

As the morning arrives, gulls croak their wired cries and I feel the subtle shake of trucks on the roads. A taste of wet dust enters through the basement windows. I hear the hoarse yell of harbor workers and the hungry cry of a baby through some open window.

I tiptoe out into the hallway so as not to wake Klaus. I find the stairs to the basement. When I open the door, a familiar musty smell wafts into my nostrils. The smell of the church basement has certainly not changed over the years; the dust remains on tomes of unread sermons. There's also the stacked disorder of half-empty boxes and the heavy cloth of sacred garments and candles and rows of shelves crammed with stage props for the youth theater groups that, year in and year out, kept performing the eternal play of the recurrence of birth and death and resurrection.

Decades ago, there had been an obvious access to the garage, but it must have been blocked off since then. I keep walking my hands along the partition in search of a hidden door in one of the recesses, but I do not find a crack or gap. I consider stepping outside onto the street in order to get into the garage, but during the night any outside access would likely be locked.

Following my futile efforts, I return to the upstairs hallway where the walls are freshly painted, the floors new and waxed, the lighting efficient.

In the basement, the musty smell of old religion kept me safe and held damnation at bay, as if the presence of guilt could save me from final judgement, as if guilt were to give my soul deliverance. But now in this blank and bleached hallway, I feel no relief.

My thoughts circle back to the moment my finger flicked the switch. Wasn't it like the moment on the beach in Algiers when *The Stranger*'s Meursault "triggered the gun to kill —to ruin the peace of a perfect day" The building might be gone, friends and foes might be dead, and even the hills might have changed, but still history can live on in the soul of a man, and in some, it lives on in a muted destiny of despair.

I sit down in a distant corner of the hallway and cry until I have shaken all the tears out of me.

I return to bed at the first sign of light.

A few sharp knocks on the door wake me from my slumber. It is Père Benoît. I squint at him with unsure eyes.

"Good morning, Yann," he says. "I have breakfast ready for you in the mess hall."

"Those Capuchin knocks could wake the dead."

"As they surely will at the resurrection."

Père Benoît's Revelation

In the breakfast hall, with its vaulted stone arches, Père Benoît waits for me at the heavy oak table, his tunic draped and folded around him like a tent. I take a seat across from him. He cuts a thick slab off a loaf of dark bread, cradles it in his left arm, then reaches over the slice with both hands extended as if he is holding up a blessed communion wafer.

"How is Karl Herrmann's son doing?"

"Klaus?"

"Yes."

"He's doing well. He's a late riser."

"I remember Karl well."

I tell him that Karl has died, and that his widow followed him in death soon thereafter. Then I explain that Klaus, their only son, is a young student of languages whose spirits I had hoped would be lifted by the Mediterranean. Father Benoît listens and, as he does, lowers his eyelids and gently widens his lips—the signs of a knowing acceptance. His face has wrinkled and furrowed over the decades, and his large figure now seems less towering, but he still emanates a sense of serenity folded into the eternal grace of God.

It may be the lack of sleep, or maybe the turmoil of hours that reeled my mind back to conflicted times, but I suddenly feel a nausea coming on, a sudden distrust of assumed meanings bestowed on measured words, the stone history of cathedrals erected by labor and despair.

"You seem troubled," Père Benoît says.

"Madeleine..."

"She was a courageous woman, wasn't she?"

He sets his elbows on the table, supports his chin with his folded hands. I tell him of the road that bends down into the valley, the rusted water tank, the herd of sheep that carried her torn body into the thicket.

"How did you learn all this?" he asks.

"An innkeeper at a bed and breakfast told me. He was a look-out in 1943. That I met him was pure coincidence."

Pére Benoît begins rubbing his fingers. "I have to tell you, Yann, how courageous she was carrying out those daring runs between Corse and the coast with her sister."

"Sister? Madeleine had a sister?"

He nods.

"A sister? What? Is she alive? What's her name?"

Pére Benoît doesn't answer me. Instead, he sits up stiffly and takes a deep breath. His chest appears to widen inside his cape.

"Oh, Yann..."

"You can't give me this information, Father Benoît, and then not answer my questions."

"You know, you and I ...we rarely talked after the war. I haven't seen you for a long time..."

"Tell me her name!"

"Her name is Annette."

"Is she alive?"

Father Benoît shifts in his chair.

"Is she alive?"

He rolls his shoulders inside the canopy of his cape and stretches his neck. His unwillingness to be forthcoming with the information begins to anger me.

"Is she alive?"

"She is."

"Tell me about her. Please."

"I haven't seen her for a long time."

"What do you know?"

Silence.

"Tell me!"

"All I know is that she does excursions from Cassis."

"Car or boat or what?"

"Boat."

"What's the name of the boat? Pequod, Nautilus, Hispaniola? Tell me!"

"I do not remember."

"Try to remember. This is important. If Madeleine has a sister, I need to find her."

Pére Benoît holds up his pointer finger, requesting me to give him a second to think.

"The name of the boat may have something to do with Madeleine's dog. Do you happen to remember its name?"

"Cursinu," I say. "One of the most loyal breeds."

"Well, it could be that Annette's boat is named The Cursinu. Or something like that. I'm sorry. I wish I could remember. Like I said, it has been years since I've seen her."

"Excuse me, but I must begin my search."

"I shall be at the church," Father Benoît says. I sense defeat in his voice.

I dash out the door and sprint down to the harbor. An official there must have a record of the registered boats.

"Harbor master!" I yell, hurrying along the quay and, in the process, nearly running over an old man who kindly points toward a yellow Citroen pulling out of a parking space. I jump over a low wall, reach the cobblestones of the main square, and run after the yellow car as it turns uphill from the harbor. I feel the morning heat bursting as the hill pushes into my legs. My chest lifts into my throat. I wheeze. There's a pounding in my head.

I keep up with the Citroen, which follows slow traffic. The blare of clonking cars erupts around me. I wave and I yell and with a final burst of energy, I dive for the handle of the passenger side door and grab it. The car pulls me a few feet, my legs still moving, like a soldier who has been shot and still manages a few last steps.

The car stops. I am still hanging sideways, clutching the door.

"What the hell are you doing?" a man shouts.

I see his face coming down toward mine as he bends down with an uncertain look in his face, trying to ascertain what has just happened. I let loose of the door handle, slide backward, and slump onto the berm.

After I put my head down and catch my breath, the driver kneels beside me.

"Man! Are you all right?"

"I'm looking for a boat and a woman named Annette!"

"You make no sense." He grows angry as the honking around his car bursts into crescendo. He looks around for some help.

"She runs tourist ...tourist ...excursions!"

"Listen, I'm afraid I can't help you. And I'm sorry, but I have to move my car now."

The man shakes his head as he drives off the sidewalk, tires screeching.

Once the gawkers have dissipated, I find my bearings and realize I have run up almost all the way to the church. I make my way to our room, where I find Klaus writing in his notebook. He snaps it shut as soon as he sees me.

"Let's go, Klaus."

"Where are we going?"

"To the café at the harbor."

"Why?"

"Don't worry about it. Just get dressed and come with me."

At the café, we order coffee and croissants.

"Stay here," I say. "I'll be right back."

I leave Klaus to his own company and hurry over to the harbor master on duty.

"Are you the man looking for *Cursinu*?" he asks, unruffled by all the radio crackle coming over the loudspeaker. "My colleague already called and told me to look out for you."

He doesn't even wait for my response. "*Cursinu* comes in at about 10:30 a.m. over at Berth 7. Does that help?"

"Does *Cursinu* belong to a woman named Annette?"

"Yes."

"Then yes, yes—your information does help. Thank you very much."

Back on the café terrace, I explain to Klaus that we may meet Madeleine's sister. I feel tense, restless thoughts plunging into history. He gives me a surprised look. "That's interesting," he says. I know I have to save any more explanations for another time and place.

"Ah! The engineer at the cathedral has a sister," he says. The news finally settling in.

"According to Father Benoît," I say.

"Hey, would you mind if I went swimming again?"

"I have to walk over to the harbor. Madeleine's sister's boat should pull in around 10:30 and I want you to be there."

"I promise I'll be back by then."

From my seat on the café terrace, I watch as Klaus walks down to the beach. He swims with wide strokes, and waves at me on occasion. Sometimes, he calls for me and I am sure he is yelling, "Come in! Come in!", but I'm comfortable on the terrace as I try to tame my wild thoughts. Why did I not know about her sister? Why hadn't Madeleine told me? My thoughts run around and around—a most awful carousel.

After a while, I stand up and begin waving my arms in an effort to get Klaus's attention. He knows it's time to get out of the water, dry off, and meet me back at the terrace, but it's obvious he would rather continue to be swept up in the sea's salty waves.

Klaus returns with a look of disbelief on his face. He furrows his forehead and sets his hands on his hips.

"Here we are finally on the beach, at the sea ...and you just sit there."

"My decision," I say, irritated.

"Do you want to tell me what happened early this morning? I heard you sneak out of the room."

"That's a long story."

I avoid Klaus's gaze and keep staring out to sea, where a few sailboats carve into the water, sails billowing. I realize how odd my behavior must appear to him.

He switches his weight from one foot to the other. "Can I at least look around the harbor while we wait?"

I nod, and off he goes.

At the harbor, Klaus takes pleasure in feeding the pigeons on the wharf, and then casually walks over to a group of men playing pétanque in a plantain tree alley. From my spot on the terrace, I can hear the click of distant collisions. To my surprise, they even let Klaus throw a few steel balls. He's warming up. And me ...well, I've still got my eyes locked on Berth 7. Any minute now.

Meeting Annette

When *Cursinu* slips into the harbor, I watch as the boat swings around into its berth. A woman lowers a plank and steps on land to tie down the stern. A young woman steps out of the cabin behind her and ties the bow. I have always enjoyed watching sailors snake those ropes with learned agility and ease, and this time is no different.

Klaus, in the meantime, has walked away from the pétanque players. I wave him over, and together we watch Annette and the young woman help three elderly couples negotiate the plank. After they carry off luggage and arrange taxi rides for the couples, Klaus and I make our way over to introduce ourselves.

"Excuse me," I say. "The harbormaster told me that you are Annette. Is that true?"

Annette looks at me suspiciously, but that doesn't stop her from answering right away.

"Yes, I'm Annette. How can I help you?"

"Well ...I'm here because I knew your sister during the war."

Annette freezes.

"My name is Yann Cedak and this is my friend Klaus." I sense that Annette wants to walk away. She must have heard my name before. From my beloved Madeleine.

But when the young woman approaches, Annette introduces her.

"This is my daughter," she says.

"Hi. I'm Pauline," the young woman says.

"Excuse us," Annette says, taking her daughter's hand, the two of them turning toward the cabin, and then disappearing from sight.

"Did Père Benoît tell you that Annette has a daughter?" Klaus says. "She is beautiful."

"I did not even know Madeleine had a sister." I am irritated as we keep waiting at the quay, irritated by this brisk wave-off, but Klaus's face is blushing with excitement. Is he infatuated? And so soon!

To my surprise Annette and Pauline re-emerge from the cabin after a very short time and Annette asks me who had told me about her.

"Father Père Benoît."

"Father Benoît? Really? I haven't seen him in years." Annette tips her head back and taps her teeth with her fingernail.

"For a time, Père Benoît and Madeleine and I worked together, but after the war, I lost contact with him. We did write letters, but it was just this morning that I saw him again in person. Anyway, Père Benoît saved many Jewish lives in those times."

"Is he at the church?" she asks.

"He is. In fact, that's where Yann and I have been staying," Klaus answers.

Pauline, who has been standing on the plankway with a box in her hands, now walks up to Klaus and says, "I noticed your German accent."

Klaus, blushing yet again, nods and smiles.

Pauline sets the box on the ground and opens it. "This was a gift from a German passenger. I don't know what to do with it."

"Pauline, I might need you here," Annette says.

Pauline does not pay her any attention. Like Klaus, she, too, seems to be captivated.

"Oh, that's a Kreisel," Klaus says. "I had one as a child."

"There's a whip that comes with the set," Pauline says.

Annette looks agitated.

"We can come back later," I say, feeling some pressure to ease the tension.

Pauline points toward the short stairs leading up to the plaza. "I want to try it out!" she says and turns toward Klaus. "Come with me."

Both run up the stairs to the plaza.

Annette tightens her lips and retreats into the cabin.

Weary, I walk up to the plaza and take a seat at a café table. From here I can easily see the berth for *Cursinu*, so I decide to wait patiently for Annette to come searching for me. Surely, she wants to know more about me. Or does she know enough already? I remain beset by the drum of obsession. What does she know? I ask myself this question over and over again. When the waiter comes by offering to refresh my cup of coffee, I dismiss him rudely, even though I don't mean to.

It is a sunny morning, but the sea looks like an interminable drab to me, and the hoarse cries of the gulls grate my nerves. I feel none of the release the sea has graciously brought me in the past.

Klaus and Pauline have unpacked the spinner in the open space of the plaza. Klaus waves at me. Pauline manages to whip the Kreisel. It starts to revolve but the spinner wobbles into wider and wider gyrations and almost right away falls onto its side. She hands Klaus the whip and, before long, I can see the surprise in her face. Klaus really is quite adept with it, snaking the long lash through the air just inches above the ground, even talking to Pauline while he is making the lash fly.

Klaus invites a few bystanders to try their hand at the Kreisel, but they can't master it; they just make it wobble. Pauline appears to know some of them, and she calls out advice and taunts them with playful insults.

Like Klaus, I'm familiar with Kreisels. And I remember Père Benoît reminding Jewish families during the occupation to hide these spinning tops used for games at Chanukah. "Do not have them around," he cautioned, "the Germans know these are Jewish toys and they may put you and your children in grave danger."

After some time, I spot Annette leaving her boat. She makes her way toward the plaza, speaks briefly to Pauline, then walks up the street and disappears behind the first building in sight. After a few more minutes, Pauline packs up her Kreisel, bids farewell to the group—including Klaus—and follows the same street her mother has taken.

Klaus, looking saddened by the sudden departure of his new friend, joins me at my table on the terrace.

"What do you think Annette said to Pauline?" I ask.

"I have no idea," Klaus says. "They were speaking mostly in Corse, I think."

"She must have told you something before she said good-bye. No?"

"Well ...I mean ...she just told me to wait."

"To wait? What was that supposed to mean?"

Klaus shrugs, but it comes across as a hopeful shrug—a new type of shrug for him.

Since there is not much to do except follow Pauline's vague order, Klaus and I enjoy a leisurely brunch, which gives me an opportunity to apologize to the poor waiter I waved off earlier. As the two of us linger, more tables and umbrellas get set up around us for the lunch crowd.

About an hour later, Annette appears at our table. Pauline steps behind her, looking pleased.

"Hello, Yann. Hello, Klaus. Pauline and I would like to invite you both to a picnic at the Calanque de Vau. The bad news is, Father Benoît will not be able to join us."

I knew it. I knew that Annette would go to Father Benoît. I wonder what she asked him. I wonder what he told her.

Regardless, I am stunned. I was almost certain that Annette was going to tell us to leave, to avoid thinking about the past when the future was more desirable in so many ways.

"I must insist that I bring food. The café at the beach has advertised some excellent take-out trays," I say.

Annette gives it a thought. "Okay. I will bring the wine, then."

They turn and walk back toward her boat.

My mouth is still agape as they duck into that protective shell of a cabin.

As we wait for the café employees to assemble the take-out trays, Klaus can't stop telling me about Pauline, her first prize in the hundred meter free-style swim, how her mother let her steer the boat one night, how she could find direction just by observing the stars.

"Isn't she pretty," he says.

"Very pretty," I say, rather absentmindedly, still shocked by Annette's unexpected invitation.

Back at *Cursinu*, Pauline wears a white blouse over a wine-colored skirt. And what I notice first about Annette is her face. Some ease seems to have settled into her expression, and for a moment I feel as though I may have found my bearings again. It's a relief of sorts as I try to prepare myself for the journey ahead—an afternoon that could go one way or the other.

Calanque D'en Vau

As the boat tuckers out of the harbor, I stand beside Annette who holds the large rudder wheel, sliding her thumbs along the spokes. I feel as if a blank wall has been erected between the two of us—a wall empty of words, empty of courage. It is the tepid hour of noon; a glazed sky hangs above us.

"Father Benoît rarely visits this region," Annette says.

"Why do you think that is?"

"I'm not sure. But I bet he has his reasons."

"So you talked with him this morning?"

"I did, but I'm not convinced he wanted to talk to me."

"Really?"

Annette doesn't answer; she merely nods her head.

I fight a sudden attack of vertigo. Everything seems to fall away in a cascade.

"How well do you know Father Benoît?" I ask.

"Well, he and I were working together during the occupation to help Jews escape to Spain."

"I see."

"And several years ago, he invited me to come to Tel Aviv for some award he was selected to receive. That's all."

"Did you go?"

"Regretfully, no. I was busy at the university."

"Do you still teach?"

"Geology. Part-time, and not on the main campus and only during the winter when the tourist business is down."

"I bet you're a great teacher."

"You teach, too?"

"I do, though lately I've been thinking my days are numbered. Let's just say some days are better than others."

Annette looks away, as if lost in thought. We have the front window tilted out, water spraying into our faces.

Pauline and Klaus, meanwhile, are sitting on the couch in the cabin. Both giggle sporadically. Klaus has never looked so comfortable, happy, and spirited.

"So, you worked with Madeleine on the cathedral project?" Annette asks.

"Yes. The Vichy government sent me there as a journalist. I worked with her off and on."

"You both did some scary stuff, didn't you?"

A brittle coldness lifts into my chest.

"Do you know what happened to Karl?" she asks.

"After France, Karl was transferred to the Russian front, where he was wounded in the abdomen. Apparently he spent the rest of the war as antiaircraft warden in Munich."

"Did he ever marry?"

"Yes. But he died recently, and his wife survived him only for a short time."

"What else do you know?"

"It was his war wound that eventually killed him. Some bowel loops became slung up into each other and it was not recognized in time."

"That must have been hard for Klaus." She turns her head back toward the cabin. "You better check on him."

I find Pauline and Klaus lying outstretched on the couches, toe to toe, tossing peanuts toward each other, trying to catch them with open mouths, laughing all the while.

I walk back up the few stairs to the bridge "They having a lot of fun, I'd say"

As we approach the narrow entry into the Calanque D'en Vau it is getting hot without the wind that now barely stipples the water's surface.

"Beaching in this Calanque requires some finesse," Annette says as she wipes sweat off her brow. "Most people come here in kayaks, but I know a mooring site that will do."

When Pauline and Klaus emerge from the cabin, Pauline seems eager to tell us about the plans they've made.

"Klaus is thinking about living in student housing in Celleneuve," she says, "and he might even be interested in learning Corse!"

Klaus and I make eye contact. It's as if he's begging me to give him my blessing.

Annette sidles the boat toward the fjord's rock wall, which is close to the narrow path that leads up to the outcrop of rocks where, in 1940, Madeleine and Karl sat cheek to cheek waiting for the Paris film crew to arrive. For the moment, this memory clips my thoughts.

"Throw the tires!" Annette calls out.

As the boat edges sidewise toward the cliff, Pauline lowers two tires alongside the hull to keep the rock from grating it. Once the anchor is set and the slipknots tied to iron rings driven into the cliff, Annette lowers the plank onto a ledge in the cliff.

My mind churns. What did Madeleine confide to Annette during the war? And how often did she get to see her sister after Madeleine had joined the Resistance? Shame floods into me in deep shivers. I feel like a pathetic appendix to a mournful history.

Debarking is difficult, given the narrow ledge the plank is set upon. The water is calm but the plank is in danger of slipping off. It keeps shifting, and I need to crawl.

Pauline cups her hands in front of her mouth, laughing.

While Annette and Pauline float drinks, food, and towels in a rubber dinghy onto the sandy beach at the base of the fjord, Klaus and I walk the path leading to the beach.

Pauline, wearing a polka dot bikini, is full of energy and decides that she doesn't want to eat. She'd rather swim, and what an excellent swimmer she is.

"I'm going to try out for the synchronized swim team," she says to Klaus. "You time me!"

Pauline executes a headstand in the water, legs stretched into the air, as she walks her hands along the bottom.

"Fifteen seconds!" Klaus yells when she surfaces, ballerina-like in her gracefulness. Klaus hands her a towel and swipes curls of hair off her forehead. Pauline holds still, unable to stop smiling as the curls immediately fall back in place.

Annette has spread a cloth on the sand and set up the lunch trays. There are cheeses of many varieties, breads, fresh tomatoes, cucumbers, and olives—some strutting in oil with their stretched skin, and others lying crumpled at the bottom of the terrine.

After lunch, Klaus and Pauline go for a swim while Annette and I stretch out on towels and let the sun grace our skin. I cannot find the words to express the endless stream of thoughts that flow through my brain. I think of what the innkeeper told me about a woman who, after the attack, walked through the torched bosque with a small child, searching for something? Was that woman Annette? Was that child Pauline?

And now she is beside me. I don't have the courage to ask, and her silence burdens me. She doesn't inquire about Klaus, doesn't ask how I wound up in Cassis. I try steadying my nerves to tell her about the memories I have of Madeleine. Maybe somehow—somehow—I can ease into what I really must say. Annette, however, seems distracted. She's got her eyes and attention on Klaus and Pauline, who are walking the narrow path toward an outcrop of rocks that overlooks the bay. Maybe something stirs in her while she watches them, maybe a sudden reminder of the chain of generations.

"You know, Yann ...Karl was lucky to survive the war. My husband died in the last days of the German-French War in June of 1940."

She leans back onto her towel, and then begins to circle her heels through the sand. She lets her hair fall over her eyes like a curtain as if nothing more needs to be said.

The woods steam in the heat; tears of resin ooze from the pines, and the fragrance wafts across the small bay. Small fish mouthing air prick the surface of the smooth water. A flock of birds shake their wings through the sandy soil, taking a dry bath.

Silence is good. I can hold on to it. Annette and I can wait for Pauline and Klaus to come back and leave it at that. Leave it at that.

But then the words tumble out.

"I am responsible for Madeleine's death," I say. "I didn't deliver the heavy machine guns that would have penetrated the Nazi tanks. I didn't deliver them because I was afraid. I didn't deliver them because I saw a comfortable life ahead of me. I didn't do what I was supposed to do and I failed. I'm so sorry."

Annette doesn't move or speak. Her face behind a curtain of fallen hair.

Then I hear a sound like strained breathing. Annette is sobbing. And for the first time in many hours, I feel a measure of relief.

"This spot is where I saw Madeleine alive for the last time," she whispers. "It was our secret cove."

There is a long pause.

"Madeleine saw a future with you. Did you know that? I can still remember her saying, 'Yann and I could do better in another life with less cruel Gods watching over us.' How beautiful that was."

"Yes. That was beautiful."

"They never found her body, Yann. Can you believe that? Never found her body."

"She was hiding among sheep, training her machine gun toward the halftracks."

"How did you know that?"

"I met a former Resistance fighter on my way to Cassis. He runs a bed and breakfast now, and he told me of the knoll where the Resistance fighters assembled, and from where they poured down with the sheep to attack the SS column. The Germans had so much firepower, so much ammunition, so much hate, that after they killed all the resistance fighters they set fire to woods far beyond the attack site. Cold blooded, senseless revenge!"

Annette lights a cigarette and takes a long drag. Then she stands up, flicks away the cigarette, and busies herself cleaning up, repackaging the food, folding the cloths. She calls for Pauline and Klaus who are hidden from view behind a bend in the path, but it seems that they do not hear her, so I offer to walk up to the overlook and tell them it's time to leave.

It was during the German occupation, at the time the film-makers from Paris made a propaganda film for the Petain regime, that Karl and Madeleine perched up there and watched as evening shadows draped over the rocky outcrop. Just like back then, hawks tilt through the sky, making the sound of flags flapping in the wind.

As I take the path now, the breeze touches me like cool silk, and between the brittle crops I can breathe in the whiff of sweet sap and the honey smell of rare herbs as salamanders rest on flat rocks, their lungs pumping life.

When I spot Pauline and Klaus from behind a thick copse of knotted trees at the bend, they are reclining against a smooth rock, their eyes closed, describing to each other what they see as their closed eyelids are lit up by the sun—a flood of unwashed colors, a world without shadows. Out in the ocean, the midday ferry sounds its hollow hoot. I watch as Pauline rubs blue blossoms into her palms and holds them up to Klaus with a smile he cannot yet see.

"Klaus! Don't you dare open your eyes!"

"How far away can you feel my skin?"

"What did you say?"

"How close is my hand?"

Klaus remains still amidst the chirping heat of the afternoon.

"I'm not sure," he says.

"Open your eyes now."

Klaus opens his eyes.

"The width of a finger," she says. "You can feel my skin that far."

He sits up.

"You want to try it on me?"

He hesitates, but then agrees.

"Well?" She lies down and closes her eyes. "Try!"

He carefully makes his hands hover over her arm, closer and closer.

"Now! Hold your hand right there!" She opens her eyes.

"The distance of two fingers!" he says.

She sits up.

"I have been fostering an idea," she says. "We all have an aura, a kind of field around us that diminishes with distance, but remains strong enough to connect all human beings if we just nurture the knowing."

He nods. "I understand."

I slowly walk backwards out from the copse that hides my presence, and then, from a distance, I call.

Back on *Cursinu,* Annette and I remain silent beside the helm. I admitted failure; I broke the seal and received no forgiveness. As I look at the rugged coastline, huge boulders tossed together, I think of Hemingway's short story, "Hills Like White Elephants." In the story, a couple waits at a train station for the Madrid-Barcelona Express. They have a troublesome history between them, but they keep drinking beer and talk and never touch on the words that smolder like hot embers between them. Staring ahead onto the sea, salt spray wetting my eyes and brows, I judge this to be the only and last time Annette and I will ever meet.

After arriving back in Cassis, Annette stays on board *Cursinu* to rest. Pauline accepts an invitation to dine with me and Klaus at the harbor café. As we enjoy an early dinner, I watch with great interest as Klaus's personality comes alive. Pauline, it appears, brings out the best in him.

In the evening, the plaza also comes to life; some young fellows pull out the hammock seats from a Renault 4, eliciting laughter from those standing around. They plop themselves down in the middle of the plaza, light their cigars, and lift them skyward: "Viva

Cuba! Viva la revolution!" From beneath plantain trees, I hear the clink of colliding Boulle balls tossed by old men with hushed gestures of dominance, friendship, and competition. Smoke uncurls from their cigarillos, beer bottles hang like clubs in their hands.

"Are your tourists mostly German?" I ask Pauline.

"Quite a lot," she answers. Then she asks what I am doing at the university. I offer her a short explanation.

"I've read *The Stranger*," she says.

Klaus's face lights up.

"What did you think of it?"

"I loved it, of course. It's such a mysterious piece of work."

Though I expect our conversation about *The Stranger* to continue, Klaus pulls out his Rolleicord to take a photo of the sea from our view at the table, and Pauline wants to know more about this small box with two lenses.

"Wait here," Klaus says.

He walks over to my car, retrieves his leather-bound photo album, and returns to our table.

"Have a look at these power lines in the Munich sky," he says.

"A grid against the sky," Pauline says.

"Do you like patterns?"

"Not views from a cage," she says.

Klaus seems startled.

Then Pauline says in hesitant German: "Ihm ist, als ob es tausend Stäbe gäbe und hinter tausend Stäben keine Welt." She is quoting the second verse of Rilke's poem, "The Panther," which describes a panther pacing in a Paris zoo cage: "As if there would be thousands of grids and behind thousands of grids no world."

Klaus sits transfixed as Pauline quotes another verse from Rilke's short poem "Like the dance of force around a center in which there waits a paralyzed will."

There are no grids, no wires in the sky above Cassis—just a sickle moon hung over a small town in this God-blessed littoral with a few fishing boats sliding away into the milky dark and the sudden, high-pitched yelps of kids playing at the harbor.

Pauline has led Klaus to the end of a journey that had kept him circling in dark gyres far too long.

Sometimes in life, we need a metaphor to carry us, and so it is on this windless night on the Mediterranean coast where slow, black waves keep turning in the harbor like gentle whales, and the cobble streets glisten silent in the ochre light that sea and sky bestow grace on men.

Annette soon joins us. She sits down, eats a plate of fried sardines, and follows up her meal with a few glasses of Retsina. Her Corse friend, the owner of the café, walks over from the now half-dark kitchen and sits down at our heavy oak table. I have no clue what they are chatting about until Pauline leans over and tells me in a low voice that they are at it again.

"What do you mean?" I ask.

"They're talking about escaping into the mountains of Corse, fishing in the coves, star filled nights and the bleating of sheep," she says.

I ask Annette if they knew Boris.

"Boris. Of course we know Boris!"

Annette's friend now pays me some attention after hearing a name that rings a bell.

"Oh, Boris. Yes," he says. "When he's not in his shack, he visits us here quite often. We have an active group of Corse friends. One foot on the mainland and the other in Corse."

After Annette finishes her drink, she tells Pauline it's time to go to sleep in the boat. Pauline wishes us sweet dreams and waves at Klaus, who stretches out his arms and says, "I've always wanted to sleep in a boat cabin."

"Someday!" Pauline says.

Back at the church, Klaus and I are assigned to a new room in the dormitory where the quarters for women and men are separated by a narrow garden with a fountain. Its splashing waters lull me to sleep.

After breakfast at the harbor the next morning, I inquire at the church office about Père Benoît, but they do not know where he is.

I leave a note with my office number and some lines that express a sincere wish for us to meet again, and sincere apologies for my sudden departure.

On our drive back to Montpellier, Klaus can't stop talking about Pauline and I, of course, can't stop thinking about Annette.

A few days later, in Montpellier, we are informed that a university housing apartment is available, so Klaus has to make up his mind: stay with me or live on his own. He decides to move into the apartment.

I do not see or speak to Klaus for a full week.

I receive most of my information about Klaus's whereabouts from Genève, who happens to live a hallway down from Klaus in the housing complex. I am surprised that, without much hesitation, she is already helping Klaus—assisting him with buying an old *Deux Chevaux* and the like. She informs me that Klaus has no telephone yet, so I drive to his apartment, but he's not there and neither is he at several consecutive visits.

It is still summer and his schedule has to be mostly free. What in the world is Klaus up to? Where has he been going?

I soon find out that he has signed up for the following courses: French, Italian, Basics of Journalism, and Introduction to Modern Existential Philosophy. He has also signed up for a course in Corse history and language, which convinces me that he's interested in pursuing his friendship with Pauline.

One evening, I finally sit down with him for supper at the Egg Café on the main square in Montpellier. Klaus appears released from some burden. He smiles at the servers and stretches out on his chair. He looks comfortable. Content, even.

"I am sorry I didn't leave you a note," he says. "I've been really busy."

"Have you been spending time with Pauline?"

"Yes. I've been visiting her a lot. We've been staying with her extended family in Corse. Most of them live in the mountains. Some herd sheep, and some of her cousins teach at the university. They're even planning to open a family restaurant soon."

"So, Pauline has uncles and sisters?"

"And cousins. A whole clan. They've all welcomed me with open arms."

"Do they ever visit the mainland?"

"Rarely."

"So what are your plans?"

Klaus pushes his fingers into his chin as if to prevent himself from speaking. I wait.

"I mean, what happens between you and Pauline?" I finally ask.

"Well, we are in love."

A hesitant smile tangles up his lips.

"She has changed my life."

"You've changed your own life," I say.

Klaus sits back in his chair and lays his hands on the table, palms up, as if he's preparing to receive a gift.

"Do you remember when you talked to me about Camus's story *Death in the Soul*?"

I nod.

"When Camus leaves Prague by train and then sees the first signs of the coast, the first houses with scaly tiles, the first vines flat against the wall made blue by sulfur dressing, he suddenly knows that light was bound to break through and he is ready for happiness."

The waiter returns to our table and serves us more Retsina. We keep listening to the collective murmur of excitement coming from the students at the tables surrounding us.

"So, what brought you back to the mainland today?" I ask.

"Spelunking, for one," he says.

"Spelunking? Who introduced you to spelunking?"

"Well, I remember you telling me about Lucienne, so I did my research, contacted her, and she is happy to take me on a few trips to St. Baume. I had to talk her father into it first."

"I think Lucienne has hopes of leaving for Corse, too," I say.

"And so does Boris."

"You know everybody now, don't you?"

Klaus smiles. "The whole Corse clan! Pauline, Annette, Lucienne, Boris, and the owner of the Cassis café."

"I had no idea."

I feel jerked from one surprise to another. All my friends seem to suddenly know each other—and what about me? Where do I fit in?

Klaus reaches for an envelope in his pocket. He opens it, and hands me a photograph.

"Here is a print of Pauline as a toddler that Lucienne helped me enlarge and sharpen. She has an excellent dark room for developing negatives, and we used it to enlarge the original print. Pauline's Corse relatives handed me a few other family photos to work on."

I look at the print and see Annette's eyes—those burning coals! Suddenly, I begin to fear the idea of Annette having a conversation with Klaus about my cowardice. What if she were to tell him everything? Unleashed the whole story onto him? This supper with Klaus could be nothing but a charade then, and history would destroy the present!

It's as if a new web of fears has just been thrown over me.

I'm tempted to outright ask Klaus what he knows, but I resist the temptation.

When it's time for him to leave, Klaus informs me that he's being picked up by two women. When they arrive in their Citroen, they stop, wave, and Klaus jumps in the backseat. I feel as if he has been ripped away from me. Alone at our table, I smoke a rare cigarette and order another Retsina and wait for the hum around me to numb me down.

I don't hear from Klaus for several days.

I drive out to Boris's hut, where a young couple has taken over the business until he is scheduled to return from a trip to Corse. And Genève ...she's occupied with searching through old files in Paris libraries for the lost works of Walter Benjamin. Everybody is busy.

I sit on my small balcony, and more and more that balcony seems to resemble the one in *The Stranger,* where Meursault spends afternoons watching the world go by impassively, without participation, without emotion. It is almost as if I can hear the screeching of the tramway beneath Klaus's balcony in Munich once more.

One evening, the phone rings. It's Father Benoît.

"Yann, I'm calling to apologize for not telling you about Annette," he says.

"You're good at keeping secrets," I say.

"So tell me—how are Pauline and Klaus getting along these days?"

"Klaus says she makes him happy."

"From all you told me, Klaus must have changed," Father Benoît says.

"It's a surprise to me, too."

"Are they moving in together?"

"Not with the housing rules of the university as they are," I explain.

"The other reason I call you is to invite you to get together over the long weekend. Pauline wants to visit the church that Madeleine intended to build.

"Pauline never visited the ruins?"

"Not as far as I know."

"Will Klaus join us?"

"I'm told he will."

"And what about Annette?"

"No, Yann. She's spending the weekend with a friend in the mountains"

After I hang up the receiver, an edgy feeling keeps lingering inside me.

I drive to Cassis and eat a slow breakfast alone at the rectory. Klaus and Pauline who have been waiting for me, pile into my car and soon enough I am reminded how rutted the road up to the Pic de St. Baume is. My rear suspension bottoms out; the steering wheel wobbles into a dance of its own; the roof of the car seems to come down on our heads more than once. I have to concentrate on the drive. There will be time to talk later.

Father Benoît is to arrive in a few hours, bringing lunch with him. When we reach the site of the old—and now abandoned—site of the youth hostel, Pauline and Klaus plead with me to drive the narrow path down to the Calanque, where we can go swimming. And no matter what technical details I throw at them—the car's low clearance, tire size, the weakly horse powers—they keep begging.

On our way down, the car is tossed about in the ruts, but what turns my stomach into knots seems to lead to a mere "Yap!" and "Wow!" and laughter from the backseat as Klaus and Pauline are thrown against each other. When we arrive at the narrow sand beach, it takes me some time to shake off my dizziness. By the time I am finally ready to go for a swim, Pauline and Klaus are already stepping out of the water, snapping towels at each other, chasing each other across the pebbles. Some kayakers have beached and now lie stretched out on top of their kayaks. And to my surprise, another car has survived the rutted road; the middle-aged couple calmly treads water in the distance.

Pauline and Klaus relax close to each other on their towels. Klaus keeps nibbling her ear and nudging her lips with gentle kisses that make her giggle. The kayakers can't stop lifting their heads to watch these two young lovers.

It takes me some time to pry them off each other, and when we eventually arrive at the Pic de St. Baume we find that Father Benoît has already laid out a picnic meal. Up here, the wind is blowing and we need some stones to weigh down the cloth. Father Benoît gives a brief blessing, but then no words are spoken for a while. I look at him, wondering what his thoughts are, trying to search for the common ground that has brought us together at this mountaintop with the remnants of a failed century.

At last, Pauline stands up and announces she wants to have a great tour.

"I'll show you what is left of the church, but it may disappoint you," I say. "I am glad to lead, but you have to stay behind me, okay? There are brittle walls and worn steps. You will have to listen to me."

After we work together to pack the food away, we enter the shell inside the metal construction and then carefully walk up the staircase to the former design room. We enter the room where the walls are still chalk white; a gypsum dust has settled all around.

Pauline finds some colored crayons on the floor beneath the white chalkboard. I stare at some panel on the opposite wall, trying to decipher old designs that might still live there. When I turn, I see Pauline standing in front of the chalkboard, her neck tilted, elbows out to her side. Klaus begins tracing her outline into the chalkboard while she tries to keep an impish expression on her face.

"Stay still," he says. "Don't turn! Don't move!"

She does not move, even when he traces her outline way up her thighs. When Pauline finally steps away from the wall, he draws a set of eyes and a mouth and a nose into the outline. Some stick figure—simple, primitive!

As we proceed into the large drawing room, Klaus, who has never seen the inside of these buildings, rushes straight to the broken drawing table in the corner. He is ahead of all of us, with Pauline close behind.

"My father's drawing table!" he yells. "I saw photos of it. Right here was the straight edge fixed to the table."

He points to a small metal joint in the upper left corner, then takes a stumpy pencil, holds it up and says: "Faber Castell! My father's favorite pencil maker!"

Father Benoît nods and smiles. "When you're done with your art work I have a surprise."

"Where are we to go?"

"You follow me to the bell tower. And be cautious!" Father Benoît says.

I stay in the room, my senses settling into the quietness.

And it seems I still can take in the smell of ammonia they used for the blue prints, and the dust seems to have preserved the smell of fresh-cut lumber reminding me of times I was younger, and the world was still fresh.

As I walk over to the bell tower, I hear Pauline's and Klaus's chatter. They have run up the stairs leading into the tower. I follow the stairs, which are so steep that I wonder how Père Benoît has made it up there.

A thin, slotted light outlines the staircase. I avoid the center of the steps, where the wood is worn down to splinters.

Halfway up, I reach a landing inside the tower where the windows are wider, and light freely floods in. Père Benoît is holding the two thick ropes that hang down from the bells, and I watch as he hands them to Pauline and Klaus.

"The bells toll loud enough to wake the whole hill country," Pére Benoît says.

He points to the top.

"A group of merchants donated these heavy bells to honor the Resistance," he says. "Rumor has it that the bells were cast from German guns."

I look out the window.

"The bells haven't been rung for a long time," Père Benoît continues. And maybe the two thick ropes have lain slack in opposite corners of the wooden floor, coiled like snakes for a long time, but now Klaus has already lifted the knotted rope that is as thick as a man's fist. No more just feeling the heft, already pulling on it, making the rope's bristles quiver in the breeze fanning in through the slotted windows.

„I've never rung bells," Klaus says.

He looks at Pauline, who, like him, has already donned gloves —God knows where they came from —and has snaked her rope around one leg.

"I can't do this alone," she says.

There is determination in the squint of her eyes and the inward curl of her lips.

Klaus looks toward Pauline, who is holding the rope in front of her, extending and pulling it toward the floor. When Klaus clamps onto the rope on his side, a gentle pull lifts him—an invitation of sorts—and there's a give in its tautness. Suddenly there's the pull upward subtle and silent at first.

We begin to hear the clucking of the joints up high in the tower as the clappers begin to sway. A faint squeak, then a sound as if a bucket has fallen. Pure steel merely clinking, not yet ringing. The ropes move up and down with increasing speed and Klaus, with his feet still firmly planted on the ground, enters into the rhythm. He glances at Pauline, whose feet are being lifted off the ground.

Then it is his moment. He closes his eyes and when he opens them he looks down at us. He is raised.

Something has burst inside Klaus, something he always had closed off. And as he flies up toward the tower, he looks down at Pauline on the floor, who is bending backward, pulling with all her weight on the rope, and letting it slide between her hands for the shortest of moments before clinging on to it and ascending upward with speed.

Klaus comes down. I see the rapture. Something is coming. Klaus is now pulling with soul and body. He feels the strength and the softness and he doesn't let go.

It isn't like a ringing—it's more like a rumble, a shiver, as if a quake has shifted the balance of this tower, his father's church.

He sees the rafters coming toward him and through the slots the sea and windsailing birds. When he comes down again, he bends his knees and places his feet flat on the boards of the landing. Dust flies off the rope, coiled on the ground where the sun is producing grids of light. Klaus gives himself to the bliss of the moment; he wants to fly.

Klaus and Pauline sail like birds between the rafters, diving between flickers of light.

Last Chapter

I spend the following weeks in cafés, reading newspapers, listening to conversations between strangers. I am a fly on the wall.

This evening, the phone rings. I hesitate to answer it. It could be anyone.

It could be Genève, telling me she's happy to take over all my courses. It could be Klaus, telling me that he has indeed moved to Corse.

"Hello?"

"Yann? It's Annette."

"Annette? Hello. How are you?"

"Listen, I need you to meet me at the railroad crossing."

"When?"

"Tomorrow. Be there at 1 p.m."

I fight a sinking feeling when I hang up the phone.

It is a sweltering afternoon. Dark clouds crowd into the horizon. Annette says hello, and when I comment on her sturdy boots, she says, "Glad to see that you came well equipped, too."

She instructs me to follow her, so we clamber the escarpment and step across screes and runnels; penetrate a chaotic topography with brushwork as thick as hedges; walk between trees of second growth, still spindle thin; step on of the rubble of thousands of years of freeze and thaw cycles, scorched by the blaze that ignited the brushwork such that for days the hills were glowing after the

Germans returned with flame throwers and torched all things living and dead.

Madeleine died in these scorched hills.

Annette is scuffing the ground with her boots, and in spots, she lifts black flakes and the soot of long-extinguished fires. Twigs and branches whip my face; brambles scrape my hands. I want to descend into some pain, but not this pain.

Finally, we reach a clearing, a last climb. The sky—the clouds are towering now—roll down into my field of vision, then I see the crowns of trees and the underwood and, before I know it, a field of flowers spills into sight. A white sea on the mountains: a field of Sabline the Provence, hundreds of five-folded petals covering the rubble and slags like a net thrown over the ground.

"Is this your handiwork?" I ask. Annette smiles and nods.

"When did you start this garden?"

"Years ago," she says. "Evil can scorch life, but we have to remember that life's roots go deeper. Here, the burnt soil has helped nourish these flowers."

I think of Madeleine. She would have appreciated this. "So will Pauline and Klaus stay together?"

"They moved in together and plan to live in Corse."

A sudden gust of wind riffles the leaves. Then we trod back down the scarred hills, cross the slopes and fields of stones. Soon, we are back to where the land has begun to heal itself, where grass has begun to cling to stones. As we step onto the paved road, it begins to rain.

Today, it rains across France, to the West, to the coast. It rains on the coast of Southern France. It rains over the sandy beaches of Saint-Brieuc and in the coves of Cassis.

I stand, not wanting to move.

If death were to come to me in this moment of wonder, not all would be lost.

Printed in the USA
CPSIA information can be obtained
at www.ICGtesting.com
LVHW050858210823
755758LV00072B/441

9 781662 811906